P.E.C.
20. A.B. - D

May 21. Reader
Darwin p. 17, Wolfe p. 26
Darwin p. 310

M⁢Cown Chap 12

English Final
109 Aggie Building
10:30

A Writer's Reader

MODELS AND MATERIALS FOR THE ESSAY

A Writer's Reader

Models and Materials for the Essay

PHILIP WEBSTER SOUERS UNIVERSITY OF OREGON

JOHN C. SHERWOOD UNIVERSITY OF OREGON

IRMA Z. SHERWOOD

HARCOURT, BRACE AND COMPANY, NEW YORK

COPYRIGHT, 1950, BY
HARCOURT, BRACE AND COMPANY, INC.

All rights reserved. No part of this book may be reproduced in any form, by mimeograph or any other means, without permission in writing from the publisher.

[b·8·50]

PRINTED IN THE UNITED STATES OF AMERICA

Contents

PART ONE: *Models*

1. ESSAYS BASED ON DIRECT OBSERVATION

Edwin P. Whipple	*Webster and the Neighbors*	3
George Crabbe, Jr.	*Life at Parham*	6
Nathaniel Hawthorne	*Two Weddings*	9
Benjamin Franklin	*Principle and Practice*	13
Charles Darwin	*Tierra del Fuego*	17
Marjorie Kinnan Rawlings	*Environment*	22
Thomas Wolfe	*Race and Occupation*	26
Theodore Roosevelt	*In the Cattle Country*	34

FIVE TRAVELERS IN THE NEAR EAST

1. Mark Twain	} *The Turkish Bath*	57
2. Lady Mary Wortley Montagu		61
3. Alexander William Kinglake	} *The Arab Camp*	63
4. Sir Richard Burton		65
5. R. B. Cunninghame Graham	*Arab Faces*	67
George Gissing	*Retrospect*	72

Robert Louis Stevenson *Despised Races* 76

Carlo Levi *Matera* 82

2. ESSAYS BASED ON READING OR INVESTIGATION

G. M. Trevelyan *The Value of History* 89

Francis Parkman *Braddock's Defeat* 95

James Anthony Froude *Sir Humfrey Gilbert* 104

Lewis Mumford *Thomas Jefferson, Architect* 114

George Orwell *The Art of Donald McGill* 124

Émile Mâle *The "Golden Legend"* 135

Sir Walter Raleigh *Robert Louis Stevenson as Romancer* 143

G. Lowes Dickinson *The Greek View of Woman* 151

Sir Walter Scott *Ghosts* 160

Ruth Benedict *The Pueblos of New Mexico* 195

3. EXPRESSION OF JUDGMENT AND OPINION

H. L. Mencken *Education* 230

Alexander Woollcott *The Archer-Shee Case* 241

Niccolo Machiavelli *Corruption in a Commonwealth* 256

Benedetto Croce *Political Honesty* 259

Abraham Lincoln *Address at Cooper Institute* 264

Winston S. Churchill *The Munich Agreement* 286

PART TWO: *Source Materials for Student Papers*

A Mysterious Disappearance FROM a Letter of Abraham Lincoln   305

The Fuegians FROM Darwin's "Voyage of the Beagle"   310

Masters and Servants FROM the Diary of Samuel Pepys   321

Aesop's *Fables*   327

Women of the Near East FROM the Letters of Lady Mary Wortley Montagu   338

The Borden Case A Summary Statement by the Editors   350

Machiavelli in Our Time A Summary Statement by the Editors   359

ANALYTICAL TABLE OF CONTENTS   361

Preface

> *When a man's thoughts are clear, the properest words will generally offer themselves first, and his own judgment will direct him in what order to place them, so that they may be best understood.* JONATHAN SWIFT

BEHIND the method of teaching composition propounded in this book lies the conviction that writing is the expression of thought and that it is good or bad as it is an accurate or inaccurate statement of the thought; in other words, all good writing is, as Huxley put it, "the clear and forcible expression of definite conceptions." Without definite conceptions, clear expression can hardly take place; and it follows that if composition is to rise above the level of mere drill on the rules of grammar and spelling, it must lay a heavy emphasis on the writer's duty to define his purpose and his ideas before he sets pen to paper. Writing can never be a mere mechanical process in which the application of a set of rules may be expected to produce invariable results. It is a complex mental process, in which the application of rules is not without importance, but in which the chief element is still the clarification of thought.

Along with this conviction, that writing is a mental process and must be taught as such, goes another conviction, that the process of writing is always the same, however much the materials may change, that such classifications as "technical" and "creative" writing, while convenient in certain situations, do not reveal any essential variations in the process of writing, but simply refer to the application of the same process to different materials and in different situations. Whether a man is writing a business letter or a scholarly treatise, he ought to have some definite conception of what he has to say, and he should endeavor to express it as clearly and exactly as possible. If this assumption is accepted, then the freshman instructor need feel himself under no obligation to try to teach all the forms of writing—the "process," the "definition," the "comparison"—and all the rhetorical patterns which have been discovered or imagined by writers of handbooks. The writer's object is not to produce an essay on such and such a rhetorical pattern; his object is to express his thought through the pattern which is most appropriate; and what the inexperienced writer needs is not a list of forms, but a command of the process by which material takes on form under the influence of thought. The editors believe that the inexperienced writer will learn the process most easily if he avoids, in the beginning at least, such complex and elaborate varieties of writing as fiction and argumentation, and embarks first on the simple exposition of ideas, based on personal experience or readily available books; and their belief that a composition course should have some dignity and cultural value has led them to avoid the purely technical and practical forms of writing. It is not likely that much is lost by these omissions; if a student can get an idea clearly defined and follow it through an essay without losing or confusing it, he will be able to keep his head through a letter or report and he will have a solid foundation for more ambitious projects. It may be hoped, too, that he will have acquired some sort of intellectual discipline and that he will not confuse the process of writing with the mere pouring out of emotion or the confused expression of opinions or prejudices.

The specific techniques employed for teaching composition in the light of the assumptions stated above are two: the analysis of models and the analysis of raw materials. Since the first technique is perhaps the most common one for teaching composition, little comment is necessary. The selection and treatment of the essays and extracts have, of course, been governed by the philosophy underlying the book. The essays are ones in which the intellectual side of the writing process is evident; each has a clear purpose (often a specific "theme idea") which is carried out by means which are capable of analysis. By studying these selections the inexperienced writer will gain some insight into those complicated workings of the mind that must take place before writing begins. The reading of good prose with care can teach the art of writing well.

Teaching composition by the analysis of models is a common practice; but teaching through the analysis of raw materials, the technique employed in Part Two, is not so common. Instead of being faced with a finished piece of writing and being asked to try to reconstruct the process by which it came into being, the inexperienced writer is brought face to face with the bare, unformed raw materials out of which an essay grows. This Part Two is made up of seven units or exercises, each of which consists of a body of quotations, all relating to some general subject, but not yet unified or assembled. One exercise, for instance, contains information, taken from Darwin's *Voyage of the Beagle,* on the Indians of Tierra del Fuego; another contains quotations from Pepys' *Diary* which illustrate the relations between masters and servants in seventeenth-century England. (The first and last exercises vary slightly from this pattern.) These exercises might very well be used as source material for student essays, but they are also intended to serve as material for class discussion—to provide, in other words, a means by which the instructor may demonstrate the process by which raw material takes on form and becomes a finished piece of writing. It is hoped that through such demonstrations the inexperienced writer will learn how to read and assimilate unformed material, how to cogitate and consider it until he is fully conscious of his attitude and point of view toward it, how to draw from it a subject that has interest and significance, and how to embody this subject in a general statement or "theme idea" which will give form and unity to the whole. The exercises are connected by cross-references with the essays with which they might most appropriately be used.

Both Part One and Part Two have been organized according to a plan appropriate to the fundamental purposes of the book. This plan is set forth in the "Analytical Table of Contents" on page 361.

In conclusion, it may be remarked that the editors have tried to select essays and extracts which not only will serve to illustrate the particular problems of composition under discussion at the moment, but which have some worth in themselves. If a composition course is to make its proper contribution toward a liberal education, then it ought to be made the occasion for bringing the student in contact with writing of real excellence and permanent human significance, and not merely with insignificant pieces of contemporary journalism whose only merit lies in their connection with some issue which seems at the moment to be especially pressing. The selections, it is hoped, do not represent the manner or thought of any particular age, for good writing comes out of all ages. It is always distinguished by what Mr. T. S. Eliot calls the "essential style of the clear mind which thinks structurally and respects the meanings of words."

University of Oregon

P. W. S.
J. C. S.
I. Z. S.

PART ONE

Models

1 Essays Based on Direct Observation

EDWIN P. WHIPPLE

Webster and the Neighbors

THAT Webster's associations from his early life in New Hampshire retained a strong hold on his mind throughout his life is well illustrated by a story which the late Mr. Peter Harvey used to tell with much zest. Some months after Webster's removal from Portsmouth to Boston, a servant knocked at his chamber door late in an April afternoon in the year 1817, with the announcement that three men were in the drawing-room who insisted on seeing him. Webster was overwhelmed with fatigue, the result of his Congressional labors and his attendance on courts of law; and he had determined, after a night's sleep, to steal a vacation in order to recruit his energies by a fortnight's fishing and hunting. He suspected that the persons below were expectant clients; and he resolved, in descending the stairs, not to accept their offer. He found in the parlor three plain, country-

"Webster and the Neighbors." Adapted from "An Essay on Daniel Webster as a Master of English Style" by Edwin P. Whipple (in *The Great Speeches and Orations of Daniel Webster*).

bred, honest-looking men, who were believers in the innocence of Levi and Laban Kenniston, accused of robbing a certain Major Goodridge on the highway, and whose trial would take place at Ipswich the next day. They could find, they said, no member of the Essex bar who would undertake the defence of the Kennistons, and they had come to Boston to engage the services of Mr. Webster. Would he go down to Ipswich and defend the accused? Mr. Webster stated that he could not and would not go. He had made arrangements for an excursion to the sea-side; the state of his health absolutely demanded a short withdrawal from all business cares; and that no fee could tempt him to abandon his purpose. "Well," was the reply of one of the delegation, "it isn't the fee that we think of at all, though we are willing to pay what you may charge; but it's justice. Here are two New Hampshire men who are believed in Exeter, and Newbury, and Newburyport, and Salem to be rascals; but we in Newmarket believe, in spite of all evidence against them, that they are the victims of some conspiracy. We think you are the man to unravel it, though it seems a good deal tangled even to us. Still we suppose that men whom we know to have been honest all their lives can't have become such desperate rogues all of a sudden." "But I cannot take the case," persisted Mr. Webster; "I am worn to death with over-work; I have not had any real sleep for forty-eight hours. Besides, I know nothing of the case." "It's hard, I can see," continued the leader of the delegation; "but you're a New Hampshire man, and the *neighbors* thought that you would not allow two innocent New Hampshire men, however humble they may be in their circumstances, to suffer for lack of your skill in exposing the wiles of this scoundrel Goodridge. The *neighbors* all desire you to take the case." That phrase "the neighbors" settled the question. No resident of a city knows what the phrase means. But Webster knew it in all the intense significance of its meaning. His imagination flew back to the scattered homesteads of a New England village, where mutual sympathy and assistance are the necessities, as they are the commonplaces, of village life. The phrase remotely meant to him the combination of neighbors to resist an assault of Indian savages, or to send volunteers to the war which wrought the independence of the nation. It specially meant to him the help of neighbor to neighbor, in times of sickness, distress, sorrow, and calamity. In his childhood and boyhood the Christian question, "Who is my neighbor?" was instantly solved the moment a matron in good health heard that the wife of Farmer A, or Farmer B, was stricken down by fever, and needed a friendly nurse to sit by her bedside all night, though she had herself been toiling hard all day. Every thing philanthropists mean when they talk of brotherhood and sisterhood among men and women was condensed in that homely phrase, "the neighbors." "Oh!" said Webster, ruefully, "if the neighbors think I may be of service, of course I must go";—and, with his three companions, he was soon seated in the stage for Ipswich, where he arrived at about midnight. The court met the next morning; and his management of the case is still considered one of his masterpieces of legal acumen and eloquence.

Questions

The passage which you have just read represents a very simple kind of writing; in it the author makes a statement about the character of Daniel Webster ("Webster's associations from his early life in New Hampshire retained a strong hold on his mind throughout his life") and then goes on to confirm the statement with a story from Webster's life. Simple as it is, however, the passage is written with pains and care; the author has been especially skillful in giving the piece unity—that is, in selecting just those details which are needed to prove his point and in excluding all others.

1. Why is it important to know that Webster was no longer living in New Hampshire? that he was tired and had planned a vacation? that he had had no sleep for forty-eight hours? Why are we told that the accused men were "humble in their circumstances" and that the three men who engaged Webster were "plain" and "country-bred"? Why is the conversation about the fee introduced? Why, since Webster finally accepted the case, need we be told that he at first refused it?

2. Why does Whipple bother to tell us that Webster started immediately for Ipswich and that the case was one of his masterpieces?
3. Naturally Webster won the case; but is it important for us to know this, considering the main purpose of the passage?
4. If Whipple had been telling the story as an illustration of Webster's popularity rather than as proof of the strength of his early associations, he would probably have given much the same facts, but the emphasis would have been different; the section about the "neighbors" would have been shortened or omitted, while the persistence of the clients in the face of several refusals would have been stressed. Suppose the story had been told as proof of Webster's vitality and capacity for hard work—which details would then have been important?

Suggested Assignments

1. Write an essay of a single paragraph in which a simple statement or "theme idea" is illustrated by a short narrative.
2. Do the exercise "A Mysterious Disappearance" on page 305.

GEORGE CRABBE, JR.

Life at Parham

AT PARHAM I was introduced to a set of manners and customs, of which there remains, perhaps, no counterpart in the present day [1834]. My great-uncle's establishment was that of the first-rate yeoman of that period—the Yeoman that already began to be styled by courtesy an Esquire. Mr. Tovell might possess an estate of some eight hundred pounds per annum, a

"Life at Parham." From *Life of the Reverend George Crabbe* by his son, the Reverend George Crabbe.

portion of which he himself cultivated. Educated at a mercantile school, he often said of himself, "Jack will never make a gentleman"; yet he had a native dignity of mind and of manners, which might have enabled him to pass muster in that character with any but very fastidious critics. His house was large, and the surrounding moat, the rookery, the ancient dovecot and the well-stored fishponds, were such as might have suited a gentleman's seat of some consequence; but one side of the house immediately overlooked a farm-yard, full of all sorts of domestic animals, and the scene of constant bustle and noise. On entering the house, one saw nothing at first sight that suggested the farm:—a spacious hall, paved with black and white marble,—at one extremity a very handsome drawing-room, and at the other a fine old staircase of black oak, polished till it was as slippery as ice, and having a chime-clock and a barrel-organ on its landing-places. But this drawing-room, a corresponding dining parlour, and a handsome sleeping apartment up stairs, were all *tabooed* ground, and made use of on great and solemn occasions only—such as rent-days, and an occasional visit with which Mr. Tovell was honoured by a neighbouring peer. At all other times the family and their visitors lived entirely in the old-fashioned kitchen along with the servants. My great-uncle occupied an armchair, or, in attacks of gout, a couch on one side of a large open chimney. Mrs. Tovell sat at a small table, on which, in the evening, stood one small candle, in an iron candlestick, plying her needle by the feeble glimmer, surrounded by her maids, all busy at the same employment; but in winter a noble block of wood, sometimes the whole circumference of a pollard, threw its comfortable warmth and cheerful blaze over the apartment.

2] At a very early hour in the morning, the alarm called the maids, and their mistress also; and if the former were tardy, a louder alarm, and more formidable, was heard chiding the delay —not that scolding was peculiar to any occasion; it regularly ran on through all the day, like bells on harness, inspiriting the work, whether it were done ill or well. After the important business of the dairy, and a hasty breakfast, their respective employments were again resumed; that which the mistress took for her especial privilege being the scrubbing of the floors of the state apartments. A new servant, ignorant of her presumption, was found one morning on her knees, hard at work on the floor of one of these preserves, and was thus addressed by her mistress— "*You* wash such floors as these? Give me the brush this instant, and troop to the scullery and wash that, madam! . . . As true as G-d's in heaven, here comes Lord Rochford, to call on Mr. Tovell.—Here, take my mantle" (a blue woollen apron), "and I'll go to the door!"

Questions

Although Crabbe's essay is a little more complex and contains a greater variety of material than Whipple's, it shows the same kind of excellence; the author has a definite idea which he wishes to elaborate and he is careful to select just the material that he needs to support the idea. Crabbe's purpose, as he suggests in the second sentence, is to discuss his uncle's peculiar social position, which is too dignified to be that of an ordinary farmer or yeoman, but not quite high enough to be that of a gentleman or wealthy landowner. The details are selected with this purpose in mind.

1. Show how Mr. Tovell's social position is exhibited in the following details:
    a. The size of his estate;
    b. The fact that he cultivates part of it himself;
    c. The exterior of his house;
    d. The interior of the house;
    e. The family's relations with the servants;
    f. Lord Rochford's call.
2. Unlike the selection by Whipple, the passage by Crabbe is divided into two paragraphs, and this arrangement is justified, since the material of the second paragraph, although clearly related to the main idea, also forms a logical unit by itself. What is the topic of paragraph 2, and why is the material properly separated from the material in paragraph 1?
3. Does the story of Lord Rochford's call make an effective conclusion for the passage?

4. Consider whether any of the following details could have been included in the passage without impairing its unity:
   a. An account of the crops grown on the farm;
   b. A list of the books in Mr. Tovell's library;
   c. A description of Mrs. Tovell's dress;
   d. An account of the love affairs of one of the maids;
   e. A description of a party given by the Tovells.

Suggested Assignment

Write an essay in which a description of some person's home is used to reveal his character or way of life.

NATHANIEL HAWTHORNE

Two Weddings

I WAS once present at the wedding of some poor English people, and was deeply impressed by the spectacle, though by no means with such proud and delightful emotions as seem to have affected all England on the recent occasion of the marriage of its Prince. It was in the Cathedral at Manchester, a particularly black and grim old structure, into which I had stepped to examine some ancient and curious wood-carvings within the choir. The woman in attendance greeted me with a smile (which always glimmers forth on the feminine visage, I know not why, when a wedding is in question), and asked me to take a seat in the nave till some poor parties were married, it being the Easter holidays, and a good time for them to marry, because no fees would be demanded by the clergyman. I sat down accordingly,

"Two Weddings." From *Our Old Home* by Nathaniel Hawthorne.

and soon the parson and his clerk appeared at the altar, and a considerable crowd of people made their entrance at a side-door, and ranged themselves in a long, huddled line across the chancel. They were my acquaintances of the poor streets, or persons in a precisely similar condition of life, and were now come to their marriage-ceremony in just such garbs as I had always seen them wear: the men in their loafers' coats, out at elbows, or their laborers' jackets, defaced with grimy toil; the women drawing their shabby shawls tighter about their shoulders, to hide the raggedness beneath; all of them unbrushed, unshaven, unwashed, uncombed, and wrinkled with penury and care; nothing virgin-like in the brides, nor hopeful or energetic in the bridegrooms; —they were, in short, the mere rags and tatters of the human race, whom some east-wind of evil omen, howling along the streets, had chanced to sweep together into an unfragrant heap. Each and all of them, conscious of his or her individual misery, had blundered into the strange miscalculation of supposing that they could lessen the sum of it by multiplying it into the misery of another person. All the couples (and it was difficult, in such a confused crowd, to compute exactly their number) stood up at once, and had execution done upon them in the lump, the clergyman addressing only small parts of the service to each individual pair, but so managing the larger portion as to include the whole company without the trouble of repetition. By this compendious contrivance, one would apprehend, he came dangerously near making every man and woman the husband or wife of every other; nor, perhaps, would he have perpetrated much additional mischief by the mistake; but, after receiving a benediction in common, they assorted themselves in their own fashion, as they only knew how, and departed to the garrets, or the cellars, or the unsheltered street-corners, where their honeymoon and subsequent lives were to be spent. The parson smiled decorously, the clerk and the sexton grinned broadly, the female attendant tittered almost aloud, and even the married parties seemed to see something exceedingly funny in the affair; but for my part, though generally apt enough to be tickled by a joke, I laid it away in my memory as one of the saddest sights I ever looked upon.

2] Not very long afterwards, I happened to be passing the same venerable Cathedral, and heard a clang of joyful bells, and beheld a bridal party coming down the steps towards a carriage and four horses, with a portly coachman and two postilions, that waited at the gate. One parson and one service had amalgamated the wretchedness of a score of paupers; a Bishop and three or four clergymen had combined their spiritual might to forge the golden links of this other marriage-bond. The bridegroom's mien had a sort of careless and kindly English pride; the bride floated along in her white drapery, a creature so nice and delicate that it was a luxury to see her, and a pity that her silk slippers should touch anything so grimy as the old stones of the churchyard avenue. The crowd of ragged people, who always cluster to witness what they may of an aristocratic wedding, broke into audible admiration of the bride's beauty and the bridegroom's manliness, and uttered prayers and ejaculations (possibly paid for in alms) for the happiness of both. If the most favorable of earthly conditions could make them happy, they had every prospect of it. They were going to live on their abundance in one of those stately and delightful English homes, such as no other people ever created or inherited, a hall set far and safe within its own private grounds, and surrounded with venerable trees, shaven lawns, rich shrubbery, and trimmest pathways, the whole so artfully contrived and tended that summer rendered it a paradise, and even winter would hardly disrobe it of its beauty; and all this fair property seemed more exclusively and inalienably their own, because of its descent through many forefathers, each of whom had added an improvement or a charm, and thus transmitted it with a stronger stamp of rightful possession to his heir. And is it possible, after all, that there may be a flaw in the title-deeds? Is, or is not, the system wrong that gives one married pair so immense a superfluity of luxurious home, and shuts out a million others from any home whatever? One day or another, safe as they deem themselves, and safe as the hereditary temper of the people really tends to make them, the gentlemen of England will be compelled to face this question.

Questions

1. *a.* What is Hawthorne's purpose in describing the two weddings? Where is this purpose indicated?

   b. State this purpose in the form of a "theme idea"—that is, a one-sentence statement of the main idea of the essay.

2. Could Hawthorne have attained his purpose through a description of the first wedding alone, without a description of the second?

3. Why does a contrast between two weddings suit Hawthorne's purpose especially well—better, say, than an account of two funerals?

4. It is easy to account for the selection of the details in the two paragraphs; in the first, they are selected to give an impression of poverty and sadness; in the second, to give an impression of richness and joy. But it is also clear that each paragraph has been put together with the other in mind and that each detail in the second paragraph corresponds to a detail in the first; thus in each case something is said about the dress and bearing of the married couples. Point out other parallels. Does the organization of paragraph 2 in any way resemble that of paragraph 1?

5. Why is the description of the poor wedding somewhat longer than the description of the rich one?

6. The whole of the first wedding ceremony is described, while only the conclusion of the second wedding is given. How do you account for this?

7. Would a detailed description of the cathedral make an appropriate addition to the passage?

8. Although the essay has only two paragraphs, the material really divides itself into three parts. What are they? Should there have been three paragraphs? Could the two paragraphs be combined?

BENJAMIN FRANKLIN

⚞ *Principle and Practice*

THE HONORABLE and learned Mr. Logan told me the following anecdote of his old master, William Penn, respecting defense. He came over from England, when a young man, with that proprietary, and as his secretary. It was war-time, and their ship was chas'd by an armed vessel, suppos'd to be an enemy. Their captain prepar'd for defense; but told William Penn, and his company of Quakers, that he did not expect their assistance, and they might retire into the cabin, which they did, except James Logan, who chose to stay upon deck, and was quarter'd to a gun. The suppos'd enemy prov'd a friend, so there was no fighting; but when the secretary went down to communicate the intelligence, William Penn rebuk'd him severely for staying upon deck, and undertaking to assist in defending the vessel, contrary to the principles of *Friends,* especially as it had not been required by the captain. This reproof, being before all the company, piqu'd the secretary, who answer'd, *"I being thy servant, why did thee not order me to come down? But thee was willing enough that I should stay and help to fight the ship when thee thought there was danger."*

2] My being many years in the Assembly, the majority of which were constantly Quakers, gave me frequent opportunities of seeing the embarrassment given them by their principle against war, whenever application was made to them, by order of the crown, to grant aids for military purposes. They were unwilling to offend government, on the one hand, by a direct re-

"Principle and Practice." From *The Autobiography of Benjamin Franklin.*

fusal; and their friends, the body of the Quakers, on the other, by a compliance contrary to their principles; hence a variety of evasions to avoid complying, and modes of disguising the compliance when it became unavoidable. The common mode at last was, to grant money under the phrase of its being *"for the king's use,"* and never to inquire how it was applied.

3] But, if the demand was not directly from the crown, that phrase was found not so proper, and some other was to be invented. As, when powder was wanting (I think it was for the garrison at Louisburg), and the government of New England solicited a grant of some from Pennsylvania, which was much urg'd on the House by Governor Thomas, they could not grant money to buy powder, because that was an ingredient of war; but they voted an aid to New England of three thousand pounds, to be put into the hands of the governor, and appropriated it for the purchasing of bread, flour, wheat, or *other grain.* Some of the council, desirous of giving the House still further embarrassment, advis'd the governor not to accept provision, as not being the thing he had demanded; but he reply'd, "I shall take the money, for I understand very well their meaning; other grain is gunpowder," which he accordingly bought, and they never objected to it.

4] These embarrassments that the Quakers suffer'd from having establish'd and published it as one of their principles that no kind of war was lawful, and which, being once published, they could not afterwards, however they might change their minds, easily get rid of, reminds me of what I think a more prudent conduct in another sect among us, that of the Dunkers. I was acquainted with one of its founders, Michael Welfare, soon after it appear'd. He complain'd to me that they were grievously calumniated by the zealots of other persuasions, and charg'd with abominable principles and practices, to which they were utter strangers. I told him this had always been the case with new sects, and that, to put a stop to such abuse, I imagin'd it might be well to publish the articles of their belief, and the rules of their discipline. He said that it had been propos'd among them, but not agreed to, for this reason: "When we were first drawn together as a society," says he, "it had pleased God to enlighten our minds so far as to see that some doctrines, which we once esteemed truths, were errors; and that others, which we had esteemed errors, were real truths. From time to time He has been pleased to afford us farther light, and our principles have been improving, and our errors diminishing. Now we are not sure that we are arrived at the end of this progression, and at the perfection of spiritual or theological knowledge; and we fear that, if we should once print our confession of faith, we should feel ourselves as if bound and confin'd by it, and perhaps be unwilling to receive farther improvement, and our successors still more so, as conceiving what we their elders and founders had done, to be something sacred, never to be departed from."

5] This modesty in a sect is perhaps a singular instance in the history of mankind, every other sect supposing itself in possession of all truth, and that those who differ are so far in the wrong; like a man traveling in foggy weather, those at some distance before him on the road he sees wrapped up in the fog, as well as those behind him, and also the people in the fields on each side, but near him all appears clear, tho' in truth he is as much in the fog as any of them.

Questions

Show that you understand what unity is by analyzing Franklin's essay. This will involve stating the theme idea of the passage and showing how the various parts of the essay are related to it. Comment also on the paragraph divisions.

Suggested Assignment

To make all actions conform to a preconceived principle, a principle not subject to modification, is a problem which confronts individuals as well as groups. In the above selection from his *Autobiography* Franklin discusses the difficulties faced by an organized group under such circumstances. Elsewhere in his *Autobiography* he lists a number of principles which he formulated for the improvement of his personal life, and discusses his troubles in trying to live up to his own ideals. Some of Franklin's rules are the following:

1. Temperance: Eat not to dullness; drink not to elevation.
2. Silence: Speak not but what may benefit others or yourself; avoid trifling conversation.
3. Order: Let all your things have their places; let each part of your business have its time.
4. Resolution: Resolve to perform what you ought; perform without fail what you resolve.
5. Frugality: Make not expense but to do good to others or yourself; i.e., waste nothing.
6. Industry: Lose no time; be always employ'd in something useful; cut off all unnecessary actions.
7. Sincerity: Use no hurtful deceit; think innocently and justly, and, if you speak, speak accordingly.
8. Justice: Wrong none by doing injuries, or omitting the benefits that are your duty.
9. Moderation: Avoid extreams; forbear resenting injuries so much as you think they deserve.
10. Tranquillity: Be not disturbed at trifles, or at accidents common or unavoidable.

From the above list select one rule which you have tried to follow yourself or which you think it might be worth while trying to follow. In a well-organized essay indicate some of the practical difficulties you might encounter in attempting to live in rigid compliance with such a rule.

CHARLES DARWIN

Tierra del Fuego

WHILE going one day on shore near Wollaston Island, we pulled alongside a canoe with six Fuegians. These were the most abject and miserable creatures I anywhere beheld. On the east coast the natives, as we have seen, have guanaco cloaks, and on the west, they possess seal-skins. Amongst these central tribes the men generally have an otter-skin, or some small scrap about as large as a pocket-handkerchief, which is barely sufficient to cover their backs as low down as their loins. It is laced across the breast by strings, and according as the wind blows, it is shifted from side to side. But these Fuegians in the canoe were quite naked, and even one full-grown woman was absolutely so. It was raining heavily, and the fresh water, together with the spray, trickled down her body. In another harbour not far distant, a woman, who was suckling a recently-born child, came one day alongside the vessel, and remained there out of mere curiosity, whilst the sleet fell and thawed on her naked bosom, and on the skin of her naked baby! These poor wretches were stunted in their growth, their hideous faces bedaubed with white paint, their skins filthy and greasy, their hair entangled, their voices discordant, and their gestures violent. Viewing such men, one can hardly make oneself believe that they are fellow-creatures, and inhabitants of the same world. It is a common subject of conjecture what pleasure in life some of the lower animals can enjoy:

"Tierra del Fuego." From the *Journal of Researches into the Natural History and Geology of the Countries Visited during the Voyage of H. M. S. Beagle Round the World, under the Command of Capt. Fitz Roy, R. N.* by Charles Darwin.

how much more reasonably the same question may be asked with respect to these barbarians! At night, five or six human beings, naked and scarcely protected from the wind and rain of this tempestuous climate, sleep on the wet ground coiled up like animals. Whenever it is low water, winter or summer, night or day, they must rise to pick shell-fish from the rocks; and the women either dive to collect sea-eggs, or sit patiently in their canoes, and with a baited hair-line without any hook, jerk out little fish. If a seal is killed, or the floating carcass of a putrid whale discovered, it is a feast; and such miserable food is assisted by a few tasteless berries and fungi.

2] They often suffer from famine: I heard Mr. Low, a sealing-master intimately acquainted with the natives of this country, give a curious account of the state of a party of one hundred and fifty natives on the west coast, who were very thin and in great distress. A succession of gales prevented the women from getting shell-fish on the rocks, and they could not go out in their canoes to catch seal. A small party of these men one morning set out, and the other Indians explained to him, that they were going a four days' journey for food: on their return, Low went to meet them, and he found them excessively tired, each man carrying a great square piece of putrid whales-blubber with a hole in the middle, through which they put their heads, like the Gauchos do through their ponchos or cloaks. As soon as the blubber was brought into a wigwam, an old man cut off thin slices, and muttering over them, broiled them for a minute, and distributed them to the famished party, who during this time preserved a profound silence. Mr. Low believes that whenever a whale is cast on shore, the natives bury large pieces of it in the sand, as a resource in time of famine; and a native boy, whom he had on board, once found a stock thus buried. The different tribes when at war are cannibals. From the concurrent, but quite independent evidence of the boy taken by Mr. Low, and of Jemmy Button,* it is certainly true, that when pressed in winter by hunger, they kill and devour their old women before they

---

* For Jemmy Button, see page 312.

kill their dogs: the boy, being asked by Mr. Low why they did this, answered, "Doggies catch otters, old women no." This boy described the manner in which they are killed by being held over smoke and thus choked; he imitated their screams as a joke, and described the parts of their bodies which are considered best to eat. Horrid as such a death by the hands of their friends and relatives must be, the fears of the old women, when hunger begins to press, are more painful to think of; we were told that they then often run away into the mountains, but that they are pursued by the men and brought back to the slaughter-house at their own fire-sides!

3] Captain Fitz Roy could never ascertain that the Fuegians have any distinct belief in a future life. They sometimes bury their dead in caves, and sometimes in the mountain forests; we do not know what ceremonies they perform. Jemmy Button would not eat land-birds, because "eat dead men": they are unwilling even to mention their dead friends. We have no reason to believe that they perform any sort of religious worship; though perhaps the muttering of the old man before he distributed the putrid blubber to his famished party, may be of this nature. Each family or tribe has a wizard or conjuring doctor, whose office we could never clearly ascertain. Jemmy believed in dreams, though not, as I have said, in the devil: I do not think that our Fuegians were much more superstitious than some of the sailors; for an old quarter-master firmly believed that the successive heavy gales, which we encountered off Cape Horn, were caused by our having the Fuegians on board. The nearest approach to a religious feeling which I heard of, was shown by York Minster, who, when Mr. Bynoe shot some very young ducklings as specimens, declared in the most solemn manner, "Oh Mr. Bynoe, much rain, snow, blow much." This was evidently a retributive punishment for wasting human food. In a wild and excited manner he also related, that his brother, one day whilst returning to pick up some dead birds which he had left on the coast, observed some feathers blown by the wind. His brother said (York imitating his manner), "What that?" and crawling onwards, he peeped over the cliff, and saw "wild man" picking his birds; he crawled a little nearer, and then hurled down a great stone and killed him. York declared for a long time afterwards storms raged, and much rain and snow fell. As far as we could make out, he seemed to consider the elements themselves as the avenging agents: it is evident in this case, how naturally, in a race a little more advanced in culture, the elements would become personified. What the "bad wild men" were, has always appeared to me most mysterious: from what York said, when we found the place like the form of a hare, where a single man had slept the night before, I should have thought that they were thieves who had been driven from their tribes; but other obscure speeches made me doubt this; I have sometimes imagined that the most probable explanation was that they were insane.

4] The different tribes have no government or chief; yet each is surrounded by other hostile tribes, speaking different dialects, and separated from each other only by a deserted border or neutral territory: the cause of their warfare appears to be the means of subsistence. Their country is a broken mass of wild rocks, lofty hills, and useless forests: and these are viewed through mists and endless storms. The habitable land is reduced to the stones on the beach; in search of food they are compelled unceasingly to wander from spot to spot, and so steep is the coast, that they can only move about in their wretched canoes. They cannot know the feeling of having a home, and still less that of domestic affection; for the husband is to the wife a brutal master to a laborious slave. Was a more horrid deed ever perpetrated, than that witnessed on the west coast by Byron, who saw a wretched mother pick up her bleeding dying infant-boy, whom her husband had mercilessly dashed on the stones for dropping a basket of sea-eggs! How little can the higher powers of the mind be brought into play: what is there for imagination to picture, for reason to compare, for judgment to decide upon? to knock a limpet from the rock does not require even cunning, that lowest power of the mind. Their skill in some respects may be compared to the instinct of animals; for it is not improved by experience: the canoe, their most ingenious work, poor as it is, has remained the same, as we know from Drake, for the last two hundred and fifty years.

5] Whilst beholding these savages, one asks, whence have they come? What could have tempted, or what change compelled a tribe of men, to leave the fine regions of the north, to travel down the Cordillera or backbone of America, to invent and build canoes, which are not used by the tribes of Chile, Peru, and Brazil, and then to enter on one of the most inhospitable countries within the limits of the globe? Although such reflections must at first seize on the mind, yet we may feel sure that they are partly erroneous. There is no reason to believe that the Fuegians decrease in number; therefore we must suppose that they enjoy a sufficient share of happiness, of whatever kind it may be, to render life worth having. Nature by making habit omnipotent, and its effects hereditary, has fitted the Fuegian to the climate and the productions of his miserable country.

Questions

The problem of selecting his material is only the first of the many problems which a writer faces. Once the material has been chosen, it must be arranged in some sort of order; in other words, the essay must be given its *organization*. The writer's purpose or his "theme idea" not only governs the choice of material but determines the organization as well.

1. Of the five paragraphs into which the passage is divided, four consist almost entirely of descriptions of things which Darwin saw and witnessed, and one consists of his own comments and reflections. Which paragraph contains the reflections?
2. Although the reflections are reserved for the latter part of the essay, there is a sentence in the first paragraph which foreshadows them. Point it out.
3. Aside from the matter of introducing his reflections at an appropriate point, Darwin's chief problem was to sort out the facts he had observed and arrange them into paragraphs. This he has done with fair success.

    a. Paragraphs 2 and 3 have limited, well-defined topics. What are they?

    b. Paragraph 1 has a looser but still fairly definite topic. What is it?

    c. Paragraph 4 is somewhat miscellaneous, as if it had been made the repository for all the material left over from the other paragraphs, but it does have a vague kind of unity. Define the topic of this paragraph as clearly as you can. (There is a hint of the topic in the next to the last sentence.)

4. The arrangement of the paragraphs in the essay is not a matter of chance; they could hardly be arranged in any other order.

   a. Why is paragraph 1 necessarily the introduction and paragraph 5 the conclusion?

   b. Why must paragraph 2 follow paragraph 1?

   c. Why do paragraphs 3 and 4 belong together? Could their order be reversed?

5. Although he does not discuss the matter in detail, Darwin seems to feel that the low mental and moral state of the Fuegians is a consequence of the hardships of their life. Suppose that he had considered their failure to create a more comfortable existence for themselves a consequence of their mental and moral deficiencies. How would this affect the organization of the essay?

Suggested Assignment

Do the exercise "The Fuegians" on page 310.

MARJORIE KINNAN RAWLINGS

Environment

THE MATTER of adjustment to physical environment is as fascinating as the adjustment of man to man, and as many-sided. The place that is right for one is wrong for another, and I think that much human unhappiness comes from ignoring the primordial relation of man to his background. Certainly the crea-

"Environment." From *Cross Creek* by Marjorie Kinnan Rawlings. Reprinted by permission of Charles Scribner's Sons.

tures are sensitive to this, and while some seem contented almost anywhere as long as food is provided, and perhaps a mate, others cannot accept the change of scene or the cage. Monkeys, I think, do not mind the zoo, but the eagle hunched on his public perch, the panther behind his bars, break the heart with their desperation. My own two animals who came to the Creek with me from urban life reacted as opposites. They were a Scottish terrier, a shy fellow, and a young tiger cat, both city-bred and reared. Both knew town apartment life, the sound of city traffic and the small bed at night behind safe walls. Both had been happy in that life.

2] Dinghy the Scotty hated the Florida backwoods from the first sandspur under his tail. He hated the sun, he hated the people, black and white, he hated the roominess of the farmhouse and the long quiet of the nights. From the beginning, he sat on his fat Scotch behind and glowered. Perhaps he sensed that his breed and pedigree were not here properly appreciated. Florida is a country of the work-dog, even where that dog is a pointer or setter and so something, always, of a pet. We live a leisurely life, but while our dogs lie, as we, in the sun, they are also expected to serve us. Dinghy was not approved. He was not even understood. There were those who did not believe he was a dog. The iceman professed to be in deadly fear of him. I took Dinghy in the car with me to Hawthorn for groceries, and the clerk came to put the packages in the car. He retreated, shrieking, "There's a varmint in that car!" I am certain that if Dinghy did not know what was meant by a varmint, he knew that humans were not impressed by him. He was accustomed to slavish overtures, the proffered tidbit and the friendly touch. He retired into his mental Highlands and stayed there.

3] Jib, his tabby companion, was of different stuff. He too had lived the languid life of a city pet, in the house most of the time, fed on ground beef and liver from the butcher, his only excitement an occasional excursion into the back yard after some intrepid city mouse. I was so busy when I took up life at the Creek that Jib was left to shift for himself. He had his warm milk fresh from old Laura, night and morning, but that was all. And where Dinghy turned into a hopeless introvert, Jib thrived.

4] The jungle that was a terror to the dog was to him enchanting. All the generations of urban life were dissolved in a moment, and he prowled the marsh and hammock as though he had known them always. He returned home with shining eyes, bearing some trophy unutterably strange, a lizard or small snake. We use the expression here, "poor as a lizard-eating cat," and I think Jib learned they were not the healthiest of foods, for as the years passed I would see him lying in the shade, watching a lizard with no attempt to catch it. He must once have been bitten by a snake, for he disappeared for two days, and came in with his head swollen to twice its size, and very wobbly on his legs. He refused food for two days more and then was himself again, but with a holy fear of anything resembling the serpent. I have seen him jump three feet in the air, like a released spring, at the sudden sight of a curving stick or a ribbon on the floor.

5] He seemed to sense the unhappiness of Dinghy and made a great effort to teach the Scotty the new delights he had discovered. He brought his lizards to the melancholy Scot and was puzzled by his disgust. He spent hours trying to teach Dinghy to catch a mouse. He would cripple it, cat-fashion, and release it under the dog's nose. Dinghy would move a few morose inches away. Jib would pick up the mouse and push it under Dinghy's belly with one paw, then sit back and wait hopefully for the mouse to slip away and Dinghy to pounce, as any rational animal would do. The mouse would begin its escape and Dinghy would look the other way. At last, with evident lack of relish, Jib would kill and eat his mouse.

6] Dinghy was returned to the city, lived happily in a bed-in-door apartment filled with the commotion of newspaper people, and fathered many broods of equally haughty and urban Scottish terriers. I am sure that if he had stayed in Florida he would have sired no progeny, out of sheer boredom. Old Jib has lived to be a veritable Egyptian mummy of a cat, lean and desiccated, with an eye cocked to watch the birds and the chameleons he has not disturbed for many years. Life will be for him always a lively matter, even when it is reduced to mere speculation. I drove over the cattle-gap into the grove late one night recently, and my lights shone two bright pairs of eyes, one on either side of the driveway. Old Jib was curled comfortably there, watching with friendly interest an opossum who had come by on his night's business.

Questions

1. *a.* What is the main idea of the essay? Where is that idea stated?
   b. How does this arrangement of facts and conclusions differ from the arrangement in Darwin's "Tierra del Fuego"? Which arrangement is superior?
2. The main idea is illustrated by the examples of Dinghy and Jib.
   a. Would the example of either animal alone serve to illustrate the idea? In other words, could the essay exist and have some point if the story of Jib or of Dinghy were omitted?
   b. If Dinghy had been unhappy in city life and Jib happy, would the story serve to illustrate the main idea? Suppose the dog had been happy in the city and the cat unhappy, would it do?
3. Most of the material on Dinghy is in paragraph 2, but there is some in paragraphs 5 and 6. Should this latter material have been moved forward and included in paragraph 2? (Compare the handling of the comparison in Hawthorne's "Two Weddings.")
4. *a.* What is there about Jib's experiences with lizards and his experience with the snake which justifies bringing the two events together in one paragraph?
   b. Paragraph 6 is partly about Dinghy, partly about Jib. Does this mean that the paragraph lacks unity?
   c. Could paragraphs 3 and 4 be combined?
5. *a.* Why is the picture of Jib watching the opossum saved for the end?
   b. Why should paragraph 4 precede paragraph 5? Is the order chronological? Suppose Jib's attempts to educate Dinghy actually occurred before his clash with the snake—would this require a change in the arrangement?

6. In which animal is the author more interested, the dog or the cat? How is this interest reflected in the organization of the essay?
7. How would the coherence of paragraph 2 be affected by the omission of the words "Perhaps he sensed that his breed and pedigree were not here properly appreciated" and "I am certain that if Dinghy did not know what was meant by a varmint, he knew that humans were not impressed by him"? Note that there is a shift in emphasis in this paragraph, from Dinghy's feelings to the feelings of human beings toward him, and back again.
8. Could the words "his tabby companion" in the first sentence of paragraph 3 and "that was a terror to the dog" in the first sentence of paragraph 4 be omitted?
9. "He retired into his mental Highlands and stayed there" (paragraph 2). If Dinghy had been a Great Dane, could this reference have been used?

THOMAS WOLFE

Race and Occupation

MYNHEER BENDIEN was obviously just a business man, a kind of Dutch Babbitt. He was, indeed, a hard-bargaining, shrewd importer who plied a constant traffic between England and Holland, and was intimately familiar with the markets and business practices of both countries. His occupation had left its mark upon him, that same mark which is revealed in a coarsening of perception and a blunting of sensitivity among people of his kind the world over.

2] As George observed the signs that betrayed what Bendien

"Race and Occupation." From *You Can't Go Home Again* by Thomas Wolfe. Copyright, 1940, by Maxwell Perkins, as executor. Reprinted by permission of Harper and Brothers.

was beyond any mistaking, he felt confirmed in an opinion that had been growing on him of late. He had begun to see that the true races of mankind are not at all what we are told in youth that they are. They are not defined either by national frontiers or by the characteristics assigned to them by the subtle investigations of anthropologists. More and more George was coming to believe that the real divisions of humanity cut across these barriers and arise out of differences in the very souls of men.

3] George had first had his attention called to this phenomenon by an observation of H. L. Mencken. In his extraordinary work on the American language, Mencken gave an example of the American sporting writers' jargon—"Babe Smacks Forty-Second with Bases Loaded"—and pointed out that such a headline would be as completely meaningless to an Oxford don as the dialect of some newly discovered tribe of Eskimos. True enough; but what shocked George to attention when he read it was that Mencken drew the wrong inference from his fact. The headline would be meaningless to the Oxford don, not because it was written in the American language, but because the Oxford don had no knowledge of baseball. The same headline might be just as meaningless to a Harvard professor, and for the same reason.

4] It seemed to George that the Oxford don and the Harvard professor had far more kinship with each other—a far greater understanding of each other's ways of thinking, feeling, and living—than either would have with millions of people of his own nationality. This observation led George to realize that academic life has created its own race of men who are set apart from the rest of humanity by the affinity of their souls. This academic race, it seemed to him, had innumerable peculiar characteristics of its own, among them the fact that, like the sporting gentry, they had invented their own private languages for communication with one another. The internationalism of science was another characteristic: there is no such thing as English chemistry or American physics or (Stalin to the contrary notwithstanding) Russian biology,* but only chemistry, physics, and

---

* Wolfe's book was published in 1940.

biology. So, too, it follows that one tells a good deal more about a man when one says he is a chemist than when one says he is an Englishman.

5] In the same way, Babe Ruth would probably feel more closely akin to the English professional cricketer, Jack Hobbs, than to a professor of Greek at Princeton. This would be true also among prize fighters. George thought of that whole world that is so complete within itself—the fighters, the trainers, the managers, the promoters, the touts, the pimps, the gamblers, the grafters, the hangers-on, the newspaper "experts" in New York, London, Paris, Berlin, Rome, and Buenos Aires. These men were not really Americans, Englishmen, Frenchmen, Germans, Italians, and Argentines. They were simply citizens of the world of prize fighting, more at home with one another than with other men of their respective nations.

6] Throughout all the years of his life, George Webber had been soaking up experience like a sponge. This process never ceased with him, but within the last few years he had noticed a change in it. Formerly, in his insatiable hunger to know everything—to see all the faces in a crowd at once, to remember every face that passed him on a city street, to hear all the voices in a room and through the vast, perplexing blur to distinguish what each was saying—he had often felt that he was drowning in some vast sea of his own sensations and impressions. But now he was no longer so overwhelmed by Amount and Number. He was growing up, and out of the very accumulation of experience he was gaining an essential perspective and detachment. Each new sensation and impression was no longer a single, unrelated thing: it took its place in a pattern and sifted down to form certain observable cycles of experience. Thus his incessantly active mind was free to a much greater degree than ever before to remember, digest, meditate, and compare, and to seek relations between all the phenomena of living. The result was an astonishing series of discoveries as his mind noted associations and resemblances, and made recognitions not only of surface similarities but of identities of concept and of essence.

7] In this way he had become aware of the world of waiters, who, more than any other class of men, seemed to him to have created a special universe of their own which had almost obliterated nationality and race in the ordinary sense of those words. For some reason George had always been especially interested in waiters. Possibly it was because his own beginnings had been small-town middle class, and because he had been accustomed from birth to the friendship of working people, and because the experience of being served at table by a man in uniform had been one of such sensational novelty that its freshness had never worn off. Whatever the reason, he had known hundreds of waiters in many different countries, had talked to them for hours at a time, had observed them intimately, and had gathered tremendous stores of knowledge about their lives—and out of all this had discovered that there are not really different nationalities of waiters but rather a separate race of waiters, whole and complete within itself. This seemed to be true even among the French, the most sharply defined, the most provincial, and the most unadaptive nationality George had ever known. It surprised him to observe that even in France the waiters seemed to belong to the race of waiters rather than to the race of Frenchmen.

8] This universe of waiterdom has produced a type whose character is as precisely distinguished as that of the Mongolian. It has a spiritual identity that unites it as no mere feelings of patriotism could ever do. And this spiritual identity—a unity of thought, of purpose, and of conduct—has produced unmistakable physical characteristics. After George became aware of this, he got so that he could recognize a waiter no matter where he saw him, whether in the New York subway or on a Paris bus or in the streets of London. He tested his observation many times by accosting men he suspected of being waiters and engaging them in conversation, and nine times out of ten he found that his guess had been right. Something in the feet and legs gave them away, something in the way they moved and walked and stood. It was not merely that these men had spent most of their lives standing on their feet and hurrying from kitchen to table in the execution of their orders. Other classes of men, such as policemen, also lived upon their feet, and yet no one could mistake a policeman in mufti for a waiter. (The police of all countries, George discovered, formed another separate race.)

9] The gait of an old waiter can best be described as gingery. It is a kind of gouty shuffle, painful, rheumatic, and yet expertly nimble, too, as if the man has learned by every process of experience to save his feet. It is the nimbleness that comes from years of "Yes, sir. Right away, sir," or of "Oui, monsieur. Je viens. Toute de suite." It is the gait of service, of despatch, of incessant haste to be about one's orders, and somehow the whole soul and mind and character of the waiter is in it.

10] If one wishes an instant insight into the emotional and spiritual differences between the race of waiters and the race of policemen, all one needs to do is to observe the gaits of each. Compare a waiter as he approaches a table at the peremptory command of an impatient customer, and a policeman, whether in New York, London, Paris, or Berlin, as he approaches the scene of a disorder or accident. A man is lying stretched out on the pavement, let us say: he has had a heart attack, or has been struck by a motor car, or has been assaulted and beaten by thugs. People are standing around in a circle. Watch the policeman as he comes up. Does he hurry? Does he rush to the scene? Does he come forward with the quick, shuffling, eager, and solicitous movement of the waiter? He does not. He advances deliberately, ponderously, with a heavy and flat-footed tread, taking the scene in slowly as he approaches, with an appraising and unrelenting look. He is coming not to take orders but to give them. He is coming to assume command of the situation, to investigate, to disperse the crowd, to do the talking, and not to be talked back to. His whole bearing expresses a certain primitive brutality of vested authority, as well as all the other related mental and spiritual qualities that proceed from the exercise of licensed power. And in all these things which issue from his own peculiar vision of life and of the world, he is almost the exact reverse of the waiter.

11] Since this is true, can anyone doubt that waiters and policemen belong to separate races? Does it not follow that a

French waiter is more closely akin to a German waiter than to a French gendarme?

12] Mynheer Bendien had attracted George's interest from the first. It was not merely that he was Dutch. That fact was unmistakable. He had a Halsian floridity, a Halsian heartiness and gusto, a Halsian heaviness—a kind of Dutch grossness that is quite different from German grossness in that it is mixed with a certain delicacy, or rather smallness. This delicacy or smallness is most often evident in the expression and shape of the mouth. So, now, with Mynheer Bendien. His lip was full and pouting, but also a little prim and smug. It was the characteristic Dutch lip—the lip of a small and cautious people, with a very good notion about which side their bread is buttered on. In any town throughout Holland one can see them behind the shuttered windows of their beautiful and delicate houses—see them quietly and privily enjoying the very best of everything and smacking those full, pouting, sensual little lips together.

13] In all these respects Mynheer Bendien was indubitably Dutch. But he was also something else as well, and this was what made George observe him with fascinated interest. For, alongside his Dutchness, he also wore that type look which George had come to recognize as belonging to the race of small business men. It was a look which he had discovered to be common to all members of this race whether they lived in Holland, England, Germany, France, the United States, Sweden, or Japan. There was a hardness and grasping quality in it that showed in the prognathous jaw. There was something a little sly and tricky about the eyes, something a little amoral in the sleekness of the flesh, something about the slightly dry concavity of the face and its vacuous expression in repose which indicated a grasping self-interest and a limited intellectual life. It was the kind of face that is often thought of as American. But it was not American. It belonged to no nationality. It belonged simply and solely to the race of small business men everywhere.

14] He was obviously the kind of man who would have found an instant and congenial place for himself among his fellow business men in Chicago, Detroit, Cleveland, St. Louis, or Kalamazoo. He would have felt completely at home at one of the weekly luncheons of the Rotary Club. He would have chewed his cigar with the best of them, wagged his head approvingly as the president spoke of some member as having "both feet on the ground," entered gleefully into all the horseplay, the heavy-handed kind of humor known as "kidding," and joined in the roars of laughter that greeted such master strokes of wit as collecting all the straw hats in the cloak room, bringing them in, throwing them on the floor, and gleefully stamping them to pieces. He would also have nodded his red face in bland agreement as the speaker aired again all the quackery about "service," "the aims of Rotary," and its "plans for world peace."

15] George could easily imagine Mynheer Bendien pounding across the continental breadth of the United States in one of the crack trains, striking up a conversation with other men of substance in the smoking room of the pullman car, pulling fat cigars from his pocket and offering them to his new-found companions, chewing on his own approvingly and nodding with ponderous affirmation as someone said: "I was talking to a man in Cleveland the other day, one of the biggest glue and mucilage producers in the country, a fellow who has learned his business from the ground up and *knows* what he's talking about—" Yes, Mynheer Bendien would have recognized his brother, his kinsman, his twin spirit wherever he found him, and would instantly have established a connection and a footing of proper familiarity with him, as Webber could never have done, even though the stranger might be an American like himself.

Questions

1. State the theme idea of the essay. Where is it first expressed?
2. List the individuals and social types who are introduced as examples to illustrate this idea, and indicate, in terms of paragraphs or parts of a paragraph, how much space is devoted to each. Which appear earlier in the essay, those to whom the most space

is devoted or those who receive less attention? Does the order go from unimportant to important, or vice versa?

3. Mynheer Bendien is discussed twice, at the beginning of the essay and at the end.

   a. What does this indicate about his importance?

   b. The first description is brief, the second rather full. How do you account for this method of treatment?

4. A comparison is usually pointless unless the things compared show resemblances as well as differences.

   a. What resemblance links the sporting fan and the professor? the waiter and the policeman?

   b. Could Wolfe have compared the waiter with the professor, and the policeman with the sporting fan?

5. *a.* Should paragraph 9 be combined with paragraph 8?

   b. Could the last three paragraphs be combined? (The resulting paragraph would not be excessively long.)

6. *a.* Is paragraph 6 an essential part of the essay? Could it be omitted without spoiling the essay?

   b. Is the present position of paragraph 6 the best one?

7. Although the essay sounds clear and logical enough on first reading, there is actually some vagueness in the thought.

   a. Does Wolfe believe that occupation molds character, or that certain occupations attract certain character types?

   b. What does Wolfe mean by "the very souls of men" (paragraph 2) and "mental and spiritual qualities" (paragraph 10)?

   c. What are the political implications of a belief that class or occupation make a man what he is? Is the essay undemocratic?

Suggested Assignment

Do the exercise "Masters and Servants" on page 321.

THEODORE ROOSEVELT

In the Cattle Country

THE GREAT grazing lands of the West lie in what is known as the arid belt, which stretches from British America on the north to Mexico on the south, through the middle of the United States. It includes New Mexico, part of Arizona, Colorado, Wyoming, Montana, and the western portion of Texas, Kansas, Nebraska, and Dakota. It must not be understood by this that more cattle are to be found here than elsewhere, for the contrary is true, it being a fact often lost sight of that the number of cattle raised on the small, thick-lying farms of the fertile Eastern States is actually many times greater than that of those scattered over the vast, barren ranches of the far West; for stock will always be most plentiful in districts where corn and other winter food can be grown. But in this arid belt, and in this arid belt only,—save in a few similar tracts on the Pacific slope,—stock-raising is almost the sole industry, except in the mountain districts where there is mining. The whole region is one vast stretch of grazing country, with only here and there spots of farm-land, in most places there being nothing more like agriculture than is implied in the cutting of some tons of wild hay or the planting of a garden patch for home use. This is especially true of the northern portion of the region, which comprises the basin of the Upper Missouri, and with which alone I am familiar. Here there are no fences to speak of, and all the land north of the Black Hills and the Big Horn Mountains and between the Rockies and the Dakota wheat-fields might be spoken of as one gigantic, un-

"In the Cattle Country." From *The Century Magazine*, 1888; reprinted in Roosevelt's *Ranch Life and the Hunting Trail.*

broken pasture, where cowboys and branding-irons take the place of fences.

2] The country throughout this great Upper Missouri basin has a wonderful sameness of character; and the rest of the arid belt, lying to the southward, is closely akin to it in its main features. A traveler seeing it for the first time is especially struck by its look of parched, barren desolation; he can with difficulty believe that it will support cattle at all. It is a region of light rainfall; the grass is short and comparatively scanty; there is no timber except along the beds of the streams, and in many places there are alkali deserts where nothing grows but sage-brush and cactus. Now the land stretches out into level, seemingly endless plains or into rolling prairies; again it is broken by abrupt hills and deep, winding valleys; or else it is crossed by chains of buttes, usually bare, but often clad with a dense growth of dwarfed pines or gnarled, stunted cedars. The muddy rivers run in broad, shallow beds, which after heavy rainfalls are filled to the brim by the swollen torrents, while in droughts the larger streams dwindle into sluggish trickles of clearer water, and the smaller ones dry up entirely, but in occasional deep pools.

3] All through the region, except on the great Indian reservation, there has been a scanty and sparse settlement, quite peculiar in its character. In the forest the woodchopper comes first; on the fertile prairies the granger is the pioneer; but on the long stretching uplands of the far West it is the men who guard and follow the horned herds that prepare the way for the settlers who come after. The high plains of the Upper Missouri and its tributary rivers were first opened, and are still held, by the stockmen, and the whole civilization of the region has received the stamp of their marked and individual characteristics. They were from the South, not from the East, although many men from the latter region came out along the great transcontinental railway lines and joined them in their northern migration.

4] They were not dwellers in towns, and from the nature of their industry lived as far apart from each other as possible. In choosing new ranges, old cow-hands, who are also seasoned plainsmen, are invariably sent ahead, perhaps a year in advance, to spy out the land and pick the best places. One of these may go by himself, or more often, especially if they have to penetrate little known or entirely unknown tracts, two or three will go together, the owner or manager of the herd himself being one of them. Perhaps their herds may already be on the border of the wild and uninhabited country: in that case they may have to take but a few days' journey before finding the stretches of sheltered, long-grass land that they seek. For instance, when I wished to move my own elkhorn steer brand on to a new ranch I had to spend barely a week in traveling north among the Little Missouri Bad Lands before finding what was then untrodden ground far outside the range of any of my neighbors' cattle. But if a large outfit is going to shift its quarters it must go much farther; and both the necessity and the chance for long wanderings were especially great when the final overthrow of the northern Horse Indians opened the whole Upper Missouri basin at one sweep to the stockmen. Then the advance-guards or explorers, each on one horse and leading another with food and bedding, were often absent months at a time, threading their way through the trackless wastes of plain, plateau, and river-bottom. If possible they would choose a country that would be good for winter and summer alike; but often this could not be done, and then they would try to find a well-watered tract on which the cattle could be summered, and from which they could be driven in fall to their sheltered winter range—for the cattle in winter eat snow, and an entirely waterless region, if broken, and with good pasturage, is often the best possible winter ground, as it is sure not to have been eaten off at all during the summer, while in the bottom the grass is always cropped down soonest. Many outfits regularly shift their herds every spring and fall; but with us in the Bad Lands all we do, when cold weather sets in, is to drive our beasts off the scantily grassed river-bottom back ten miles or more among the broken buttes and plateaux of the uplands to where the brown hay, cured on the stalk, stands thick in the winding *coulées*.

5] These lookouts or forerunners having returned, the herds are set in motion as early in the spring as may be, so as to get on the ground in time to let the travel-worn beasts rest and gain flesh before winter sets in. Each herd is accompanied by a dozen, or a score, or a couple of score, of cowboys, according to its size, and beside it rumble and jolt the heavy four-horse wagons that hold the food and bedding of the men and the few implements they will need at the end of their journey. As long as possible they follow the trails made by the herds that have already traveled in the same direction, and when these end they strike out for themselves. In the Upper Missouri basin, the pioneer herds soon had to scatter out and each find its own way among the great dreary solitudes, creeping carefully along so that the cattle might not be overdriven and might have water at the halting-places. An outfit might thus be months on its lonely journey, slowly making its way over melancholy, pathless plains, or down the valleys of the lonely rivers. It was tedious, harassing work, as the weary cattle had to be driven carefully and quietly during the day and strictly guarded at night, with a perpetual watch kept for Indians or white horse-thieves. Often they would skirt the edges of the streams for days at a time, seeking for a ford or a good swimming crossing, and if the water was up and the quicksand deep the danger to the riders was serious and the risk of loss among the cattle very great.

6] At last, after days of excitement and danger and after months of weary, monotonous toil, the chosen ground is reached and the final camp pitched. The footsore animals are turned loose to shift for themselves, outlying camps of two or three men each being established to hem them in. Meanwhile the primitive ranch-house, out-buildings, and corrals are built, the unhewn cottonwood logs being chinked with moss and mud, while the roofs are of branches covered with dirt, spades and axes being the only tools needed for the work. Bunks, chairs, and tables are all home-made, and as rough as the houses they are in. The supplies of coarse, rude food are carried perhaps two or three hundred miles from the nearest town, either in the ranch-wagons or else by some regular freighting outfit, whose huge canvas-topped prairie schooners are each drawn by several yoke of oxen, or perhaps by six or eight mules. To guard against the numerous mishaps of prairie travel, two or three of these prairie schooners usually go together, the brawny teamsters, known either as "bull-whackers" or as "mule-skinners," stalking beside their slow-moving teams.

7] The small outlying camps are often tents, or mere dug-outs in the ground. But at the main ranch there will be a cluster of log buildings, including a separate cabin for the foreman or ranchman; often another in which to cook and eat; a long house for the men to sleep in; stables, sheds, a blacksmith's shop, etc.,— the whole group forming quite a little settlement, with the corrals, the stacks of natural hay, and the patches of fenced land for gardens or horse pastures. This little settlement may be situated right out in the treeless, nearly level open, but much more often is placed in the partly wooded bottom of a creek or river, sheltered by the usual background of somber brown hills.

8] When the northern plains began to be settled, such a ranch would at first be absolutely alone in the wilderness, but others of the same sort were sure soon to be established within twenty or thirty miles on one side or the other. The lives of the men in such places were strangely cut off from the outside world, and, indeed, the same is true to a hardly less extent at the present day. Sometimes the wagons are sent for provisions, and the beef-steers are at stated times driven off for shipment. Parties of hunters and trappers call now and then. More rarely small bands of emigrants go by in search of new homes, impelled by the restless, aimless craving for change so deeply grafted in the breast of the American borderer: the white-topped wagons are loaded with domestic goods, with sallow, dispirited-looking women, and with tow-headed children; while the gaunt, moody frontiermen slouch alongside, rifle on shoulder, lank, homely, uncouth, and yet with a curious suggestion of grim strength underlying it all. Or cowboys from neighboring ranches will ride over, looking for lost horses, or seeing if their cattle have strayed off the range. But this is all. Civilization seems as remote as if we were living in an age long past. The whole existence is patriarchal in character: it is the life of men who live in the open, who tend their herds on horseback, who go armed and ready to guard their lives by their own prowess, whose wants are very simple, and who call no man master. Ranching is an occupation like those of vigorous, primitive pastoral peoples, having little in common with the humdrum, workaday business world of the nineteenth century; and the free ranchman in his manner of life shows more kinship to an Arab sheik than to a sleek city merchant or tradesman.

9] By degrees the country becomes what in a stock-raising region passes for well settled. In addition to the great ranches smaller ones are established, with a few hundred, or even a few score, head of cattle apiece; and now and then miserable farmers straggle in to fight a losing and desperate battle with drought, cold, and grasshoppers. The wheels of the heavy wagons, driven always over the same course from one ranch to another, or to the remote frontier towns from which they get their goods, wear ruts in the soil, and roads are soon formed, perhaps originally following the deep trails made by the vanished buffalo. These roads lead down the river-bottoms or along the crests of the divides or else strike out fairly across the prairie, and a man may sometimes travel a hundred miles along one without coming to a house or camp of any sort. If they lead to a shipping point whence the beeves are sent to market, the cattle, traveling in single file, will have worn many and deep paths on each side of the wheel-marks; and the roads between important places which are regularly used either by the United States Government, by stage-coach lines, or by freight teams become deeply worn landmarks—as, for instance, near us, the Deadwood and the old Fort Keogh trails.

10] Cattle-ranching can only be carried on in its present form while the population is scanty; and so in stock-raising regions, pure and simple, there are usually few towns, and these are almost always at the shipping points for cattle. But, on the other hand, wealthy cattlemen, like miners who have done well, always spend their money freely; and accordingly towns like Denver, Cheyenne, and Helena, where these two classes are the most influential in the community, are far pleasanter places of residence than cities of five times their population in the exclusively agricultural States to the eastward.

11] A true "cow town" is worth seeing,—such a one as Miles City, for instance, especially at the time of the annual meeting of the great Montana Stock-raisers' Association. Then the whole place is full to overflowing, the importance of the meeting and the fun of the attendant frolics, especially the horse-races, drawing from the surrounding ranch country many hundreds of men of every degree, from the rich stock-owner worth his millions to the ordinary cowboy who works for forty dollars a month. It would be impossible to imagine a more typically American assemblage, for although there are always a certain number of foreigners, usually English, Irish, or German, yet they have become completely Americanized; and on the whole it would be difficult to gather a finer body of men, in spite of their numerous shortcomings. The ranch-owners differ more from each other than do the cowboys; and the former certainly compare very favorably with similar classes of capitalists in the East. Anything more foolish than the demagogic outcry against "cattle kings" it would be difficult to imagine. Indeed, there are very few businesses so absolutely legitimate as stock-raising and so beneficial to the nation at large; and a successful stock-grower must not only be shrewd, thrifty, patient, and enterprising, but he must also possess qualities of personal bravery, hardihood, and self-reliance to a degree not demanded in the least by any mercantile occupation in a community long settled. Stockmen are in the West the pioneers of civilization, and their daring and adventurousness make the after settlement of the region possible. The whole country owes them a great debt.

12] The most successful ranchmen are those, usually Southwesterners, who have been bred to the business and have grown up with it; but many Eastern men, including not a few college graduates, have also done excellently by devoting their whole time and energy to their work,—although Easterners who invest their money in cattle without knowing anything of the business, or who trust all to their subordinates, are naturally enough likely to incur heavy losses. Stockmen are learning more and more to act together; and certainly the meetings of their associations are conducted with a dignity and good sense that would do credit to any parliamentary body.

13] But the cowboys resemble one another much more and outsiders much less than is the case even with their employers, the ranchmen. A town in the cattle country, when for some cause it is thronged with men from the neighborhood round about, always presents a picturesque sight on the wooden sidewalks of the broad, dusty streets. The men who ply the various industries known only to frontier existence jostle one another as they saunter to and fro or lounge lazily in front of the straggling, cheap-looking board houses: hunters, in their buckskin shirts and fur caps, greasy and unkempt, but with resolute faces and sullen, watchful eyes, that are ever on the alert; teamsters, surly and self-contained, with slouch hats and great cowhide boots; stage-drivers, their faces seamed by hardship and exposure during their long drives with every kind of team, through every kind of country, and in every kind of weather, who, proud of their really wonderful skill as reinsmen and conscious of their high standing in any frontier community, look down on and sneer at the plodding teamsters; trappers and wolfers, whose business is to poison wolves, with shaggy, knock-kneed ponies to carry their small bales and bundles of furs—beaver, wolf, fox, and occasionally otter; silent sheep-herders, with cast-down faces, never able to forget the absolute solitude and monotony of their dreary lives, nor to rid their minds of the thought of the woolly idiots they pass all their days in tending,—these are the men who have come to town, either on business or else to frequent the flaunting saloons and gaudy hells of all kinds in search of the coarse, vicious excitement that in the minds of many of them does duty as pleasure, the only form of pleasure they have ever had a chance to know. Indians too, wrapped in blankets and with stolid, emotionless faces, stalk silently round among the whites, or join in the gambling and horse-racing. If the town is on the borders of the mountain country, there will also be sinewy lumbermen, rough-looking miners and packers, whose business it is to guide the long mule trains that go where wagons can not and whose work in packing needs special and peculiar skill; and mingled with and drawn from all these classes are desperadoes of every grade, from the gambler up through the horse-thief to the murderous professional bully, or, as he is locally called, "bad man"—now, however, a much less conspicuous object than formerly.

14] But everywhere among these plainsmen and mountainmen, and more important than any, are the cowboys,—the men who follow the calling that has brought such towns into being. Singly, or in twos or threes, they gallop their wiry little horses down the street, their lithe, supple figures erect or swaying slightly as they sit loosely in the saddle; while their stirrups are so long that their knees are hardly bent, the bridles not taut enough to keep the chains from clanking. They are smaller and less muscular than the wielders of ax and pick; but they are as hardy and self-reliant as any men who ever breathed—with bronzed, set faces, and keen eyes that look all the world straight in the face without flinching as they flash out from under the broad-brimmed hats. Peril and hardship, and years of long toil broken by weeks of brutal dissipation, draw haggard lines across their eager faces, but never dim their reckless eyes nor break their bearing of defiant self-confidence. They do not walk well, partly because they so rarely do any work out of the saddle, partly because their *chaparajos* or leather overalls hamper them when on the ground; but their appearance is striking for all that, and picturesque too, with their jingling spurs, the big revolvers stuck in their belts, and bright silk handkerchiefs knotted loosely round their necks over the open collars of the flannel shirts. When drunk on the villainous whisky of the frontier towns, they cut mad antics, riding their horses into the saloons, firing their pistols right and left, from boisterous light-heartedness rather than from any viciousness, and indulging too often in deadly shooting affrays, brought on either by the accidental contact of the moment or on account of some long-standing grudge, or perhaps because of bad blood between two ranches or localities; but except while on such sprees they are quiet, rather self-contained men, perfectly frank and simple, and on their own ground treat a stranger with the most whole-souled hospitality, doing all in their power for him and scorning to take any reward in return. Although prompt to resent an injury, they are not at all apt to be rude to outsiders, treating them with what can almost be called a grave courtesy. They are much better fellows and pleasanter companions than small farmers or agricultural laborers; nor are the mechanics and workmen of a great city to be mentioned in the same breath.

15] The bulk of the cowboys themselves are South-westerners; but there are also many from the Eastern and the Northern States, who if they begin young do quite as well as the Southerner. The best hands are fairly bred to the work and follow it from their youth up. Nothing can be more foolish than for an Easterner to think he can become a cowboy in a few months' time. Many a young fellow comes out hot with enthusiasm for life on the plains, only to learn that his clumsiness is greater than he could have believed possible; that the cowboy business is like any other and has to be learned by serving a painful apprenticeship; and that this apprenticeship implies the endurance of rough fare, hard living, dirt, exposure of every kind, no little toil, and month after month of the dullest monotony. For cowboy work there is need of special traits and special training, and young Easterners should be sure of themselves before trying it: the struggle for existence is very keen in the far West, and it is no place for men who lack the ruder, coarser virtues and physical qualities, no matter how intellectual or how refined and delicate their sensibilities. Such are more likely to fail there than in older communities. Probably during the past few years more than half of the young Easterners who have come West with a little money to learn the cattle business have failed signally and lost what they had in the beginning. The West, especially the far West, needs men who have been bred on the farm or in the workshop far more than it does clerks or college graduates.

16] Some of the cowboys are Mexicans, who generally do the actual work well enough, but are not trustworthy; moreover, they are always regarded with extreme disfavor by the Texans in an outfit, among whom the intolerant caste spirit is very strong. Southern-born whites will never work under them, and look down upon all colored or half-caste races. One spring I had with my wagon a Pueblo Indian, an excellent rider and roper, but a drunken, worthless, lazy devil; and in the summer of 1886 there were with us a Sioux half-breed, a quiet, hard-working, faithful fellow, and a mulatto, who was one of the best cow-hands in the whole round-up.

17] Cowboys, like most Westerners, occasionally show remarkable versatility in their tastes and pursuits. One whom I know has abandoned his regular occupation for the past nine months, during which time he has been in succession a bartender, a school-teacher, and a probate judge! Another, whom I once employed for a short while, had passed through even more varied experiences, including those of a barber, a sailor, an apothecary, and a buffalo-hunter.

18] As a rule the cowboys are known to each other only by their first names, with, perhaps, as a prefix, the title of the brand for which they are working. Thus I remember once overhearing a casual remark to the effect that "Bar Y Harry" had married "the seven Open A girl," the latter being the daughter of a neighboring ranchman. Often they receive nicknames, as, for instance, Dutch Wannigan, Windy Jack, and Kid Williams, all of whom are on the list of my personal acquaintances.

19] No man traveling through or living in the country need fear molestation from the cowboys unless he himself accompanies them on their drinking-bouts, or in other ways plays the fool, for they are, with us at any rate, very good fellows, and the most determined and effective foes of real law-breakers, such as horse and cattle thieves, murderers, etc. Few of the outrages quoted in Eastern papers as their handiwork are such in reality, the average Easterner apparently considering every individual who wears a broad hat and carries a six-shooter a cowboy. These outrages are, as a rule, the work of the roughs and criminals who always gather on the outskirts of civilization and who infest every frontier town until the decent citizens become sufficiently numerous and determined to take the law into their own hands and drive them out. The old buffalo-hunters, who formed a distinct class, became powerful forces for evil once they had destroyed the vast herds of mighty beasts whose pursuit had been their means of livelihood. They were absolutely shiftless and improvident; they had no settled habits; they were inured to peril and hardship, but entirely unaccustomed to steady work; and so they afforded just the materials from which to make the bolder and more desperate kinds of criminals. When the game was gone they hung round the settlements for some little time, and then many of them naturally took to horse-stealing, cattle-killing, and highway robbery, although others, of course, went into honest pursuits. They were men who died off rapidly, however; for it is curious to see how many of these plainsmen, in spite of their iron nerves and thews, have their constitutions completely undermined, as much by the terrible hardships they have endured as by the fits of prolonged and bestial revelry with which they have varied them.

20] The "bad men," or professional fighters and man-killers, are of a different stamp, quite a number of them being, according to their light, perfectly honest. These are the men who do most of the killing in frontier communities; yet it is a noteworthy fact that the men who are killed generally deserve their fate. These men are, of course, used to brawling, and are not only sure shots, but, what is equally important, able to "draw" their weapons with marvelous quickness. They think nothing whatever of murder, and are the dread and terror of their associates; yet they are very chary of taking the life of a man of good standing, and will often weaken and back down at once if confronted fearlessly. With many of them their courage arises from confidence in their own powers and knowledge of the fear in which they are held; and men of this type often show the white feather when they get in a tight place. Others, however, will face any odds without flinching. On the other hand, I have known of these men fighting, when mortally wounded, with a cool, ferocious despair that was terrible. As elsewhere, so here, very quiet men are often those who in an emergency show themselves best able to hold their own. These desperadoes always try to "get the drop" on a foe— that is, to take him at a disadvantage before he can use his own weapon. I have known more men killed in this way, when the affair was wholly one-sided, than I have known to be shot in fair fight; and I have known fully as many who were shot by accident. It is wonderful, in the event of a street-fight, how few bullets seem to hit the men they are aimed at.

21] During the last two or three years the stockmen have united to put down all these dangerous characters, often by the most summary exercise of lynch law. Notorious bullies and murderers have been taken out and hung, while the bands of horse and cattle thieves have been regularly hunted down and destroyed in pitched fights by parties of armed cowboys; and as a consequence most of our territory is now perfectly law-abiding. One such fight occurred north of me early last spring. The horse-thieves were overtaken on the banks of the Missouri; two of their number were slain, and the others were driven on the ice, which broke, and two more were drowned. A few months previously another gang, whose headquarters were near the Canadian line, were surprised in their hut; two or three were shot down by the cowboys as they tried to come out, while the rest barricaded themselves in and fought until the great log-hut was set on fire, when they broke forth in a body, and nearly all were killed at once, only one or two making their escape. A little over a year ago one committee of vigilantes in eastern Montana shot or hung nearly sixty—not, however, with the best judgment in all cases.

22] A stranger in the North-western cattle country is especially struck by the resemblance the settlers show in their pursuits and habits to the Southern people. Nebraska and Dakota, east of the Missouri, resemble Minnesota and Iowa and the States farther east, but Montana and the Dakota cow country show more kinship with Texas; for while elsewhere in America settlement has advanced along the parallels of latitude, on the great plains it has followed the meridians of longitude and has gone northerly rather than westerly. The business is carried on as it is in the South. The rough-rider of the plains, the hero of rope and revolver, is first cousin to the backwoodsman of the southern Alleghanies, the man of the ax and the rifle; he is only a unique offshoot of the frontier stock of the South-west. The very term "round-up" is used by the cowboys in the exact sense in which it is employed by the hill people and mountaineers of Kentucky, Tennessee, and

North Carolina, with whom also labor is dear and poor land cheap, and whose few cattle are consequently branded and turned loose in the woods exactly as is done with the great herds on the plains.

23] But the ranching industry itself was copied from the Mexicans, of whose land and herds the South-western frontiermen of Texas took forcible possession; and the traveler in the North-west will see at a glance that the terms and practices of our business are largely of Spanish origin. The cruel curb-bit and heavy stock-saddle, with its high horn and cantle, prove that we have adopted Spanish-American horse-gear; and the broad hat, huge blunt spurs, and leather *chaparajos* of the rider, as well as the corral in which the stock are penned, all alike show the same ancestry. Throughout the cattle country east of the Rocky Mountains, from the Rio Grande to the Saskatchewan, the same terms are in use and the same system is followed; but on the Pacific slope, in California, there are certain small differences, even in nomenclature. Thus, we of the great plains all use the double *cincha* saddle, with one girth behind the horse's fore legs and another farther back, while Californians prefer one with a single *cincha*, which seems to us much inferior for stock-work. Again, Californians use the Spanish word "lasso," which with us has been entirely dropped, no plainsman with pretensions to the title thinking of any word but "rope," either as noun or verb.

24] The rope, whether leather lariat or made of grass, is the one essential feature of every cowboy's equipment. Loosely coiled, it hangs from the horn or is tied to one side of the saddle in front of the thigh, and is used for every conceivable emergency, a twist being taken round the stout saddle-horn the second the noose settles over the neck or around the legs of a chased animal. In helping pull a wagon up a steep pitch, in dragging an animal by the horns out of a bog-hole, in hauling up logs for the fire, and in a hundred other ways aside from its legitimate purpose, the rope is of invaluable service, and dexterity with it is prized almost or quite as highly as good horsemanship, and is much rarer. Once a cowboy is a good roper and rider, the only other accomplishment he values is skill with his great army revolver, it being taken for granted that he is already a thorough plainsman and has long mastered the details of cattle-work; for the best roper and rider alive is of little use unless he is hard-working, honest, keenly alive to his employer's interest, and very careful in the management of the cattle.

25] All cowboys can handle the rope with more or less ease and precision, but great skill in its use is only attained after long practice, and for its highest development needs that the man should have begun in earliest infancy. A really first-class roper can command his own price, and is usually fit for little but his own special work.

26] It is much the same with riding. The cowboy is an excellent rider in his own way, but his way differs from that of a trained school horseman or cross-country fox-hunter as much as it does from the horsemanship of an Arab or of a Sioux Indian, and, as with all these, it has its special merits and special defects —schoolman, fox-hunter, cowboy, Arab, and Indian being all alike admirable riders in their respective styles, and each cherishing the same profound and ignorant contempt for every method but his own. The flash riders, or horse-breakers, always called "bronco busters," can perform really marvelous feats, riding with ease the most vicious and unbroken beasts, that no ordinary cowboy would dare to tackle. Although sitting seemingly so loose in the saddle, such a rider can not be jarred out of it by the wildest plunger, it being a favorite feat to sit out the antics of a bucking horse with silver half-dollars under each knee or in the stirrups under each foot. But their method of breaking is very rough, consisting only in saddling and bridling a beast by main force and then riding him, also by main force, until he is exhausted, when he is turned over as "broken." Later on the cowboy himself may train his horse to stop or wheel instantly at a touch of the reins or bit, to start at top speed at a signal, and to stand motionless when left. An intelligent pony soon picks up a good deal of knowledge about the cow business on his own account.

27] All cattle are branded, usually on the hip, shoulder, and side, or on any one of them, with letters, numbers, or figures, in every combination, the outfit being known by its brand. Near me, for instance, are the Three Sevens, the Thistle, the Bellows, the OX, the VI., the Seventy-six Bar ($\overline{76}$), and the Quarter Circle Diamond ($\overset{\frown}{\diamond}$) outfits. The dew-lap and the ears may also be cut, notched, or slit. All brands are registered, and are thus protected against imitators, any man tampering with them being punished as severely as possible. Unbranded animals are called *mavericks,* and when found on the round-up are either branded by the owner of the range on which they are, or else are sold for the benefit of the association. At every shipping point, as well as where the beef cattle are received, there are stock inspectors who jealously examine all the brands on the live animals or on the hides of the slaughtered ones, so as to detect any foul play, which is immediately reported to the association. It becomes second nature with a cowboy to inspect and note the brands of every bunch of animals he comes across.

28] Perhaps the thing that seems strangest to the traveler who for the first time crosses the bleak plains of this Upper Missouri grazing country is the small number of cattle seen. He can hardly believe he is in the great stock region, where for miles upon miles he will not see a single head, and will then come only upon a straggling herd of a few score. As a matter of fact, where there is no artificial food put up for winter use cattle always need a good deal of ground per head; and this is peculiarly the case with us in the North-west, where much of the ground is bare of vegetation and where what pasture there is is both short and sparse. It is a matter of absolute necessity, where beasts are left to shift for themselves in the open during the bitter winter weather, that they then should have grass that they have not cropped too far down; and to insure this it is necessary with us to allow on the average about twenty-five acres of ground to each animal. This means that a range of country ten miles square will keep between two and three thousand head of stock only, and if more are put on, it is at the risk of seeing a severe winter kill off half or three-quarters of the whole number. So a range may be in reality overstocked when to an Eastern and unpracticed eye it seems hardly to have on it a number worth taking into account.

29] Overstocking is the great danger threatening the stock-raising industry on the plains. This industry has only risen to be of more than local consequence during the past score of years, as before that time it was confined to Texas and California; but during these two decades of its existence the stockmen in different localities have again and again suffered the most ruinous losses, usually with overstocking as the ultimate cause. In the south the drought, and in the north the deep snows, and everywhere unusually bad winters, do immense damage; still, if the land is fitted for stock at all, they will, averaging one year with another, do very well so long as the feed is not cropped down too close.

30] But, of course, no amount of feed will make some countries worth anything for cattle that are not housed during the winter; and stockmen in choosing new ranges for their herds pay almost as much attention to the capacity of the land for yielding shelter as they do to the abundant and good quality of the grass. High up among the foot-hills of the mountains cattle will not live through the winter; and an open, rolling prairie land of heavy rainfall, and where in consequence the snow lies deep and there is no protection from the furious cold winds, is useless for winter grazing, no matter how thick and high the feed. The three essentials for a range are grass, water, and shelter: the water is only needed in summer and the shelter in winter, while it may be doubted if drought during the hot months has ever killed off more cattle than have died in consequence of exposure on shelterless ground to the icy weather, lasting from November to April.

31] The finest summer range may be valueless either on account of its lack of shelter or because it is in a region of heavy snowfall—portions of territory lying in the same latitude and not very far apart often differing widely in this respect; or extraordinarily severe weather may cause a heavy death-rate utterly unconnected with overstocking. This was true of the loss that visited the few herds which spent the very hard winter of 1880 on the northern cattle plains. These were the pioneers of their kind, and the grass was all that could be desired; yet the extraordinary severity of the weather proved too much for the cattle.

This was especially the case with those herds consisting of "pilgrims," as they are called—that is, of animals driven up on to the range from the south, and therefore in poor condition. One such herd of pilgrims on the Powder River suffered a loss of thirty-six hundred out of a total of four thousand, and the survivors kept alive only by browsing on the tops of cottonwoods felled for them. Even seasoned animals fared very badly. One great herd in the Yellowstone Valley lost about a fourth of its number, the loss falling mainly on the breeding cows, calves, and bulls,—always the chief sufferers, as the steers, and also the dry cows, will get through almost anything. The loss here would have been far heavier than it was had it not been for a curious trait shown by the cattle. They kept in bands of several hundred each, and during the time of the deep snows a band would make a start and travel several miles in a straight line, plowing their way through the drifts and beating out a broad track; then, when stopped by a frozen watercourse or chain of buttes, they would turn back and graze over the trail thus made, the only place where they could get at the grass.

32] A drenching rain, followed by a severe snap of cold, is even more destructive than deep snow, for the saturated coats of the poor beasts are turned into sheets of icy mail, and the grass-blades, frozen at the roots as well as above, change into sheaves of brittle spears as uneatable as so many icicles. Entire herds have perished in consequence of such a storm. Mere cold, however, will kill only very weak animals, which is fortunate for us, as the spirit in the thermometer during winter often sinks to fifty degrees below zero, the cold being literally arctic; yet though the cattle become thin during such a snap of weather, and sometimes have their ears, tails, and even horns frozen off, they nevertheless rarely die from the cold alone. But if there is a blizzard blowing in at such a time, the cattle need shelter, and if caught in the open, will travel for scores of miles before the storm, until they reach a break in the ground, or some stretch of dense woodland, which will shield them from the blasts. If cattle traveling in this manner come to some obstacle that they can not pass, as, for instance, a wire fence or a steep railway embankment, they will not try to make their way back against the storm, but will simply stand with their tails to it until they drop dead in their tracks; and, accordingly, in some parts of the country—but luckily far to the south of us—the railways are fringed with countless skeletons of beasts that have thus perished, while many of the long wire fences make an almost equally bad showing. In some of the very open country of Kansas and Indian Territory, many of the herds during the past two years have suffered a loss of from sixty to eighty per cent., although this was from a variety of causes, including drought as well as severe winter weather. Too much rain is quite as bad as too little, especially if it falls after the 1st of August, for then, though the growth of grass is very rank and luxuriant, it yet has little strength and does not cure well on the stalk; and it is only possible to winter cattle at large at all because of the way in which the grass turns into natural hay by this curing on the stalk.

33] But scantiness of food, due to overstocking, is the one really great danger to us in the north, who do not have to fear the droughts that occasionally devastate portions of the southern ranges. In a fairly good country, if the feed is plenty, the natural increase of a herd is sure shortly to repair any damage that may be done by an unusually severe winter—unless, indeed, the latter should be one such as occurs but two or three times in a century. When, however, the grass becomes cropped down, then the loss in even an ordinary year is heavy among the weaker animals, and if the winter is at all severe it becomes simply appalling. The snow covers the shorter grass much quicker, and even when there is enough, the cattle, weak and unfit to travel around, have to work hard to get it by exertion tending to enfeeble them and render them less able to cope with the exposure and cold. Again, the grass is, of course, soonest eaten off where there is shelter; and, accordingly, the broken ground to which the animals cling during winter may be grazed bare of vegetation though the open plains, to which only the hardiest will at this season stray, may have plenty; and insufficiency of food, although not such as actually to starve them, weakens them so that they succumb readily to the cold or to one of the numerous accidents to which they are liable—as slipping off an icy butte or getting cast in a frozen washout. The cows in calf are those that suffer most, and so heavy is the loss among these and so light the calf crop that it is yet an open question whether our northern ranges are as a whole fitted for breeding. When the animals get weak they will huddle into some nook or corner or empty hut and simply stay there till they die.

34] Overstocking may cause little or no harm for two or three years, but sooner or later there comes a winter which means ruin to the ranches that have too many cattle on them; and in our country, which is even now getting crowded, it is merely a question of time as to when a winter will come that will understock the ranges by the summary process of killing off about half of all the cattle throughout the North-west.

35] In our northern country we have "free grass"; that is, the stockmen rarely own more than small portions of the land over which their cattle range, the bulk of it being unsurveyed and still the property of the National Government—for the latter refuses to sell the soil except in small lots, acting on the wise principle of distributing it among as many owners as possible. Here and there some ranchman has acquired title to narrow strips of territory peculiarly valuable as giving water-right; but the amount of land thus occupied is small with us,—although the reverse is the case farther south,—and there is practically no fencing to speak of. As a consequence, the land is one vast pasture, and the man who overstocks his own range damages his neighbors as much as himself. These huge northern pastures are too dry and the soil too poor to be used for agriculture until the rich, wet lands to the east and west are occupied; and at present we have little fear from grangers. Of course, in the end much of the ground will be taken up for small farms, but the farmers that so far have come in have absolutely failed to make even a living, except now and then by raising a few vegetables for the use of the stockmen; and we are inclined to welcome the incoming of an occasional settler, if he is a decent man, especially as, by the laws of the Territories in which the great grazing plains lie, he is obliged to fence in his own patch of cleared ground, and we do not have to keep our cattle out of it.

36] At present we are far more afraid of each other. There are always plenty of men who for the sake of the chance of gain they themselves run are willing to jeopardize the interests of their neighbors by putting on more cattle than the land will support—for the loss, of course, falls as heavily on the man who has put on the right number as on him who has put on too many; and it is against these individuals that we have to guard so far as we are able. To protect ourselves completely is impossible, but the very identity of interest that renders all of us liable to suffer for the fault of a few also renders us as a whole able to take some rough measures to guard against the wrong-doing of a portion of our number; for the fact that the cattle wander intermixed over the ranges forces all the ranchmen of a locality to combine if they wish to do their work effectively. Accordingly, the stockmen of a neighborhood, when it holds as many cattle as it safely can, usually unitedly refuse to work with any one who puts in another herd. In the cow country a man is peculiarly dependent upon his neighbors, and a small outfit is wholly unable to work without their assistance when once the cattle have mingled completely with those of other brands. A large outfit is much more master of its destiny, and can do its own work quite by itself; but even such a one can be injured in countless ways if the hostility of the neighboring ranchmen is incurred. So a certain check is put to undue crowding of the ranges; but it is only partial.

37] The best days of ranching are over; and though there are many ranchmen who still make money, yet during the past two or three years the majority have certainly lost. This is especially true of the numerous Easterners who went into the business without any experience and trusted themselves entirely to their Western representatives; although, on the other hand, many of those who have made most money at it are Easterners, who, however, have happened to be naturally fitted for the work and who have deliberately settled down to learning the business as they would have learned any other, devoting their whole time and energy to it. As the country grows older, stock-raising will in some places die out, and in others entirely change its character; the ranches will be broken up, will be gradually modified into stock-farms, or, if on good soil, may even fall under the sway of the husbandman.

38] In its present form stock-raising on the plains is doomed, and can hardly outlast the century. The great free ranches, with their barbarous, picturesque, and curiously fascinating surroundings, mark a primitive stage of existence as surely as do the great tracts of primeval forests, and like the latter must pass away before the onward march of our people; and we who have felt the charm of the life, and have exulted in its abounding vigor and its bold, restless freedom, will not only regret its passing for our own sakes, but must also feel real sorrow that those who come after us are not to see, as we have seen, what is perhaps the pleasantest, healthiest, and most exciting phase of American existence.

Questions

Roosevelt's article is not the kind of essay which is built around a theme idea; its object is not to prove a point, but to present a large body of information about a given topic—in this case, life on the Western plains in the 80's of the last century. In such an essay, especially in one which assembles such a large and varied body of facts as this one does, the main problem is naturally that of organization; the mass of facts must be sorted into logical divisions and some kind of form imposed. Roosevelt's success in handling this problem of sorting and assembling should be made evident by the answers to the questions which follow.

1. Although the organization of the essay is somewhat informal, it can easily be divided into six sections. The first section covers paragraphs 1-2; the second, paragraphs 3-9; the third, paragraphs 10-21; the fourth, paragraphs 22-27; the fifth, paragraphs 28-36; and the sixth, paragraphs 37-38. Give a title to each section.

2. *a.* The second section really combines two topics: the process of settlement and the layout of a ranch. How does Roosevelt manage to treat these two subjects together?

b. The third section also deals with two distinct subjects. What are they, and why was it convenient for Roosevelt to discuss the two together?

c. Would it be more appropriate to transfer the discussion of the cowboy's character to the second section?

3. The order in which the sections are arranged is not the only possible one, but it is probably as good as any.

    a. What is there about the first section which makes it an appropriate beginning?

    b. Why does the fifth section naturally come just before the conclusion?

    c. Why should the description of the ranch come before the description of the town?

    d. Another writer might have preferred to place the present fourth section after the second section. What would be the advantage of this arrangement, and what would be one objection to it?

4. Why should paragraph 13 precede paragraphs 14-19—in other words, why does Roosevelt discuss the other miscellaneous Western types before he discusses the cowboys, who are, as he says, "more important than any"?

5. The transitions from topic to topic in this essay are especially good.

    a. How does Roosevelt manage the transition from the description of the cowboy to the description of the "bad man" (paragraph 19)?

    b. How does the discussion of trails and roads in paragraph 9 help to lead from the second section to the third?

6. Although the physical appearance of a ranch is given in some detail, the towns of the third section are hardly described at all. Can you see any reason for this?

7. In his last sentence Roosevelt concludes that ranch life was "perhaps the pleasantest, healthiest, and most exciting phase of American existence."

    a. Is he justified in speaking of a life which includes blizzards, lynchings, and gun frays as pleasant and healthy?

    b. Has Roosevelt's enthusiastic attitude toward ranch life been evident throughout the essay or does it come as a surprise at the end? In other words, is the conclusion properly prepared for?

Suggested Assignment

Write an extended description of life in some region or locality with which you are familiar. Collect as much detail as you can, and do not begin writing until you have evolved a suitable plan for organizing the material.

FIVE TRAVELERS IN THE NEAR EAST *

Mark Twain
Lady Mary Wortley Montagu
Alexander William Kinglake
Sir Richard Burton
R. B. Cunninghame Graham

1. MARK TWAIN   [The Turkish Bath]

WHEN I think how I have been swindled by books of Oriental travel, I want a tourist for breakfast. For years and years I have dreamed of the wonders of the Turkish bath; for years and years I have promised myself that I would yet enjoy one. Many and many a time, in fancy, I have lain in the marble bath, and breathed the slumbrous fragrance of Eastern spices that filled the air; then passed through a weird and complicated system of pulling and hauling and drenching and scrubbing, by a gang of naked savages who loomed vast and vaguely through

---

* The five selections that follow are to be studied as a unit. Questions will be found at the end of the fifth selection.
Mark Twain. From *The Innocents Abroad* by Mark Twain (Samuel L. Clemens). Reprinted by permission of Harper and Brothers.

the steaming mists, like demons; then rested for a while on a divan fit for a king; then passed through another complex ordeal, and one more fearful than the first; and, finally, swathed in soft fabrics, been conveyed to a princely saloon and laid on a bed of eiderdown, where eunuchs, gorgeous of costume, fanned me while I drowsed and dreamed, or contentedly gazed at the rich hangings of the apartment, the soft carpets, the sumptuous furniture, the pictures, and drank delicious coffee, smoked the soothing narghili, and dropped, at the last, into tranquil repose, lulled by sensuous odors from unseen censers, by the gentle influence of the narghili's Persian tobacco, and by the music of fountains that counterfeited the pattering of summer rain.

2] That was the picture, just as I got it from incendiary books of travel. It was a poor, miserable imposture. The reality is no more like it than the Five Points are like the Garden of Eden. They received me in a great court, paved with marble slabs; around it were broad galleries, one above another, carpeted with seedy matting, railed with unpainted balustrades, and furnished with huge rickety chairs, cushioned with rusty old mattresses, indented with impressions left by the forms of nine successive generations of men who had reposed upon them. The place was vast, naked, dreary; its court a barn, its galleries stalls for human horses. The cadaverous, half-nude varlets that served in the establishment had nothing of poetry in their appearance, nothing of romance, nothing of Oriental splendor. They shed no entrancing odors—just the contrary. Their hungry eyes and their lank forms continually suggested one glaring, unsentimental fact—they wanted what they term in California "a square meal."

3] I went into one of the racks and undressed. An unclean starveling wrapped a gaudy table-cloth about his loins, and hung a white rag over my shoulders. If I had had a tub then, it would have come natural to me to take in washing. I was then conducted down-stairs into the wet, slippery court, and the first things that attracted my attention were my heels. My fall excited no comment. They expected it, no doubt. It belonged in the list of softening, sensuous influences peculiar to this home of Eastern luxury. It was softening enough, certainly, but its application was not happy. They now gave me a pair of wooden clogs—benches in miniature, with leather straps over them to confine my feet (which they would have done, only I do not wear No. 13's). These things dangled uncomfortably by the straps when I lifted up my feet, and came down in awkward and unexpected places when I put them on the floor again, and sometimes turned sideways and wrenched my ankles out of joint. However, it was all Oriental luxury, and I did what I could to enjoy it.

4] They put me in another part of the barn and laid me on a stuffy sort of pallet, which was not made of cloth of gold, or Persian shawls, but was merely the unpretending sort of thing I have seen in the Negro quarters of Arkansas. There was nothing whatever in this dim marble prison but five more of these biers. It was a very solemn place. I expected that the spiced odors of Araby were going to steal over my senses, now, but they did not. A copper-colored skeleton, with a rag around him, brought me a glass decanter of water, with a lighted tobacco pipe in the top of it, and a pliant stem a yard long, with a brass mouthpiece to it.

5] It was the famous "narghili" of the East—the thing the Grand Turk smokes in the pictures. This began to look like luxury. I took one blast at it, and it was sufficient; the smoke went in a great volume down into my stomach, my lungs, even into the uttermost parts of my frame. I exploded one mighty cough, and it was as if Vesuvius had let go. For the next five minutes I smoked at every pore, like a frame house that is on fire on the inside. Not any more narghili for me. The smoke had a vile taste, and the taste of a thousand infidel tongues that remained on that brass mouthpiece was viler still. I was getting discouraged. Whenever, hereafter, I see the cross-legged Grand Turk smoking his narghili, in pretended bliss, on the outside of a paper of Connecticut tobacco, I shall know him for the shameless humbug he is.

6] This prison was filled with hot air. When I had got warmed up sufficiently to prepare me for a still warmer temperature, they took me where it was—into a marble room, wet, slippery, and steamy, and laid me out on a raised platform in the center. It was very warm. Presently my man sat me down by a tank of hot water, drenched me well, gloved his hand with a coarse mitten, and began to polish me all over with it. I began to smell disagreeably. The more he polished the worse I smelt. It was alarming. I said to him:

7] "I perceive that I am pretty far gone. It is plain that I ought to be buried without any unnecessary delay. Perhaps you had better go after my friends at once, because the weather is warm, and I cannot 'keep' long."

8] He went on scrubbing, and paid no attention. I soon saw that he was reducing my size. He bore hard on his mitten, and from under it rolled little cylinders, like macaroni. It could not be dirt, for it was too white. He pared me down in this way for a long time. Finally I said:

9] "It is a tedious process. It will take hours to trim me to the size you want me; I will wait; go and borrow a jack-plane."

10] He paid no attention at all.

11] After a while he brought a basin, some soap, and something that seemed to be the tail of a horse. He made up a prodigious quantity of soap-suds, deluged me with them from head to foot, without warning me to shut my eyes, and then swabbed me viciously with the horse-tail. Then he left me there, a snowy statue of lather, and went away. When I got tired of waiting I went and hunted him up. He was propped against the wall, in another room, asleep. I woke him. He was not disconcerted. He took me back and flooded me with hot water, then turbaned my head, swathed me with dry table-cloths, and conducted me to a latticed chicken-coop in one of the galleries, and pointed to one of those Arkansas beds. I mounted it, and vaguely expected the odors of Araby again. They did not come.

12] The blank, unornamented coop had nothing about it of that Oriental voluptuousness one reads of so much. It was more suggestive of the county hospital than anything else. The skinny servitor brought a narghili, and I got him to take it out again without wasting any time about it. Then he brought the world-renowned Turkish coffee that poets have sung so rapturously for many generations, and I seized upon it as the last hope that was left of my old dreams of Eastern luxury. It was another fraud.

Of all the unchristian beverages that ever passed my lips, Turkish coffee is the worst. The cup is small, it is smeared with grounds; the coffee is black, thick, unsavory of smell, and execrable in taste. The bottom of the cup has a muddy sediment in it half an inch deep. This goes down your throat, and portions of it lodge by the way, and produce a tickling aggravation that keeps you barking and coughing for an hour.

13] Here endeth my experience of the celebrated Turkish bath, and here also endeth my dream of the bliss the mortal revels in who passes through it. It is a malignant swindle. The man who enjoys it is qualified to enjoy anything that is repulsive to sight or sense, and he that can invest it with a charm of poetry is able to do the same with anything else in the world that is tedious, and wretched, and dismal, and nasty.

2. LADY MARY WORTLEY MONTAGU
[*The Turkish Bath*]

I WENT to the bagnio about ten o'clock. It was already full of women. It is built of stone, in the shape of a dome, with no windows but in the roof, which gives light enough. There were five of these domes joined together, the outmost being less than the rest, and serving only as a hall, where the portress stood at the door. Ladies of quality generally give this woman the value of a crown or ten shillings; and I did not forget that ceremony. The next room is a very large one paved with marble, and all around it, raised, two sofas of marble, one above another. There were four fountains of cold water in this room, falling first into marble basins, and then running on the floor in little channels made for that purpose, which carried the streams into the next room, something less than this, with the same sort of marble sofas, but so hot with steams of sulphur proceeding from

Lady Mary Wortley Montagu. Adapted from a letter to the Lady ——, Adrianople, April 1, 1717.

the baths joining to it, it was impossible to stay there with one's clothes on. The two other domes were the hot baths, one of which had cocks of cold water turning into it, to temper it to what degree of warmth the bathers have a mind to.

2] I was in my travelling habit, which is a riding dress, and certainly appeared very extraordinary to them. Yet there was not one of them that shewed the least surprise or impertinent curiosity, but received me with all the obliging civility possible. I know no European court where the ladies would have behaved themselves in so polite a manner to a stranger. I believe in the whole, there were two hundred women, and yet none of those disdainful smiles, or satiric whispers, that never fail in our assemblies when any body appears that is not dressed exactly in the fashion. They repeated over and over to me, "Uzelle, pék uzelle," which is nothing but Charming, very charming.

3] The first sofas were covered with cushions and rich carpets, on which sat the ladies; and on the second, their slaves behind them, but without any distinction of rank by their dress, all being in the state of nature, that is, in plain English, stark naked, without any beauty or defect concealed. Yet there was not the least wanton smile or immodest gesture amongst them. They walked and moved with the same majestic grace which Milton describes of our general mother. There were many amongst them as exactly proportioned as ever any goddess was drawn by the pencil of Guido or Titian,—and most of their skins shiningly white, only adorned by their beautiful hair divided into many tresses, hanging on their shoulders, braided either with pearl or ribbon, perfectly representing the figures of the Graces. They were in different postures, some in conversation, some working, others drinking coffee or sherbet, and many negligently lying on their cushions, while their slaves (generally pretty girls of seventeen or eighteen) were employed in braiding their hair in several pretty fancies. In short, it is the women's coffee-house, where all the news of the town is told, scandal invented, etc. They generally take this diversion once a week, and stay there at least four or five hours, without getting cold by immediate coming out of the hot bath into the cold room, which was very surprising to me.

4] The lady that seemed the most considerable among them, entreated me to sit by her, and would fain have undressed me for the bath. I excused myself with some difficulty. They being all so earnest in persuading me, I was at last forced to open my shirt, and shew them my stays; which satisfied them very well, for, I saw, they believed I was so locked up in that machine, that it was not in my own power to open it, which contrivance they attributed to my husband. I was charmed with their civility and beauty, and should have been very glad to pass more time with them; but Mr. Wortley resolving to pursue his journey the next morning early, I was in haste to see the ruins of Justinian's church, which did not afford me so agreeable a prospect as I had left, being little more than a heap of stones.

3. ALEXANDER WILLIAM KINGLAKE
[*The Arab Camp*]

BEFORE sunset I came up with an encampment of Arabs (the encampment from which my camels had been brought), and my tent was pitched amongst theirs. I was now amongst the true Bedouins. Almost every man of this race closely resembles his brethren; almost every man has large and finely formed features, but his face is so thoroughly stripped of flesh, and the white folds from his head-gear fall down by his haggard cheeks so much in the burial fashion, that he looks quite sad and ghastly; his large, dark orbs roll slowly and solemnly over the white of his deep-set eyes; his countenance shows painful thought and long suffering—the suffering of one fallen from a high estate. His gait is strangely majestic, and he marches along with his simple blanket as though he were wearing the purple.

Alexander William Kinglake. From *Eothen* by Alexander William Kinglake.

His common talk is a series of piercing screams and cries, very painful to hear.

2] The Bedouin women are not treasured up like the wives and daughters of other Orientals, and indeed they seemed almost entirely free from the restraints imposed by jealousy. The feint which they made of concealing their faces from me was always slight. When they first saw me, they used to hold up a part of their drapery with one hand across their faces, but they seldom persevered very steadily in subjecting me to this privation. They were sadly plain. The awful haggardness that gave something of character to the faces of the men was sheer ugliness in the poor women. It is a great shame, but the truth is that, except when we refer to the beautiful devotion of the mother to her child, all the fine things we say and think about woman apply only to those who are tolerably good-looking or graceful. These Arab women were not within the scope of the privilege, and indeed were altogether much too plain and clumsy for this vain and lovesome world. They may have been good women enough, so far as relates to the exercise of the minor virtues, but they had so grossly neglected the prime duty of looking pretty in this transitory life that I could not at all forgive them; they seemed to feel the weight of their guilt, and to be truly and humbly penitent. I had the complete command of their affections, for at any moment I could make their young hearts bound and their old hearts jump by offering a handful of tobacco; yet, believe me, it was not in the first soirée that my store of latakia was exhausted!

3] The Bedouin women have no religion. This is partly the cause of their clumsiness. Perhaps if from Christian girls they would learn how to pray, their souls might become more gentle, and their limbs be clothed with grace.

4] You who are going into their country have a direct personal interest in knowing something about "Arab hospitality"; but the deuce of it is that the poor fellows with whom I have happened to pitch my tent were scarcely ever in a condition to exercise that magnanimous virtue with much éclat; indeed, Mysseri's *

---

* Kinglake's interpreter and the manager of his party.

canteen generally enabled me to outdo my hosts in the matter of entertainment. They were always courteous, however, and were never backward in offering me the *youart*, a kind of whey, which is the principal delicacy to be found amongst the wandering tribes.

5] Practically, I think, Childe Harold would have found it a dreadful bore to make "the desert his dwelling-place," for, at all events, if he adopted the life of the Arabs he would have tasted no solitude. The tents are partitioned, not so as to divide the Childe and the "fair spirit" who is his "minister" from the rest of the world, but so as to separate the twenty or thirty brown men that sit screaming in the one compartment from the fifty or sixty brown women and children that scream and squeak in the other. If you adopt the Arab life for the sake of seclusion, you will be horribly disappointed, for you will find yourself in perpetual contact with a mass of hot fellow-creatures. It is true that all who are inmates of the same tent are related to each other, but I am not quite sure that that circumstance adds much to the charm of such a life.

4. SIR RICHARD BURTON [*The Arab Camp*]

THIS WORK [his translation of the *Arabian Nights*], laborious as it may appear, has been to me a labour of love, an unfailing source of solace and satisfaction. During my long years of official banishment to the luxuriant and deadly deserts of Western Africa, and to the dull and dreary half-clearings of South America, it proved itself a charm, a talisman against ennui and despondency. Impossible even to open the pages without a vision starting into view; without drawing a picture from the pinacothek of the brain; without reviving a host of memories and reminiscences which are not the common property of   10

Sir Richard Burton. From the Introduction to *The Book of the Thousand Nights and a Night*, translated by Richard F. Burton.

travellers, however widely they may have travelled. From my dull and commonplace and "respectable" surroundings, the Jinn bore me at once to the land of my predilection, Arabia, a region so familiar to my mind that even at first sight, it seemed a reminiscence of some by-gone metempsychic life in the distant Past. Again I stood under the diaphanous skies, in air glorious as ether, whose every breath raises men's spirits like sparkling wine. Once more I saw the evening star hanging like a solitaire from the pure front of the western firmament; and the after-glow transfiguring and transforming, as by magic, the homely and rugged features of the scene into a fairy-land lit with a light which never shines on other soils or seas. Then would appear the woollen tents, low and black, of the true Badawin, mere dots in the boundless waste of lion-tawny clays and gazelle-brown gravels, and the camp-fire dotting like a glow-worm the village centre. Presently, sweetened by distance, would be heard the wild weird song of lads and lasses, driving or rather pelting, through the gloaming their sheep and goats; and the measured chant of the spearsmen gravely stalking behind their charge, the camels; mingled with the bleating of the flocks and the bellowing of the humpy herds; while the reremouse flitted overhead with his tiny shriek, and the rave of the jackal resounded through deepening glooms, and—most musical of music—the palm trees answered the whispers of the night-breeze with the softest tones of falling water.

2] And then a shift of scene. The Shaykhs and "white-beards" of the tribe gravely take their places, sitting with outspread skirts like hillocks on the plain, as the Arabs say, around the camp-fire, whilst I reward their hospitality and secure its continuance by reading or reciting a few pages of their favourite tales. The women and children stand motionless as silhouettes outside the ring; and all are breathless with attention; they seem to drink in the words with eyes and mouths as well as with ears. The most fantastic flights of fancy, the wildest improbabilities, the most impossible of impossibilities, appear to them utterly natural, mere matters of every-day occurrence. They enter thoroughly into each phase of feeling touched upon by the author:

they take a personal pride in the chivalrous nature and knightly prowess of Taj al-Mulúk; they are touched with tenderness by the self-sacrificing love of Azizah; their mouths water as they hear of heaps of untold gold given away in largess like clay; they chuckle with delight every time a Kázi or Fakir—a judge or a reverend—is scurvily entreated by some Pantagruelist of the Wilderness; and, despite their normal solemnity and impassibility, all roar with laughter, sometimes rolling upon the ground till the reader's gravity is sorely tried, at the tales of the garrulous Barber and of Ali and the Kurdish Sharper. To this magnetizing mood the sole exception is when a Badawi of superior accomplishments, who sometimes says his prayers, ejaculates a startling "Astagh-faru'llah"—I pray Allah's pardon!—for listening, not to Carlyle's "downright lies," but to light mention of the sex whose name is never heard amongst the nobility of the Desert.

5. R. B. CUNNINGHAME GRAHAM [*Arab Faces*]

AT THE entrance of the town stood the palace of the Kaid, an enormous structure made of mud and painted light rose-pink, but all in ruins, the crenellated walls a heap of rubbish, the machicolated towers blown up with gunpowder. The Kaid, it seems, oppressed the people of the town and district beyond the powers of even Arabs and Berbers to endure; so they rebelled, and to the number of twelve thousand besieged the place, took it by storm, and tore it all to pieces to search for money in the walls.

2] Most people in Morocco if they have money, hide it in the walls of their abode, but the Kaid of Amsmiz was wiser, and had sent all his to Mogador. He fought to the last, then cutting

R. B. Cunninghame Graham. From *Mogreb-el-Acksa, A Journey in Morocco*, by R. B. Cunninghame Graham. Reprinted by permission of the Viking Press, Inc.

all his women's throats, mounted his favourite horse and almost unattended "maugre all his enemies, through the thickest of them he rode," leaving his stores well-dressed with arsenic, so that, like Samson in his fall, he killed more of his enemies than in his life. Today he is said to live in Fez, greatly respected, a quiet old Arab with a fine white beard, whose greatest pleasure is to tell his rosary.

3] Curious how little the Oriental face is altered by the storms of life. I knew one, Haj Mohammed el ——, —a scoundrel of the deepest dye—who in his youth had poisoned many people, had tortured others, assassinated several with his own hand, and yet was a kindly, courteous, venerable gentleman, whose hobby was to buy any eligible young girl he heard of, to stock his harem. One day I ventured to remark that he was getting rather well on in years to think of such commodities. He answered; "Yes, but then I buy them as you Christians buy pictures—to adorn my house; by Allah, my heirs will be the gainers by my mania." Yet the man's face was quiet and serene, his eyes bright as a sailor's, his countenance as little marred by wrinkles as those one sees upon the Bishops' benches in the House of Lords; and as he stroked his beard, and told his beads, he seemed to me a patriarch after the type of those depicted in the Old Testament. Perhaps it is the lack of railways, with their clatter, smoke, and levelling of all mankind to the most common multiple; but still it is the case—an Eastern scoundrel's face is finer far than that a Nonconformist Cabinet Minister displays, all spoiled with lines, with puckers round the mouth, a face in which you see all natural passion stultified, and greed and piety—the two most potent factors in his life—writ large and manifest.

Questions

The idea which dominates a prose selection and the feeling which runs through it are not separable. The impact of something—whether it be an occurrence, a series of occurrences, a place, a person, or perhaps information he has gathered—induces the writer to set down his thoughts. True, his reaction may be much more intellectual than emotional; or much more emotional than intellectual. But, whatever element predominates, both will be present; and consistency of feeling, no less than singleness of idea, is necessary to produce a unified impression. In the last analysis, then, the personality of the author, or more particularly his personality as reflected in his attitude toward some specific thing, helps to unify his writing. Even if he does not use the first person singular or give any direct information about himself, we sense his presence behind the thing he observes.

A thorough understanding of the writer's attitude toward his material is of practical importance—both to the writer and to the reader. The writer who is not completely conscious of his own point of view is likely to produce a blurred piece of prose. The expressions "shift in point of view" or "shift in attitude," frequent comments on student themes, refer to this uncertainty of feeling. On the other hand, the reader who fails to realize that a selection is permeated by feeling may accept all the details given as pure, objective facts. Facts are commonly the basis of the writing, to be sure—but facts interpreted and hence unified by a particular temperament.

This importance of feeling and personality is well illustrated by the five selections "Travelers in the Orient." All are the reactions of persons of Western culture to the strangeness of the Near East; all are written in the first person singular. Moreover, the selections from Mark Twain and Lady Mary Wortley Montagu can be compared with each other, as can those from Alexander Kinglake and Sir Richard Burton. Certainly, in these comparable selections, there are differences other than personality to be taken into account. There is, for example, the question of time: Lady Mary Wortley Montagu was in Adrianople in 1717, whereas Mark Twain is reporting an experience that occurred in the second half of the nineteenth century. The degree of likeness between the actual experiences must also be considered: Mark Twain and Lady Montagu describe different Turkish baths; Kinglake and Burton are reporting facts about the same Arab tribes, but whereas Kinglake, as a "tourist," encountered them only once, Burton lived among them.

These differences having been conceded, however, the fact remains that Lady Montagu's bath differs from Mark Twain's, and Kinglake's camp differs from Burton's not merely because the baths or camps were different, but because the persons who wrote of them were different and described the objects in a manner which was dictated by their own ideas and personalities.

1 & 2. THE TURKISH BATH

1. What did Mark Twain expect the Turkish bath to be like? What did Lady Mary Wortley Montagu expect? Of what value is an introductory paragraph devoted wholly to the subject of expectation?
2. The bath which Lady Montagu visited seems intrinsically pleasanter than that which Mark Twain describes, but actually some of the details are precisely the same. For example, Lady Montagu speaks of a room "paved with marble" (paragraph 1), Mark Twain of "a great court, paved with marble slabs" (paragraph 2). Point out other similar details in the two selections. In each instance, how does Mark Twain manage to make his description sound so distasteful?
3. Assume the last sentence of paragraph 2 in Mark Twain's selection were written as follows:

   Their hungry eyes and their lank forms continually suggested one glaring, unsentimental fact—they hadn't had enough to eat.

   Do you sense any difference in tone? What is the point of mentioning California?
4. It is natural for the traveler to compare what he sees to what is familiar to him in his own country. Find three or four instances in which Mark Twain does this. What do all the examples which you have selected have in common?
5. Where does Lady Montagu introduce such a comparison? What is the important difference between her comparison and those Mark Twain uses?
6. Mark Twain assumes that his fall (paragraph 3) elicited no comment because it was expected. Might he have interpreted this fact in any other way? Is there any reason why the court should not have been wet and slippery?
7. Who is in the right about the "narghili"—Mark Twain or the Grand Turk (paragraph 5)? Who is more to be trusted in the matter of Turkish coffee—the poets who have sung so rapturously for many generations or Mark Twain (paragraph 12)?
8. Do you think that Mark Twain's remarks in paragraphs 7 and 9 are recorded verbatim? What is the nature of their humor? In what way is this humor an integral part of Twain's whole point of view?

Five Travelers in the Near East

9. Lady Montagu's conclusion, that she was "charmed with their civility and beauty" (paragraph 4) is evident throughout her description of the women's bagnio. What other attitudes might another European woman, of a different temperament, have assumed toward this experience?

3 & 4. THE ARAB CAMP

1. The phrase "before sunset" constitutes Kinglake's entire description of his surroundings. How much space does Burton devote to a description of place? What in the nature of the two selections explains this difference?

2. What do you think is revealed about Kinglake by each of the following phrases or sentences?

    a. ". . . they had so grossly neglected the prime duty of looking pretty in this transitory life that I could not at all forgive them" (paragraph 2).

    b. ". . . the deuce of it is that the poor fellows with whom I have happened to pitch my tent were scarcely ever in a condition to exercise that magnanimous virtue with much éclat" (paragraph 4).

    c. "They were always courteous . . ." (paragraph 4).

    d. ". . . you will find yourself in perpetual contact with a mass of hot fellow-creatures" (paragraph 5).

3. Explain the reference to Childe Harold in paragraph 5. Childe Harold may be taken as a symbol of the romantic attitude toward experience. Is Kinglake's attitude romantic? Is Burton's?

4. In the light of your general impression of Kinglake's personality, how do you think he would have reacted to the following details mentioned by Burton: the tents in the boundless waste (lines 23-24)? the color of the clays and gravels (lines 24-25)? *the wild weird song of lads and lasses* (lines 26-27)? the women and children standing outside the ring (lines 41-42)? the rolling upon the ground with laughter (lines 55-56)?

5. Substitute a matter-of-fact phrase for each of the following expressions in Burton: *the Jinn bore me* (lines 12-13); *from the pure front of the western firmament* (lines 18-19); *through the gloaming* (line 28); *answered the whispers of the night breeze* (line 34); *Pantagruelist of the Wilderness* (lines 53-54).

5. ARAB FACES

1. What does Cunninghame Graham think of the Kaid of Amsmiz (paragraph 2)? Does he condemn his conduct?
2. What do the Kaid of Amsmiz and Haj Mohammed el —— (paragraph 3) have in common? What does Cunninghame Graham think of Haj Mohammed?
3. Which interests Cunninghame Graham more—admiration for the serene Arab face or condemnation of the shortcomings of the English? or is he equally interested in both? Explain your answer.
4. In attitude, which of the four other authors in this section does Cunninghame Graham most closely resemble?

Suggested Assignment

Find and analyze the reports of the same event in two or more different newspapers. It will be best to take an event about which there has been some controversy and to use newspapers which differ widely in their editorial policies.

GEORGE GISSING

Retrospect

I SOMETIMES think I will go and spend the sunny half of a twelvemonth in wandering about the British Isles. There is so much of beauty and interest that I have not seen, and I grudge to close my eyes on this beloved home of ours, leaving any corner of it unvisited. Often I wander in fancy over all the parts I know, and grow restless with desire at familiar names

"Retrospect." From *The Private Papers of Henry Ryecroft* by George Gissing, published by E. P. Dutton and Co., Inc., New York.

which bring no picture to memory. My array of county guide-
books (they have always been irresistible to me on the stalls)
sets me roaming; the only dull pages in them are those that treat
of manufacturing towns. Yet I shall never start on that
pilgrimage. I am too old, too fixed in habits. I dislike the railway: I dislike hotels. I should grow homesick for my library, my
garden, the view from my windows. And then—I have such a
fear of dying anywhere but under my own roof.

2] As a rule, it is better to re-visit only in imagination the
places which have greatly charmed us, or which, in the retrospect, seem to have done so. Seem to have charmed us, I say; for
the memory we form, after a certain lapse of time, of places
where we lingered, often bears but a faint resemblance to the
impression received at the time. What in truth may have
been very moderate enjoyment, or enjoyment greatly disturbed
by inner or outer circumstances, shows in the distance as a keen
delight, or as deep, still happiness. On the other hand, if memory creates no illusion, and the name of a certain place is associated with one of the golden moments of life, it were rash to
hope that another visit would repeat the experience of a bygone
day. For it was not merely the sights that one beheld which were
the cause of joy and peace; however lovely the spot, however
gracious the sky, these things external would not have availed,
but for contributory movements of mind and heart and
blood, the essentials of the man as then he was.

3] Whilst I was reading this afternoon my thoughts strayed,
and I found myself recalling a hillside in Suffolk, where, after a
long walk, I rested drowsily one midsummer day twenty years
ago. A great longing seized me; I was tempted to set off at once,
and find again that spot under the high elm trees, where, as I
smoked a delicious pipe, I heard about me the crack, crack, crack
of broom-pods bursting in the glorious heat of the noontide sun.
Had I acted upon the impulse, what chance was there of my
enjoying such another hour as that which my memory
cherished? No, no; it is not the *place* that I remember; it is the
time of life, the circumstances, the mood, which at that moment
fell so happily together. Can I dream that a pipe smoked on that

same hillside, under the same glowing sky, would taste as it then did, or bring me the same solace? Would the turf be so soft beneath me? Would the great elm-branches temper so delightfully the noontide rays beating upon them? And, when the hour of rest was over, should I spring to my feet as then I did, eager to put forth my strength again? No, no; what I remember is just one moment of my earlier life, linked by accident with that picture of the Suffolk landscape. The place no longer exists; it never existed save for me. For it is the mind which creates the world about us, and, even though we stand side by side in the same meadow, my eyes will never see what is beheld by yours, my heart will never stir to the emotions with which yours is touched.

Questions

On a first reading, Gissing's essay may seem to be too simple to deserve analysis. It consists of but three paragraphs; there is nothing difficult about the vocabulary; the prose is straightforward, without rhetorical flourishes. Yet, in its interweaving of concrete experiences with abstract ideas it is a finished and artistic prose selection.

1. Of the three paragraphs, one is devoted chiefly to a single, specific experience; another, to repeated experiences, all similar in kind; another, to the development of an abstract idea, with no concrete experience mentioned. Identify the content of each paragraph.

2. *a.* What hints does the reader get of the author's personality as he writes this essay? What paragraph contains most of these hints?

   b. What was the author like in his youth? What paragraph contains this information?

   c. Is the general idea of the essay a thought suggested by the experiences of youth or by the experiences of age?

3. Starting with one specific experience and proceeding from the experience to the ideas it suggests is often a very satisfactory pattern for a personal essay. Could this method be followed here? that is, if you assume that the transitions were rewritten, could paragraphs 1 and 3 be switched? Defend your answer.

4. More than one idea is suggested in the essay. All the following, for example, are perfectly good theme ideas, each of which might be worthy of development in a single essay.

a. "It is better to re-visit only in imagination the places which have greatly charmed us" (lines 15-16).

b. "The memory we form, after a certain lapse of time, of places where we lingered, often bears but a faint resemblance to the impression received at the time" (lines 18-20).

c. "It is the mind which creates the world about us" (lines 52-53). Which of these three sentences best expresses the theme idea of the essay? Does any one of them express the idea completely? If, in your opinion, neither *a, b,* nor *c* is a complete theme idea for the essay, construct a sentence which is. Which of the three ideas is the most abstract?

5. Suppose that lines 43-49 in paragraph 3 were rewritten as follows:

A pipe smoked on that same hillside, under the same glowing sky, would not taste as it then did, or bring me the same solace. The turf would not be so soft beneath me. The great elm-branches would not temper so delightfully the noontide rays beating upon them. And, when the hour of rest was over, I should not spring to my feet as then I did, eager to put forth my strength again.

a. What is the difference in rhetorical effect between this version and the one the author uses?

b. Under what circumstances is a series of questions more desirable than a series of positive statements?

6. It would be possible for this essay to end with the sentence "The place no longer exists; it never existed save for me" (lines 51-52). If the last sentence of the essay were omitted, what would be the difference in the impression left on the reader's mind?

7. Write another title for Gissing's essay.

ROBERT LOUIS STEVENSON

❧ Despised Races

OF ALL stupid ill-feelings, the sentiment of my fellow Caucasians towards our companions in the Chinese car was the most stupid and the worst. They seemed never to have looked at them, listened to them, or thought of them, but hated them *à priori*. The Mongols were their enemies in that cruel and treacherous battle-field of money. They could work better and cheaper in half a hundred industries, and hence there was no calumny too idle for the Caucasians to repeat, and even to believe. They declared them hideous vermin, and affected a kind of choking in the throat when they beheld them. Now, as a matter of fact, the young Chinese man is so like a large class of European women, that on raising my head and suddenly catching sight of one at a considerable distance, I have for an instant been deceived by the resemblance. I do not say it is the most attractive class of our women, but for all that many a man's wife is less pleasantly favoured. Again, my emigrants declared that the Chinese were dirty. I cannot say they were clean, for that was impossible upon the journey; but in their efforts after cleanliness they put the rest of us to shame. We all pigged and stewed in one infamy, wet our hands and faces for half a minute daily on the platform, and were unashamed. But the Chinese never lost an opportunity, and you would see them washing their feet—an

---

"Despised Races." From *Across the Plains* by Robert Louis Stevenson. The book describes a railroad journey across the Western plains in the nineteenth century. Of the three passenger cars on the train, one was reserved for family groups, one for single "Caucasians," and one for Chinese; hence the references to the "Chinese car."

act not dreamed of among ourselves—and going as far as decency permitted to wash their whole bodies. I may remark, by the way, that the dirtier people are in their persons, the more delicate is their sense of modesty. A clean man strips in a crowded boathouse; but he who is unwashed slinks in and out of bed without uncovering an inch of skin. Lastly, these very foul and malodorous Caucasians entertained the surprising illusion that it was the Chinese waggon, and that alone, which stank. I have said already that it was the exception, and notably the freshest of the three.

2] These judgments are typical of the feeling in all Western America. The Chinese are considered stupid, because they are imperfectly acquainted with English. They are held to be base, because their dexterity and frugality enable them to underbid the lazy, luxurious Caucasian. They are said to be thieves; I am sure they have no monopoly of that. They are called cruel; the Anglo-Saxon and the cheerful Irishman may each reflect before he bears the accusation. It comes amiss from John Bull, who the other day forced the unhappy Zazel, all bruised and tottering from a dangerous escape, to come forth again upon the theatre, and continue to risk her life for his amusement; or from Pat, who makes it his pastime to shoot down the complainant farmer from behind a wall in Europe, or to stone the solitary Chinaman in California. I am told, again, that they are of the race of river pirates, and belong to the most despised and dangerous class in the Celestial Empire. But if this be so, what remarkable pirates have we here! and what must be the virtues, the industry, the education, and the intelligence of their superiors at home!

3] Awhile ago it was the Irish, now it is the Chinese, that must go. Such is the cry. It seems, after all, that no country is bound to submit to immigration any more than to invasion: each is war to the knife, and resistance to either but legitimate defence. Yet we may regret the free tradition of the republic, which loved to depict herself with open arms, welcoming all unfortunates. And certainly, as a man who believed that he loves freedom, I may be excused some bitterness when I find her sacred name misused in the contention. It was but the other day that

I heard a vulgar fellow in the Sand-lot, the popular tribune of San Francisco, roaring for arms and butchery. "At the call of Abraham Lincoln," said the orator, "ye rose in the name of freedom to set free the Negroes; can ye not rise and liberate yourselves from a few dirty Mongolians?" It exceeds the license of an Irishman to rebaptise our selfish interests by the name of virtue. Defend your bellies, if you must; I, who do not suffer, am no judge in your affairs; but let me defend language, which is the dialect and one of the ramparts of virtue.

4] For my own part, I could not look but with wonder and respect on the Chinese. Their forefathers watched the stars before mine had begun to keep pigs. Gunpowder and printing, which the other day we imitated, and a school of manners which we never had the delicacy so much as to desire to imitate, were theirs in a long-past antiquity. They walk the earth with us, but it seems they must be of a different clay. They hear the clock strike the same hour, yet surely of a different epoch. They travel by steam conveyance, yet with such a baggage of old Asiatic thoughts and superstitions as might check the locomotive in its course. Whatever is thought within the circuit of the Great Wall; what the wry-eyed, spectacled schoolmaster teaches in the hamlets round Pekin; religions so old that our language looks a halfing boy alongside; philosophy so wise that our best philosophers find things therein to wonder at; all this travelled alongside of me for thousands of miles over plain and mountain. Heaven knows if we had one common thought or fancy all that way; or whether our eyes, which yet were formed upon the same design, beheld the same world out of the railway windows. And when either of us turned his thoughts to home and childhood, what a strange dissimilarity must there not have been in these pictures of the mind—when I beheld that old, grey, castled city, high throned above the firth, with the flag of Britain flying, and the red-coat sentry pacing over all; and the man in the next car to me would conjure up some junks and a pagoda and a fort of porcelain, and call it, with the same affection, home.

5] Another race shared among my fellow-passengers in the disfavour of the Chinese; and that, it is hardly necessary to say, was the noble red man of old story—he over whose own hereditary continent we had been steaming all these days. I saw no wild or independent Indian; indeed, I hear that such avoid the neighbourhood of the train; but now and again at way-stations, a husband and wife and a few children, disgracefully dressed out with the sweepings of civilisation, came forth and stared upon the emigrants. The silent stoicism of their conduct, and the pathetic degradation of their appearance, would have touched any thinking creature; but my fellow-passengers danced and jested round them with a truly cockney baseness. I was ashamed for the thing we call civilisation. We should carry upon our consciences so much, at least, of our forefathers' misconduct, as we continue to profit by ourselves.

6] If oppression drives a wise man mad, what should be raging in the hearts of these poor tribes, who have been driven back and back, step after step, their promised reservations torn from them one after another as the States extended westward, until at length they are shut up into these hideous mountain deserts of the centre—and even there find themselves invaded, insulted, and hunted out by ruffianly diggers? The eviction of the Cherokees (to name but an instance), the extortion of Indian agents, the outrages of the wicked, the ill faith of all, nay, down to the ridicule of such poor beings as were here with me upon the train, make up a chapter of injustice and indignity such as a man must be in some ways base if his heart will suffer him to pardon or forget. These old well-founded, historical hatreds have a savour of nobility for the independent. That the Jew should not love the Christian, nor the Irishman love the English, nor the Indian brave tolerate the thought of the American, is not disgraceful to the nature of man; rather, indeed, honourable, since it depends on wrongs ancient like the race, and not personal to him who cherishes the indignation.

7] As for the Indians, there are of course many unteachable and wedded to war and their wild habits; but many also who, with fairer usage, might learn the virtues of the peaceful state. You will find a valley in the county of Monterey, drained by the river of Carmel: a true Californian valley, bare, dotted with chaparral, overlooked by quaint, unfinished hills. The Carmel runs by many pleasant farms, a clear and shallow river, loved by wading kine; and at last, as it is falling towards a quicksand and the great Pacific, passes a ruined mission on a hill. From the church the eye embraces a great field of ocean, and the ear is filled with a continuous sound of distant breakers on the shore. The roof has fallen; the ground squirrel scampers on the graves; the holy bell of St. Charles is long dismounted; yet one day in every year the church awakes from silence, and the Indians return to worship in the church of their converted fathers. I have seen them trooping thither, young and old, in their clean print dresses, with those strange, handsome, melancholy features, which seem predestined to a national calamity and it was notable to hear the old Latin words and old Gregorian music sung, with nasal fervour, and in a swift, staccato style, by a trained chorus of Red Indian men and women. In the huts of the Rancherie they have ancient European Mass-books, in which they study together to be perfect. An old blind man was their leader. With his eyes bandaged, and leaning on a staff, he was led into his place in church by a little grandchild. He had seen changes in the world since first he sang that music sixty years ago, when there was no gold and no Yankees, and he and his people lived in plenty under the wing of the kind priests. The mission church is in ruins; the Rancherie, they tell me, encroached upon by Yankee newcomers; the little age of gold is over for the Indian; but he has had a breathing-space in Carmel valley before he goes down to the dust with his red fathers.

Questions

1. Although the unity of this essay is not easy to express in terms of a theme idea, yet there is unity of a definite kind. Consider first the section dealing with the Chinese:

   a. Is Stevenson more interested in the feelings of the persecuted Chinese, or of the persecuting Caucasians?

   b. Is he more interested in race prejudice as a moral wrong, or as an offense against logic and common sense?

c. What is the topic of the first paragraph? the second? the third? What does the orator of paragraph 3 have in common with the travelers in paragraph 1 besides a lack of Christian charity?

d. What is the method of attack which Stevenson employs in paragraph 1? in paragraph 2? In what way does the approach used in paragraph 4 resemble that used in paragraph 1?

2. *a.* Why does Stevenson spend more time exposing the falsehoods told about the appearance and cleanliness of the Chinese than he does with the lies about their morals?

   b. There are many aspects of the life of the Chinese which Stevenson might have touched on in paragraph 4, but he chooses to concentrate on their intellectual achievements. Explain this choice.

3. Would it be wise to place paragraph 4 between paragraphs 1 and 2 instead of in its present position?

4. Does Stevenson analyze the prejudice against the Indian in the same way that he does the prejudice against the Chinese? Is there any attempt to contrast the "despised race" as it really is with the picture of the race as it exists in the minds of the persecutors?

5. In what ways is the tone and method of approach in paragraph 6 different from that in the rest of the essay?

6. Instead of giving a complete account of the life of the Indians on the Carmel, Stevenson limits himself to their religious activities. Explain this choice.

7. The description of the Carmel valley (paragraph 7) tells us nothing about racial prejudice but it is not therefore irrelevant. What does this description contribute to the paragraph and to the essay as a whole? In what ways is the setting appropriate for the Indians whom Stevenson is about to describe?

Suggested Assignment

Man's ability to hold to beliefs which are hopelessly at variance with the facts he sees before him appears in many matters other than race relations. Find another example of this characteristic and describe it in a short essay.

CARLO LEVI

Matera

MY SISTER had come from Turin and she could stay for only four or five days.

2] "I wasted entirely too much time getting here," she said, "because I had to come by way of Matera in order to have the police there stamp my permit to visit you. Instead of coming directly through Naples and Potenza, which would have taken me only two days, I had to take the roundabout route via Bari to Matera, and at Matera I lost a whole day waiting for the bus. What a place that is! From the glimpse I had of Gagliano just now I'd say it wasn't so bad; it couldn't be worse than Matera, anyhow."

3] She was horrified and frightened by what she had seen. I told her that the violence of her reaction must be due to the fact that she had never before been in these parts and that Matera had been the scene of her first meeting with this landscape and the desolate race of men that lived in it.

NOTE: Because of his opposition to Fascism, Carlo Levi, an Italian painter, writer, and physician, was banished at the beginning of the Abyssinian War (1935) to a small village of Lucania in southern Italy. *Christ Stopped at Eboli* is a record of the year he spent in this region and of the miserable and poverty-stricken life of its inhabitants. The book is full of memorable passages; one of the most affecting is the account which Levi's sister gives of a visit to Matera, one of the principal towns in the district. It is something more than a picture of sordid conditions; in the end it becomes a symbol of the meaning of Fascism for a certain section of Italy.

"Matera." From *Christ Stopped at Eboli: The Story of a Year* by Carlo Levi. Copyright 1947 by Carlo Levi and reprinted by permission of Farrar, Straus & Company, Inc.

4] "I didn't know this part of the country, to be sure," she answered, "but I did somehow picture it in my mind. Only Matera. . . . Well, it was beyond anything I could possibly have imagined. I got there at about eleven in the morning. I had read in the guidebook that it was a picturesque town, quite worth a visit, that it had a museum of ancient art and some curious cave dwellings. But when I came out of the railway station, a modern and rather sumptuous affair, and looked around me, I couldn't for the life of me see the town; it simply wasn't there. I was on a sort of deserted plateau, surrounded by bare, low hills of a grayish earth covered with stones. In the middle of this desert there rose here and there eight or ten big marble buildings built in the style made fashionable in Rome by Piacentini, with massive doors, ornate architraves, solemn Latin inscriptions, and pillars gleaming in the sun. Some of them were unfinished and seemed to be quite empty, monstrosities entirely out of keeping with the desolate landscape around them. A jerry-built housing project, for the benefit, no doubt, of government employees, which had already fallen into a state of filth and disrepair, filled up the empty space around the buildings and shut off my view on one side. The whole thing looked like an ambitious bit of city planning, begun in haste and interrupted by the plague, or else like a stage set, in execrable taste, for a tragedy by d'Annunzio. These enormous twentieth-century imperial palaces housed the prefecture, the police station, the post office, the town hall, the barracks of the *carabinieri*, the Fascist Party headquarters, the Fascist Scouts, the Corporations, and so on. But where was the town? Matera was nowhere to be seen.

5] "I decided to attend at once to my business. I went to the police station, of resplendent marble without but dirty and bug-ridden within, its ill-kept rooms piled up with dust and sweepings. I was received, for the purpose of getting a stamp on my permit, by the assistant chief, who was also the head of the local political police. I was worried about the danger of malaria and so I asked him whether there was any chance of your being transferred to a healthier climate. Another officer who was in the room burst into the conversation abruptly: 'Malaria? There isn't any such thing. It's all imagination. One case a year, perhaps. Your brother is quite well off where he is.' But when he realized that I was a doctor he was silent, and his superior answered me in an entirely different tone: 'There's malaria everywhere,' he said. 'We can transfer your brother, if you like, but he'll find conditions just the same as at Gagliano. There's only one place in the whole province that's free of malaria, and that's Stigliano, because it's almost three thousand feet above sea level. Perhaps later we can send him there, but for the time being it's impossible.' (I caught on to the fact that only dissident Fascists were sent to Stigliano.) 'No, your brother had better stay put. Look at us; we live here in Matera, and we're not political prisoners. And it's no better here, as far as malaria is concerned, than at Gagliano. If we can stick it, then he can stick it too.'

6] "To this argument there was really no answer, so I pursued the matter no further, and went out. I wanted to buy you a stethoscope as I had forgotten to bring one from Turin and I knew that you needed one for your medical practice. Since there were no dealers in medical instruments I decided to look for one in a pharmacy. Among the government buildings and the cheap new houses I found two pharmacies, the only ones, I was told, in the town. Neither had what I was looking for and what's more their proprietors disclaimed all knowledge of what it might be. 'A stethoscope? What's that?' After I had explained that it was a simple instrument for listening to the heart, made like an ear trumpet, usually out of wood, they told me that I might find such a thing in Bari, but that here in Matera no one had ever heard of it.

7] "By now it was noon and I repaired to the restaurant that was pointed out to me as the best in town. There, all at one table with a soiled cloth on it and napkin rings that showed they came there every day, sat the assistant chief of police with several of his subordinates, looking bored to tears. You know that I'm not hard to please, but I swear that when I got up to leave I was just as hungry as when I came.

8] "I set out at last to find the town. A little beyond the station I found a street with a row of houses on one side and on the other a deep gully. In the gully lay Matera. From where I was, higher up, it could hardly be seen because the drop was so sheer. All I could distinguish as I looked down were alleys and terraces, which concealed the houses from view. Straight across from me there was a barren hill of an ugly gray color, without a single tree or sign of cultivation upon it, nothing but sun-baked earth and stones. At the bottom of the gully a sickly, swampy stream, the Bradano, trickled among the rocks. The hill and the stream had a gloomy, evil appearance that caught at my heart. The gully had a strange shape: it was formed by two half-funnels, side by side, separated by a narrow spur and meeting at the bottom, where I could see a white church, Santa Maria de Idris, which looked half-sunk in the ground. The two funnels, I learned, were called Sasso Caveoso and Sasso Barisano. They were like a schoolboy's idea of Dante's Inferno. And, like Dante, I too began to go down from circle to circle, by a sort of mule path leading to the bottom. The narrow path wound its way down and around, passing over the roofs of the houses, if houses they could be called. They were caves, dug into the hardened clay walls of the gully, each with its own façade, some of which were quite handsome, with eighteenth-century ornamentation. These false fronts, because of the slope of the gully, were flat against its side at the bottom, but at the top they protruded, and the alleys in the narrow space between them and the hillside did double service: they were a roadway for those who came out of their houses from above and a roof for those who lived beneath. The houses were open on account of the heat, and as I went by I could see into the caves, whose only light came in through the front doors. Some of them had no entrance but a trapdoor and ladder. In these dark holes with walls cut out of the earth I saw a few pieces of miserable furniture, beds, and some ragged clothes hanging up to dry. On the floor lay dogs, sheep, goats, and pigs. Most families have just one cave to live in and there they sleep all together; men, women, children, and animals. This is how twenty thousand people live.

9] "Of children I saw an infinite number. They appeared from everywhere, in the dust and heat, amid the flies, stark naked or clothed in rags; I have never in all my life seen such a picture of poverty. My profession has brought me in daily contact with dozens of poor, sick, ill-kempt children, but I never even dreamed of seeing a sight like this. I saw children sitting on the doorsteps, in the dirt, while the sun beat down on them, with their eyes half-closed and their eyelids red and swollen; flies crawled across the lids, but the children stayed quite still, without raising a hand to brush them away. Yes, flies crawled across their eyelids, and they seemed not even to feel them. They had trachoma. I knew that it existed in the South, but to see it against this background of poverty and dirt was something else again. I saw other children with the wizened faces of old men, their bodies reduced by starvation almost to skeletons, their heads crawling with lice and covered with scabs. Most of them had enormous, dilated stomachs and faces yellow and worn with malaria.

10] "The women, when they saw me look in the doors, asked me to come in, and in the dark, smelly caves where they lived I saw children lying on the floor under torn blankets, with their teeth chattering from fever. Others, reduced to skin and bones by dysentery, could hardly drag themselves about. I saw children with waxen faces who seemed to me to have something worse than malaria, perhaps some tropical disease such as Kala Azar, or black fever. The thin women, with dirty, undernourished babies hanging at their flaccid breasts, spoke to me mildly and with despair. I felt, under the blinding sun, as if I were in a city stricken by the plague. I went on down toward the church at the bottom of the gully; a constantly swelling crowd of children followed a few steps behind me. They were shouting something, but I could not understand their incomprehensible dialect. I kept on going; still they followed and called after me. I thought they must want pennies, and I stopped for a minute. Only then did I make out the words they were all shouting together: '*Signorina, dammi 'u chinì!* Signorina, give me some quinine!' I gave them what coins I had with me to buy candy, but that was not what they wanted; they kept on asking, with sorrowful insistence, for quinine. Meanwhile we had reached Santa Maria de Idris, a handsome baroque church. When I lifted my eyes to see the way

I had come, I at last saw the whole of Matera, in the form of a slanting wall. From here it seemed almost like a real town. The façades of the caves were like a row of white houses; the holes of the doorways stared at me like black eyes. The town is indeed a beautiful one, picturesque and striking. I reached the museum with its Greek vases, statuettes, and coins found in the vicinity. While I was looking at them the children still stood out in the sun, waiting for me to bring them quinine."

Questions

1. It is important to see clearly Levi's attitude toward the manifestations of Fascism in Matera.

    a. Why does Levi bother to describe the government buildings (paragraph 4)? Why do the "massive doors, ornate architraves, solemn Latin inscriptions, and pillars gleaming in the sun" fail to make the proper impression? What is the significance of the fact that some of the splendid buildings are unfinished and that the marble police station is "dirty and bug-ridden"? (Does a town of twenty thousand usually have such a collection of government buildings?)

    b. What is the state of mind of the Fascist officials? Is the officer who says there is no malaria (paragraph 5) meant to appear mean or brutal? Is the assistant chief's "If we can stick it, then he can stick it too" a mere excuse for not helping? Why does Levi introduce the picture of the police officers at lunch in the best restaurant in town (paragraph 7)?

    c. Why does it seem appropriate that the town should be invisible from the government buildings?

2. The description of the town in the gully must have been relatively easy to write; the facts are so striking in themselves that they need little coloring. Nevertheless, there are some indications of conscious artistry.

    a. Why is the emphasis throughout on the children rather than the adults? Why, among all the hardships of life in Matera, is disease given the most emphasis?

    b. Why is the insistent demand of the children for quinine so pathetic? (How does Levi's sister first interpret their cry?)

c. What suggestions do we have of a somewhat less depressing period or periods in the past of Matera? Do the traces of past glory relieve the impression of present misery or do they accentuate it?

3. *a.* "I felt, under the blinding sun, as if I were in a city stricken by the plague" (paragraph 10). Where else in the selection does Levi speak of the city as stricken by plague? What is the value of such repeated references?

　　b. What is there about the state of mind of the women in the gully which reminds one of the Fascists on the hill?

4. What would be the effect of removing the last sentence?

5. What is the advantage of seeing Matera through the eyes of a stranger who has never been there before?

6. To sum up, what is Levi trying to say about the reign of Fascism in southern Italy?

2 Essays Based on Reading or Investigation

G. M. TREVELYAN

The Value of History

WHAT, then, are the various ways in which history can educate the mind?
2] The first, or at least the most generally acknowledged educational effect of history, is to train the mind of the citizen into a state in which he is capable of taking a just view of political problems. But, even in this capacity, history cannot prophesy the future; it cannot supply a set of invariably applicable laws for the guidance of politicians; it cannot show, by the deductions of historical analogy, which side is in the right in any quarrel of our own day. It can do a thing less, and yet greater than all these. It can mould the mind itself into the capability of understanding great affairs and sympathising with other men. The information given by history is valueless in itself, unless it produce a new state of mind. The value of Lecky's Irish history did not consist

"The Value of History." From "Clio, a Muse," in *Clio, a Muse and Other Essays Literary and Pedestrian* by George Macaulay Trevelyan. Reprinted by permission of Longmans, Green & Co., Inc.

in the fact that he recorded in a book the details of numerous massacres and murders, but that he produced sympathy and shame, and caused a better understanding among us all of how the sins of the fathers are often visited upon the children, unto the third and fourth generations of them that hate each other. He does not prove that Home Rule is right or wrong, but he trains the mind of Unionists and Home Rulers to think sensibly about that and other problems.

3] For it is in this political function of history that the study of cause and effect is of some real use. Though such a study can be neither scientific nor exact, common sense sometimes points to an obvious causal connection. Thus it was supposed, even before the invention of scientific history, that Alva's policy was in some causal connection with the revolt of the Netherlands, that Brunswick's manifesto had something to do with the September Massacres, and the September Massacres with the spread of reaction. Such suggestions of cause and effect in the past help to teach political wisdom. When a man of the world reads history, he is called on to form a judgment on a social or political problem, without previous bias, and with some knowledge of the final protracted result of what was done. The exercise of his mind under such unwonted conditions, sends him back to the still unsettled problems of modern politics and society, with larger views, clearer head and better temper. The study of past controversies, of which the final outcome is known, destroys the spirit of prejudice. It brings home to the mind the evils that are likely to spring from violent policy, based on want of understanding of opponents. When a man has studied the history of the Democrats and Aristocrats of Corcyra, of the English and Irish, of the Jacobins and anti-Jacobins, his political views may remain the same, but his political temper and his way of thinking about politics may have improved, if he is capable of receiving an impression.

4] And so, too, in a larger sphere than politics, a review of the process of historical evolution teaches a man to see his own age, with its peculiar ideals and interests, in proper perspective as one among other ages. If he can learn to understand that other ages had not only a different social and economic structure but correspondingly different ideals and interests from those of his own age, his mind will have veritably enlarged. I have hopes that ere long the Workers' Educational Association will have taught its historical students not to ask, "What was Shakespeare's attitude to Democracy?" and to perceive that the question no more admits of an answer than the inquiry, "What was Dante's attitude to Protestantism?" or, "What was Archimedes' attitude to the steam-engine?"

5] The study of cause and effect is by no means the only, and perhaps not the principal means, of broadening the mind. History does most to cure a man of political prejudice, when it enables him, by reading about men or movements in the past, to understand points of view which he never saw before, and to respect ideals which he had formerly despised. Gardiner's *History of the Civil War* has done much to explain Englishmen to each other, by revealing the rich variety of our national life, far nobler than the unity of similitude. Forms of idealism, considerations of policy and wisdom, are acceptable or at least comprehensible, when presented by the historian to minds which would reject them if they came from the political opponent or the professed sage.

6] But history should not only remove prejudice, it should breed enthusiasm. To many it is an important source of the ideas that inspire their lives. With the exception of a few creative minds, men are too weak to fly by their own unaided imagination beyond the circle of ideas that govern the world in which they are placed. And since the ideals of no one epoch can in themselves be sufficient as an interpretation of life, it is fortunate that the student of the past can draw upon the purest springs of ancient thought and feeling. Men will join in associations to propagate the old-new idea, and to recast society again in the ancient mould, as when the study of Plutarch and the ancient historians rekindled the breath of liberty and of civic virtue in modern Europe; as when in our own day men attempt to revive mediæval ideals of religious or of corporate life, or to rise to the Greek standard of the individual. We may like or dislike such revivals, but at least they bear witness to the potency of history as something quite other than a science. And outside the circle of these larger influences, history supplies us each with private ideals, only too varied and too numerous for complete realisation. One may aspire to the best characteristics of a man of Athens or a citizen of Rome; a Churchman of the twelfth century, or a Reformer of the sixteenth; a Cavalier of the old school, or a Puritan of the Independent party; a Radical of the time of Castlereagh, or a public servant of the time of Peel. Still more are individual great men the model and inspiration of the smaller. It is difficult to appropriate the essential qualities of these old people under new conditions; but whatever we study with strong loving conception, and admire as a thing good in itself and not merely good for its purpose or its age, we do in some measure absorb.

7] This presentation of ideals and heroes from other ages is perhaps the most important among the educative functions of history. For this purpose, even more than for the purpose of teaching political wisdom, it is requisite that the events should be both written and read with intellectual passion. Truth itself will be the gainer, for those by whom history was enacted were in their day passionate.

8] Another educative function of history is to enable the reader to comprehend the historical aspect of literature proper. Literature can no doubt be enjoyed in its highest aspects even if the reader is ignorant of history. But on those terms it cannot be enjoyed completely, and much of it cannot be enjoyed at all. For much of literature is allusion, either definite or implied. And the allusions, even of the Victorian age, are by this time historical. For example, the last half dozen stanzas of Browning's *Old Pictures in Florence,* the fifth stanza of his *Lovers' Quarrel,* and half his wife's best poems are already meaningless unless we know something of the continental history of that day. Political authors like Burke, Sydney Smith, and Courier, the prose of Milton, one-half of Swift, the best of Dryden, and the best of Byron (his satires and letters) are enjoyed *ceteris paribus,* in exact proportion to the amount we know of the history of their times. And since allusions to classical history and mythology, and even to the Bible, are no longer, as they used to be, familiar ground for all educated readers, there is all the more reason, in the interest of literature, why allusions to modern history should be generally understood. History and literature cannot be fully comprehended, still less fully enjoyed, except in connection with one another. I confess I have little love either for "Histories of Literature," or for chapters on "the literature of the period," hanging at the end of history books like the tail from a cow. I mean, rather, that those who write or read the history of a period should be soaked in its literature, and that those who read or expound literature should be soaked in history. The "scientific" view of history that discouraged such interchange and desired the strictest specialisation by political historians, has done much harm to our latter-day culture. The mid-Victorians at any rate knew better than that.

9] The substitution of a pseudo-scientific for a literary atmosphere in historical circles, has not only done much to divorce history from the outside public, but has diminished its humanising power over its own devotees in school and university. Not a few university teachers are already conscious of this and are trying to remedy it, having seen that historical "science" for the undergraduate means the text-book, that is, the "crammer" in print. At one university as I know, and at others I dare say, literature already plays a greater part in historical teaching and reading than it played some years ago. Historical students are now encouraged to read the "literary" historians of old, who were recently *taboo,* and still more to read the contemporary literature of periods studied. But for all that, there is much leeway to be made up.

10] The value and pleasure of travel, whether at home or abroad, is doubled by a knowledge of history. For places, like books, have an interest or a beauty of association, as well as an absolute or æsthetic beauty. The garden front of St. John's, Oxford, is beautiful to every one; but, for the lover of history, its outward charm is blent with the intimate feelings of his own mind, with images of that same College as it was during the Great Civil War. Given over to the use of a Court whose days of royalty were numbered, its walks and quadrangles were filled, as the end came near, with men and women learning to accept sorrow as their lot through life, the ambitious abandoning hope of power, the wealthy hardening themselves to embrace poverty, those who loved England preparing to sail for foreign shores, and lovers to be parted forever. There they strolled through the garden, as the hopeless evenings fell, listening, at the end of all, while the siege-guns broke the silence with ominous iteration. Behind the cannon on those low hills to northward were ranked the inexorable men who came to lay their hands on all this beauty, hoping to change it to strength and sterner virtue. And this was the curse of the victors, not to die, but to live, and almost to lose their awful faith in God, when they saw the Restoration, not of the old gaiety that was too gay for them and the old loyalty that was too loyal for them, but of corruption and selfishness that had neither country nor king. The sound of the Roundhead cannon has long ago died away, but still the silence of the garden is heavy with unalterable fate, brooding over besiegers and besieged, in such haste to destroy each other and permit only the vile to survive. St. John's College is not mere stone and mortar, tastefully compiled, but an appropriate and mournful witness between those who see it now and those by whom it once was seen. And so it is, for the reader of history, with every ruined castle and ancient church throughout the wide, mysterious lands of Europe.

Questions

1. What are the principal ways in which history educates the mind? What does the word "educate" mean in this context?
2. In what sense is history "a school of political wisdom"?
3. Of the uses of history enumerated by Trevelyan, which are the more important, which less important? Are the more important ones discussed first, or the less important ones? Comment on this arrangement.
4. Why would it be wrong to insert the section on history and travel between the section on history as a school of political wis-

dom and the section on history as a source of enthusiasm and ideals?

5. Comment on the unity of the passage. Is the fact that history can increase the pleasures of travel too trivial a matter to be discussed along with grave political questions?

FRANCIS PARKMAN

Braddock's Defeat

THUS began that memorable war which, kindling among the forests of America, scattered its fires over the kingdoms of Europe, and the sultry empire of the Great Mogul; the war made glorious by the heroic death of Wolfe, the victories of Frederic, and the exploits of Clive; the war which controlled the destinies of America, and was first in the chain of events which led on to her Revolution with all its vast and undeveloped consequences. On the old battle-ground of Europe, the contest bore the same familiar features of violence and horror which had marked the strife of former generations—fields ploughed by the cannon ball, and walls shattered by the exploding mine, sacked towns and blazing suburbs, the lamentations of women, and the license of a maddened soldiery. But in America, war assumed a new and striking aspect. A wilderness was its sublime arena. Army met army under the shadows of primeval woods; their cannon resounded over wastes unknown to civilized man. And before the hostile powers could join in battle, endless forests must be traversed, and morasses passed, and everywhere the axe of the pioneer must hew a path for the bayonet of the soldier.

"Braddock's Defeat." From *The Conspiracy of Pontiac* by Francis Parkman.

2] Before the declaration of war, and before the breaking off of negotiations between the courts of France and England, the English ministry formed the plan of assailing the French in America on all sides at once, and repelling them, by one bold push, from all their encroachments.[1] A provincial army was to advance upon Acadia, a second was to attack Crown Point, and a third Niagara; while the two regiments which had lately arrived in Virginia under General Braddock, aided by a strong body of provincials, were to dislodge the French from their newly-built fort of Du Quesne. To Braddock was assigned the chief command of all the British forces in America; and a person worse fitted for the office could scarcely have been found. His experience had been ample, and none could doubt his courage; but he was profligate, arrogant, perverse, and a bigot to military rules.[2] On his first arrival in Virginia, he called together the governors of the several provinces, in order to explain his instructions and adjust the details of the projected operations. These

---

[1] Instructions of General Braddock. See *Précis des Faits*, 160, 168.

[2] The following is Horace Walpole's testimony, and writers of better authority have expressed themselves, with less liveliness and piquancy, to the same effect:—

"Braddock is a very Iroquois in disposition. He had a sister, who, having gamed away all her little fortune at Bath, hanged herself with a truly English deliberation, leaving only a note upon the table with those lines, 'To die is landing on some silent shore,' &c. When Braddock was told of it, he only said, 'Poor Fanny! I always thought she would play till she would be forced *to tuck herself up.*'"

Here follows a curious anecdote of Braddock's meanness and profligacy, which I omit. The next is more to his credit. "He once had a duel with Colonel Gumley, Lady Bath's brother, who had been his great friend. As they were going to engage, Gumley, who had good humor and wit (Braddock had the latter), said, 'Braddock, you are a poor dog! Here, take my purse. If you kill me, you will be forced to run away, and then you will not have a shilling to support you.' Braddock refused the purse, insisted on the duel, was disarmed, and would not even ask his life. However, with all his brutality, he has lately been governor of Gibraltar, where he made himself adored, and where scarce any governor was endured before."—*Letters to Sir H. Mann*, CCLXV. CCLXVI.

Washington's opinion of Braddock may be gathered from his Writings, II. 77.

arrangements complete, Braddock advanced to the borders of Virginia, and formed his camp at Fort Cumberland, where he spent several weeks in training the raw backwoodsmen, who joined him, into such discipline as they seemed capable of; in collecting horses and wagons, which could only be had with the utmost difficulty; in railing at the contractors, who scandalously cheated him; and in venting his spleen by copious abuse of the country and the people. All at length was ready, and early in June, 1755, the army left civilization behind, and struck into the broad wilderness as a squadron puts out to sea.

3] It was no easy task to force their way over that rugged ground, covered with an unbroken growth of forest; and the difficulty was increased by the needless load of baggage which encumbered their march. The crash of falling trees resounded in the front, where a hundred axemen labored with ceaseless toil to hew a passage for the army.[3] The horses strained their utmost strength to drag the ponderous wagons over roots and stumps, through gullies and quagmires; and the regular troops were daunted by the depth and gloom of the forest which hedged them in on either hand, and closed its leafy arches above their heads. So tedious was their progress, that, by the advice of Washington, twelve hundred chosen men moved on in advance with the lighter baggage and artillery, leaving the rest of the army to follow, by slower stages, with the heavy wagons. On the eighth of July, the advanced body reached the Monongahela, at a point not far distant from Fort du Quesne. The rocky and impracticable ground on the eastern side debarred their passage, and the general resolved to cross the river in search of a smoother path, and recross it a few miles lower down, in order to gain the fort. The first passage was easily made, and the troops moved, in glittering array, down the western margin of the water, rejoicing that their goal was well nigh reached, and the hour of their expected triumph close at hand.

4] Scouts and Indian runners had brought the tidings of Braddock's approach to the French at Fort du Quesne. Their

[3] MS. *Diary of the Expedition,* in the British Museum.

dismay was great, and Contrecœur, the commander, thought only of retreat; when Beaujeu, a captain in the garrison, made the bold proposal of leading out a party of French and Indians to waylay the English in the woods, and harass or interrupt their march. The offer was accepted, and Beaujeu hastened to the Indian camps.

5] Around the fort and beneath the adjacent forest were the bark lodges of savage hordes, whom the French had mustered from far and near; Ojibwas and Ottawas, Hurons and Caughnawagas, Abenakis and Delawares. Beaujeu called the warriors together, flung a hatchet on the ground before them, and invited them to follow him out to battle; but the boldest stood aghast at the peril, and none would accept the challenge. A second interview took place with no better success; but the Frenchman was resolved to carry his point. "I am determined to go," he exclaimed. "What, will you suffer your father to go alone?" [4] His daring proved contagious. The warriors hesitated no longer; and when, on the morning of the ninth of July, a scout ran in with the news that the English army was but a few miles distant, the Indian camps were at once astir with the turmoil of preparation. Chiefs harangued their yelling followers, braves bedaubed themselves with war-paint, smeared themselves with grease, hung feathers in their scalp-locks, and whooped and stamped till they had wrought themselves into a delirium of valor.

6] That morning, James Smith, an English prisoner recently captured on the frontier of Pennsylvania, stood on the rampart, and saw the half-frenzied multitude thronging about the gateway, where kegs of bullets and gunpowder were broken open, that each might help himself at will.[5] Then band after band hastened away towards the forest, followed and supported by nearly two hundred and fifty French and Canadians, commanded

[4] Sparks's *Life and Writings of Washington*, II. 473. I am indebted to the kindness of President Sparks for copies of several French manuscripts, which throw much light on the incidents of the battle. These manuscripts are alluded to in the Life and Writings of Washington.

[5] *Smith's Narrative*. This interesting account has been several times published. It may be found in Drake's *Tragedies of the Wilderness*.

by Beaujeu. There were the Ottawas, led on, it is said, by the remarkable man [Pontiac] whose name stands on the title-page of this history; there were the Hurons of Lorette under their chief, whom the French called Athanase,[6] and many more, all keen as hounds on the scent of blood. At about nine miles from the fort, they reached a spot where the narrow road descended to the river through deep and gloomy woods, and where two ravines, concealed by trees and bushes, seemed formed by nature for an ambuscade. Beaujeu well knew the ground; and it was here that he had resolved to fight; but he and his followers were well nigh too late; for as they neared the ravines, the woods were resounding with the roll of the British drums.

7] It was past noon of a day brightened with the clear sunlight of an American midsummer, when the forces of Braddock began, for a second time, to cross the Monongahela, at the fording-place, which to this day bears the name of their ill-fated leader. The scarlet columns of the British regulars, complete in martial appointment, the rude backwoodsmen with shouldered rifles, the trains of artillery and the white-topped wagons, moved on in long procession through the shallow current, and slowly mounted the opposing bank.[7] Men were there whose names have become historic: Gage, who, twenty years later, saw his routed battalions recoil in disorder from before the breastwork on Bunker Hill; Gates, the future conqueror of Burgoyne; and

[6] "Went to Lorette, an Indian village about eight miles from Quebec. Saw the Indians at mass, and heard them sing psalms tolerably well—a dance. Got well acquainted with Athanase, who was commander of the Indians who defeated General Braddock, in 1755—a very sensible fellow."— *MS. Journal of an English Gentleman on a Tour through Canada, in* 1765.

[7] "My feelings were heightened by the warm and glowing narration of that day's events, by Dr. Walker, who was an eye-witness. He pointed out the ford where the army crossed the Monongahela (below Turtle Creek, 800 yards). A finer sight could not have been beheld,—the shining barrels of the muskets, the excellent order of the men, the cleanliness of their appearance, the joy depicted on every face at being so near Fort du Quesne—the highest object of their wishes. The music re-echoed through the hills. How brilliant the morning—how melancholy the evening!"—*Letter of Judge Yeates, dated August,* 1776. See Haz. *Pa. Reg.*, VI. 104.

one destined to a higher fame,—George Washington, a boy in years, a man in calm thought and self-ruling wisdom.

8] With steady and well ordered march, the troops advanced into the great labyrinth of woods which shadowed the eastern borders of the river. Rank after rank vanished from sight. The forest swallowed them up, and the silence of the wilderness sank down once more on the shores and waters of the Monongahela.

9] Several engineers and guides and six light horsemen led the way; a body of grenadiers under Gage was close behind, and the army followed in such order as the rough ground would permit, along a narrow road, twelve feet wide, tunnelled through the dense and matted foliage. There were flanking parties on either side, but no scouts to scour the woods in front, and with an insane confidence Braddock pressed on to meet his fate. The van had passed the low grounds that bordered the river, and were now ascending a gently rising ground, where, on either hand, hidden by thick trees, by tangled undergrowth and rank grasses, lay the two fatal ravines. Suddenly, Gordon, an engineer in advance, saw the French and Indians bounding forward through the forest and along the narrow track, Beaujeu leading them on, dressed in a fringed hunting-shirt, and wearing a silver gorget on his breast. He stopped, turned, and waved his hat, and his French followers, crowding across the road, opened a murderous fire upon the head of the British column, while, screeching their war-cries, the Indians thronged into the ravines, or crouched behind rocks and trees on both flanks of the advancing troops. The astonished grenadiers returned the fire, and returned it with good effect; for a random shot struck down the brave Beaujeu, and the courage of the assailants was staggered by his fall. Dumas, second in command, rallied them to the attack; and while he, with the French and Canadians, made good the pass in front, the Indians from their lurking places opened a deadly fire on the right and left. In a few moments, all was confusion. The advance guard fell back on the main body, and every trace of subordination vanished. The fire soon extended along the whole length of the army, from front to rear.

Scarce an enemy could be seen, though the forest resounded with their yells; though every bush and tree was alive with incessant flashes; though the lead flew like a hailstorm, and the men went down by scores. The regular troops seemed bereft of their senses. They huddled together in the road like flocks of sheep; and happy did he think himself who could wedge his way into the midst of the crowd, and place a barrier of human flesh between his life and the shot of the ambushed marksmen. Many were seen eagerly loading their muskets, and then firing them into the air, or shooting their own comrades in the insanity of their terror. The officers, for the most part, displayed a conspicuous gallantry; but threats and commands were wasted alike on the panic-stricken multitude. It is said that at the outset Braddock showed signs of fear; but he soon recovered his wonted intrepidity. Five horses were shot under him, and five times he mounted afresh.[8] He stormed and shouted, and, while the Virginians were fighting to good purpose, each man behind a tree, like the Indians themselves, he ordered them with furious menace to form in platoons, where the fire of the enemy mowed them down like grass. At length, a mortal shot silenced him, and two provincials bore him off the field. Washington rode through the tumult calm and undaunted. Two horses were killed under him, and four bullets pierced his clothes;[9] but his hour was not come, and he escaped without a wound. Gates was shot through the body, and Gage also was severely wounded. Of eighty-six officers, only twenty-three remained unhurt; and of twelve hundred soldiers who crossed the Monongahela, more than seven hundred were killed and wounded. None suffered more severely than the Virginians, who had displayed throughout a degree of courage and steadiness which put the cowardice of the regulars to shame. The havoc among them was terrible, for of their whole number scarcely one-fifth left the field alive.[10]

[8] Letter—*Captain Orme, his aide-de-camp, to* —, July 18.
[9] Sparks, I. 67.
[10] "The Virginia troops showed a good deal of bravery, and were nearly all killed; for I believe, out of three companies that were there, scarcely thirty men are left alive. Captain Peyrouny, and all his officers, down to a

10] The slaughter lasted three hours; when, at length, the survivors, as if impelled by a general impulse, rushed tumultuously from the place of carnage, and with dastardly precipitation fled across the Monongahela. The enemy did not pursue beyond the river, flocking back to the field to collect the plunder, and gather a rich harvest of scalps. The routed troops pursued their flight until they met the rear division of the army, under Colonel Dunbar; and even then their senseless terrors did not abate. Dunbar's soldiers caught the infection. Cannon, baggage, provisions and wagons were destroyed, and all fled together, eager to escape from the shadows of those awful woods, whose horrors haunted their imagination. They passed the defenceless settlements of the border, and hurried on to Philadelphia, leaving the unhappy people to defend themselves as they might against the tomahawk and scalping-knife.

11] The calamities of this disgraceful rout did not cease with the loss of a few hundred soldiers on the field of battle; for it brought upon the provinces all the miseries of an Indian war. Those among the tribes who had thus far stood neutral, wavering between the French and English, now hesitated no longer. Many of them had been disgusted by the contemptuous behavior of Braddock. All had learned to despise the courage of the English, and to regard their own prowess with unbounded complacency. It is not in Indian nature to stand quiet in the midst of war; and the defeat of Braddock was a signal for the western savages to snatch their tomahawks and assail the English settlements with one accord, murdering and pillaging with ruthless fury, and turning the frontier of Pennsylvania and Virginia into one wide scene of havoc and desolation.

corporal, were killed. Captain Polson had nearly as hard a fate, for only one of his was left. In short, the dastardly behavior of those they call regulars exposed all others, that were inclined to do their duty, to almost certain death; and at last, in despite of all the efforts of the officers to the contrary, they ran, as sheep pursued by dogs, and it was impossible to rally them."—*Writings of Washington*, II. 87.

The English themselves bore reluctant testimony to the good conduct of the Virginians.—See Entick, *Hist. Late War*, 147.

Questions

Parkman's account of Braddock's famous disaster is an example of historical narrative pure and simple; the author is not trying to illustrate an idea or prove a point, but simply to tell what happened on a certain occasion. This does not mean, however, that there was no problem of selection or arrangement. Parkman could not tell *all* that happened, but only a part, and the way in which he has selected the facts which are to be included reveals something about his interests and his purpose in writing. And even though the passage is a narrative of a succession of events in time, there remains a certain latitude in the ordering of the details.

1. Although the passage tells of the fate of a British commander and a largely British army, it is evident that Parkman is chiefly interested in the battle as an event in American history. The reference to the American Revolution in the first paragraph is one indication of this. Find others.
2. Although the French were the victors, it is obvious that Parkman is much more interested in what happened to the British and Americans. Show how this interest is revealed in the very structure of the passage.
3. At one point only is the center of interest shifted over to the French. Find this section and explain its insertion at this point. By what device does Parkman shift the attention back to the English?
4. Although the selection of the material depends in part on Parkman's interests as a historian, many of the details are included simply because they increase the vividness and excitement of the story. Point out a number of such details.
5. What were the chief causes of the defeat? Show that these causes are indicated in the earlier part of the passage and brought out in the account of the battle itself.
6. Why are Horace Walpole's account of Braddock's character and Washington's report of the losses of the Virginians consigned to footnotes instead of being embodied in the text?
7. Compare the form of the references to sources in Parkman's footnotes with the forms prescribed in your composition handbook.

In what ways would Parkman's footnotes be considered unsatisfactory today?
8. Does Parkman's narrative fulfill any of the functions of history which Trevelyan enumerates in his essay?

Suggested Assignment

The world is full of men who, like Braddock, involve themselves and others in disaster because they cannot adapt themselves to circumstances. Discuss this problem in a short essay, using examples from your own experience. It would be well to limit the discussion to one field—war, business, education, or whatever it may be.

JAMES ANTHONY FROUDE

Sir Humfrey Gilbert

SOME two miles above the port of Dartmouth, once among the most important harbors in England, on a projecting angle of land which runs out into the river at the head of one of its most beautiful reaches, there has stood for some centuries the Manor House of Greenaway. The largest vessels may ride with safety within a stone's throw of the windows. In the latter half of the sixteenth century there must have met, in the hall of this mansion, a party as remarkable as could have been found anywhere in England. Humfrey and Adrian Gilbert, with their half-brother, Walter Raleigh, here, when little boys, played at sailors in the reaches of Long Stream; in the summer evenings doubtless rowing down with the tide to the port, and wondering at the quaint figure-heads and carved prows of the ships which

"Sir Humfrey Gilbert." Adapted from "England's Forgotten Worthies," in *Short Studies on Great Subjects* by James Anthony Froude.

thronged it; or climbing on board, and listening, with hearts beating, to the mariners' tales of the new earth beyond the sunset. And here in later life, matured men, whose boyish dreams had become heroic action, they used again to meet in the intervals of quiet, and the rock is shown underneath the house where Raleigh smoked the first tobacco.

2] Of this party, for the present we confine ourselves to the host and owner, Humfrey Gilbert, knighted afterwards by Elizabeth. Led by the scenes of his childhood to the sea and to sea adventures, and afterwards, as his mind unfolded, to study his profession scientifically, we find him as soon as he was old enough to think for himself, or make others listen to him, "amending the great errors of naval sea-cards, whose common fault is to make the degree of longitude in every latitude of one common bigness"; inventing instruments for taking observations, studying the form of the earth, and convincing himself that there was a northwest passage; and studying the necessities of his country, and discovering the remedies for them in colonization and extended markets for home manufactures.

3] Gilbert was examined before the Queen's Majesty and the Privy Council, and the record of his examination he has himself left to us in a paper which he afterwards drew up, and strange enough reading it is. The most admirable conclusions stand side by side with the wildest conjectures. Homer and Aristotle are pressed into service to prove that the ocean runs round the three old continents, and that America therefore is necessarily an island. The Gulf Stream, which he had carefully observed, eked out by a theory of the *primum mobile*, is made to demonstrate a channel to the north, corresponding to Magellan's Straits in the south, Gilbert believing, in common with almost everyone of his day, that these straits were the only opening into the Pacific, and the land to the south was unbroken to the Pole. He prophesies a market in the East for our manufactured linen and calicos:—

> The Easterns greatly prizing the same, as appeareth in Hester, where the pomp is expressed of the great King of India, Ahasuerus, who matched the colored clothes wherewith his houses and tents were appareled, with gold and silver, as part of his greatest treasure.

4] These and other such arguments were the best analysis which Sir Humfrey had to offer of the spirit which he felt to be working in him. We may think what we please of them; but we can have but one thought of the great grand words with which the memorial concludes, and they alone would explain the love which Elizabeth bore him:—

> Never, therefore, mislike with me for taking in hand any laudable and honest enterprise, for if through pleasure or idleness we purchase shame, the pleasure vanisheth, but the shame abideth forever.
>
> Give me leave, therefore, without offense, always to live and die in this mind: that he is not worthy to live at all that for fear or danger of death, shunneth his country's service and his own honor, seeing that death is inevitable and the fame of virtue immortal, wherefore in this behalf *mutare vel timere sperno.**

5] Two voyages which he undertook at his own cost, which shattered his fortune, and failed, as they naturally might, since inefficient help or mutiny of subordinates, or other disorders, are inevitable conditions under which more or less great men must be content to see their great thoughts mutilated by the feebleness of their instruments, did not dishearten him, and in June, 1583, a last fleet of five ships sailed from the port of Dartmouth, with commission from the queen to discover and take possession from latitude 45° to 50° North—a voyage not a little noteworthy, there being planted in the course of it the first English colony west of the Atlantic. Elizabeth had a foreboding that she would never see him again. She sent him a jewel as a last token of her favor, and she desired Raleigh to have his picture taken before he went.

6] The history of the voyage was written by a Mr. Edward Hayes, of Dartmouth, one of the principal actors in it, and as a composition it is more remarkable for fine writing than any very commendable thought in the author. But Sir Humfrey's nature shines through the infirmity of his chronicler; and in the end, indeed, Mr. Hayes himself is subdued into a better mind. He had

---

* I scorn to change or fear.

lost money by the voyage, and we will hope his higher nature was only under a temporary eclipse. The fleet consisted (it is well to observe the ships and the size of them) of the *Delight*, 120 tons; the bark *Raleigh*, 200 tons (this ship deserted off the Land's End); the *Golden Hinde* and the *Swallow*, 40 tons each; and the *Squirrel*, which was called the frigate, 10 tons. For the uninitiated in such matters, we may add, that if in a vessel the size of the last, a member of the Yacht Club would consider that he had earned a club-room immortality if he had ventured a run in the depth of summer from Cowes to the Channel Islands.

We were in all (says Mr. Hayes) 260 men, among whom we had of every faculty good choice. Besides, for solace of our own people, and allurement of the savages, we were provided of music in good variety, not omitting the least toys, as morris-dancers, hobby-horses, and May-like conceits to delight the savage people.

7] The expedition reached Newfoundland without accident. St. John's was taken possession of, and a colony left there; and Sir Humfrey then set out exploring along the American coast to the south, he himself doing all the work in his little 10-ton cutter, the service being too dangerous for the larger vessels to venture on. One of these had remained at St. John's. He was now accompanied only by the *Delight* and the *Golden Hinde*, and these two keeping as near the shore as they dared, he spent what remained of the summer examining every creek and bay, marking the soundings, taking the bearings of the possible harbors, and risking his life, as every hour he was obliged to risk it in such a service, in thus leading, as it were, the forlorn hope in the conquest of the New World. How dangerous it was we shall presently see. It was towards the end of August.

The evening was fair and pleasant, yet not without token of storm to ensue, and most part of this Wednesday night, like the swan that singeth before her death, they in the *Delight* continued in sounding of drums and trumpets and fifes, also winding the cornets and hautboys, and in the end of their jollity left with the battell and ringing of doleful knells.

8] Two days after came the storm; the *Delight* struck upon a bank, and went down in sight of the other vessels, which were unable to render her any help. Sir Humfrey's papers, among other things, were all lost in her; at the time considered by him an irreparable misfortune. But it was little matter: he was never to need them. The *Golden Hinde* and the *Squirrel* were now left alone of the five ships. The provisions were running short, and the summer season was closing. Both crews were on short allowance; and with much difficulty Sir Humfrey was prevailed upon to be satisfied for the present with what he had done, and to lay off for England.

So upon Saturday, in the afternoon, the 31st of August, we changed our course, and returned back for England, at which very instant, even in winding about, there passed along between us and the land, which we now forsook, a very lion, to our seeming, in shape, hair, and color; not swimming after the manner of a beast by moving of his feet, but rather sliding upon the water with his whole body, except his legs, in sight, neither yet diving under and again rising as the manner is of whales, porpoises, and other fish, but confidently showing himself without hiding, notwithstanding that we presented ourselves in open view and gesture to amaze him. Thus he passed along, turning his head to and fro, yawning and gaping wide, with ougly demonstration of long teeth and glaring eyes; and to bidde us farewell, coming right against the *Hinde*, he sent forth a horrible voice, roaring and bellowing as doth a lion, which spectacle we all beheld so far as we were able to discern the same, as men prone to wonder at every strange thing. What opinion others had thereof, and chiefly the General himself, I forbear to deliver. But he took it for *Bonum Omen*, rejoicing that he was to war against such an enemy, if it were the devil.

9] We have no doubt that he did think it was the devil; men in those days believing really that evil was more than a principle or a necessary accident, and that in all their labor for God and for right, they must make their account to have to fight with the devil in his proper person. But if we are to call it superstition, and if this were no devil in the form of a roaring lion, but a mere great seal or sea-lion, it is a more innocent superstition to impersonate so real a power, and it requires a bolder heart to rise up against it and defy it in its living terror, than to sublimate it away into a philosophical principle, and to forget to battle with it in speculating on its origin and nature. But to follow the brave Sir Humfrey, whose work of fighting with the devil was now over, and who was passing to his reward. The 2d of September the General came on board the *Golden Hinde* "to make merry with us." He greatly deplored the loss of his books and papers, but he was full of confidence from what he had seen, and talked with eagerness and warmth of the new expedition for the following spring. Apocryphal gold-mines still occupying the minds of Mr. Hayes and others, they were persuaded that Sir Humfrey was keeping to himself some such discovery which he had secretly made, and they tried hard to extract it from him. They could make nothing, however, of his odd, ironical answers, and their sorrow at the catastrophe which followed is sadly blended with disappointment that such a secret should have perished. Sir Humfrey doubtless saw America with other eyes than theirs, and gold-mines richer than California in its huge rivers and savannas.

Leaving the issue of this good hope (about the gold), (continues Mr. Hayes), to God, who only knoweth the truth thereof, I will hasten to the end of this tragedy, which must be knit up in the person of our General, and as it was God's ordinance upon him, even so the vehement persuasion of his friends could nothing avail to divert him from his willful resolution of going in his frigate; and when he was entreated by the captain, master, and others, his well-wishers in the *Hinde,* not to venture, this was his answer—"I will not forsake my little company going homewards, with whom I have passed so many storms and perils."

10] Two thirds of the way home they met foul weather and terrible seas, "breaking short and pyramidwise." Men who had all their lives "occupied the sea" had never seen it more outrageous. "We had also upon our mainyard an apparition of a little fier by night, which seamen do call Castor and Pollux."

Monday, the ninth of September, in the afternoon, the frigate was near cast away oppressed by waves, but at that time recovered, and giving forth signs of joy, the General, sitting abaft with a book in his hand, cried out unto us in the *Hinde* so often as we did approach within hearing, "We are as near to heaven by sea as by land," reiterating the same speech, well beseeming a soldier resolute in Jesus Christ, as I can testify that he was. The same Monday night, about twelve of the clock, or not long after, the frigate being ahead of us in the *Golden Hinde*, suddenly her lights were out, whereof as it were in a moment we lost the sight; and withal our watch cried, "The General was cast away," which was too true.

Thus faithfully (concludes Mr. Hayes, in some degree rising above himself) I have related this story, wherein some spark of the knight's virtues, though he be extinguished, may happily appear; he remaining resolute to a purpose honest and godly as was this, to discover, possess, and reduce unto the service of God and Christian piety, those remote and heathen countries of America. Such is the infinite bounty of God, who from every evil deriveth good, that fruit may grow in time of our travelling in these Northwestern lands (as has it not grown?), and the crosses, turmoils, and afflictions, both in the preparation and execution of the voyage, did correct the intemperate humors which before we noted to be in this gentleman, and made unsavory and less delightful his other manifold virtues.

Thus as he was refined and made nearer unto the image of God, so it pleased the Divine will to resume him unto Himself, whither both his and every other high and noble mind have always aspired.

11] Such was Sir Humfrey Gilbert; still in the prime of his years when the Atlantic swallowed him. Like the gleam of a landscape lit suddenly for a moment by the lightning, these few scenes flash down to us across the centuries: but what a life must that have been of which this was the conclusion! We have glimpses of him a few years earlier, when he won his spurs in Ireland—won them by deeds which to us seem terrible in their ruthlessness, but which won the applause of Sir Henry Sidney as too high for praise or even reward. Checkered like all of us with lines of light and darkness, he was nevertheless one of a race which has ceased to be. We look round for them, and we can hardly believe that the same blood is flowing in our veins. Brave we may still be, and strong perhaps as they, but the high moral grace which made bravery and strength so beautiful is departed from us forever.

Questions

Although both Parkman ("Braddock's Defeat," p. 95) and Froude are historians, the selections by which they are here represented differ greatly in purpose and method. Parkman, writing historical narrative, is interested in telling simply *what happened;* he relates his facts in chronological order. Froude's essay, it is true, is based upon a narrative and relies in part on the chronological method; but Froude makes use of his source only to expound an idea.

Froude's essay rests largely on a single source. With the exception of the first three quotations, all the material is drawn from the account written by Sir Humfrey Gilbert's rear admiral, Edward Hayes.* Despite the fact that he is dependent on one source, however, Froude is not merely condensing the original account or selecting its most exciting parts and linking them with a few comments of his own. Rather, he has a definite attitude toward his material and a specific idea which he wishes to emphasize. His attitude and his idea determine the quotations he selects and the way in which he handles them.

1. *a.* What evidence does Froude have for the information that he gives in the first paragraph—that the Gilberts and Raleigh in their childhood rowed down to the port, wondered at the appearance of the ships, and listened to the mariners' tales?

   b. What is the purpose of the first paragraph?

2. If you have answered 1*b* by saying "as an introduction to the essay," explain your meaning further. Does the first paragraph state the idea of the essay? Does it present the facts about the sources which Froude is using?

3. In his discussion of Gilbert's examination before the Privy Council (paragraph 3) Froude writes, "The most admirable conclusions stand side by side with the wildest conjectures." Of the facts given in paragraphs 3 and 4, which are "admirable conclusions"? which are "wild conjectures"?

4. Consider each of the following as possible revisions for the first sentence in paragraph 5.

* *A Report of the Voyage and Success Thereof, Attempted in the Year of Our Lord 1583, by Sir Humfrey Gilbert, Knight* by Edward Hayes. (Students may refer to the original in the *Principal Navigations* of Hakluyt.)

a. Two voyages, which he undertook at his own cost, were failures and shattered his fortune. His third expedition was launched in June, 1583, when a last fleet of five ships sailed from the port of Dartmouth, with commission from the queen to discover and take possession from latitude 45° to 50° North.

b. Although he had already shattered his fortune by two unsuccessful voyages, Sir Humfrey never seemed to be assailed by any doubts concerning his ability as a seaman or as a commander of men. In June, 1583, he launched a third abortive expedition. An ill-fated fleet of five ships sailed from the port of Dartmouth, with commission from the queen to discover and take possession from latitude 45° to 50° North.

Explain the difference in tone between each of the revisions printed above and the original. Point out those phrases in the original which reveal Froude's opinion.

5. Reread paragraphs 6 through 10 carefully. In each, point out those sentences or phrases which reveal Froude's attitude toward the facts he is reporting.

6. *a.* The long quotation in paragraph 8 relates an extraordinary occurrence, but no more extraordinary than other parts of Hayes's narrative. What reason, other than the fact that the event was unusual, does Froude have for quoting this passage?

b. The long quotation in paragraph 10 gives the essential facts about Gilbert's death. What other reasons does Froude have for quoting it in full?

7. Explain the meaning of the following: "It is a more innocent superstition to impersonate so real a power, and it requires a bolder heart to rise up against it and defy it in its living terror, than to sublimate it away into a philosophical principle, and to forget to battle with it in speculating on its origin and nature" (paragraph 9).

8. In a research paper, the material quoted is as much a part of the essay as are the writer's own words. If the essay is to hold together as a unit, the reader should not have the feeling that the quotations are thrust upon him. Achieving smoothness depends upon deft transitions from text to quotation and from quotation to text. Some of the devices useful in effecting easy transitions are these: summarizing or giving a clue to the material in the quotation; commenting on the quoted material; selecting a key word or

phrase from the quoted material and carrying it over into the writer's next sentence; characterizing the quotation by a summarizing phrase; indicating that the quoted material is representative of many similar instances.

Analyze each of Froude's quotations, explaining how he introduces it and how he proceeds to the next point.

9. *a.* After having answered questions 1 through 8, what do you think Froude means by "the spirit which he felt to be working in him" (paragraph 4)? What does Froude see in Sir Humfrey besides bravery and a readiness for adventure?

   b. Summarize the theme idea of the essay in a single sentence.

10. In your opinion does this essay fulfill any of the functions of history itemized by Trevelyan (pp. 89-94)?

Suggested Assignments

1. If copies are available in the college library, read Edward Hayes's narrative. His account is fairly brief but rich in material—information on the means of establishing a claim to new territory, on the religious beliefs of the age, on the conduct of the sailors, and so on. Evolve a theme idea of your own and write an essay based on the narrative, following Froude's method of quoting only what is pertinent to your purpose.

2. Read another one of the accounts of early voyages in Hakluyt's collection, *Principal Navigations,* and follow the procedure suggested in 1.

LEWIS MUMFORD

Thomas Jefferson, Architect

IN EVERY respect, the University of Virginia was the crowning episode in Jefferson's life: the seal of his conviction as a statesman and a political philosopher, the proof of his greatness as an architect. The University itself was one of his most persistent dreams; for he wished his native state, in his own words, to "give every citizen the information he needs for the transaction of his daily business . . . and, in general, to observe with intelligence and faithfulness all the social relations under which he shall be placed." We know that Jefferson, while a student at William and Mary, had come directly under the influence of three redoubtable tutors, who stood in the relation of friends, whilst he was still a student; and Jefferson, from the beginning, had it constantly in mind to create a series of buildings which would, by their very spacing and arrangement, favor the intimate kind of relation between professor and student by which he himself had profited.

2] Here we have, I think, one of the reasons for the imaginative sweep and formal clarity of Jefferson's design for the University. Almost all great works of art—I think one may safely generalize—have a long period of hidden gestation. They do not arise out of sudden and superficial demands that come from the outside; they are rather the mature working out of inner convictions and beliefs that the artist has long held, has mulled over, has perhaps sought to embody in preliminary essays. In short, the

"Thomas Jefferson, Architect." From *The South in Architecture*, copyright, 1941, by Lewis Mumford. Reprinted by permission of Harcourt, Brace and Company, Inc.

artist must live with his form, so that it becomes flesh of his flesh and bone of his bone, before he can start it on its independent career. Jefferson began his plans for the University with no formal structure, like the Maison Carrée, in his mind's eye: he began, rather, with the program of the new university, as a place in which professors and students would become partners in the exchange and pursuit of knowledge; and his problem was not to imitate a Greek temple or an Italian villa or even an Oxford college; but to find a fresh form which would mirror his purpose. In a letter to Governor Nicholas of Virginia, dated April 12, 1816, Jefferson wrote: "I would strongly recommend . . . instead of one immense building, to have a small one for every professorship, arranged at proper distances around a square, to admit of extensions, connected by a piazza, so that they may go dry from one school to another. The village form is preferable to a single great building for many reasons, particularly on account of fire, health, economy, peace, and quiet." Those were the words of a man who had a firm grip on every part of his problem.

3] The few precedents that existed in America did not hamper or guide Jefferson: the separate collegiate buildings of Harvard, Princeton, or William and Mary did not impress him: he made a clean departure from the current tradition. Nor was Jefferson influenced by the medieval quadrangles of Oxford, with their cloistered quiet and their carefully guarded enclosures. In the richness of his old age, his architectural thought had become purposeful and integrated, sure enough of its foundations to permit him to create a truly native form. Though he drew upon his architectural acquaintances like Dr. William Thornton and that excellent professional Benjamin Latrobe, what he sought were only specific suggestions for details: the main lines were already laid down in his mind. His letter to Dr. William Thornton, dated May 9, 1817, leaves no doubt as to this:

4] "We are commencing here," he wrote, "the establishment of a college. Instead of building a magnificent house which would exhaust all our funds, we propose to lay off a square of seven or eight hundred feet, in the outside of which we shall arrange separate pavilions, one for each professor and his scholars. Each pavilion will have a school room below and two rooms for the professor above, and between pavilion and pavilion a range of dormitories for the boys, one story high, giving to each a room 10 feet wide and 14 feet deep. The pavilions about 36 feet wide in front and 26 feet in depth. . . . The whole of the pavilions to be united by a colonnade in front, of the height of the lower story of the pavilions." A few of these details underwent change: the distance between the rows was reduced from 800 to 200 feet, with both an esthetic and a social gain; and Jefferson, finding that not all professors were bachelors, had to provide bigger quarters for the professors' families, with four private rooms instead of two; but the main outlines of the scheme remained.

5] In designing the University Jefferson had the opportunity he had lacked in the Richmond State Capitol. Not merely was he constantly at hand to supervise the work, but he began with an adequate site, and from the beginning was able to control the use of the site no less than the individual designs of the buildings. Here again his common sense and imagination triumphed over his bias toward purely geometrical figures. As a lover of squared paper, he was inclined to favor the checkerboard plan in the design of cities; he had even thought of combating the plague of yellow fever by building cities on a literal checkerboard plan, in which only the black squares would be used for building and the white ones left open, in turf and trees. When the ancient site of Babylon was re-discovered and its strictly rectangular plan was brought to light, Jefferson had hailed it as a model and thought it should serve as a precedent for Washington: indeed, he never fully reconciled himself to L'Enfant's starlike pattern of radial avenues which were superimposed on that design. Fortunately, not merely was Jefferson forced to narrow the space between the rows; he was also forced to meet a drop in the land by building low transverse terraces. This slight irregularity, this modification of pure form to meet the exigencies of life, adds to the esthetic effectiveness of the plan itself.

6] If the palace of Versailles was one of the first examples of an open order of planning, in which the building stretched in a straight line, instead of making a quadrangle or a court, the University of Virginia buildings are the first, as far as I know, in which this kind of open plan was repeated in four parallel rows, of equal length. Here was a better suggestion for city planning than the suggestion for an open checkerboard, which Jefferson had made to Volney in 1805. This form of planning is what the Germans now call Seilenbau, which merely means building in parallel rows open at the ends; and during recent years it has almost become a symbol of modern town planning, since, if the buildings are properly oriented, it permits the fullest exposure to the prevailing winds and the view. But Jefferson's open rows have a characteristic feature that most modern forms of Seilenbau have not. The dormitories, instead of stretching in unbroken lines, are punctuated by the houses of the professors, which also contained the classrooms; or, on the further ranges, the students' rows are broken by the individual boarding houses, in which the students boarded. This interruption of the uniform façade is logical: it is functional; and it is esthetic; in other words, it embodies Sir Henry Wotton's often quoted definition of the essentials of architecture: commodity, firmness, and delight. No one of these reasons alone would have been sufficient to make the rows the masterly architectural achievement that they are: it is the conjuncture of all three, and their perfect embodiment in the buildings themselves, that establish their success.

7] I would emphasize, even at the risk of being tedious, how much the beauty of the University of Virginia depends upon Jefferson's insight into the human needs that these buildings serve. That is obvious, for example, in the very intimate scale of the colonnades, with their succession of low arches; there is no effort to blow up this attractive architectural feature into monumental proportions. But it should be even more obvious when one sees how the principle of designing the college on a village pattern, rather than a palatial institutional one, leads naturally to breaking up both the professors' houses and the boarding houses into separate buildings.

8] Note how Jefferson avoided that characteristic monstrosity of our more recent American colleges, the huge dining hall; noisy, institutionalized, barrackslike. He provided, again in his own words, for "six hotels for dieting the students, with a single room in each for a refectory, and two rooms, a garden, and offices for the tenants." That introduces into the business of eating, a human, an intimate note; eating under these circumstances must have lent itself to conversation and friendship; and it probably lent itself likewise to a better sort of life for the people who cooked and served the food, and were by reason of the human scale, on more amiable terms with the boarders. As a member of a college building committee, I have fought to establish that principle in modern American practice; and though I have so far fought in vain, I am convinced that Jefferson was right, right both as an architect and as an educator; and that if we are interested in the whole process of education, we will pay as much attention to the conditions under which students eat, as we do to the conditions under which they take physical exercise; though it is the cultivation of the whole personality rather than the body alone that should be our main object in "dieting" the students.

9] The one place where Jefferson went wrong in the design of the University of Virginia was where he lost sight of his own fundamental principles, and as a result committed even an esthetic error. Jefferson, in his deference for high architectural authority, took over Latrobe's suggestion for a central domed building which should close up the axis and dominate the group. His original plans made no such provision: both ends of the rows left the landscape open to the eye. And though he had the good sense to transform Latrobe's proposed auditorium into a library, the scale and character of the building—the Rotunda—are entirely out of keeping with the village plan that Jefferson so wisely had in mind. Granting that a library building was a necessity, it would have been better sense and better architecture to have treated it as an integral part of the rest of the design; one can imagine a central stack room, with wings to serve the special departments of knowledge and provide more intimate reading and study alcoves—all conceived on the scale of the pavilions and dormitories, with such appropriate changes in windows and lighting as the storing and reading of books would naturally suggest.

Such a building would have completed the design of the rows: whereas Jefferson's attempt to reproduce the Pantheon, despite its more modest scale, is entirely out of keeping both in design and in bulk with the modest buildings that were erected; neither in its original form, nor in McKim, Mead and White's reproduction, is it anything but an awkward overgrown structure, which mars the general picture and could not from the first, in the very nature of its composition, serve its own function adequately.

10] The library is the only real weakness, however, in the whole conception; in every other respect the design is a masterpiece. For if the plan and the general order were good, the execution of the details was no less admirable. Jefferson designed each of the professors' pavilions to be a replica, as far as possible, of some noble classic temple; in order that the students of architecture might have a model of the best taste of the past always before their eyes. Though his purpose here has ceased to be relevant, the actual effect is still charming: the variations he introduced in those buildings, now with a flat, now with a gabled roof, now with small, superimposed columns for the front porches, now with a full-scale temple portico, the austere ancient pattern sometimes broken in the balconies by a diamond pattern or a Chinese fret—all these variations on the central theme are music for the eye. The pavilions, again, lost some of that bleakness and gawkiness that the austere temple form sometimes has in the American landscape, by reason of the fact that they are supported by the low horizontal façades of the dormitories. The success of these buildings applies even to the smallest details. Consider his famous wall, with its undulating curves; this was an astonishing piece of virtuosity; for it is only one brick thick; and by laying a series of arches on the ground, as it were, he not only gave an interesting ripple of movement to what was otherwise just a barrier, but provided a sheltered, twice-warmed place for the more tender plantations.

11] In short, the University of Virginia was the marvelous embodiment of three great architectural essentials. The first was a well-conceived and well-translated program, based upon a fresh conception of the functions of a modern university. A good building serves as the physical and symbolic setting for a scheme of life: to build well, the first step is to understand the purposes, the motives, the habits, and the desires of those who are to be housed. Architecture, if it is to be anything better than scene painting, must be evolved from the inside out; and the architect must therefore begin, not with the land or the structure, but with the needs that the land or the structure are finally to satisfy. Unlike modern millionaires, who so often put up collegiate buildings for the pleasure of seeing their names on the façades, and who imagine that the more money they spend, the more highly their names will be edified, Jefferson began with certain definite convictions about the needs of students and scholars. Hence a certain modesty and economy of detail; hence a respect for human proportions. Although Jefferson spent freely when the need arose—I have told how he imported stonecutters from Italy to carve the capitals—there was no splurging in these buildings, if one perhaps excepts the unfortunate library. Jefferson had a carefully thought-out program; and he carried it through.

12] The second great architectural essential is that individual buildings should never be conceived as isolated units; they should always be conceived and executed as parts of the whole. Buildings exist in a landscape, in a village, or in a city; they are parts of a natural or an urban setting; they are elements in a whole. The individual unit must always be conceived and modified in terms of the whole. This cannot be done by architects who have their nose on the draughting board, and who, in their own conceit, have no regard for the principle of neighborliness and no interest in the surrounding works of nature or man.

13] A certain discipline, a certain restraint, even a certain sacrifice of private tastes and preferences is necessary if an individual is going to develop a positive character: people who do what they like, when and how they like, are not merely a nuisance to their neighbors, but they turn out to be weak characters, to boot. It is the same in architecture. The beauty of the University of Virginia buildings that Jefferson designed does not lie in any single detail; it does not lie in any single building; it does not even lie in any single row: it derives from the order and purpose that underlies the whole and creates a harmony, practical and esthetic, between its various parts. That is a lesson which the architects and builders largely forgot in the two generations that followed Jefferson's death. To pick up that tradition and re-instate it has been one of the main tasks of our own time, and it is one that is still only imperfectly performed.

14] The third great quality that Jefferson showed was his ability to modify details to meet a special situation, while holding to a rigorous and consistent plan. This is a quality that has special meaning for us today; for we are too often the helpless victims of the very mechanical order we have created. Now Jefferson was as much enamored as our most machine-minded contemporaries of regularity, of mathematical proportions, of mechanical accuracy; and his readiness to make departures from such order, when necessity arose, is one of the proofs of his mastership. Geometry satisfies a deep desire of the human mind: the desire for order, certainty, regularity, for form and stability in a world of flux. When this order is embodied in building, it satisfies the mind that man is for the moment on top and in control of the situation. But that victory of order always has its dangers, as the Greeks, who so well mastered geometry, were aware: the danger is that it may flout human needs, as completely as Procrustes did when he chopped off human legs in order to make his guests fit the beds they were to sleep in. Life without order is chaotic; but order without life is the end of everything, and eventually the end of order, too, since the purpose of order in building is to sustain human life. In the University of Virginia, Jefferson struck a balance between formal order and vital order, between the logic of building and the logic of life. And that is why this achievement of his ranks, not merely as one of the highest achievements of American architecture, but as one of the high points of architecture anywhere in the world in the nineteenth century. It dwarfs all of Jefferson's other buildings. It puts the work of his contemporaries and successors for the next fifty years distinctly into third rank. If Jefferson's achievement here had been studied by his successors with some of the reverence and love and understanding that it has belatedly received, the course of American architecture might have been appreciably changed; and changed, of course, for the better.

Questions

Mumford's essay is especially interesting as a model for composition since it represents a pattern common in critical articles. Briefly, Mumford is engaged in setting up a standard of judgment and in applying that standard to a particular work. Such an essay involves certain problems, and Mumford has solved them very well.

1. The essay clearly divides itself into two main parts. At what paragraph does the division occur? Indicate the difference in content between parts 1 and 2.
2. *a.* Using a single sentence for each paragraph, write a sentence outline of paragraphs 11 through 14. *Write sentences.*

    b. Which two of these paragraphs might be combined into one? Why?
3. Combine the sentences which you have written in answer to question 2a into a single, well-constructed sentence.
4. Which is a better summary of the main idea of the essay—the first sentence of paragraph 1 or the sentence which you have written in answer to question 3? Defend your choice.
5. What is the logical relationship between the first sentence of the essay and your summarizing sentence?
6. The architectural principles which Mumford establishes in paragraphs 11 through 14 might have been explained in abstract terms in a single introductory paragraph preceding paragraph 1. In other words, Mumford might have started with theory rather than with the concrete example. Would this procedure have been advisable? Why? or why not?
7. Preparation for each of the principles established in the concluding part of the essay has been made by certain of the details in part 1.

    a. Point out those details in part 1 which support the idea of a well-conceived plan based on a conception of the function of a university.

    b. Point out those details which support the idea of the harmony of the whole group of buildings.

c. Point out those details which support the idea of the modification of a plan to meet special situations.

8. Could Mumford have omitted any paragraph in 1 through 10 without weakening the preparation for his conclusions? If so, what paragraph or paragraphs might best have been omitted? Why?

9. A student is often faced with a problem similar to that which Mumford solves in paragraph 9: the problem of discussing a minor point which weakens or partially refutes the main theory of his paper. To omit the point completely may involve intellectual dishonesty. To handle it skillfully, placing it in a suitably subordinate position, is a sign of mature writing.

   a. Should Mumford have introduced the problem of the library earlier in his essay? Why? or why not?

   b. Could paragraphs 9 and 10 be reversed? Explain.

10. Could the following sentence be substituted for sentence 1 in paragraph 10?
    "Although in every other respect the design is a masterpiece, the library is a real weakness."

11. The phrase *in short* (paragraph 11) is Mumford's only transition between the two main parts of his essay. Substitute a more adequate summarizing phrase.

Suggested Assignment

Write an essay on one of the following subjects. To uphold your thesis, you will undoubtedly find it necessary to inspect the buildings you are interested in and jot down pertinent details.

1. The campus as a whole judged according to Mumford's three architectural principles.

2. A particular group of college buildings judged according to Mumford's three architectural principles.

3. A single college building judged according to one or more of Mumford's principles.

You may follow Mumford's plan, which is a fairly elaborate one, or plan your paper according to your own needs. Here are some possibilities: a detailed description of the buildings, followed by a discussion of their architectural value in terms of Mumford's principles (Mumford's method); a discussion of the principles followed by the illustrations; a discussion of each principle, with the illustrative material pertinent to that principle, handled separately.

GEORGE ORWELL

The Art of Donald McGill

WHO DOES not know the "comics" of the cheap stationers' windows, the penny or twopenny coloured post cards with their endless succession of fat women in tight bathing-dresses and their crude drawing and unbearable colours, chiefly hedge-sparrow's egg tint and Post Office red?

2] This question ought to be rhetorical, but it is a curious fact that many people seem to be unaware of the existence of these things, or else to have a vague notion that they are something to be found only at the seaside, like Negro minstrels or peppermint rock. Actually they are on sale everywhere—they can be bought at nearly any Woolworth's, for example—and they are evidently produced in enormous numbers, new series constantly appearing. They are not to be confused with the various other types of comic illustrated post card, such as the sentimental ones dealing with puppies and kittens or the Wendyish, subpornographic ones which exploit the love-affairs of children. They are a *genre* of their own, specialising in very "low" humour, the mother-in-law, baby's nappy, policemen's boots type of joke, and distinguishable from all the other kinds by having no artistic pretensions. Some

"The Art of Donald McGill." Abridged from *Dickens, Dali and Others*, copyright, 1946, by George Orwell. Reprinted by permission of Harcourt, Brace and Co. The essay has been abridged by arrangement with the author.

half-dozen publishing houses issue them, though the people who draw them seem not to be numerous at any one time.

3] I have associated them especially with the name of Donald McGill because he is not only the most prolific and by far the best of contemporary post card artists, but also the most representative, the most perfect in the tradition. Who Donald McGill is, I do not know. He is apparently a trade name, for at least one series of post cards is issued simply as "The Donald McGill Comics," but he is also unquestionably a real person with a style of drawing which is recognisable at a glance. Anyone who examines his post cards in bulk will notice that many of them are not despicable even as drawings, but it would be mere dilettantism to pretend that they have any direct æsthetic value. A comic post card is simply an illustration to a joke, invariably a "low" joke, and it stands or falls by its ability to raise a laugh. Beyond that it has only "ideological" interest. McGill is a clever draughtsman with a real caricaturist's touch in the drawing of faces, but the special value of his post cards is that they are so completely typical. They represent, as it were, the norm of the comic post card. Without being in the least imitative, they are exactly what comic post cards have been any time these last forty years, and from them the meaning and purpose of the whole *genre* can be inferred.

4] Get hold of a dozen of these things, preferably McGill's— if you pick out from a pile the ones that seem to you funniest, you will probably find that most of them are McGill's—and spread them out on a table. What do you see?

5] Your first impression is of overpowering vulgarity. This is quite apart from the ever-present obscenity, and apart also from the hideousness of the colours. They have an utter lowness of mental atmosphere which comes out not only in the nature of the jokes but, even more, in the grotesque, staring, blatant quality of the drawings. The designs, like those of a child, are full of heavy lines and empty spaces, and all the figures in them, every gesture and attitude, are deliberately ugly, the faces grinning and vacuous, the women monstrously parodied, with bottoms like Hottentots. Your second impression, however, is of indefinable familiarity. What do these things remind you of? What are they so like? In the first place, of course, they remind you of the barely different post cards which you probably gazed at in your childhood. But more than this, what you are really looking at is something as traditional as Greek tragedy, a sort of sub-world of smacked bottoms and scrawny mothers-in-law which is a part of Western European consciousness. Not that the jokes, taken one by one, are necessarily stale. Not being debarred from smuttiness, comic post cards repeat themselves less often than the joke columns in reputable magazines, but their basic subject-matter, the *kind* of joke they are aiming at, never varies. A few are genuinely witty, in a Max Millerish style.

6] In general, however, they are not witty but humorous, and it must be said for McGill's post cards, in particular, that the drawing is often a good deal funnier than the joke beneath it. Obviously the outstanding characteristic of comic post cards is their obscenity, and I must discuss that more fully later. But I give here a rough analysis of their habitual subject-matter, with such explanatory remarks as seem to be needed:

7] *Sex.*—More than half, perhaps three-quarters, of the jokes are sex jokes, ranging from the harmless to the all but unprintable. First favourite is probably the illegitimate baby. Also newly-weds, old maids, nude statues and women in bathing-dresses. All of these are *ipso facto* funny, mere mention of them being enough to raise a laugh. The cuckoldry joke is very seldom exploited.

Conventions of the sex joke:

(i) Marriage only benefits the women. Every man is plotting seduction and every woman is plotting marriage. No woman ever remains unmarried voluntarily.

(ii) Sex-appeal vanishes at about the age of twenty-five. Well-preserved and good-looking people beyond their first youth are never represented. The amorous honey-mooning couple reappear as the grim-visaged wife and shapeless, moustachioed, red-nosed husband, no intermediate stage being allowed for.

8] *Home life.*—Next to sex, the henpecked husband is the favourite joke. Typical caption: "Did they get an X-ray of your wife's jaw at the hospital?"—"No, they got a moving picture instead."

Conventions:

(i) There is no such thing as a happy marriage.

(ii) No man ever gets the better of a woman in argument.

9] *Drunkenness.*—Both drunkenness and teetotalism are *ipso facto* funny.

Conventions:

(i) All drunken men have optical illusions.

(ii) Drunkenness is something peculiar to middle-aged men. Drunken youths or women are never represented.

10] *Inter-working-class snobbery.*—Much in these post cards suggests that they are aimed at the better-off working class and poorer middle class. There are many jokes turning on malapropisms, illiteracy, dropped aitches and the rough manners of slum-dwellers. Countless post cards show draggled hags of the stage-charwoman type exchanging "unladylike" abuse. A certain number produced since the war treat evacuation from the anti-evacuee angle. There are the usual jokes about tramps, beggars and criminals, and the comic maidservant appears fairly frequently. Also the comic navvy, bargee, etc.; but there are no anti trade union jokes. Broadly speaking, everyone with much over or much under £5 a week is regarded as laughable. The "swell" is almost as automatically a figure of fun as the slum-dweller.

11] *Stock figures.*—Foreigners seldom or never appear. The chief locality joke is the Scotsman, who is almost inexhaustible. The lawyer is always a swindler, the clergyman always a nervous idiot who says the wrong thing. The "knut" or "masher" still appears, almost as in Edwardian days, in out-of-date-looking evening-clothes and an opera hat, or even with spats and a knobby cane. Another survival is the Suffragette, one of the big jokes of the pre-1914 period and too valuable to be relinquished. She has reappeared, unchanged in physical appearance, as the Feminist lecturer or Temperance fanatic. A feature of the last few years is the complete absence of anti-Jew post cards. The "Jew joke," always somewhat more ill-natured than the "Scotch joke," disappeared abruptly soon after the rise of Hitler.

12] *Politics.*—Any contemporary event, cult or activity which has comic possibilities (for example, "free love," feminism, A.R.P., nudism) rapidly finds its way into the picture post cards, but their general atmosphere is extremely old-fashioned. The implied political outlook is a Radicalism appropriate to about the year 1900. At normal times they are not only not patriotic, but go in for a mild guying of patriotism, with jokes about "God save the King," the Union Jack, etc. The European situation only began to reflect itself in them at some time in 1939, and first did so through the comic aspects of A.R.P. Even at this date few post cards mention the war except in A.R.P. jokes (fat woman stuck in the mouth of Anderson shelter: wardens neglecting their duty while young woman undresses at window she has forgotten to black out, etc., etc.). A few express anti-Hitler sentiments of a not very vindictive kind. Unlike the twopenny weekly papers, comic post cards are not the product of any great monopoly company, and evidently they are not regarded as having any importance in forming public opinion. There is no sign in them of any attempt to induce an outlook acceptable to the ruling class.

13] Here one comes back to the outstanding, all-important feature of comic post cards—their obscenity. It is by this that everyone remembers them, and it is also central to their purpose, though not in a way that is immediately obvious. But at the same time the McGill post card—and this applies to all other post cards in this *genre*—is not intended as pornography but, a subtler thing, as a skit on pornography. The Hottentot figures of the women are caricatures of the Englishman's secret ideal, not portraits of it. When one examines McGill's post cards more closely, one notices that his brand of humour only has meaning in relation to a fairly strict moral code. Whereas in papers like *Esquire,* for instance, or *La Vie Parisienne,* the imaginary background of the jokes is always promiscuity, the utter breakdown of all standards, the background of the McGill post card is marriage. The four leading jokes are nakedness, illegitimate babies, old maids and newly married couples, none of which would seem funny in a really dissolute or even "sophisticated" society. The implication—and this is just the implication the *Esquire* or the *New Yorker* would avoid at all costs—is that marriage is something profoundly exciting and important, the biggest event in the average human being's life. So also with jokes about nagging wives and tyrannous mothers-in-law. They do at least imply a stable society in which marriage is indissoluble and family loyalty taken for granted. And bound up with this is something I noted earlier, the fact that there are no pictures, or hardly any, of good-looking people beyond their first youth. There is the "spooning" couple and the middle-aged, cat-and-dog couple, but nothing in between. The liaison, the illicit but more or less decorous love-affair which used to be the stock joke of French comic papers, is not a post card subject. And this reflects, on a comic level, the working-class outlook which takes it as a matter of course that youth and adventure—almost, indeed, individual life—end with marriage. One of the few authentic class-differences, as opposed to class-distinctions, still existing in England is that the working classes age very much earlier. They do not live less long, provided that they survive their childhood, nor do they lose their physical activity earlier, but they do lose very early their youthful appearance. This fact is observable everywhere, but can be most easily verified by watching one of the higher age groups registering for military service; the middle- and upper-class members look, on average, ten years younger than the others. It is usual to attribute this to the harder lives that the working classes have to live, but it is doubtful whether any such difference now exists as would account for it. More probably the truth is that the working classes reach middle age earlier because they accept it earlier. For to look young after, say, thirty is largely a matter of wanting to do so. This generalisation is less true of the better-paid workers, especially those who live in council houses and labour-saving flats, but it is true enough even of them to point to a difference of outlook. And in this, as usual, they are more traditional, more in accord with the Christian past than the well-to-do women who try to stay young at forty by means of physical jerks, cosmetics and avoidance of child-bearing. The impulse to cling to youth at all costs, to attempt to preserve your sexual attraction, to see even in middle age a future for yourself and not merely for your children, is a thing of recent growth and has only precariously established itself. It will probably disappear again when our standard of living drops and our birth-rate rises. "Youth's a stuff will not endure" expresses the normal, traditional attitude. It is this ancient wisdom that McGill and his colleagues are reflecting, no doubt unconsciously, when they allow for no transition stage between the honeymoon couple and those glamourless figures, Mum and Dad.

14] I have said that at least half McGill's post cards are sex jokes, and a proportion, perhaps ten per cent., are far more obscene than anything else that is now printed in England. Newsagents are occasionally prosecuted for selling them, and there would be many more prosecutions if the broadest jokes were not invariably protected by double meanings. It is doubtful whether there is any paper in England that would print jokes of this kind, and certainly there is no paper that does so habitually. There is an immense amount of pornography of a mild sort, countless illustrated papers cashing in on women's legs, but there is no popular literature specialising in the "vulgar," farcical aspect of sex. On the other hand, jokes exactly like McGill's are the ordinary small change of the revue and music-hall stage, and are also to be heard on the radio, at moments when the censor happens to be nodding. In England the gap between what can be said and what can be printed is rather exceptionally wide. Remarks and gestures which hardly anyone objects to on the stage would raise a public outcry if any attempt were made to reproduce them on paper. (Compare Max Miller's stage patter with his weekly column in the *Sunday Dispatch*.) The comic post cards are the only existing exception to this rule, the only medium in which really "low" humour is considered to be printable. Only in post cards and on the variety stage can the stuck-out behind, dog and lamppost, baby's nappy type of joke be freely exploited. Remembering that, one sees what function these post cards, in their humble way, are performing.

15] What they are doing is to give expression to the Sancho Panza view of life, the attitude to life that Miss Rebecca West once summed up as "extracting as much fun as possible from smacking behinds in basement kitchens." The Don Quixote-Sancho Panza combination, which of course is simply the ancient dualism of body and soul in fiction form, recurs more frequently in the literature of the last four hundred years than can be explained by mere imitation. It comes up again and again, in endless variations, Bouvard and Pécuchet, Jeeves and Wooster, Bloom and Dedalus, Holmes and Watson (the Holmes-Watson variant is an exceptionally subtle one, because the usual physical characteristics of two partners have been transposed). Evidently it corresponds to something enduring in our civilisation, not in the sense that either character is to be found in a "pure" state in real life, but in the sense that the two principles, noble folly and base wisdom, exist side by side in nearly every human being. If you look into your own mind, which are you, Don Quixote or Sancho Panza? Almost certainly you are both. There is one part of you that wishes to be a hero or a saint, but another part of you is a little fat man who sees very clearly the advantages of staying alive with a whole skin. He is your unofficial self, the voice of the belly protesting against the soul. His tastes lie towards safety, soft beds, no work, pots of beer and women with "voluptuous" figures. He it is who punctures your fine attitudes and urges you to look after Number One, to be unfaithful to your wife, to bilk your debts, and so on and so forth. Whether you allow yourself to be influenced by him is a different question. But it is simply a lie to say that he is not part of you, just as it is a lie to say that Don Quixote is not part of you either, though most of what is said and written consists of one lie or the other, usually the first.

16] But though in varying forms he is one of the stock figures of literature, in real life, especially in the way society is ordered, his point of view never gets a fair hearing. There is a constant world-wide conspiracy to pretend that he is not there, or at least that he doesn't matter. Codes of law and morals, or religious systems, never have much room in them for a humorous view of life. Whatever is funny is subversive, every joke is ultimately a custard pie, and the reason why so large a proportion of jokes centre round obscenity is simply that all societies, as the price of survival, have to insist on a fairly high standard of sexual morality. A dirty joke is not, of course, a serious attack upon morality, but it is a sort of mental rebellion, a momentary wish that things were otherwise. So also with all other jokes, which always centre round cowardice, laziness, dishonesty or some other quality which society cannot afford to encourage. Society has always to demand a little more from human beings than it will get in practice. It has to demand faultless discipline and self-sacrifice, it must expect its subjects to work hard, pay their taxes, and be faithful to their wives, it must assume that men think it glorious to die on the battlefield and women want to wear themselves out with child-bearing. The whole of what one may call official literature is founded on such assumptions. I never read the proclamations of generals before battle, the speeches of führers and prime ministers, the solidarity songs of public schools and Left Wing political parties, national anthems, Temperance tracts, papal encyclicals and sermons against gambling, without seeming to hear in the background a chorus of raspberries from all the millions of common men to whom these high sentiments make no appeal. Nevertheless the high sentiments always win in the end, leaders who offer blood, toil, tears and sweat always get more out of their followers than those who offer safety and a good time. When it comes to the pinch, human beings are heroic. Women face childbed and the scrubbing brush, revolutionaries keep their mouths shut in the torture chamber, battleships go down with their guns still firing when their decks are awash. It is only that the other element in man, the lazy, cowardly, debt-bilking adulterer who is inside all of us, can never be suppressed altogether and needs a hearing occasionally.

17] The comic post cards are one expression of his point of view, a humble one, less important than the music halls, but still worthy of attention. In a society which is still basically Christian they naturally concentrate on sex jokes; in a totalitarian society, if they had any freedom of expression at all, they would probably concentrate on laziness or cowardice, but at any rate on the unheroic in one form or another. It will not do to condemn them on the ground that they are vulgar and ugly. That is exactly what they are meant to be. Their whole meaning and virtue is in their unredeemed lowness, not only in the sense of obscenity, but lowness of outlook in every direction whatever. The slightest hint of "higher" influences would ruin them utterly. They stand for the worm's-eye view of life, for the music-hall world where marriage is a dirty joke or a comic disaster, where the rent is always behind and the clothes are always up the spout, where the lawyer is always a crook and the Scotsman always a miser, where the newlyweds make fools of themselves on the hideous beds of seaside lodging-houses and the drunken, red-nosed husbands roll home at four in the morning to meet the linen-nightgowned wives who wait for them behind the front door, poker in hand. Their existence, the fact that people want them, is symptomatically important. Like the music halls, they are a sort of saturnalia, a harmless rebellion against virtue. They express only one tendency in the human mind, but a tendency which is always there and will find its own outlet, like water. On the whole, human beings want to be good, but not too good, and not quite all the time. For:

there is a just man that perishes in his righteousness, and there is a wicked man that prolongeth his life in his wickedness. Be not righteous over much; neither make thyself over wise; why shouldst thou destroy thyself? Be not overmuch wicked, neither be thou foolish: why shouldst thou die before thy time?

18] In the past the mood of the comic post card could enter into the central stream of literature, and jokes barely different from McGill's could casually be uttered between the murders in Shakespeare's tragedies. That is no longer possible, and a whole category of humour, integral to our literature till 1800 or thereabouts, has dwindled down to these ill-drawn post cards, leading a barely legal existence in cheap stationers' windows. The corner of the human heart that they speak for might easily manifest itself in worse forms, and I for one should be sorry to see them vanish.

Questions

A serious essay, even of the research type, need not necessarily concern itself with matters remote from ordinary experience. Human nature reveals itself in small things as well as great, in common activities as well as in great events; and even such a trivial and vulgar thing as the comic post card can become, in the hands of a sober and thoughtful critic like Orwell, the occasion for some acute comments on man and society.

1. Unless the essay is read with some care, it is easy to misunderstand the author's point of view.

    a. Does Orwell wish to encourage the practice of any of the vices depicted in the comic post cards?

    b. Does he believe that the cards themselves encourage laziness, drunkenness, immorality, and so forth?

    c. Why does McGill's brand of humor have meaning only "in relation to a fairly strict moral code"?

    d. "[The comic post cards] are a sort of saturnalia, a harmless rebellion against virtue" (paragraph 17). What were the Saturnalia? Is the allusion appropriate? What is meant by "a harmless rebellion against virtue"?

2. Identify Sancho Panza and Don Quixote and explain just what each stands for. Is the section in which they appear (paragraphs 15-18) an essential part of the essay? If it were omitted, would the essay still give an adequate report of the general character of the comic post card? In what way would this omission weaken the essay, aside from giving it a very abrupt conclusion?

3. Why is this section (paragraphs 15-18) properly placed at the end of the essay?

4. Paragraphs 1-4 constitute a kind of introduction to the essay. What kind of information is given in these paragraphs and why is it to be regarded as introductory? Why, for instance, is the brief discussion of the "aesthetic value" of the cards not to be considered one of the main points of the essay?

Suggested Assignment

The exercise "Aesop's Fables," which is suggested for use with the essay by Mâle, is also suitable for use with Orwell's essay.

ÉMILE MÂLE

The "Golden Legend"

THE *Golden Legend* remains one of the most interesting books of its time for those who seek in mediæval literature for the spirit of the age to which it belonged. Its fidelity in reproducing earlier stories, and its very absence of originality make it of special value to us, and in re-editing it Graesse rendered a valuable service to the history of art, if not also to the history of religion.[1] So we will take the *Golden Legend* as our chief guide, seeking in that popular book the interpretation of the works of art made for the people.

2] One can easily imagine the charm such a book had for the Middle Ages, and the moral sustenance men found in it.

3] To begin with, the numerous biographies presented a varied picture of human life. To know the lives of the saints was to know life from many sides, for in them every age and every condition could be studied. Modern novels or French *comédies humaines* are less varied and less rich in their presentation of life than the immense collection of the *Acta Sanctorum,* and of this great storehouse the *Golden Legend* gives us the essential part. There was no business or profession which had not had its saint. Saints had been kings like St. Louis, popes like St. Gregory, knights-errant like St. George, shoemakers like St. Crispin, beg-

"The *Golden Legend.*" Taken from *Religious Art in France, XIII Century,* by Émile Mâle, translated by Dora Nussey, published by E. P. Dutton & Co., Inc., New York.

[1] *Legenda aurea,* Ed. Graesse, Wratislaw, 1890, 8vo. Brunet translated the *Leg. aurea* into French, Paris, 1843, 2 vols. 12vo. Th. de Myzewa has made a more recent translation. [See Caxton's version, published in the Temple Classics.]

gars like St. Alexis. Even a canonised lawyer could be found, and in the hymn sung in honour of St. Yves the people showed their good-humoured surprise:

> Advocatus et non latro,
> Res miranda populo.*

4] In that great company deemed worthy to sit at the right hand of God there were shepherds, cattle-drovers, carters, serving men of all kinds, and the lives of these humble Christians showed the seriousness and the depth of which all human life is capable. For the student in the Middle Ages it was a rich storehouse of wisdom. To the simplest it offered a model after which to fashion his life.

5] The *Golden Legend* taught the Christian something not only of life but of other times and other countries. It is true that the universe is there presented after a vague and chaotic fashion, distorted as in the old maps, but still it was an image of reality, and it gave the Middle Ages some dim notion of history and geography. According to the day of the week the book transported the reader to the desert of the Thebaid, among the tombs which the hermits inhabited in company with the jackals, or to the Rome of St. Gregory, deserted, in ruins, devastated by the plague. At another time the story-teller led the reader to the banks of the rivers of Germany, or made him fly with him to the "Isle of the saints." By the end of the Christian year all countries and all times had been traversed in imagination, and the humble peasant who knew nothing of the world beyond the street in which he lived and its clock-tower, had shared the life of the whole of Christendom.

6] But the book's greatest charm lay less in the true than in the marvellous. The lives of many of the saints equalled the most romantic of novels, and the legends of eastern saints compiled by Greek or Coptic hagiographers read like fairy-tales. Among them the stories of St. Eustace, St. George and St. Christopher are remarkable for their strange and unexpected features.

---

* A lawyer who is not a thief—
A thing that passes all belief! [Ed.]

7] The legend tells how one day when pursuing a stag, Placidas, Trajan's general, saw the figure of the Christ between its horns. The miracle converted him. He was baptized with his wife, and took the name of Eustace. Then God brought him to ruin, that he might prove him as He had proved His servant Job. Eustace, penniless, took ship with his family and reached Egypt, but he had no money to pay his passage and the owner of the boat kept his wife as hostage. Overcome with sorrow Eustace plunged into the unknown country, and arrived with his two children on the bank of a river. One of them he carried over, and he was returning to fetch the second, when as he was half-way across the river, he saw one child being carried off by a wolf and the other by a lion. The wretched Eustace found his way to a neighbouring village, and found work as a labourer. There he stayed for some years, lamenting the sons whom he believed to be dead, while all the time they were living not far from him with the peasants who had saved their lives. The story ends like the classical romances and comedies. The dramatic device to which Menander and Terence so often had recourse, the recognition, is skilfully handled by the hagiographer. Some of Trajan's soldiers passing through the village in which Eustace had taken refuge, saw and recognised their general. Eustace, whom it seems the emperor had reinstated at the head of the legions, recognised his long-lost sons among the soldiers. In their turn the two young men are recognised by their mother, who had overheard them in an inn telling tales of their childhood. And so after many trials Eustace was at last reunited to his wife and children. But their happiness was short-lived. On learning that Eustace was a Christian, Trajan's successor imprisoned him with his wife and children in a bull of bronze, and inflicted on them the torment devised by Phalaris.

8] For the man of the Middle Ages such stories had all the charm of our tales of adventure.[2]

9] The legend of St. George, which arose in the Greek world,

[2] The legend of St. Eustace was a favourite one with the mediæval artist (see the windows at Sens, Auxerre, Le Mans, Tours). At Chartres two windows are dedicated to him, in addition to a bas-relief in the south porch.

is the fragment of an epic, for in Greece the epic spirit had never lost its vitality. St. George is the Perseus of the Christian east. The story goes that near to Silenus in Libya there was a pond inhabited by a monster to whom the town regularly sent a tribute of sheep. If by misadventure they failed to do so, the monster came even to the walls of the city and poisoned the air with its breath. When there were no more sheep young men and maidens were offered to the monster. Now it happened that the lot fell on the king's own daughter. Nothing could save her, and after a week's delay, clothed in royal apparel she walked towards the pond, watched by the whole town. St. George, who was passing by, saw that she was weeping and asked her whither she went. "Young man," she said, "I believe that thou hast a noble and great heart, but haste thee to depart." And George replied, "I will not depart until thou hast told me the cause of thy tears." When she had told him all, he answered, "Fear nothing, for I will come to thine aid in the name of Jesus Christ." "Brave knight," she said, "do not seek death with me. It is enough that I should perish, for thou canst neither help me nor deliver me, but will succumb with me." At this moment the monster came out of the water. Then the maiden trembling said, "Flee with all speed, knight." For reply George mounted his horse, made the sign of the cross, and advanced towards the monster. Then commending himself to God he charged it bravely, flinging his lance with such force that it passed through the dragon and pinned it to the ground. Then turning to the princess he told her to fear nothing, and to put her girdle round the monster's neck. When this had been done the dragon followed her like a friendly dog.[3] Surely this romantic story equals the finest adventure of Lancelot or Gawain, for what knight-errant could compare with St. George?

10] The story of St. Christopher is even more amazing. Christopher was a giant twelve cubits high and of a terrible appear-

---

[3] *Leg. aur.*, taken from Brunet's translation [*Golden Legend*, iii. p. 126 sq.]. St. George is represented three times at Chartres (see the statue in the south porch, window in the nave, window in the choir). At Lyons two bas-reliefs in the porch are devoted to him.

ance, who lived in the land of Canaan. He entered the service of a king because it was said that this king was the most powerful in the world. One day, however, the king crossed himself on hearing the name of the devil, and thereby Christopher knew that there was in the world one more powerful than his master. So he set forth and put himself at the service of the devil. He met him in a desert place and accompanied him on his way. On reaching the cross-roads they came on a crucifix, and the devil suddenly fled. When Christopher rejoined him, he would fain know the cause of this sudden terror, and when pressed with questions the devil had to confess that there was one more powerful than he, and that one was Jesus Christ. Without loss of time Christopher went forth to seek this master who was more powerful than the devil, and he met a hermit who taught him the truths of the Christian faith and baptized him. Then the hermit, desirous of advancing him on the path of perfection, recommended him to fast, but of this the good giant was quite incapable. He then enjoined the reciting of prayers, but Christopher became confused and could not remember them. Being now better acquainted with his convert, the hermit established this man of goodwill on the bank of a fast-flowing river, where year after year many travellers were drowned. Christopher took the passers-by on his back, and with the help of a stick he managed to carry them across the stream. One day he heard himself called by a child; he came out of his hut, and taking the child on his shoulders he began to ford the stream. But when he was in the midst of it, the child became so heavy that the giant, bent double with his weight, could hardly struggle to the other side. When he had reached the bank he asked the child who he was. "So great was thy weight," he said, "that had I carried the whole world on my shoulders I should have had no heavier burden." "Be not surprised, Christopher," was the answer, "for thou hast carried on thy shoulders not only the whole world but the creator of the world. Know that I am Jesus Christ." And the child disappeared, and Christopher, who had stuck his stick into the sand, saw that it was covered with flowers and leaves. A short time after this Christopher died the death of a brave martyr in the town of Samos in Lycia.[4] If St. George was the Perseus, St. Christopher was the Hercules of Christendom, like him born to serve. The old-time heroes, who were believed to be dead and gone, lived again under new forms in mediæval Greece.

11] Primitive people delighted in these stories. Almost all the legends of saints of eastern origin read like romances. Saint Theodora disguises herself as a monk, and for twenty years lives unsuspected in a monastery; St. Alexis goes to beg at his father's palace door, sleeps under the stairs with the dogs, and is recognised by no one. The legend of the Seven Sleepers of Ephesus is as charming as a tale from the "Thousand and one Nights," for in it neither cave nor treasure is forgotten.

12] The stories of the western saints were less rich in adventure, but a few biographies of saints of Germanic or Celtic origin stirred men's imagination. The legend of the saintly king Gontran of Burgundy, who guided by rats found a subterranean passage filled with gold, was no doubt a popular song of the Burgundian tribes.[5] The life of St. Patrick of Ireland and that of St. Brandon were apparently written by Celtic bards not long converted to Christianity.[6] The poet (he deserves the name) constantly transports his reader to the confines of the known world. Before the time of Marco Polo St. Brandon's adventures on the sea was the only book of travels possessed by the Middle Ages, and even fifteenth-century navigators dreamed over the magic islands which the Irish saint was reputed to have discovered in the ocean.

13] If there were fewer adventures in the lives of the western saints, there were at least as many miracles. Even in the Middle Ages the Church held as suspicious several of the miracles in the *Golden Legend,* though the people accepted them all and attrib-

[4] *Leg. aur., De Sanct. Christoph.* Window at Chartres. Figures of St. Christopher became numerous at the end of the Middle Ages.

[5] The legend of Gontran, like that of several saints of whom we shall have occasion to speak in this chapter, does not appear in the *Golden Legend,* but as we have already pointed out the name "Golden Legend" is for us a convenient title for all the collections of lives of the saints in use in the Middle Ages.

[6] St. Patrick changed a king of Ireland into a fox.

uted new ones to their favourite saints.[7] A St. Vincent de Paul or a St. François de Sales would have hardly been acceptable to the Christian of the thirteenth century. A true saint was a man who saw angels and demons face to face. The story that the devil extinguished her candle at one side while an angel relighted it at the other, was the one episode in the legend of St. Geneviève which the people of Paris remembered.

14] The continual intervention of angels gives a great charm to these legends. The angels come to serve the saints in all humility, for through conflict and suffering these heroic men have become greater than they. Angels gently bear the old St. Peter Nolasco, founder of the Mercedarians, to the choir stalls, when his limbs will no longer support him. They finish the furrow which St. Isidore had left in order to pray, and after her martyrdom they carry the body of St. Catherine to Mount Sinai. Earth and heaven meet. Christ descends to His prison, and communicates St. Denis with His own hands.

15] The miracles in which the saints showed their power over nature were the people's favourites. The world seemed to regain its primitive innocence, and the hermits who lived in the forests of Gaul lived in Eden. St. Calais's companion on the plain of Le Perche is an auroch, the wild bull of ancient Gaul. St. Gilles is fed by a hart, and his hand is pierced with an arrow in defending it against the king's huntsmen, for many a time when hunting the Merovingian kings found themselves face to face with the hermits. St. Blaise cures the sick beasts, but before approaching him they wait until he has finished his prayers, and St. Bridget caresses the swans of the northern seas which fall on the frozen pond at Kildare.

16] In the Vitae Sanctorum man is reconciled with nature and the most savage of beasts becomes the gentlest. A lion follows St. Gerasimus in the desert,[8] a wolf leads the blind St. Hervaeus through Brittany, and when St. Gervase sleeps in the open air an eagle hovers over his head to shelter him from the rays of the sun.

17] Virtue, it seems, proceeds from the saints, and even inani-

[7] The miracle of the three school-children resuscitated by St. Nicholas is, as we shall presently show, a popular invention.

[8] The painters early confused St. Gerasimus with St. Jerome, and the latter is also painted with a lion as companion.

mate nature leaps with joy as they pass by. The trees, stripped of their leaves by the winter winds, suddenly become green at the passage of the relics of St. Firmin, and nowhere is the grass so fine as where St. Ulphia of Picardy goes by on her way to church. Everywhere about them the saints re-establish the world's ancient harmony. Many of the legends which had sprung from the hearts of the people testify to a profound feeling for nature, and they are to the honour both of those who created and of those who adopted them.

18] Such is the charm of the *Golden Legend.* In the thirteenth century men found there all that they loved best: a picture of human life, a summary of the world's history, strange adventures, and wonderful miracles.

19] Since the Council of Trent the Church has dealt severely with these simple stories, judging no doubt that so many marvels tended to hide the true greatness of the saints. The seventeenth-century scholars understood their time, and they were anxious that the lives of the saints should not become an occasion for scandal to minds made critical by Protestant influence. The formidable Launoi deserved his nickname of *dénicheur de saints,* and as he bowed low before him the curé of St. Eustache trembled for his church's patron. Such scruples could not occur to the mediæval Church. And, moreover, under the trappings of legend the people's insight almost always divined the truly sublime. The endless stories of St. Martin's miracles did not blind the craftsmen to the most human feature of his life, and they immortalised the heroic action of the young Roman soldier who took his sword to cut in half his military cloak, that he might clothe a poor man.

Questions

1. As the title of his book suggests, Mâle's chief interest is the history of art rather than the history of literature. What indications are there in the passage that Mâle is taking care to keep the reader's mind from straying too far from the subject of art? (Look especially in the footnotes.)

2. What is the main idea of the passage? What sentence comes nearest to expressing it?
3. What is the function of the first paragraph?
4. Is the last paragraph essential to the development of the thought? Is its present position the logical one? Why is the legend of St. Martin introduced at this point?
5. What are the principal divisions of the main body of the essay? Why are the sections arranged in this order?
6. In one section only does Mâle illustrate his discussion with summaries of entire legends; why is this method particularly appropriate to this section?
7. *a.* Why does Mâle bother to inform us that the tale of St. Eustace employs a device used by the playwrights Menander and Terence?
   b. Who is Perseus, and why is St. George compared to him? Why is St. Christopher compared to Hercules?
8. There are several one-sentence paragraphs in the essay. For what purpose does Mâle employ them?

Suggested Assignment

Do the exercise "Aesop's Fables" on page 327.

SIR WALTER RALEIGH

❧ *Robert Louis Stevenson as Romancer*

THE FACULTY of romance, the greatest of the gifts showered on Stevenson's cradle by the fairies, will suffer no course of development; the most that can be done with it is to preserve it on from childhood unblemished and undiminished.

"Robert Louis Stevenson as Romancer." From *Robert Louis Stevenson,* by Sir Walter Raleigh.

It is of a piece with Stevenson's romantic ability that his own childhood never ended; he could pass back into that airy world without an effort. In his stories his imagination worked on the old lines, but it became conscious of its working. And the highest note of these stories is not drama, nor character, but romance. In one of his essays he defines the highest achievement of romance to be the embodiment of "character, thought, or emotion in some act or attitude that shall be remarkably striking to the mind's eye." His essay on Victor Hugo shows how keenly conscious he was that narrative romance can catch and embody emotions and effects that are for ever out of the reach of the drama proper, and of the essay or homily, just as they are out of the reach of sculpture and painting. Now, it is precisely in these effects that the chief excellence of romance resides; it was the discovery of a world of these effects, insusceptible of treatment by the drama, neglected entirely by the character-novel, which constituted the Romantic revival of the end of last century. "The artistic result of a romance," says Stevenson, "what is left upon the memory by any powerful and artistic novel, is something so complicated and refined that it is difficult to put a name upon it, and yet something as simple as nature. . . . The fact is, that art is working far ahead of language as well as of science, realizing for us, by all manner of suggestions and exaggerations, effects for which as yet we have no direct name, for the reason that these effects do not enter very largely into the necessities of life. Hence alone is that suspicion of vagueness that often hangs about the purpose of a romance; it is clear enough to us in thought, but we are not used to consider anything clear until we are able to formulate it in words, and analytical language has not been sufficiently shaped to that end." He goes on to point out that there is an epical value about every great romance, an underlying idea, not presentable always in abstract or critical terms, in the stories of such masters of pure romance as Victor Hugo and Nathaniel Hawthorne.

2] The progress of romance in the present century * has consisted chiefly in the discovery of new exercises of imagination

---

* I.e., the nineteenth.

and new subtle effects in story. Fielding, as Stevenson says, did not understand that the nature of a landscape or the spirit of the times could count for anything in a story; all his actions consist of a few simple personal elements. With Scott vague influences that qualify a man's personality begin to make a large claim; "the individual characters begin to occupy a comparatively small proportion of that canvas on which armies manœuvre and great hills pile themselves upon each other's shoulders." And the achievements of the great masters since Scott—Hugo, Dumas, Hawthorne, to name only those in Stevenson's direct line of ancestry—have added new realms to the domain of romance.

3] What are the indescribable effects that romance, casting far beyond problems of character and conduct, seeks to realise? What is the nature of the great informing, underlying idea that animates a truly great romance—*The Bride of Lammermoor, Monte Cristo, Les Misérables, The Scarlet Letter, The Master of Ballantrae?* These questions can only be answered by deforming the impression given by each of these works to present it in the chop-logic language of philosophy. But an approach to an answer may be made by illustration.

4] In his *American Notebooks* Nathaniel Hawthorne used to jot down subjects for stories as they struck him. His successive entries are like the souls of stories awaiting embodiment, which many of them never received; they bring us very near to the workings of the mind of a great master. Here are some of them:

A sketch to be given of a modern reformer, a type of the extreme doctrines on the subject of slaves, cold water, and the like. He goes about the streets haranguing most eloquently, and is on the point of making many converts, when his labours are suddenly interrupted by the appearance of the keeper of a madhouse whence he has escaped. Much may be made of this idea.

The scene of a story or sketch to be laid within the light of a street lantern; the time when the lamp is near going out; and the catastrophe to be simultaneous with the last flickering gleam.

A person to be writing a tale and to find it shapes itself against his intentions; that the characters act otherwise than he thought, and a catastrophe comes which he strives in vain to avert. It might shadow forth his own fate—he having made himself one of the personages.

Two persons to be expecting some occurrence and watching for the two principal actors in it, and to find that the occurrence is even then passing, and that they themselves are the two actors.

A satire on ambition and fame from a statue of snow.

Hawthorne used this idea in one of his sketches.

A moral philosopher to buy a slave, or otherwise get possession of a human being, and to use him for the sake of experiment by trying the operation of a certain vice on him.

5] M. Bourget, the French romancer, has made use of this idea in his novel called *Le Disciple*. Only it is not a slave, but a young girl whom he pretends to love, that is the subject of the moral philosopher's experiment; and a noisy war has been waged round the book in France. Hawthorne would plainly have seized the romantic essence of the idea and would have avoided the boneyard of "problem morality."

A story the principal personage of which shall seem always on the point of entering on the scene, but shall never appear.

6] This is the device that gives fascination to the figures of Richelieu in *Marion Delorme*, and of Captain Flint in *Treasure Island*.

The majesty of death to be exemplified in a beggar, who, after being seen humble and cringing in the streets of a city for many years, at length by some means or other gets admittance into a rich man's mansion, and there dies—assuming state, and striking awe into the breasts of those who had looked down upon him.

7] These are all excellent instances of the sort of idea that gives life to a romance—of acts or attitudes that stamp themselves upon the mind's eye. Some of them appeal chiefly to the mind's eye, others are of value chiefly as symbols. But, for the most part, the romantic kernel of a story is neither pure picture nor pure allegory, it can neither be painted nor moralised. It makes its most irresistible appeal neither to the eye that searches for form and colour, nor to the reason that seeks for abstract truth, but to the blood, to all that dim instinct of danger, mystery, and sympathy in things that is man's oldest inheritance—to the superstitions of the heart. Romance vindicates the supernatural against science and rescues it from the palsied tutelage of morality.

8] Stevenson's work is a gallery of romantic effects that haunt the memory. Some of these are directly pictorial: the fight in the round-house on board the brig *Covenant;* the duel between the two brothers of Ballantrae in the island of light thrown up by the candles from that abyss of windless night; the flight of the Princess Seraphina through the dark mazes of the wood,—all these, although they carry with them subtleties beyond the painter's art, yet have something of picture in them. But others make entrance to the corridors of the mind by blind and secret ways, and there awaken the echoes of primæval fear. The cry of the parrot—"Pieces of eight"—the tapping of the stick of the blind pirate Pew as he draws near the inn-parlour, and the similar effects of inexplicable terror wrought by the introduction of the blind catechist in *Kidnapped,* and of the disguise of a blind leper in *The Black Arrow,* are beyond the reach of any but the literary form of romantic art. The last appearance of Pew, in the play of *Admiral Guinea,* written in collaboration with Mr. W. E. Henley, is perhaps the masterpiece of all the scenes of terror. The blind ruffian's scream of panic fear, when he puts his groping hand into the burning flame of the candle in the room where he believed that he was unseen, and so realises that his every movement is being silently watched, is indeed "the horrors come alive."

9] The animating principle or idea of Stevenson's longer stories is never to be found in their plot, which is generally built carelessly and disjointedly enough around the central romantic situation or conception. The main situation in *The Wrecker* is a splendid product of romantic aspiration, but the structure of the story is incoherent and ineffective, so that some of the best passages in the book—the scenes in Paris, for instance —have no business there at all. The story in *Kidnapped* and *Catriona* wanders on in a single thread, like the pageant of a dream, and the reader feels and sympathises with the author's obvious difficulty in leading it back to the scene of the trial and execution of James Stewart. *The Master of Ballantrae* is stamped with a magnificent unity of conception, but the story illuminates that conception by a series of scattered episodes. That lurid embodiment of fascinating evil, part vampire, part Mephistopheles, whose grand manner and heroic abilities might have made him a great and good man but for "the malady of not wanting," is the light and meaning of the whole book. Innocent and benevolent lives are thrown in his way that he may mock or distort or shatter them. Stevenson never came nearer than in this character to the sublime of power.

10] But an informing principle of unity is more readily to be apprehended in the shorter stories, and it is a unity not so much of plot as of impression and atmosphere. His islands, whether situated in the Pacific or off the coast of Scotland, have each of them a climate of its own, and the character of the place seems to impose itself on the incidents that occur, dictating subordination or contrast. The events that happen within the limits of one of these magic isles could in every case be cut off from the rest of the story and framed as a separate work of art. The long starvation of David Balfour on the island of Earraid, the sharks of crime and monsters of blasphemy that break the peace of the shining tropical lagoons in *Treasure Island* and *The Ebb Tide*, the captivity on the Bass Rock in *Catriona*, the supernatural terrors that hover and mutter over the island of *The Merry Men* —these imaginations are plainly generated by the scenery against which they are thrown; each is in some sort the genius of the place it inhabits.

11] In his search for the treasures of romance, Stevenson adventured freely enough into the realm of the supernatural. When he is handling the superstitions of the Scottish people, he allows his humorous enjoyment of their extravagance to peep out from behind the solemn dialect in which they are dressed. The brief tale of *Thrawn Janet*, and Black Andy's story of Tod Lapraik in *Catriona*, are grotesque imaginations of the school of *Tam o' Shanter* rather than of the school of Shakespeare, who deals in no comedy ghosts. They are turnip-lanterns swayed by a laughing urchin, proud of the fears he can awaken. Even *The Strange Case of Dr. Jekyll and Mr. Hyde* and the story of *The Bottle Imp* are manufactured bogeys, that work on the nerves and not on the heart, whatever may be said by those who insist on seeing allegory in what is only dream-fantasy. The supernatural must be rooted deeper than these in life and experience if it is to reach an imposing stature: the true ghost is the shadow of the man. And Stevenson shows a sense of this in two of his very finest stories, the exquisite idyll of *Will o' the Mill* and the grim history of *Markheim*. Each of these stories is the work of a poet, by no means of a goblin-fancier. The personification of Death is as old as poetry; it is wrought with moving gentleness in that last scene in the arbour of Will's inn. The wafted scent of the heliotropes, which had never been planted in the garden since Marjory's death, the light in the room that had been hers, prelude the arrival at the gate of the stranger's carriage, with the black pine tops standing above it like plumes. And Will o' the Mill makes the acquaintance of his physician and friend, and goes at last upon his travels. In the other story, Markheim meets with his own double in the house of the dealer in curiosities, whom he has murdered. It is not such a double as Rossetti prayed for to the god of Sleep:

> Ah! might I, by thy good grace,
> Groping in the windy stair
> (Darkness and the breath of space
> Like loud waters everywhere),
> Meeting mine own image there
> Face to face,
> Send it from that place to her!

but a clear-eyed critic of the murderer, not unfriendly, who lays bare before him his motives and history. At the close of that wonderful conversation, one of the most brilliant of its author's achievements, Markheim gives himself into the hands of the police. These two stories, when compared with the others, serve to show how Stevenson's imagination quickened and strengthened when it played full upon life. For his best romantic effects, like all great romance, are illuminative of life, and no mere idle games.

Questions

Literary criticism, dealing as it does with elusive feelings and effects, is one of the most difficult kinds of writing. To feel and comprehend a great work of art is one thing; to communicate the feeling and comprehension to others is a different matter. As a result of this fundamental critical difficulty of analyzing a highly personal impression, a good deal of literary criticism is necessarily vague and "impressionistic." Raleigh's task, to analyze "romance," which lies almost wholly within the realm of feeling, is a peculiarly exacting one; his essay should be judged accordingly.

1. What is Stevenson's definition of romance? Is it the same as Mâle's (pages 135-142)?
2. *a.* Why should paragraphs 1-7 precede paragraphs 8-11?
   b. Why should paragraphs 4-7 follow paragraphs 1-3?
3. The insertion of a passage on Hawthorne into an essay on Stevenson requires some explanation.
   a. Raleigh himself says that the passage was put in for "illustration" (paragraph 3). What was it meant to illustrate?
   b. Why, according to Raleigh, was this method of approach necessary?
   c. How well do the examples from Hawthorne's notebooks live up to Stevenson's definition of romance?
4. What does Raleigh mean by saying that "a true ghost is the shadow of a man" (paragraph 11)? How does this fit in with the definition of romance given earlier in the essay? Why are the ghosts in *Markheim* and *Will o' the Mill* "true ghosts"?
5. One difficulty in writing literary criticism is to know how far to go in describing the works under discussion. A detailed summary will take up too much room and bore the reader who is already acquainted with the original, while a reader lacking this acquaintance will be puzzled if the description is too general.
   a. Does Raleigh give enough of the plot of *Markheim* (paragraph 11) to make his point clear?

b. Is it necessary to have read *Treasure Island* and *Admiral Guinea* to appreciate the references to Pew in paragraph 8?

6. Raleigh says that Stevenson's stories have a unity of "impression and atmosphere." What other kinds of unity are there?

G. LOWES DICKINSON

The Greek View of Woman

NOTHING more profoundly distinguishes the Hellenic from the modern view of life than the estimate in which women were held by the Greeks. Their opinion on this point was partly the cause and partly the effect of that preponderance of the idea of the state on which we have already dwelt, and from which it followed naturally enough that marriage should be regarded primarily as a means of producing healthy and efficient citizens. This view is best illustrated by the institutions of such a state as Sparta, where, as we saw, the woman was specially trained for maternity, and connections outside the marriage tie were sanctioned by custom and opinion, if they were such as were likely to lead to healthy offspring. Further it may be noted that in almost every state the exposure of deformed or sickly infants was encouraged by law, the child being thus regarded, from the beginning, as a member of the state, rather than as a member of the family.

2] The same view is reflected in the speculations of political philosophers. Plato, indeed, in his Republic, goes so far as to eliminate the family relation altogether. Not only is the whole connection between men and women to be regulated by the

"The Greek View of Woman." From *The Greek View of Life* by G. Lowes Dickinson. Reprinted by permission of Methuen & Co., Ltd.

state, in respect both of the persons and of the limit of age within which they may associate, but the children as soon as they are born are to be carried off to a common nursery, there to be reared together, undistinguished by the mothers, who will suckle indifferently any infant that might happen to be assigned to them for the purpose. Here, as in other instances, Plato goes far beyond the limits set by the current sentiment of the Greeks, and in his later work is reluctantly constrained to abandon his scheme of community of wives and children. Yet even there he makes it compulsory on every man to marry between the ages of thirty and thirty-five, under penalty of fine and civil disabilities. Plato, no doubt, as we have said, exaggerates the opinions of his time; but the view, which he pushes to its extreme, of the subordination of the family to the state, was one, as we have already pointed out, which did predominate in Greece. It reappears in a soberer form in the treatise of Aristotle. He too would regulate by law both the age at which marriages should take place and the number of children that should be produced, and would have all deformed infants exposed. And here, no doubt, he is speaking in conformity if not with the practice, at least with the feeling of Greece. The modern conception that the marriage relation is a matter of private concern, and that any individual has a right to wed whom and when he will, and to produce children at his own discretion, regardless of all considerations of health and decency, was one altogether alien to the Greeks. In theory at least, and to some extent in practice (as for example in the case of Sparta), they recognized that the production of children was a business of supreme import to the state, and that it was right and proper that it should be regulated by law with a view to the advantage of the whole community.

3] And if now we turn from considering the family in its relation to the state to regard it in its relation to the individual, we are struck once more by a divergence from the modern point of view, or rather from the view which is supposed to prevail, particularly by writers of fiction, at any rate in modern English life. In ancient Greece, so far as our knowledge goes, there was little or no romance connected with the marriage tie. Marriage was a means of producing legitimate children; that is how it is defined by Demosthenes; and we have no evidence that it was ever regarded as anything more. In Athens we know that marriages were commonly arranged by the father, much as they are in modern France, on grounds of age, property, connection and the like, and without any regard for the inclination of the parties concerned. And an interesting passage in Xenophon indicates a point of view quite consonant with this accepted practice. God, he says, ordained the institution of marriage; but on what grounds? Not in the least for the sake of the personal relation that might be established between the husband and wife, but for ends quite external and indifferent to any affection that might exist between them. First, for the perpetuation of the human race; secondly, to raise up protectors for the father in his old age; thirdly, to secure an appropriate division of labour, the man performing the outdoor work, the women guarding and superintending at home, and each thus fulfilling duly the function for which they were designed by nature. This eminently prosaic way of conceiving the marriage relation is also, it would seem, eminently Greek; and it leads us to consider more particularly the opinion prevalent in Greece of the nature and duty of women in general.

4] Here the first point to be noticed is the wide difference of the view represented in the Homeric poems from that which meets us in the historic period. Readers of the Iliad and the Odyssey will find depicted there, amid all the barbarity of an age of rapine and war, relations between men and women so tender, faithful and beautiful, that they may almost stand as universal types of the ultimate human ideal. Such for example is the relation between Odysseus and Penelope, the wife waiting year by year for the husband whose fate is unknown, wooed in vain by suitors who waste her substance and wear her life, nightly "watering her bed with her tears" for twenty weary years, till at last the wanderer returns, and "at once her knees were loosened and her heart melted within her . . . and she fell a weeping and ran straight towards him, and cast her hands about his neck, and kissed his head;" for "even as the sight of the land is welcome to mariners, so welcome to her was the sight of her lord, and her white arms would never quite leave hold of his neck."

5] Such, again, is the relation between Hector and Andromache as described in the well-known scene of the Iliad, where the wife comes out with her babe to take leave of the husband on his way to battle. "It were better for me," she cries, "to go down to the grave if I lose thee; for never will any comfort be mine when once thou, even thou, hast met thy fate, but only sorrow. . . . Thou art to me father and lady mother, yea, and brother, even as thou art my goodly husband. Come now, have pity and abide here upon the tower, lest thou make thy child an orphan and thy wife a widow." Hector answers with the plea of honour. He cannot draw back, but he foresees defeat; and in his anticipation of the future nothing is so bitter as the fate he fears for his wife. "Yet doth the conquest of the Trojans hereafter not so much trouble me, neither Hekabe's own, neither King Priam's, neither my brethren's, the many and brave that shall fall in the dust before their foemen, as doth thine anguish in the day when some mail-clad Achaian shall lead thee weeping and rob thee of the light of freedom. . . . But me in death may the heaped-up earth be covering, ere I hear thy crying and thy carrying into captivity."

6] But most striking of all the portraits of women to be found in Homer, and most typical of a frank and healthy relation between the sexes, is the account of Nausicaa given in the Odyssey. Ulysses, shipwrecked and naked, battered and covered with brine, surprises Nausicaa and her maidens as they are playing at ball on the shore. The attendants run away, but Nausicaa remains to hear what the stranger has to say. He asks her for shelter and clothing; and she grants the request, with an exquisite courtesy and a freedom from all embarrassment which becomes only the more marked and the more delightful when, as she sees him emerge from the bath, clothed and beautiful, she cannot restrain the exclamation "would that such a one might be called my husband, dwelling here, and that it may please him here to abide." About the whole scene there is a freshness and a fragrance as of early morning, and a tone so natural, free and frank, that in the face of this rustic idyl the later centuries sicken and faint, like candle-light in the splendour of the dawn.

7] If we had only Homer to give us our ideas of the Greeks, we might conclude, from such passages as these, that they had a conception of woman and of her relation to man, finer and nobler in some respects, than that of modern times. But in fact the Homeric poems represent a civilization which had passed away before the opening of the period with which at present we are chiefly concerned. And in the interval, for reasons which we need not here attempt to state, a change had taken place in the whole way of regarding the female sex. So far, at any rate, as our authorities enable us to judge, woman in the historic age was conceived to be so inferior to man that he recognized in her no other end than to minister to his pleasure or to become the mother of his children. Romance and the higher championship of intellect and spirit do not appear (with certain notable exceptions) to have been commonly sought or found in this relation. Woman, in fact, was regarded as a means, not as an end; and was treated in a manner consonant with this view. Of this estimate many illustrations might be adduced from the writers of the fifth and fourth centuries. Plato, for example, classes together "children, women, and servants," and states generally that, there is no branch of human industry in which the female sex is not inferior to the male. Similarly, Aristotle insists again and again on the natural inferiority of woman, and illustrates it by such quaint observations as the following: "A man would be considered a coward who was only as brave as a brave woman, and a woman as a chatterbox who was only as modest as a good man." But the most striking example, perhaps, because the most unconscious, of this habitual way of regarding women is to be found in the funeral oration put by Thucydides into the mouth of Pericles, where the speaker, after suggesting what consolation he can to the fathers of the slain, turns to the women with the brief but significant exhortation: "If I am to speak of womanly virtues to those of you who will henceforth be widows, let me sum them up in one short admonition: To a woman not to show more weakness than is natural to her sex is a great glory, and not to be talked about for good or for evil among men."

8] The sentiments of the poets are less admissible as evidence; but some of them are so extreme that they may be adduced as a further indication of a point of view whose prevalence alone could render them even dramatically plausible. Such for example is the remark of one of the characters in Menander, "a woman is necessarily an evil, and he is a lucky man who catches her in the mildest form." While the general Greek view of the dependence of woman on man is well expressed in the words of Aethra, in the "Suppliants" of Euripides: "It is proper for women who are wise to let men act for them in everything."

9] In accordance with this conception of the inferiority of the female sex, and partly as a cause, partly as an effect of it, we find that the position of the wife in ancient Greece was simply that of the domestic drudge. To stay at home and mind the house was her recognized ideal. "A free woman should be bounded by the street door," says one of the characters in Menander; and another writer discriminates as follows the functions of the two sexes: "War, politics, and public speaking are the sphere of man; that of woman is to keep house, to stay at home and to receive and tend her husband." We are not surprised, therefore, to find that the symbol of woman is the tortoise; and in the following burlesque passage from Aristophanes we shall recognize, in spite of the touch of caricature, the genuine features of the Greek wife. Praxagora is recounting the merits and services of women:

> They dip their wool in hot water according to the ancient plan, all of them without exception, and never make the slightest innovation. They sit and cook, as of old. They carry upon their heads, as of old. They conduct the Themophoriae, as of old. They wear out their husbands, as of old. They buy sweets, as of old.

10] And that this was also the kind of ideal approved by their lords and masters, and that any attempt to pass beyond it was resented, is amusingly illustrated in the following extract from the same poet, where Lysistrata explains the growing indignation of the women at the bad conduct of affairs by the men, and the way in which their attempts to interfere were resented. The comments of the "magistrate" typify, of course, the man's point of view.

> Think of our old moderation and gentleness, think how we bore with your pranks, and were still,
> All through the days of your former prognacity, all through the war that is over and spent:
> Not that (be sure) we approved of your policy; never our griefs you allowed us to vent.
> Well we perceived your mistakes and mismanagement. Often at home on our housekeeping cares,
> Often we heard of some foolish proposal you made for conducting the public affairs.
> Then would we question you mildly and pleasantly, inwardly grieving, but outwardly gay;
> "Husband, how goes it abroad?" we would ask of him; "what have ye done in Assembly today?"
> "What would ye write on the side of the Treaty-stone?" Husband says angrily, "What's that to you?
> You hold your tongue!" And I held it accordingly.

STRATYLLIS

> That is a thing which I never would do!

MAGISTRATE

> Ma'am, if you hadn't you'd soon have repented it.

LYSISTRATA

> Therefore I held it, and spake not a word.
> Soon of another tremendous absurdity, wilder and worse than the former, we heard.
> "Husband," I say, with a tender solicitude, "why have you passed such a foolish decree?"
> Viciously, moodily, glaring askance at me, "Stick to your spinning, my mistress," says he,

"Else you will speedily find it the worse for you! war is the care and business of men!"

MAGISTRATE

Zeus! 'twas a worthy reply, and an excellent!

LYSISTRATA

What! you unfortunate, shall we not then,
Then, when we see you perplexed and incompetent, shall we not tender advice to the state! [1]

11] The conception thus indicated in burlesque of the proper place of woman is expressed more seriously, from the point of view of the average man, in the "Oeconomicus" of Xenophon. Ischomachus, the hero of that work, with whom we have already made acquaintance, gives an account of his own wife, and of the way in which he had trained her. When he married her, he explains, she was not yet fifteen, and had been brought up with the utmost care "that she might see, hear, and ask as little as possible." Her accomplishments were weaving and a sufficient acquaintance with all that concerns the stomach; and her attitude towards her husband she expressed in the single phrase: "Everything rests with you; my duty, my mother said, is simply to be modest." Ischomachus proceeds to explain to her the place he expects her to fill; she is to suckle his children, to cook, and to superintend the house; and for this purpose God has given her special gifts, different from but not necessarily inferior to those of man. Husband and wife naturally supply one another's deficiencies; and if the wife perform her function worthily she may even make herself the ruling partner, and be sure that as she grows older she will be held not less but more in honour, as the guardian of her children and the stewardess of her husband's goods.—In Xenophon's view, in fact, the inferiority of the woman almost disappears; and the sentiment approximates closely to that of Tennyson—

[1] Aristoph. Lysistrata. 507.—Translated by B. B. Rogers.

> either sex alone
> Is half itself, and in true marriage lies
> Nor equal, nor unequal: each fulfils
> Defect in each.

12] Such a conception, however, of the "complementary" relation of woman to man, does not exclude a conviction of her essential inferiority. And this conviction, it can hardly be disputed, was a cardinal point in the Greek view of life.

Questions

1. State the main idea of the passage in a single sentence.
2. Would "Women's Life in Ancient Greece" be a suitable title for the passage? What about "The Greek View of Marriage"?
3. What is the relation of the first three paragraphs to the rest of the essay?
4. What would be the effect of omitting the last paragraph altogether?
5. To what classes of writers do most of the authorities cited by Dickinson belong? Are writers of this kind usually regarded as reliable sources for a historian? What is there about the nature of the essay which makes the use of such authorities allowable and even necessary?
6. Pick out those quotations and summaries of sources which are long enough to be worth discussing and tell what point each is meant to illustrate.
7. Since the life described by Homer is that of a period long before the one with which Dickinson is concerned and since the works of Homer can therefore offer no evidence either for or against Dickinson's thesis, why is the section on Homer inserted at all?
8. Why is the Greek conception of woman as an inferior being partly the cause and partly the effect of her being a mere "domestic drudge" (paragraph 9)?
9. Why is an "unconscious" statement more striking (paragraph 7)?

Suggested Assignments

1. Write a short essay defining as exactly as possible what you consider to be the "American View of Women."
2. Do the exercise "Women of the Near East" on page 338.

SIR WALTER SCOTT

Ghosts

SOMETHING remains to be said upon a species of superstition, so general, that it may be called proper to mankind in every climate; so deeply rooted also in human belief, that it is found to survive in states of society during which all other fictions of the same order are entirely dismissed from influence. Mr Crabbe, with his usual felicity, has called the belief in ghosts "the last lingering fiction of the brain."

2] Nothing appears more simple at the first view of the subject, than that human memory should recall and bring back to the eye of the imagination, in perfect similitude, even the very form and features of a person with whom we have been long conversant, or which have been imprinted in our minds with indelible strength, by some striking circumstances touching our meeting in life. The son does not easily forget the aspect of an affectionate father; and, for reasons opposite, but equally powerful, the countenance of a murdered person is engraved upon the recollection of his slayer. A thousand additional circumstances, far too obvious to require recapitulation, render the supposed apparition of the dead the most ordinary spectral phenomenon which is ever believed to occur among the living. All that we

"Ghosts." From *Letters on Demonology and Witchcraft* by Sir Walter Scott.

have formerly said respecting supernatural appearances in general, applies with peculiar force to the belief of ghosts; for whether the cause of delusion exists in an excited imagination or a disordered organic system, it is in this way that it commonly exhibits itself. Hence Lucretius himself, the most absolute of sceptics, considers the existence of ghosts, and their frequent apparition, as facts so undeniable, that he endeavours to account for them at the expense of assenting to a class of phenomena very irreconcilable to his general system. As he will not allow of the existence of the human soul, and at the same time cannot venture to question the phenomena supposed to haunt the repositories of the dead, he is obliged to adopt the belief that the body consists of several coats like those of an onion, and that the outmost and thinnest, being detached by death, continues to wander near the place of sepulture, in the exact resemblance of the person while alive.

3] We have said there are many ghost stories which we do not feel at liberty to challenge as impostures, because we are confident that those who relate them on their own authority actually believe what they assert, and may have good reason for doing so, though there is no real phantom after all. We are far, therefore, from averring that such tales are necessarily false. It is easy to suppose the visionary has been imposed upon by a lively dream, a waking reverie, the excitation of a powerful imagination, or the misrepresentation of a diseased organ of sight; and, in one or other of these causes, to say nothing of a system of deception which may in many instances be probable, we apprehend a solution will be found for all cases of what are called real ghost stories.

4] In truth, the evidence with respect to such apparitions is very seldom accurately or distinctly questioned. A supernatural tale is, in most cases, received as an agreeable mode of amusing society, and he would be rather accounted a sturdy moralist than an entertaining companion, who should employ himself in assailing its credibility. It would indeed be a solecism in manners, something like that of impeaching the genuine value of the antiquities exhibited by a good-natured collector, for the gratification of his guests. This difficulty will appear greater, should a company have the rare good fortune to meet the person who himself witnessed the wonders which he tells; a well-bred or prudent man will, under such circumstances, abstain from using the rules of cross-examination practised in a court of justice; and if in any case he presumes to do so, he is in danger of receiving answers, even from the most candid and honourable persons, which are rather fitted to support the credit of the story which they stand committed to maintain, than to the pure service of unadorned truth. The narrator is asked, for example, some unimportant question with respect to the apparition; he answers it on the hasty suggestion of his own imagination, tinged as it is with belief of the general fact, and by doing so, often gives a feature of minute evidence which was before wanting, and this with perfect unconsciousness on his own part. It is a rare occurrence, indeed, to find an opportunity of dealing with an actual ghost-seer; such instances, however, I have certainly myself met with, and that in the case of able, wise, candid, and resolute persons, of whose veracity I had every reason to be confident. But in such instances, shades of mental aberration have afterwards occurred, which sufficiently accounted for the supposed apparitions, and will incline me always to feel alarmed in behalf of the continued health of a friend, who should conceive himself to have witnessed such a visitation.

5] The nearest approximation which can be generally made to exact evidence in this case, is the word of some individual who has had the story, it may be, from the person to whom it has happened, but most likely from his family, or some friend of the family. Far more commonly, the narrator possesses no better means of knowledge than that of dwelling in the country where the thing happened, or being well acquainted with the outside of the mansion in the inside of which the ghost appeared.

6] In every point, the evidence of such a second-hand retailer of the mystic story must fall under the adjudged case in an English court. The judge stopped a witness who was about to give an account of the murder upon trial, as it was narrated to him by the ghost of the murdered person. "Hold, sir," said his lordship; "the ghost is an excellent witness, and his evidence the best possible; but he cannot be heard by proxy in this court. Summon him hither, and I'll hear him in person; but your communication is mere hearsay, which my office compels me to reject." Yet it is upon the credit of one man, who pledges it upon that of three or four persons who have told it successively to each other, that we are often expected to believe an incident inconsistent with the laws of nature, however agreeable to our love of the wonderful and the horrible.

7] In estimating the truth or falsehood of such stories, it is evident we can derive no proofs from that period of society when men affirmed boldly, and believed stoutly, all the wonders which could be coined or fancied. That such stories are believed and told by grave historians, only shows that the wisest men cannot rise in all things above the general ignorance of their age. Upon the evidence of such historians, we might as well believe the portents of ancient, or the miracles of modern, Rome. For example, we read in Clarendon, of the apparition of the ghost of Sir George Villiers to an ancient dependant. This is, no doubt, a story told by a grave author, at a time when such stories were believed by all the world; but does it follow that our reason must acquiesce in a statement so positively contradicted by the voice of Nature, through all her works? The miracle of raising a dead man was positively refused by our Saviour to the Jews, who demanded it as a proof of his mission; because they had already sufficient grounds of conviction, and, as they believed them not, it was irresistibly argued by the Divine Person whom they tempted, that neither would they believe if one arose from the dead. Shall we suppose that a miracle refused for the conversion of God's chosen people, was sent on a vain errand, to save the life of a profligate spend-thrift? I lay aside, you observe, entirely, the not unreasonable supposition that Towers, or whatever was the ghost-seer's name, desirous to make an impression upon Buckingham, as an old servant of his house, might be tempted to give him his advice, of which we are not told the import, in the character of his father's spirit, and authenticate the tale by the mention of some token known to him as a former retainer of the family. The Duke was superstitious, and the ready dupe of astrologers and soothsayers. The manner in which he had provoked the fury of the people, must have warned every reflecting person of his approaching fate; and, the age considered, it was not unnatural that a faithful friend should take this mode of calling his attention to his perilous situation. Or, if we suppose that the incident was not a mere pretext to obtain access to the Duke's ear, the messenger may have been imposed upon by an idle dream—in a word, numberless conjectures might be formed for accounting for the event in a natural way, the most extravagant of which is more probable, than that the laws of nature were broken through in order to give a vain and fruitless warning to an ambitious minion.

8] It is the same with all those that are called accredited ghost stories usually told at the fireside. They want evidence. It is true, that the general wish to believe, rather than power of believing, has given some such stories a certain currency in society. I may mention, as one of the class of tales I mean, that of the late Earl St Vincent, who watched, with a friend, it is said, a whole night, in order to detect the cause of certain nocturnal disturbances which took place in a certain mansion. The house was under lease to Mrs Ricketts, his sister. The result of his lordship's vigil is said to have been, that he heard the noises, without being able to detect the causes, and insisted on his sister giving up the house. This is told as a real story, with a thousand different circumstances. But who has heard or seen an authentic account from Earl St Vincent, or from his "companion of the watch," or from his lordship's sister? And as in any other case, such sure species of direct evidence would be necessary to prove the facts, it seems unreasonable to believe such a story on slighter terms. When the particulars are precisely fixed and known, it might be time to enquire whether Lord St Vincent, amid the other eminent qualities of a first-rate seaman, might not be in some degree tinged with their tendency to superstition: and still farther, whether, having ascertained the existence of disturbances not immediately or easily detected, his lordship might not advise his sister rather to remove, than to remain in a house so haunted, though he might believe that poachers or smugglers were the worst ghosts by whom it was disturbed.

9] The story of two highly respectable officers in the British army, who are supposed to have seen the spectre of the brother of one of them in a hut, or barrack, in America, is also one of those accredited ghost tales, which attain a sort of brevet rank as true, from the mention of respectable names as the parties who witnessed the vision. But we are left without a glimpse when, how, and in what terms, this story obtained its currency; as also by whom, and in what manner, it was first circulated; and among the numbers by whom it has been quoted, although all agree in the general event, scarcely two, even of those who pretend to the best information, tell the story in the same way.

10] Another such story, in which the name of a lady of condition is made use of as having seen an apparition in a country-seat in France, is so far better borne out than those I have mentioned, that I have seen a narrative of the circumstances, attested by the party principally concerned. That the house was disturbed seems to be certain, but the circumstances (though very remarkable) did not, in my mind, by any means exclude the probability that the disturbance and appearances were occasioned by the dexterous management of some mischievously-disposed persons.

11] The remarkable circumstance of Thomas, the second Lord Lyttelton, prophesying his own death within a few minutes, upon the information of an apparition, has been always quoted as a true story. But of late it has been said and published, that the unfortunate nobleman had previously determined to take poison, and of course had it in his own power to ascertain the execution of the prediction. It was no doubt singular that a man, who meditated his exit from the world, should have chosen to play such a trick on his friends. But it is still more credible that a whimsical man should do so wild a thing, than that a messenger should be sent from the dead, to tell a libertine at what precise hour he should expire.

12] To this list other stories of the same class might be added. But it is sufficient to show that such stories as these, having gained a certain degree of currency in the world, and bearing creditable names on their front, walk through society unchallenged, like bills through a bank, when they bear respectable indorsations, although, it may be, the signatures are forged after all. There is, indeed, an unwillingness very closely to examine such subjects, for the secret fund of superstition in every man's bosom, is gratified by believing them to be true, or at least induces him to abstain from challenging them as false. And no doubt it must happen that the transpiring of incidents, in which men have actually seen, or conceived that they saw, apparitions which were invisible to others, contributes to the increase of such stories,—which do accordingly sometimes meet us in a shape of veracity difficult to question.

13] The following story was narrated to me by my friend Mr William Clerk, chief clerk to the Jury Court, Edinburgh, when he first learned it, now nearly thirty years ago, from a passenger in the mail coach. With Mr Clerk's consent, I gave the story at that time to poor Mat Lewis, who published it with a ghost-ballad which he adjusted on the same theme. From the minuteness of the original detail, however, the narrative is better calculated for prose than verse; and more especially as the friend to whom it was originally communicated, is one of the most accurate, intelligent, and acute persons whom I have known in the course of my life, I am willing to preserve the precise story in this place.

14] It was about the eventful year 1800, when the Emperor Paul laid his ill-judged embargo on British trade, that my friend Mr William Clerk, on a journey to London, found himself in company, in the mail coach, with a seafaring man of middle age and respectable appearance, who announced himself as master of a vessel in the Baltic trade, and a sufferer by the embargo. In the course of the desultory conversation which takes place on such occasions, the seaman observed, in compliance with a common superstition, "I wish we may have good luck on our journey —there is a magpie."—"And why should that be unlucky?" said my friend.—"I cannot tell you that," replied the sailor; "but all the world agrees that one magpie bodes bad luck—two are not so bad, but three are the devil. I never saw three magpies but twice, and once I had near lost my vessel, and the second I fell from a horse, and was hurt." This conversation led Mr Clerk to observe, that he supposed he believed also in ghosts, since he credited such auguries. "And if I do," said the sailor, "I may have my own reasons for doing so;" and he spoke this in a deep and serious manner, implying that he felt deeply what he was saying. On being further urged, he confessed that, if he could believe his own eyes, there was one ghost at least which he had seen repeatedly. He then told his story as I now relate it.

15] Our mariner had, in his youth, gone mate of a slave vessel from Liverpool, of which town he seemed to be a native. The captain of the vessel was a man of a variable temper, sometimes kind and courteous to his men, but subject to fits of humour, dislike, and passion, during which he was very violent, tyrannical, and cruel. He took a particular dislike at one sailor aboard, an elderly man, called Bill Jones, or some such name. He seldom spoke to this person without threats and abuse, which the old man, with the license which sailors take in merchant vessels, was very apt to return. On one occasion, Bill Jones appeared slow in getting out on the yard to hand a sail. The captain, according to custom, abused the seaman as a lubberly rascal, who got fat by leaving his duty to other people. The man made a saucy answer, almost amounting to mutiny, on which, in a towering passion, the captain ran down to his cabin, and returned with a blunderbuss loaded with slugs, with which he took deliberate aim at the supposed mutineer, fired, and mortally wounded him. The man was handed down from the yard, and stretched on the deck, evidently dying. He fixed his eyes on the captain, and said, "Sir, you have done for me, but *I will never leave you.*" The captain, in return, swore at him for a fat lubber, and said he would have him thrown into the slave-kettle, where they made food for the Negroes, and see how much fat he had got. The man died; his body was actually thrown into the slave-kettle, and the narrator observed, with a *naïveté* which confirmed the extent of his own belief in the truth of what he told, "There was not much fat about him after all."

16] The captain told the crew they must keep absolute silence on the subject of what had passed; and as the mate was not willing to give an explicit and absolute promise, he ordered him to be confined below. After a day or two, he came to the mate, and demanded if he had an intention to deliver him up for trial when the vessel got home. The mate, who was tired of close confinement in that sultry climate, spoke his commander fair, and obtained his liberty. When he mingled among the crew once more, he found them impressed with the idea, not unnatural in their situation, that the ghost of the dead man appeared among them when they had a spell of duty, especially if a sail was to be handed, on which occasion the spectre was sure to be out upon the yard before any of the crew. The narrator had seen this apparition himself repeatedly—he believed the captain saw it also, but he took no notice of it for some time, and the crew, terrified at the violent temper of the man, dared not call his attention to it. Thus, they held on their course homeward, with great fear and anxiety.

17] At length the captain invited the mate, who was now in a sort of favour, to go down to the cabin and take a glass of grog with him. In this interview, he assumed a very grave and anxious aspect. "I need not tell you, Jack," he said, "what sort of hand we have got on board with us— He told me he would never leave me, and he has kept his word— You only see him now and then, but he is always by my side, and never out of my sight. At this very moment I see him—I am determined to bear it no longer, and I have resolved to leave you."

18] The mate replied, that his leaving the vessel while out of the sight of any land was impossible. He advised, that if the captain apprehended any bad consequences from what had happened, he should run for the west of France or Ireland, and there go ashore, and leave him, the mate, to carry the vessel into Liverpool. The captain only shook his head gloomily, and reiterated his determination to leave the ship. At this moment, the mate was called to the deck for some purpose or other, and the instant he got up the companion-ladder, he heard a splash in the water, and looking over the ship's side, saw that the captain had thrown himself into the sea from the quarter-gallery, and was running astern at the rate of six knots an hour. When just about to sink, he seemed to make a last exertion, sprung half out of the water, and clasped his hands towards the mate, calling, "By ——, Bill is with me now!" and then sunk, to be seen no more.

19] After hearing this singular story, Mr Clerk asked some questions about the captain, and whether his companion considered him as at all times rational. The sailor seemed struck with the question, and answered, after a moment's delay, that in general *he conversationed well enough.*

20] It would have been desirable to have been able to ascertain how far this extraordinary tale was founded on fact; but want of time, and other circumstances prevented Mr Clerk from learning the names and dates, that might, to a certain degree, have verified the events. Granting the murder to have taken place, and the tale to have been truly told, there was nothing more likely to arise among the ship's company than the belief in the apparition; as the captain was a man of a passionate and irritable disposition, it was nowise improbable that he, the victim of remorse, should participate in the horrible visions of those less concerned, especially as he was compelled to avoid communicating his sentiments with any one else; and the catastrophe would in such a case be but the natural consequence of that superstitious remorse, which has conducted so many criminals to suicide or the gallows. If the fellow-traveller of Mr Clerk be not allowed this degree of credit, he must at least be admitted to have displayed a singular talent for the composition of the horrible in fiction. The tale, properly detailed, might have made the fortune of a romancer.

21] I cannot forbear giving you, as congenial to this story, another instance of a guilt-formed phantom, which made considerable noise about twenty years ago or more. I am, I think tolerably correct in the details, though I have lost the account of the trial. Jarvis Matcham—such, if I am not mistaken, was the name of my hero—was pay-sergeant in a regiment, where he was so highly esteemed as a steady and accurate man, that he was permitted opportunity to embezzle a considerable part of the money lodged in his hands for pay of soldiers, bounty of recruits, then a large sum, and other charges which fell within his duty. He was summoned to join his regiment from a town where he had been on the recruiting service, and this perhaps under some shade of suspicion. Matcham perceived discovery was at hand, and would have deserted, had it not been for the presence of a little drummer lad, who was the only one of his party appointed to attend him. In the desperation of his crime, he resolved to murder the poor boy, and avail himself of some balance of money to make his escape. He meditated this wickedness the more readily, that the drummer, he thought, had been put as a spy on him. He perpetrated his crime, and, changing his dress after the deed was done, made a long walk across the country to an inn on the Portsmouth road, where he halted, and went to bed, desiring to be called when the first Portsmouth coach came. The waiter summoned him accordingly; but long after remembered, that when he shook the guest by the shoulder, his first words as he awoke were, "My God! I did not kill him."

22] Matcham went to the seaport by the coach, and instantly entered as an able-bodied landsman or marine, I know not which. His sobriety and attention to duty gained him the same good opinion of the officers in his new service which he had enjoyed in the army. He was afloat for several years, and behaved remarkably well in some actions. At length the vessel came into Plymouth, was paid off, and some of the crew, amongst whom was Jarvis Matcham, were dismissed as too old for service. He and another seaman resolved to walk to town, and took the route by Salisbury. It was when within two or three miles of this celebrated city, that they were overtaken by a tempest so sudden, and accompanied with such vivid lightning, and thunder so dreadfully loud, that the obdurate conscience of the old sinner began to be awakened. He expressed more terror than seemed natural for one who was familiar with the war of elements, and began to look and talk so wildly, that his companion became aware that something more than usual was the matter. At length Matcham complained to his companion that the stones rose from the road and flew after him. He desired the man to walk on the other side of the highway, to see if they would follow him when he was alone. The sailor complied, and Jarvis Matcham complained that the stones still flew after him, and did not pursue the other. "But what is worse," he added, coming up to his companion, and whispering, with a tone of mystery and fear, "who is that little drummer boy, and what business has he to follow us so closely?"—"I can see no one," answered the seaman, infected by the superstition of his associate. "What! not see that little boy with the bloody pantaloons!" exclaimed the secret murderer, so much to the terror of his comrade, that he conjured him, if he had any thing on his mind, to make a clear conscience as far as confession could do it. The criminal fetched a deep groan, and declared that he was unable longer to endure the life which he had led for years. He then confessed the murder of the drummer, and added, that as a considerable reward had been offered, he wished his comrade to deliver him up to the magistrates of Salisbury, as he would desire a shipmate to profit by his fate, which he was now convinced was inevitable. Having overcome his friend's objections to this mode of proceeding, Jarvis Matcham was surrendered to justice accordingly, and made a full confession of his guilt. But before the trial the love of life returned. The prisoner denied his confession, and pleaded Not Guilty. By this time, however, full evidence had been procured from other quarters. Witnesses appeared from his former regiment to prove his identity with the murderer and deserter, and the waiter remembered the ominous words which he had spoken when he awoke him to join the Portsmouth coach. Jarvis Matcham was found guilty, and executed. When his last chance of life was over, he returned to his confession, and with his dying breath averred, and truly, as he thought, the truth of the vision on Salisbury plain. Similar stories might be produced, showing plainly that, under the direction of Heaven, the influence of superstitious fear may be the appointed means of bringing the criminal to repentance for his own sake, and to punishment for the advantage of society.

23] Cases of this kind are numerous, and easily imagined, so I shall dwell on them no further; but rather advert to at least an equally abundant class of ghost stories, in which the apparition is pleased not to torment the actual murderer, but proceeds in a very circuitous manner, acquainting some stranger or ignorant old woman with the particulars of his fate, who, though perhaps unacquainted with all the parties, is directed by the phantom to lay the facts before a magistrate. In this respect, we must certainly allow that ghosts have, as we are informed by the facetious Captain Grose, forms and customs peculiar to themselves.

24] There would be no edification, and little amusement, in treating of clumsy deceptions of this kind, where the grossness of the imposture detects itself. But occasionally cases occur like the following, with respect to which it is more difficult, to use James Boswell's phrase, "to know what to think."

25] Upon the 10th of June, 1754, Duncan Terig, *alias* Clark, and Alexander Bain MacDonald, two Highlanders, were tried before the Court of Justiciary, Edinburgh, for the murder of Arthur Davis, sergeant in Guise's regiment, on the 28th September, 1749. The accident happened not long after the Civil War, the embers of which were still reeking, so there existed too many reasons on account of which an English soldier, straggling far from assistance, might be privately cut off by the inhabitants of these wilds. It appears that Sergeant Davis was missing for years, without any certainty as to his fate. At length, an account of the murder appeared from the evidence of one Alexander MacPherson, (a Highlander, speaking no language but Gaelic, and sworn by an interpreter,) who gave the following extraordinary account of his cause of knowledge:—He was, he said, in bed in his cottage, when an apparition came to his bedside, and commanded him to rise and follow him out of doors. Believing his visitor to be one Farquharson, a neighbour and friend, the witness did as he was bid; and when they were without the cottage, the appearance told the witness he was the ghost of Sergeant Davis, and requested him to go and bury his mortal remains, which lay concealed in a place he pointed out, in a moorland tract called the hill of Christie. He desired him to take Farquharson with him as an assistant. Next day the witness went to the place specified, and there found the bones of a human body much decayed. The witness did not at that time bury the bones so found, in consequence of which negligence the sergeant's ghost again appeared to him, upbraiding him with his breach of promise. On this occasion the witness asked the ghost who were the murderers, and received for answer that he had been slain by the prisoners at the bar. The witness, after this second visitation, called the assistance of Farquharson, and buried the body.

26] Farquharson was brought in evidence, to prove that the preceding witness, MacPherson, had called him to the burial of the bones, and told him the same story which he repeated in court. Isabel MacHardie, a person who slept in one of the beds which run along the wall in an ordinary Highland hut, declared, that upon the night when MacPherson said he saw the ghost, she saw a naked man enter the house, and go towards MacPherson's bed.

27] Yet though the supernatural incident was thus fortified, and although there were other strong presumptions against the prisoners, the story of the apparition threw an air of ridicule on the whole evidence for the prosecution. It was followed up by the counsel for the prisoners asking, in the cross-examination of MacPherson, "What language did the ghost speak in?" The witness, who was himself ignorant of English, replied, "As good Gaelic as I ever heard in Lochaber."—"Pretty well for the ghost of an English sergeant," answered the counsel. The inference was rather smart and plausible than sound, for, the apparition of the ghost being admitted, we know too little of the other world to judge whether all languages may not be alike familiar to those who belong to it. It imposed, however, on the jury, who found the accused parties Not Guilty, although their counsel and solicitor, and most of the court, were satisfied of their having committed the murder. In this case, the interference of the ghost seems to have rather impeded the vengeance which it was doubtless the murdered sergeant's desire to obtain. Yet there may be various modes of explaining this mysterious story, of which the following conjecture may pass for one.

28] The reader may suppose that MacPherson was privy to the fact of the murder, perhaps as an accomplice, or otherwise and may also suppose, that from motives of remorse for the action, or of enmity to those who had committed it, he entertained a wish to bring them to justice. But through the whole Highlands there is no character more detestable than that of an informer, or one who takes what is called Tascal-money, or reward for discovery of crimes. To have informed against Terig and MacDonald might have cost MacPherson his life; and it is far from being impossible, that he had recourse to the story of the ghost, knowing well that his superstitious countrymen would pardon his communicating the commission intrusted to him by a being from the other world, although he might probably have been murdered, if his delation of the crime had been supposed voluntary. This explanation, in exact conformity with the sentiments of the Highlanders on such subjects, would reduce the whole story to a stroke of address on the part of the witness.

29] It is therefore of the last consequence, in considering the truth of stories of ghosts and apparitions, to consider the possibility of wilful deception, whether on the part of those who are agents in the supposed disturbances, or the author of the legend. We shall separately notice an instance or two of either kind.

30] The most celebrated instance in which human agency was used to copy the disturbances imputed to supernatural beings, refers to the ancient palace of Woodstock, when the Commissioners of the Long Parliament came down to dispark what had been lately a royal residence. The Commissioners arrived at Woodstock 13th October, 1649, determined to wipe away the memory of all that connected itself with the recollection of monarchy in England. But in the course of their progress, they were encountered by obstacles which apparently came from the next world. Their bedchambers were infested with visits of a thing resembling a dog, but which came and passed as mere earthly dogs cannot do. Logs of wood, the remains of a very large tree called the King's Oak, which they had splintered into billets for burning, were tossed through the house, and the chairs displaced and shuffled about. While they were in bed, the feet of their couches were lifted higher than their heads, and then dropped with violence. Trenchers "without a wish" flew at their heads, of free will. Thunder and lightning came next, which were set down to the same cause. Spectres made their appearance, as they thought, in different shapes, and one of the party saw the apparition of a hoof, which kicked a candlestick and lighted candle into the middle of the room, and then politely scratched on the red snuff to extinguish it. Other and worse tricks were practised on the astonished Commissioners, who, considering that all the fiends of hell were let loose upon them, retreated from Woodstock without completing an errand, which was, in their opinion, impeded by infernal powers, though the opposition offered was rather of a playful and malicious, than of a dangerous cast.

31] The whole matter was, after the Restoration, discovered to be the trick of one of their own party, who had attended the Commissioners as a clerk, under the name of Giles Sharp. This man, whose real name was Joseph Collins of Oxford, called *Funny Joe,* was a concealed loyalist, and well acquainted with the old mansion of Woodstock, where he had been brought up before the Civil War. Being a bold, active, spirited man, Joe availed himself of his local knowledge of trap-doors and private passages, so as to favour the tricks which he played off upon his masters by aid of his fellow-domestics. The Commissioners' personal reliance on him made his task the more easy, and it was all along remarked, that trusty Giles Sharp saw the most extraordinary sights and visions among the whole party. The unearthly terrors experienced by the Commissioners are detailed with due gravity by Sinclair, and also, I think, by Dr Plott. But although the detection, or explanation of the real history of the Woodstock demons, has also been published, and I have myself seen it, I have at this time forgotten whether it exists in a separate collection, or where it is to be looked for.

32] Similar disturbances have been often experienced, while it was the custom to believe in and dread such frolics of the invisible world, and under circumstances which induce us to wonder, both at the extreme trouble taken by the agents in these impostures, and the slight motives from which they have been induced to do much wanton mischief. Still greater is our modern surprise at the apparently simple means by which terror has been excited to so general an extent, that even the wisest and most prudent have not escaped its contagious influence.

33] On the first point, I am afraid there can be no better reason assigned than the conscious pride of superiority, which induces the human being in all cases to enjoy and practise every means of employing an influence over his fellow mortals; to which we may safely add, that general love of tormenting, as common to our race, as to that noble mimick of humanity, the monkey. To this is owing the delight with which every schoolboy anticipates the effects of throwing a stone into a glass shop; and to this we must also ascribe the otherwise unaccountable pleasure which individuals have taken in practising the tricksy pranks of a goblin, and filling a household, or neighbourhood, with anxiety and dismay, with little gratification to themselves besides the consciousness of dexterity if they remain undiscovered, and with the risk of loss of character, and punishment, should the imposture be found out.

34] In the year 1772, a train of transactions commencing upon Twelfth Day, threw the utmost consternation into the village of Stockwell, near London, and impressed upon some of its inhabitants the inevitable belief that they were produced by invisible agents. The plates, dishes, china, and glass-ware, and small movables of every kind, contained in the house of Mrs Golding, an elderly lady, seemed suddenly to become animated, shifted their places, flew through the room, and were broken to pieces. The particulars of this commotion were as curious, as the loss and damage occasioned in this extraordinary manner were alarming and intolerable. Amidst this combustion, a young woman, Mrs Golding's maid, named Anne Robinson, was walking backwards and forwards, nor could she be prevailed on to sit down for a moment, excepting while the family were at prayers, during which time no disturbance happened. This Anne Robinson had been but a few days in the old lady's service, and it was remarkable that she endured with great composure the extraordinary display which others beheld with terror, and coolly advised her mistress not to be alarmed or uneasy, as these things could not be helped. This excited an idea that she had some reason for being so composed, not inconsistent with a degree of connexion with what was going forward. The afflicted Mrs Golding, as she might be well termed, considering such a commotion and demolition among her goods and chattels, invited neighbours to stay in her house, but they soon became unable to bear the sight of these supernatural proceedings, which went so far, that not above two cups and saucers remained out of a valuable set of china. She next abandoned her dwelling, and took refuge with a neighbour, but, finding his movables were seized with the same sort of St Vitus's dance, her landlord reluctantly refused to shelter any longer a woman who seemed to be persecuted by so strange a subject of vexation. Mrs Golding's suspicions against Anne Robinson now gaining ground, she dismissed her maid, and the hubbub among her movables ceased once and for ever.

35] This circumstance of itself indicates that Anne Robinson was the cause of these extraordinary disturbances, as has been since more completely ascertained by a Mr Brayfield, who persuaded Anne, long after the events had happened, to make him her confident. There was a love story connected with the case, in which the only magic was the dexterity of Anne Robinson, and the simplicity of the spectators. She had fixed long horse hairs to some of the crockery, and placed wires under others, by which she could throw them down without touching them. Other things she dexterously threw about, which the spectators, who did not watch her motions, imputed to invisible agency. At times, when the family were absent, she loosened the hold of the strings by which the hams, bacon, and similar articles were suspended, so that they fell on the slightest motion. She employed some simple chemical secrets; and, delighted with the success of her pranks, pushed them farther than she at first intended. Such was the solution of the whole mystery, which, known by the name of the Stockwell ghost, terrified many well-meaning persons, and had been nearly as famous as that of Cocklane, which may be hinted at as another imposture of the same kind. So many and wonderful are the appearances described, that, when I first met with the original publication, I was strongly impressed with the belief that the narrative was like some of Swift's advertisements, a jocular experiment upon the credulity of the public. But it was certainly published "bona fide," and Mr Hone, on the authority of Mr Brayfield, has since fully explained the wonder.[1]

36] Many such impositions have been detected, and many others have been successfully concealed; but to know what has been discovered in many instances, gives us the assurance of the ruling cause in all. I remember a scene of the kind attempted to be got up near Edinburgh, but detected at once by a sheriff's officer, a sort of persons whose habits of incredulity and suspicious observation render them very dangerous spectators on such occasions. The late excellent Mr Walker, minister at Dunottar, in the Mearns, gave me a curious account of an imposture of this kind, practised by a young country girl, who was surprisingly quick at throwing stones, turf, and other missiles, with such dexterity, that it was for a long time impossible to ascertain her agency in the disturbances of which she was the sole cause.

37] The belief of the spectators that such scenes of disturbance arise from invisible beings, will appear less surprising, if we consider the common feats of jugglers, or professors of legerdemain, and recollect that it is only the frequent exhibition of such powers which reconciles us to them as matters of course, although they are wonders at which, in our fathers' time, men would have cried out either sorcery or miracles. The spectator also, who has been himself duped, makes no very respectable appearance when convicted of his error; and thence, if too candid to add to the evidence of supernatural agency, is yet unwilling to stand convicted, by cross-examination, of having been imposed on, and unconsciously becomes disposed rather to colour more highly than the truth, than acquiesce in an explanation resting on his having been too hasty a believer. Very often, too, the detection depends upon the combination of certain circumstances, which, apprehended, necessarily explain the whole story.

38] For example, I once heard a sensible and intelligent friend in company, express himself convinced of the truth of a wonderful story told him by an intelligent and bold man, about an ap-

---

[1] See Hone's Every-Day Book, p. 62.

parition. The scene lay in an ancient castle on the coast of Morven, or the Isle of Mull, where the ghost-seer chanced to be resident. He was given to understand by the family, when betaking himself to rest, that the chamber in which he slept was occasionally disquieted by supernatural appearances. Being at that time no believer in such stories, he attended little to this hint, until the witching hour of night, when he was awakened from a dead sleep by the pressure of a human hand on his body. He looked up at the figure of a tall Highlander in the antique and picturesque dress of his country, only that his brows were bound with a bloody bandage. Struck with sudden and extreme fear, he was willing to have sprung from bed, but the spectre stood before him in the bright moonlight, its one arm extended, so as to master him if he attempted to rise; the other hand held up in a warning and grave posture, as menacing the Lowlander if he should attempt to quit his recumbent posture. Thus he lay in mortal agony for more than an hour, after which it pleased the spectre of ancient days to leave him to more sound repose. So singular a story had on its side the usual number of votes from the company, till, upon cross-examination, it was explained that the principal person concerned was an exciseman; after which *éclaircissement,* the same explanation struck all present, viz., that the Highlanders of the mansion had chosen to detain the exciseman by the apparition of an ancient heroic ghost, in order to disguise from his vigilance the removal of certain modern enough spirits, which his duty might have called upon him to seize. Here a single circumstance explained the whole ghost story.

39] At other times it happens that the meanness and trifling nature of a cause not very obvious to observation, has occasioned it to be entirely overlooked, even on account of that very meanness, since no one is willing to acknowledge that he has been alarmed by a cause of little consequence, and which he would be ashamed of mentioning. An incident of this sort happened to a gentleman of birth and distinction, who is well known in the political world, and was detected by the precision of his observation. Shortly after he succeeded to his estate and title, there was a rumour among his servants concerning a strange noise heard in the family mansion at night, the cause of which they had found it impossible to trace. The gentleman resolved to watch himself, with a domestic who had grown old in the family, and who had begun to murmur strange things concerning the knocking having followed so close upon the death of his old master. They watched until the noise was heard, which they listened to with that strange uncertainty attending midnight sounds, which prevents the hearers from immediately tracing them to the spot where they arise, while imputing to them more than the due importance which they would receive, if mingled with the usual noises of daylight. At length the gentleman and his servant traced the sounds which they had repeatedly heard, to a small store-room used as a place for keeping provisions of various kinds for the family, of which the old butler had the key. They entered this place, and remained there for some time, without hearing the noises which they had traced thither; at length the sound was heard, but much lower than it had formerly seemed to be, while acted upon at a distance by the imagination of the hearers. The cause was immediately discovered. A rat caught in an old-fashioned trap had occasioned this tumult, by its efforts to escape, in which it was able to raise the trap-door of its prison to a certain height, but was then obliged to drop it. The noise of the fall resounding through the house, had occasioned the disturbance which, but for the cool investigation of the proprietor, might easily have established an accredited ghost story. The circumstance was told me by the gentleman to whom it happened.

40] There are other occasions in which the ghost story is rendered credible by some remarkable combination of circumstances very unlikely to have happened, and which no one could have supposed, unless some particular fortune occasioned a discovery.

41] An apparition which took place at Plymouth is well known, but it has been differently related; and having some reason to think the following edition correct, it is an incident so much to my purpose, that you must pardon its insertion.

42] A club of persons connected with science and literature, was formed at the great sea-town we have named. During the summer months, the society met in a cave by the sea-shore; during those of autumn and winter, they convened within the premises of a tavern, but, for the sake of privacy, had their meetings in a summer-house situated in the garden, at a distance from the main building. Some of the members to whom the position of their own dwellings rendered this convenient, had a pass key to the garden-door, by which they could enter the garden and reach the summer-house without the publicity or trouble of passing through the open tavern. It was the rule of this club that its members presided alternately. On one occasion, in the winter, the president of the evening chanced to be very ill; indeed, was reported to be on his death-bed. The club met as usual, and, from a sentiment of respect, left vacant the chair which ought to have been occupied by him, if in his usual health; for the same reason, the conversation turned upon the absent gentleman's talents, and the loss expected to the society by his death. While they were upon this melancholy theme, the door suddenly opened, and the appearance of the president entered the room. He wore a white wrapper, a nightcap round his brow, the appearance of which was that of death itself. He stalked into the room with unusual gravity, took the vacant place of ceremony, lifted the empty glass which stood before him, bowed around, and put it to his lips; then replaced it on the table, and stalked out of the room as silent as he had entered it. The company remained deeply appalled; at length, after many observations on the strangeness of what they had seen, they resolved to dispatch two of their number as ambassadors, to see how it fared with the president, who had thus strangely appeared among them. They went, and returned with the frightful intelligence, that the friend, after whom they had enquired, was that evening deceased.

43] The astonished party then resolved that they would remain absolutely silent respecting the wonderful sight which they had seen. Their habits were too philosophical to permit them to believe that they had actually seen the ghost of their deceased brother, and at the same time they were too wise men, to wish to confirm the superstition of the vulgar, by what might seem indubitable evidence of a ghost. The affair was therefore kept a strict secret, although, as usual, some dubious rumours of the tale found their way to the public. Several years afterwards, an old woman who had long filled the place of a sick-nurse, was taken very ill, and on her death-bed was attended by a medical member of the philosophical club. To him, with many expressions of regret, she acknowledged that she had long before attended Mr ——, naming the president, whose appearance had surprised the club so strangely, and that she felt distress of conscience on account of the manner in which he died. She said, that as his malady was attended by light-headedness, she had been directed to keep a close watch upon him during his illness. Unhappily she slept, and during her sleep the patient had awaked, and left the apartment. When, on her own awaking, she found the bed empty and the patient gone, she forthwith hurried out of the house to seek him, and met him in the act of returning. She got him, she said, replaced in bed, but it was only to die there. She added, to convince her hearer of the truth of what she said, that immediately after the poor gentleman expired, a deputation of two members from the club came to enquire after their president's health, and received for answer that he was already dead. This confession explained the whole matter. The delirious patient had very naturally taken the road to the club, from some recollections of his duty of the night. In approaching and retiring from the apartment, he had used one of the pass keys already mentioned, which made his way shorter. On the other hand, the gentlemen sent to enquire after his health had reached his lodging by a more circuitous road; and thus there had been time for him to return to what proved his death-bed, long before they reached his chamber. The philosophical witnesses of this strange scene, were now as anxious to spread the story as they had formerly been to conceal it, since it showed in what a remarkable manner men's eyes might turn traitors to them, and impress them with ideas far different from the truth.

44] Another occurrence of the same kind, although scarcely so striking in its circumstances, was yet one which, had it remained unexplained, might have passed as an indubitable instance of a supernatural apparition.

45] A Teviotdale farmer was riding from a fair, at which he had indulged himself with John Barleycorn, but not to that extent of defying goblins which it inspired into the gallant Tam O'Shanter. He was pondering with some anxiety upon the dangers of travelling alone on a solitary road, which passed the corner of a churchyard, now near at hand, when he saw before him, in the moonlight, a pale female form standing upon the very wall which surrounded the cemetery. The road was very narrow, with no opportunity of giving the apparent phantom what seamen call a wide berth. It was, however, the only path which led to the rider's home, who therefore resolved, at all risks to pass the apparition. He accordingly approached, as slowly as possible, the spot where the spectre stood, while the figure remained, now perfectly still and silent, now brandishing its arms, and gibbering at the moon. When the farmer came close to the spot, he dashed off upon a gallop; but the spectre did not miss its opportunity. As he passed the corner where she was perched, she contrived to drop behind the horseman, and seize him round the waist; a manœuvre which greatly increased the speed of the horse, and the terror of the rider; for the hand of her who sat behind him, when pressed upon his, felt as cold as that of a corpse. At his own house at length he arrived, and bid the servants who came to attend him, "Tak aff the ghaist!" They took off accordingly a female in white, and the poor farmer himself was conveyed to bed, where he lay struggling for weeks with a strong nervous fever. The female was found to be a maniac, who had been left a widow very suddenly by an affectionate husband, and the nature and cause of her malady induced her, when she could make her escape, to wander to the churchyard wall, where she sometimes wildly wept over his grave, and sometimes standing on the corner of the churchyard wall, looked out, and mistook every stranger on horseback for the husband she had lost. If this woman, which was very possible, had dropt from the horse unobserved by him, whom she had made her involuntary companion, it would have been very hard to have convinced the honest farmer that he had not actually performed part of his journey with a ghost behind him.

46] There is also a large class of stories of this sort, where various secrets of Chemistry, of Acoustics, Ventriloquism, or other arts, have been either employed to dupe the spectators, or have tended to do so though mere accident and coincidence. Of these it is scarce necessary to quote instances; but the following may be told as a tale recounted by a foreign nobleman, known to me nearly thirty years ago, whose life, lost in the service of his sovereign, proved too short for his friends, and his native land.

47] At a certain old castle on the confines of Hungary, the lord to whom it belonged had determined upon giving an entertainment worthy of his own rank, and of the magnificence of the antique mansion which he inhabited. The guests of course were numerous, and among them was a veteran officer of Hussars, remarkable for his bravery. When the arrangements for the night were made, this officer was informed that there would be difficulty in accommodating the company in the castle, large as it was, unless some one would take the risk of sleeping in a room supposed to be haunted; and that as he was known to be above such prejudices, the apartment was, in the first place, proposed for his occupation, as the person least likely to suffer a bad night's rest from such a cause. The Major thankfully accepted the preference, and having shared the festivity of the evening, retired after midnight, having denounced vengeance against any one who should presume by any trick to disturb his repose; a threat which his habits would, it was supposed, render him sufficiently ready to execute. Somewhat contrary to the custom in these cases, the Major went to bed, having left his candle burning, and laid his trusty pistols carefully loaded on the table by his bedside.

48] He had not slept an hour when he was awakened by a solemn strain of music—he looked out. Three ladies, fantastically dressed in green, were seen in the lower end of the apartment, who sung a solemn requiem. The Major listened for some time with delight; at length he tired—"Ladies," he said, "this is very well, but somewhat monotonous—will you be so kind as to change the tune?" The ladies continued singing; he expostulated, but the music was not interrupted. The Major began to grow angry: "Ladies," he said, "I must consider this as a trick for the purpose of terrifying me, and as I regard it as an impertinence, I shall take a rough mode of stopping it." With that he began to handle his pistols. The ladies sung on. He then got seriously angry—"I will but wait five minutes," he said, "and then fire without hesitation." The song was uninterrupted—the five minutes were expired—"I still give you law, ladies," he said, "while I count twenty." This produced as little effect as his former threats. He counted one, two, three, accordingly; but on approaching the end of the number, and repeating more than once his determination to fire, the last numbers, seventeen—eighteen—nineteen, were pronounced with considerable pauses between, and an assurance that the pistols were cocked. The ladies sung on. As he pronounced the word twenty he fired both pistols against the musical damsels;—but the ladies sung on! The Major was overcome by the unexpected inefficacy of his violence, and had an illness which lasted more than three weeks. The trick put upon him may be shortly described by the fact, that the female choristers were placed in an adjoining room, and that he only fired at their reflection thrown forward into that in which he slept by the effect of a concave mirror.

49] Other stories of the same kind are numerous and well known. The apparition of the Brocken mountain, after having occasioned great admiration and some fear, is now ascertained by philosophers to be a gigantic reflection, which makes the traveller's shadow, represented upon the misty clouds, appear a colossal figure of almost immeasurable size. By a similar deception, men have been induced, in Westmoreland and other mountainous countries, to imagine they saw troops of horse and armies marching and countermarching, which were in fact only the reflection of horses pasturing upon an opposite height, or of the forms of peaceful travellers.

50] A very curious case of this kind was communicated to me by the son of the lady principally concerned, and tends to show out of what mean materials a venerable apparition may be sometimes formed. In youth this lady resided with her father, a man of sense and resolution. Their house was situated in the principal street of a town of some size. The back part of the house ran at right angles to an Anabaptist chapel, divided from it by a small cabbage-garden. The young lady used sometimes to indulge the romantic love of solitude, by sitting in her own apartment in the evening till twilight, and even darkness, was approaching. One evening while she was thus placed, she was surprised to see a gleamy figure, as of some aerial being hovering, as it were, against the arched window in the end of the Anabaptist chapel. Its head was surrounded by that halo which painters give to the Catholic saints; and, while the young lady's attention was fixed on an object so extraordinary, the figure bent gracefully towards her more than once, as if intimating a sense of her presence, and then disappeared. The seer of this striking vision descended to her family, so much discomposed as to call her father's attention. He obtained an account of the cause of her disturbance, and expressed his intention to watch in the apartment next night. He sat, accordingly, in his daughter's chamber, where she also attended him. Twilight came, and nothing appeared; but as the gray light faded into darkness, the same female figure was seen hovering on the window; the same shadowy form; the same pale light around the head; the same inclinations, as the evening before. "What do you think of this?" said the daughter to the astonished father.—"Anything, my dear," said the father, "rather than allow that we look upon what is supernatural."—A strict research established a natural cause for the appearance on the window. It was the custom of an old woman, to whom the garden beneath was rented, to go out at night to gather cabbages. The lantern she carried in her hand threw up the refracted reflection of her form on the chapel window. As she stooped to gather her cabbages, the reflection appeared to bend forward; and that was the whole matter.

51] Another species of deception affecting the credit of such supernatural communications, arises from the dexterity and skill of the authors who have made it their business to present such stories in the shape most likely to attract belief. Defoe—whose power in rendering credible that which was in itself very much the reverse was so peculiarly distinguished—has not failed to show his superiority in this species of composition. A bookseller of his acquaintance had, in the tradephrase, rather overprinted an edition of Drelincourt on Death, and complained to Defoe of the loss which was likely to ensue. The experienced bookmaker, with the purpose of recommending the edition, advised his friend to prefix the celebrated narrative of Mrs Veal's ghost, which he wrote for the occasion, with such an air of truth, that although, in fact, it does not afford a single tittle of evidence properly so called, it nevertheless was swallowed so eagerly by the people, that Drelincourt's work on death, which the supposed spirit recommended to the perusal of her friend Mrs Bargrave, instead of sleeping on the editor's shelf, moved off by thousands at once; the story, incredible in itself, and unsupported as it was by evidence or enquiry, was received as true, merely from the cunning of the narrator, and the addition of a number of adventitious circumstances, which no man alive could have conceived as having occurred to the mind of a person composing a fiction.

52] It did not require the talents of Defoe, though in that species of composition he must stand unrivalled, to fix the public attention on a ghost story. John Dunton, a man of scribbling celebrity at the time, succeeded to a great degree in imposing upon the public a tale which he calls the Apparition Evidence. The beginning of it at least, for it is of great length, has something in it a little new. At Mynehead, in Somersetshire, lived an ancient gentlewoman, named Mrs Leckie, whose only son and daughter resided in family with her. The son traded to Ireland, and was supposed to be worth eight or ten thousand pounds. They had a child about five or six years old. This family was generally respected in Mynehead; and especially Mrs Leckie, the old lady, was so pleasant in society, that her friends used to say to her, and to each other, that it was a thousand pities such an excellent, good-humoured gentlewoman must, from her age, be soon lost to her friends. To which Mrs Leckie often made the somewhat startling reply: "For as much as you now seem to like me, I am afraid you will but little care to see or speak with me after my death, though I believe you may have that satisfaction." Die, however, she did, and after her funeral, was repeatedly seen in her personal likeness, at home and abroad, by night and by noon-day.

53] One story is told, of a doctor of physic walking into the fields, who in his return met with this spectre, whom he at first accosted civilly, and paid her the courtesy of handing her over a stile; observing, however, that she did not move her lips in speaking, or her eyes in looking round, he became suspicious of the condition of his companion, and showed some desire to be rid of her society. Offended at this, the hag at the next stile planted herself upon it, and obstructed his passage. He got through at length with some difficulty, and not without a sound kick, and an admonition to pay more attention to the next aged gentlewoman whom he met. "But this," says John Dunton, "was a petty and inconsiderable prank to what she played in her son's house, and elsewhere. She would at noon-day appear upon the key of Mynehead, and cry, 'A boat, a boat, ho! a boat, a boat, ho!' If any boatmen or seamen were in sight and did not come, they were sure to be cast away; and if they did come, 'twas all one, they were cast away. It was equally dangerous to please and displease her. Her son had several ships sailing between Ireland and England; no sooner did they make land, and come in sight of England, but this ghost would appear in the same garb and likeness as when she was alive, and, standing at the mainmast, would blow with a whistle, and though it were never so great a calm, yet immediately there would arise a most dreadful storm, that would break, wreck, and drown the ship and goods, only the seamen would escape with their lives—the devil had no permission from God to take them away. Yet at this rate, by her frequent apparitions and disturbances, she had made a poor merchant of her son, for his fair estate was all buried in the sea, and he that was once worth thousands, was reduced to a very poor and low condition in the world; for whether the ship were his own or hired, or he had but goods on board it to the value of twenty shillings, this troublesome ghost would come as before, whistle in a calm at the mainmast at noon-day, when they had descried land, and then ship and goods went all out of hand to wreck; insomuch that he could at last get no ships wherein to stow his goods, nor any mariner to sail in them; for, knowing what an uncomfortable, fatal, and losing voyage they should make of it, they did all decline his service. In her son's house she hath her constant haunts by day and night; but whether he did not, or would not own, if he did see her, he always professed he never saw her. Sometimes when in bed with his wife, she would cry out, 'Husband, look, there's your mother!' And when he would turn to the right side, then was she gone to the left; and when to the left side of the bed, then was she gone to the right: only one evening their only child, a girl of about five or six years old, lying in a truckle-bed under them cries out, 'O help me, father! help me, mother, for grandmother will choke me!' and before they could get to their child's assistance, she had murdered it; they finding the poor girl dead, her throat having been pinched by two fingers, which stopped her breath and strangled her. This was the sorest of all their afflictions; their estate is gone, and now their child is gone also; you may guess at their grief and great sorrow. One morning after the child's funeral, her husband being abroad, about eleven in the forenoon, Mrs Leckie the younger goes up into her chamber to dress her head, and, as she was looking into the glass, she spies her mother-in-law, the old beldam, looking over her shoulder. This cast her into a great horror; but recollecting her affrighted spirits, and recovering the exercise of her reason, faith and hope, having cast up a short and silent prayer to God, she turns about, and bespeaks her: 'In the name of God, mother, why do you trouble me?'— 'Peace!' says the spectrum; 'I will do thee no hurt.'— 'What will you have of me?' says the daughter," &c.[2] Dunton, the narrator, and probably the contriver of the story, proceeds to inform us, at length, of a commission which the wife of Mr Leckie receives from the ghost to deliver to Atherton, Bishop of Waterford, a guilty and unfortunate man, who afterwards died by the hands of the executioner; but that part of the subject is too disagreeable and tedious to enter upon.

[2] Apparition Evidence.

54] So deep was the impression made by the story on the inhabitants of Mynehead, that it is said the tradition of Mrs Leckie still remains in that port, and that mariners belonging to it often, amid tempestuous weather, conceive they hear the whistle-call of the implacable hag who was the source of so much mischief to her own family. However, already too desultory, and too long, it would become intolerably tedious were we to insist farther on the peculiar sort of genius by which stories of this kind may be embodied and prolonged.

55] I may, however, add, that the charm of the tale depends much upon the age of the person to whom it is addressed; and that the vivacity of fancy which engages us in youth to pass over much that is absurd, in order to enjoy some single trait of imagination, dies within us when we obtain the age of manhood, and the sadder and graver regions which lie beyond it. I am the more conscious of this, because I have been myself, at two periods of my life, distant from each other, engaged in scenes favourable to that degree of superstitious awe which my countrymen expressively call being *eerie*.

56] On the first of these occasions, I was only nineteen or twenty years old, when I happened to pass a night in the magnificent old baronial castle of Glammis, the hereditary seat of the Earls of Strathmore. The hoary pile contains much in its appearance, and in the traditions connected with it, impressive to the imagination. It was the scene of the murder of a Scottish king of great antiquity; not, indeed, the gracious Duncan, with whom the name naturally associates itself, but Malcolm the Second. It contains also a curious monument of the peril of feudal times, being a secret chamber, the entrance of which, by the law or custom of the family must only be known to three persons at once, viz. the Earl of Strathmore, his heir apparent, and any third person whom they may take into their confidence. The extreme antiquity of the building is vouched by the immense thickness of the walls, and the wild and straggling arrangement of the accommodation within doors. As the late Earl of Strathmore seldom resided in that ancient mansion, it was, when I was there, but half furnished, and that with movables of great antiquity, which, with the pieces of chivalric armour hanging upon the walls, greatly contributed to the general effect of the whole. After a very hospitable reception from the late Peter Proctor, Esq., then seneschal of the castle, in Lord Strathmore's absence, I was conducted to my apartment in a distant corner of the building. I must own, that as I heard door after door shut, after my conductor had retired, I began to consider myself too far from the living, and somewhat too near the dead. We had passed through what is called "the King's room," a vaulted apartment, garnished with stags' antlers, and similar trophies of the chase, and said by tradition to be the spot of Malcolm's murder, and I had an idea of the vicinity of the castle chapel.

57] In spite of the truth of history, the whole night scene in Macbeth's castle rushed at once upon my mind, and struck my imagination more forcibly than even when I have seen its terrors represented by the late John Kemble and his inimitable sister. In a word, I experienced sensations, which, though not remarkable either for timidity or superstition, did not fail to affect me to the point of being disagreeable, while they were mingled at the same time with a strange and indescribable kind of pleasure, the recollection of which affords me gratification at this moment.

58] In the year 1814, accident placed me, then past middle life, in a situation somewhat similar to that which I have described.

59] I had been on a pleasure voyage with some friends around the north coast of Scotland, and in that course had arrived in the salt-water lake under the Castle of Dunvegan, whose turrets, situated upon a frowning rock, rise immediately above the waves of the loch. As most of the party, and I myself in particular, chanced to be well known to the Laird of Macleod, we were welcomed to the castle with Highland hospitality, and glad to find ourselves in polished society, after a cruise of some duration. The most modern part of the castle was founded in the days of James VI.; the more ancient is referred to a period "whose birth tradition notes not." Until the present Macleod connected by a drawbridge the site of the castle with the mainland of Skye, the access must have been extremely difficult. Indeed, so much greater was the regard paid to security than to convenience, that in former times the only access to the mansion arose through a vaulted cavern in a rock, up which a staircase ascended from the sea shore, like the buildings we read of in the romances of Mrs Radcliffe.

60] Such a castle in the extremity of the Highlands was of course furnished with many a tale of tradition, and many a superstitious legend, to fill occasional intervals in the music and song, as proper to the halls of Dunvegan as when Johnson commemorated them. We reviewed the arms and ancient valuables of this distinguished family—saw the dirk and broadsword of Rorie Mhor, and his horn, which would drench three chiefs of these degenerate days. The solemn drinking cup of the Kings of Man must not be forgotten, nor the fairy banner given to Macleod by the Queen of Fairies; that magic flag, which has been victorious in two pitched fields, and will still float in a third, the bloodiest and the last, when the Elfin Sovereign shall, after the fight is ended, recall her banner, and carry off the standard-bearer.

61] Amid such tales of ancient tradition, I had from Macleod and his lady the courteous offer of the haunted apartment of the castle, about which, as a stranger, I might be supposed interested. Accordingly, I took possession of it about the witching hour. Except perhaps some tapestry hangings, and the extreme thickness of the walls, which argued great antiquity, nothing could have been more comfortable than the interior of the apartment; but if you looked from the windows, the view was such as to correspond with the highest tone of superstition. An autumnal blast, sometimes clear, sometimes driving mist before it, swept along the troubled billows of the lake, which it occasionally concealed, and by fits disclosed. The waves rushed in wild disorder on the shore, and covered with foam the steep piles of rock, which, rising from the sea in forms something resembling the human figure, have obtained the name of Macleod's Maidens, and in such a night, seemed no bad representatives of the Norwegian goddesses, called Choosers of the Slain, or Riders of the Storm. There was something of the dignity of danger in the scene; for on a platform beneath the windows lay an ancient battery of cannon, which had sometimes been used against privateers even of late years. The distant scene was a view of that part of the Quillan mountains which are called, from their form, Macleod's Dining-Tables. The voice of an angry cascade, termed the Nurse of Rorie Mhor, because that chief slept best in its vicinity, was heard from time to time mingling its notes with those of wind and wave. Such was the haunted room at Dunvegan, and as such, it well deserved a less sleepy inhabitant. In the language of Dr Johnson, who has stamped his memory on this remote place, "I looked around me, and wondered that I was not more affected; but the mind is not at all times equally ready to be moved." In a word, it is necessary to confess, that of all I heard or saw, the most engaging spectacle was the comfortable bed, in which I hoped to make amends for some rough nights on shipboard, and where I slept accordingly without thinking of ghost or goblin till I was called by my servant in the morning.

62] From this I am taught to infer, that tales of ghosts and demonology are out of date at forty years and upwards; that it is only in the morning of life that this feeling of superstition "comes o'er us like a summer cloud," affecting us with fear, which is solemn and awful rather than painful; and I am tempted to think, that if I were to write on the subject at all, it should have been during a period of life when I could have treated it with more interesting vivacity, and might have been at least amusing, if I could not be instructive. Even the present fashion of the world seems to be ill suited for studies of this fantastic nature; and the most ordinary mechanic has learning sufficient to laugh at the figments which in former times were believed by persons far advanced in the deepest knowledge of the age.

63] I cannot, however, in conscience carry my opinion of my countrymen's good sense so far as to exculpate them entirely from the charge of credulity. Those who are disposed to look for them may, without much trouble, see such manifest signs, both of superstition and the disposition to believe in its doctrines, as may render it no useless occupation to compare the follies of our fathers with our own. The sailors have a proverb that every man in his lifetime must eat a peck of impurity; and it seems yet more clear that every generation of the human race must swallow a certain measure of nonsense. There remains hope, however, that the grosser faults of our ancestors are now out of date; and that whatever follies the present race may be guilty of, the sense of humanity is too universally spread to permit them to think of tormenting wretches till they confess what is impossible, and then burning them for their pains.

Questions

1. What specifically is Scott trying to prove in his essay, and how does he go about proving it?
2. What is there about his method which forces him to accumulate such a vast number of examples? Why does every example have to be analyzed?
3. A casual reader might well come away with the impression that Scott was telling tale after tale without bothering to classify or arrange his material. Actually the stories are classified; there is a broad division between the stories which rest upon no evidence and can be discarded and those which actually occurred and must be explained away. Where does the division come?
4. The second section, which contains the more or less authentic stories, has several subdivisions. What are they?
5. Is the anecdote of the exciseman (paragraph 38) in the section where it properly belongs? Are any other stories misplaced?
6. Scott has six subdivisions in the second section, but three would serve. What would they be? If we put all the cases in which deception is involved together in one section, this section could in turn be divided into two subsections. What would they be?
7. Does Scott's rather informal organization actually detract much from the effectiveness of the essay?
8. Is there anything to make you suspect that Scott is less interested in making his point than in telling marvelous tales? Compare his narrative method with Whipple's or Froude's; does he limit himself to those details which are really essential to his point?
9. What does the personal reminiscence at the end add to the essay?

RUTH BENEDICT

⚜ *The Pueblos of New Mexico*

THE BASIC contrast between the Pueblos and the other cultures of North America is the contrast that is named and described by Nietzsche in his studies of Greek tragedy. He discusses two diametrically opposed ways of arriving at the values of existence. The Dionysian pursues them through "the annihilation of the ordinary bounds and limits of existence"; he seeks to attain in his most valued moments escape from the boundaries imposed upon him by his five senses, to break through into another order of experience. The desire of the Dionysian, in personal experience or in ritual, is to press through it toward a certain psychological state, to achieve excess. The closest analogy to the emotions he seeks is drunkenness, and he values the illuminations of frenzy. With Blake, he believes "the path of excess leads to the palace of wisdom." The Apollonian distrusts all this, and has often little idea of the nature of such experiences. He finds means to outlaw them from his conscious life. He "knows but one law, measure in the Hellenic sense." He keeps the middle of the road, stays within the known map, does not meddle with disruptive psychological states. In Nietzsche's fine phrase, even in the exaltation of the dance he "remains what he is, and retains his civic name."

2] The Southwest Pueblos are Apollonian. Not all of Nietzsche's discussion of the contrast between Apollonian and

"The Pueblos of New Mexico." Adapted from *Patterns of Culture* by Ruth Benedict. Copyright 1934, by Ruth Benedict. Reprinted by permission of and arrangement with Houghton Mifflin Company, the authorized publisher.

Dionysian applies to the contrast between the Pueblos and the surrounding peoples. There were refinements of the types in Greece that do not occur among the Indians of the Southwest, and among these latter, again, there are refinements that did not occur in Greece. It is with no thought of equating the civilization of Greece with that of aboriginal America that I use, in describing the cultural configurations of the latter, terms borrowed from the culture of Greece. I use them because they are categories that bring clearly to the fore the major qualities that differentiate Pueblo culture from those of other American Indians, not because all the attitudes that are found in Greece are found also in aboriginal America.

3] Apollonian institutions have been carried much further in the pueblos than in Greece. Greece was by no means as single-minded. In particular, Greece did not carry out as the Pueblos have the distrust of individualism that the Apollonian way of life implies, but which in Greece was scanted because of forces with which it came in conflict. Zuñi ideals and institutions on the other hand are rigorous on this point. The known map, the middle of the road, to any Apollonian is embodied in the common tradition of his people. To stay always within it is to commit himself to precedent, to tradition. Therefore those influences that are powerful against tradition are uncongenial and minimized in their institutions, and the greatest of these is individualism. It is disruptive, according to Apollonian philosophy in the Southwest, even when it refines upon and enlarges the tradition itself. That is not to say that the Pueblos prevent this. No culture can protect itself from additions and changes. But the process by which these come is suspect and cloaked, and institutions that would give individuals a free hand are outlawed.

4] It is not possible to understand Pueblo attitudes toward life without some knowledge of the culture from which they have detached themselves: that of the rest of North America. It is by the force of the contrast that we can calculate the strength of their opposite drive and the resistances that have kept out of the Pueblos the most characteristic traits of the American aborigines. For the American Indians as a whole, and including those of Mexico, were passionately Dionysian. They valued all violent experience, all means by which human beings may break through the usual sensory routine, and to all such experiences they attributed the highest value.

5] The Indians of North America outside the Pueblos have, of course, anything but uniform culture. They contrast violently at almost every point, and there are eight of them that it is convenient to differentiate as separate culture areas. But throughout them all, in one or another guise, there run certain fundamental Dionysian practices. The most conspicuous of these is probably their practice of obtaining supernatural power in a dream or vision. On the western plains men sought these visions with hideous tortures. They cut strips from the skin of their arms, they struck off fingers, they swung themselves from tall poles by straps inserted under the muscles of their shoulders. They went without food and water for extreme periods. They sought in every way to achieve an order of experience set apart from daily living. It was grown men, on the plains, who went out after visions. Sometimes they stood motionless, their hands tied behind them, or they staked out a tiny spot from which they could not move till they had received their blessing. Sometimes, in other tribes, they wandered over distant regions, far out into dangerous country. Some tribes chose precipices and places especially associated with danger. At all events a man went alone, or, if he was seeking his vision by torture and someone had to go out with him to tie him to the pole from which he was to swing till he had his supernatural experience, his helper did his part and left him alone for his ordeal.

6] It was necessary to keep one's mind fixed upon the expected visitation. Concentration was the technique above all others upon which they relied. "Keep thinking it all the time," the old medicine men said always. Sometimes it was necessary to keep the face wet with tears so that the spirits would pity the sufferer and grant him his request. "I am a poor man. Pity me," is a constant prayer. "Have nothing," the medicine men taught, "and the spirits will come to you."

7] On the western plains they believed that when the vision came it determined their life and the success they might expect. If no vision came, they were doomed to failure. "I was going to be poor; that is why I had no vision." If the experience was of curing, one had curing powers; if of warfare, one had warrior's powers. If one encountered Double Woman, one was a transvestite and took woman's occupations and habits. If one was blessed by the mythical Water Serpent, one had supernatural power for evil and sacrificed the lives of one's wife and children in payment for becoming a sorcerer. Any man who desired general strengthening or success in particular ventures sought visions often. They were necessary for warpaths and for curings and for all kinds of miscellaneous occasions: calling the buffalo, naming children, mourning, revenge, finding lost articles.

8] When the vision came, it might be visual or auditory hallucination, but it need not be. Most of the accounts tell of the appearance of some animal. When it first appeared it was often in human form, and it talked with the suppliant and gave him a song and a formula for some supernatural practice. As it was leaving, it turned into an animal, and the suppliant knew what animal it was that had blessed him, and what skin or bone or feathers he must get to keep as a memento of the experience and preserve for life as his sacred medicine bundle. On the other hand some experiences were much more casual. There were tribes that valued especially moments of intimacy with nature, occasions when a person alone by the edge of a river or following the trail felt in some otherwise simple event a compelling significance.

9] It might be from a dream that the supernatural power came to them. Some of the accounts of visions are unmistakable dream experiences, whether they occurred in sleep or under less normal conditions. Some tribes valued the dreams of sleep more highly than any other experiences. Lewis and Clark complained when they crossed the western plains in the early days that no night was fit for sleeping; some old man was always rousing to beat on his drum and ceremonially rehearse the dream he had just had. It was a valuable source of power.

10] In any case the criterion of whether or not the experience had power was necessarily a matter for the individual to decide. It was recognized as subjective, no matter what other social curbs were imposed upon its subsequent practice. Some experiences had power and some had not, and they distinguished by the flash of significance that singled out those that were valuable. If it did not communicate this thrill, an experience they had sought even with torture was counted valueless, and they dared not claim power from it for fear that the animal claimed as guardian spirit would visit death and disgrace upon them.

11] This belief in the power of a vision experience on the western plains is a cultural mechanism which gives a theoretically unlimited freedom to the individual. He might go out and get this supremely coveted power, no matter to what family he belonged. Besides this, he might claim his vision as authority for any innovation, any personal advantage which he might imagine, and this authority he invoked was an experience in solitude which in the nature of the case could not be judged by another person. It was, moreover, probably the experience of greatest instability that he could achieve. It gave individual initiative a scope which is not easily equalled. Practically, of course, the authority of custom remained unchallenged. Even given the freest scope by their institutions, men are never inventive enough to make more than minute changes. From the point of view of an outsider the most radical innovations in any culture amount to no more than a minor revision, and it is a commonplace that prophets have been put to death for the difference between Tweedledum and Tweedledee. In the same way, the cultural license that the vision gave was used to establish, according to the instructions of the vision, a Strawberry Order of the Tobacco Society where before there had been a Snowbird Order, or the power of the skunk in warfare where the usual reliance was upon the buffalo. Other limitations were also inevitable. The emphasis might be placed upon trying out the vision. Only those could claim supernatural power for war who had put their vision to the test and had led a successful war party. In some tribes even the proposition to put the vision to the test had to go before the elders, and the body of elders was guided by no mystic communications.

12] In cultures other than those of the western plains these limitations upon Dionysian practices were carried much further. Wherever vested rights and privileges were important in any community the conflict occasioned by such a cultural trait as the vision is obvious enough. It is a frankly disruptive cultural mechanism. In tribes where the conflict was strong a number of things might happen. The supernatural experience, to which they still gave lip service, might become an empty shell. If prestige was vested in cult groups and in families, these could not afford to grant individuals free access to the supernatural and teach them that all power came from such contact. There was no reason why they could not still teach the dogma of the free and open vision, and they did. But it was an hypocrisy. No man could exercise power by any authority except that of succession to his father's place in the cult in which he had membership. Among the Omaha, although all power passed down strictly within the family line and was valued for the sorcery that it was, they did not revise their traditional dogma of absolute and sole dependence upon the solitary vision as a sanction for supernatural power. On the Northwest Coast, and among the Aztecs of Mexico, where prestige was also a guarded privilege, different compromises occurred, but they were compromises which did not outlaw the Dionysian values.

13] The Dionysian bent in the North American vision quest, however, did not usually have to make compromise with prestige groups and their privileges. The experience was often sought openly by means of drugs and alcohol. Among the Indian tribes of Mexico the fermented juice of the fruit of the giant cactus was used ceremonially to obtain the blessed state which was to them supremely religious. The great ceremony of the year among the related Pima, by means of which all blessings were obtained, was the brewing of this cactus beer. The priests drank first, and then all the people, "to get religious." Intoxication, in their practice and in their poetry, is the synonym of religion. It has the same mingling of clouded vision and of insight. It gives the whole tribe, together, the exaltation that it associated with religion.

14] Drugs were much commoner means of attaining this experience. The peyote or mescal bean is a cactus button from the highlands of Mexico. The plant is eaten fresh by the Indian tribes within pilgrimage distance, but the button is traded as far as the Canadian border. It is always used ceremonially. Its effect is well known. It gives peculiar sensations of levitation and brilliant colour images, and is accompanied by very strong affect, either ultimate despair or release from all inadequacy and insecurity. There is no motor disturbance and no erotic excitation.

15] The cult of the peyote among the American Indians is still spreading. It is incorporated as the Indian Church in Oklahoma and among many tribes the older tribal rituals have paled before this cult. It is associated everywhere with some attitude toward the whites, either a religious opposition to their influence, or a doctrine of speedy acceptance of white ways, and it has many Christian elements woven into its fabric. The peyote is passed and eaten in the manner of the sacrament, first the peyote, then the water, round and round, with songs and prayers. It is a dignified all-night ceremony, and the effects prolong themselves during the following day. In other cases it is eaten for four nights, with four days given up to the excitation. Peyote, within the cults that espouse it, is identified with god. A large button of it is placed upon the ground altar and worshipped. All good comes from it. "It is the only holy thing I have known in my life"; "this medicine alone is holy, and has rid me of all evil." And it is the Dionysian experience of the peyote trance that constitutes its appeal and its religious authority.

16] The datura or the jimson weed is a more drastic poison. It is more local, being used in Mexico and among the tribes of Southern California. In this latter region it was given to boys at initiation, and under its influence they received their visions. I have been told of boys who died as a result of the drink. The boys were comatose, and some tribes speak of this condition continuing for one day and some for four. The Mojave, the eastern neighbours of these tribes, used datura to get luck in gambling and were said to be unconscious for four days. During this time the dream came which gave them the luck they sought.

17] Everywhere among the North American Indians, therefore, except in the southern Pueblos, we encounter this Dionysian dogma and practice of the vision-dream from which comes supernatural power. The Southwest is surrounded by peoples who seek the vision by fasting, by torture, by drugs and alcohol. But the Pueblos do not accept disruptive experiences and they do not derive supernatural power from them. If a Zuñi Indian has by chance a visual or auditory hallucination it is regarded as a sign of death. It is an experience to avoid, not one to seek by fasting. Supernatural power among the Pueblos comes from cult membership, a membership which has been bought and paid for and which involves the learning of verbatim ritual. There is no occasion when they are expected to overpass the boundaries of sobriety either in preparation for membership, or in initiation, or in the subsequent rise, by payment, to the higher grades, or in the exercise of religious prerogatives. They do not seek or value excess. Nevertheless the elements out of which the widespread vision quest is built up are present: the seeking of dangerous places, the friendship with a bird or animal, fasting, the belief in special blessings from supernatural encounters. But they are no longer integrated as a Dionysian experience. There is complete reinterpretation. Among the Pueblos men go out at night to feared or sacred places and listen for a voice, not that they may break through to communication with the supernatural, but that they may take the omens of good luck and bad. It is regarded as a minor ordeal during which they are badly frightened, and the great tabu connected with it is that they must not look behind on the way home, no matter what seems to be following. The objective performance is much the same as in the vision quest; in each case, they go out during the preparation for a difficult undertaking—in the Southwest, often a foot-race—and make capital of the darkness, the solitariness, the appearance of animals. But the experience which is elsewhere conceived as Dionysian, among the Pueblos is a mechanical taking of omens.

18] Fasting, the technique upon which the American Indian

most depended in attaining a self-induced vision, has received the same sort of reinterpretation. It is no longer utilized to dredge up experiences that normally lie below the level of consciousness; among the Pueblos it is a requirement for ceremonial cleanness. Nothing could be more unexpected to a Pueblo Indian than any theory of a connection between fasting and any sort of exaltation. Fasting is required during all priestly retreats, before participation in a dance, in a race, and on endless ceremonial occasions, but it is never followed by power-giving experience; it is never Dionysian.

19] The fate of the jimson-weed poisoning in the Southwest pueblos is much like that of the technique of fasting. The practice is present, but its teeth are drawn. The one-to-four-day jimson-weed trances of the Indians of Southern California are not for them. The drug is used as it was in ancient Mexico in order to discover a thief. In Zuñi the man who is to take the drug has a small quantity put into his mouth by the officiating priest, who then retires to the next room and listens for the incriminating name from the lips of the man who has taken the jimson-weed. He is not supposed to be comatose at any time; he alternately sleeps and walks about the room. In the morning he is said to have no memory of the insight he has received. The chief care is to remove every trace of the drug and two common desacratizing techniques are employed to take away the dangerous sacredness of the plant; first, he is given an emetic, four times, till every vestige of the drug is supposed to be ejected; then his hair is washed in yucca suds. The other Zuñi use of jimson weed is even further from any Dionysian purpose; members of the priestly orders go out at night to plant prayer-sticks on certain occasions "to ask the birds to sing for rain," and at such times a minute quantity of the powdered root is put into the eyes, ears, and mouth of each priest. Here all connections with the physical properties of the drug are lost sight of.

20] Peyote has had an even more drastic fate. The Pueblos are close to the Mexican plateau where the peyote button is obtained, and the Apache and the tribes of the plains with which they came most in contact were peyote-eaters. But the practice gained no foothold in the pueblos. A small anti-government group in Taos, the most atypical and Plains-like of the Pueblos, has recently taken it up. But elsewhere it has never been accepted. In their strict Apollonian *ethos,* the Pueblos distrust and reject those experiences which take the individual in any way out of bounds and forfeit his sobriety.

21] This repugnance is so strong that it has even been sufficient to keep American alcohol from becoming an administrative problem. Everywhere else on Indian reservations in the United States alcohol is an inescapable issue. There are no government regulations that can cope with the Indian's passion for whiskey. But in the pueblos the problem has never been important. They did not brew any native intoxicant in the old days, nor do they now. Nor is it a matter of course, as it is for instance with the near-by Apaches, that every trip to town, for old men or young, is a debauch. It is not that the Pueblos have a religious tabu against drinking. It is deeper than that. Drunkenness is repulsive to them. In Zuñi after the early introduction of liquor, the old men voluntarily outlawed it and the rule was congenial enough to be honoured.

22] Torture was even more consistently rejected. The Pueblos, especially the eastern Pueblos, were in contact with two very different cultures in which self-torture was of the greatest importance, the Plains Indians and the Mexican Penitentes. Pueblo culture also shares many traits with the now extinct torture-using civilization of ancient Mexico, where on all occasions one drew blood from parts of one's own body, especially from the tongue, as an offering to the gods. On the plains, self-torture was specialized as a technique for obtaining states of self-oblivion during which one obtained a vision. The Penitentes of New Mexico are the last surviving sect, in a far corner of the world, of the Flagellants of mediæval Spain, and they have retained to the present day the Good Friday observances of identification with the crucified Saviour. The climax of the rite is the crucifixion of the Christ, impersonated by one of the members of the cult. The procession emerges from the house of the Penitentes at dawn of Good Friday, the Christ staggering under the weight of the tremendous cross. Behind him are his brethren with bared backs who lash themselves at every slow step with their great whips of bayonet cactus to which are fastened barbs of the cholla. From a distance their backs look as if covered with a rich red cloth. The "way" is about a mile and a half, and when they reach the end the Christ is bound upon the cross and raised. If he, or one of the whippers, dies, his shoes are placed upon his doorstep, and no mourning is allowed for him.

23] The Pueblos do not understand self-torture. Every man's hand has its five fingers, and unless they have been tortured to secure a sorcery confession they are unscarred. There are no cicatrices upon their backs, no marks where strips of skin have been taken off. They have no rites in which they sacrifice their own blood, or use it for fertility. They used to hurt themselves to a certain extent in a few initiations at the moments of greatest excitement, but in such cases the whole matter was almost an affair of collegiate exuberance. In the Cactus Society, a warrior cult, they dashed about striking themselves and each other with cactus-blade whips; in the Fire Society they tossed fire about like confetti. Neither psychic danger nor abnormal experience is sought in either case. Certainly in the observed fire tricks of the Pueblos—as also in the fire tricks of the Plains—it is not self-torture that is sought. In the Fire Walk, whatever the means employed, feet are not burned, and when the fire is taken into the mouth the tongue is not blistered.

24] The Pueblo practice of beating with stripes is likewise without intent to torture. The lash does not draw blood. Far from glorying in any such excesses, as the Plains Indians do, a Zuñi child, whipped at adolescence or earlier, at the tribal initiation, may cry out and even call for his mother when he is struck by the initiating masked gods. The adults repudiate with distress the idea that the whips might raise welts. Whipping is "to take off the bad happenings"; that is, it is a trusted rite of exorcism. The fact that it is the same act that is used elsewhere for self-torture has no bearing upon the use that is made of it in this culture.

25] If ecstasy is not sought by fasting, by torture, or by drugs or alcohol, or under the guise of the vision, neither is it induced in the dance. Perhaps no people in North America spend more time in the dance than the Southwest Pueblos. But their object in it never is to attain self-oblivion. It is by the frenzy of the dance that the Greek cult of Dionysus was best known, and it recurs over and over in North America. The Ghost Dance of the Indians that swept the country in the 1870's was a round dance danced monotonously till the dancers, one after the other, fell rigid, prostrate on the ground. During their seizure they had visions of deliverance from the whites, and meanwhile the dance continued and others fell. It was the custom in most of the dozens of tribes to which it penetrated to hold the dance every Sunday. There were other and older dances also that were thoroughly Dionysian. The tribes of northern Mexico danced, frothing at the mouth, upon the altar. The shamans' dances of California required a cataleptic seizure. The Maidu used to hold shamans' contests in which that one was victor who danced down the others; that is, who did not succumb to the hypnotic suggestions of the dance. On the Northwest Coast the whole winter ceremonial was thought of as being designed to tame the man who had returned mad and possessed by the spirits. The initiates played out their rôle with the frenzy that was expected of them. They danced like Siberian shamans, tethered by four ropes strung to the four directions so that they could be controlled if they ran into harm to themselves or others.

26] Of all this there is no suggestion in all the dance occasions of Zuñi. The dance, like their ritual poetry, is a monotonous compulsion of natural forces by reiteration. The tireless pounding of their feet draws together the mist in the sky and heaps it into the piled rain clouds. It forces out the rain upon the earth. They are bent not at all upon an ecstatic experience, but upon so thorough-going an identification with nature that the forces of nature will swing to their purposes. This intent dictates the form and spirit of Pueblo dances. There is nothing wild about them. It is the cumulative force of the rhythm, the perfection of forty men moving as one, that makes them effective.

27] No one has conveyed this quality of Pueblo dancing more precisely than D. H. Lawrence. "All the men sing in unison, as they move with the soft, yet heavy bird tread which is the whole of the dance, with bodies bent a little forward, shoulders and heads loose and heavy, feet powerful but soft, the men tread the rhythm into the centre of the earth. The drums keep up the pulsating heart beat and for hours, hours, it goes on." Sometimes they are dancing the sprouting corn up out of the earth, sometimes they are calling the game animals by the tramp of their feet, sometimes they are constraining the white cumulus clouds that are slowly piling up the sky on a desert afternoon. Even the presence of these in the sky, whether or not they vouchsafe rain, is a blessing from the supernaturals upon the dance, a sign that their rite is accepted. If rain comes, that is the sign and seal of the power of their dance. It is the answer. They dance on through the swift Southwest downpour, their feathers wet and heavy, their embroidered kilts and mantles drenched. But they have been favoured by the gods. The clowns make merry in the deep adobe mud, sliding at full length in the puddles and paddling in the half-liquid earth. It is their recognition that their feet in the dance have the compulsion of natural forces upon the storm clouds and have been powerful to bring the rain.

28] Even where the Pueblos share with their near neighbours dance patterns the very forms of which are instinct with Dionysian meaning, they are used among the Pueblos with complete sobriety. The Cora of northern Mexico have a whirling dance, like so many other tribes of that part of the country, and the climax of it comes when the dancer, having reached the greatest velocity and obliviousness of which he is capable, whirls back and back and upon the very ground altar itself. At any other moment, on any other occasion, this is sacrilege. But of such things the highest Dionysian values are made. In his madness the altar is destroyed, trampled into the sand again. At the end the dancer falls upon the destroyed altar.

29] In the sets of dances in the underground kiva chamber in the Hopi Snake Dance they also dance upon the altar. But there is no frenzy. It is prescribed, like a movement of a Virginia

Reel. One of the commonest formal dance patterns of the Pueblos is built up of the alternation of two dance groups who in each set vary a similar theme, appearing from alternate sides of the dancing space. Finally for the last set the two come out simultaneously from both directions. In this kiva snake dance, the Antelope Society dancers are opposed to the Snake dancers. In the first set the Antelope priest dances, squatting, the circuit of the altar, and retires. The Snake priest repeats. In the second set Antelope receives a vine in his mouth and dances before the initiates, trailing it over their knees. He retires. Snake follows, receiving a live rattlesnake in his mouth in the same fashion and trailing it over the initiates' knees. In the final set Antelope and Snake come out together, still in the squatting position, and dance not the circuit of the altar but upon it, ending the dance. It is a formal sequence like that of a Morris dance, and it is danced in complete sobriety.

30] Nor is the dancing with snakes a courting of the dangerous and the terrible in Hopi. There is current in our civilization so common a horror of snakes that we misread the Snake Dance. We readily attribute to the dancers the emotions we should feel in like case. But snakes are not often regarded with horror by the American Indians. They are often reverenced, and occasionally their holiness makes them dangerous, as anything may be that is sacred or *manitou*. But our unreasoned repulsion is no part of their reaction. Nor are snakes especially feared for their attack. There are Indian folktales that end, "and that is why the rattlesnake is not dangerous." The habits of the rattlesnake make it easy to subdue and Indians readily cope with it. The feeling tone of the dancers toward the snakes in the Snake Dance is not that of unholy dread or repulsion, but that of cult members toward their animal patron. Moreover, it has been repeatedly verified that the poison sacs of the rattlesnakes are removed for the dance. They are bruised or pinched out, and when the snakes are released after the dance, the sacs grow again and fill with poison as before. But for the period of the dance the snakes are harmless. The situation, therefore, in the mind of the Hopi dancer is not Dionysian either in its secular or in its supernatural aspect.

It is an excellent example of the fact that the same objective behaviour may be according to inculcated ideas, either a Dionysian courting of dangerous and repulsive experience, or a sober and formal ceremonial.

31] Whether by the use of drugs, of alcohol, of fasting, of torture, or of the dance, no experiences are sought or tolerated among the Pueblos that are outside of ordinary sensory routine. The Pueblos will have nothing to do with disruptive individual experiences of this type. The love of moderation to which their civilization is committed has no place for them. Therefore they have no shamans.

32] Shamanism is one of the most general human institutions. The shaman is the religious practitioner who, by whatever kind of personal experience is recognized as supernatural in his tribe, gets his power directly from the gods. He is often, like Cassandra and others of those who spoke with tongues, a person whose instability has marked him out for his profession. In North America shamans are characteristically those who have the experience of the vision. The priest, on the other hand, is the depository of ritual and the administrator of cult activities. The Pueblos have no shamans; they have only priests.

33] The Zuñi priest holds his position because of relationship claims, or because he has bought his way up through various orders of a society, or because he has been chosen by the chief priests to serve for the year as impersonator of the kachina priests. In any case he has qualified by learning vast quantity of ritual, both of act and of word. All his authority is derived from the office he holds, from the ritual he administers. It must be word-perfect, and he is responsible for the traditional correctness of each complicated ceremony he performs. The Zuñi phrase for a person with power is "one who knows how." There are persons who "know how" in the most sacred cults, in racing, in gambling, and in healing. In other words, they have learned their power verbatim from traditional sources. There is no point at which they are licensed to claim the power of their religion as the sanction for any act of their own initiative. They may not even approach the supernatural except with group warrant at stated intervals. Every prayer, every cult act, is performed at an authorized and universally known season, and in the traditional fashion. The most individual religious act in Zuñi is the planting of prayer-sticks, those delicately fashioned offerings to the gods which are half-buried in sacred places and carry their specific prayer to the supernaturals. But even prayer-sticks may not be offered on the initiative even of the highest priests. One of the folk-tales tells of the chief priest of Zuñi who made prayer-sticks and went out to bury them. It was not the time of the moon when prayer-sticks are planted by the members of the medicine societies, and the people said, "Why does the chief priest plant prayer-sticks? He must be conjuring." As a matter of fact, he was using his power for a private revenge. If the most personal of all religious acts may not be performed on the private initiative even of the chief priest, more formal acts are doubly fenced about with public sanctions. No one must ever wonder why an individual is moved to pray.

34] The Pueblos in their institution of the priest, and the rest of aboriginal America in its institution of the shaman, select and reward two opposing types of personality. The Plains Indians in all their institutions gave scope to the self-reliant man who could easily assume authority. He was rewarded beyond all others. The innovations the returned Crow Indian brought back from his vision might be infinitesimal. That is not the point. Every Buddhist monk and every mediæval Christian mystic saw in his vision what his brethren had seen before. But they and the aboriginal Crow claimed power—or godliness—on the authority of their private experience. The Indian went back to his people in the strength of his vision, and the tribe carried out as a sacred privilege the instructions he had received. In healing, each man knew his own individual power, and asked nothing of any other votary. This dogma was modified in practice, for man perpetuates tradition even in those institutions that attempt to flaunt it. But the dogmas of their religion gave cultural warrant for an amazing degree of self-reliance and personal authority.

35] This self-reliance and personal initiative on the plains were expressed not only in shamanism but in their passionate enthusiasm for the guerrilla warfare that occupied them. Their war parties were ordinarily less than a dozen strong, and the individual acted alone in their simple engagements in a way that stands at the other pole from the rigid discipline and subordination of modern warfare. Their war was a game in which each individual amassed counts. These counts were for cutting loose a picketed horse, or touching an enemy, or taking a scalp. The individual, usually by personal dare-deviltry, acquired as many as he could, and used them for joining societies, giving feasts, qualifying as a chief. Without initiative and the ability to act alone, an Indian of the plains was not recognized in his society. The testimony of early explorers, the rise of outstanding individuals in their conflicts with the whites, the contrast with the Pueblos, all go to show how their institutions fostered personality, almost in the Nietzschean sense of the superman. They saw life as the drama of the individual progressing upward through grades of men's societies, through acquisitions of supernatural power, through feasts and victories. The initiative rested always with him. His deeds of prowess were counted for him personally, and it was his prerogative to boast of them on ritual occasions, and to use them in every way to further his personal ambitions.

36] The ideal man of the Pueblos is another order of being. Personal authority is perhaps the most vigorously disparaged trait in Zuñi. "A man who thirsts for power or knowledge, who wishes to be as they scornfully phrase it 'a leader of his people,' receives nothing but censure and will very likely be persecuted for sorcery," and he often has been. Native authority of manner is a liability in Zuñi, and witchcraft is the ready charge against a person who possesses it. He is hung by the thumbs until he "confesses." It is all Zuñi can do with a man of strong personality. The ideal man in Zuñi is a person of dignity and affability who has never tried to lead, and who has never called forth comment from his neighbours. Any conflict, even though all right is on his side, is held against him. Even in contests of skill like their foot races, if a man wins habitually he is debarred from running. They are interested in a game that a number can play with even chances, and an outstanding runner spoils the game: they will have none of him.

37] A good man has, in Dr. Bunzel's words, "a pleasing address, a yielding disposition, and a generous heart." The highest praise, describing an impeccable townsman, runs: "He is a nice polite man. No one ever hears anything from him. He never gets into trouble. He's Badger clan and Muhekwe kiva, and he always dances in the summer dances." He should "talk lots," as they say —that is, he should always set people at their ease—and he should without fail co-operate easily with others either in the field or in ritual, never betraying a suspicion of arrogance or a strong emotion.

38] He avoids office. He may have it thrust upon him, but he does not seek it. When the kiva offices must be filled, the hatchway of the kiva is fastened and all the men are imprisoned until someone's excuses have been battered down. The folktales always relate of good men their unwillingness to take office—though they always take it. A man must avoid the appearance of leadership. When the chosen person has been prevailed upon and has been initiated in the office, he has not been given authority in our sense. His post carries with it no sanction for important action. The council of Zuñi is made up of the highest priests, and priests have no jurisdiction in cases of conflict or violence. They are holy men and must not have a quarrel put before them. Only the war chiefs have some measure of executive authority, not in war so much as in peace-time policing powers. They make proclamation of a coming rabbit hunt, or coming dances, they summon priests and co-operate with the medicine societies. The crime that they traditionally have to deal with is witchcraft. Another crime, that of betraying to the uninitiated boys the secret of the kachinas, is punished by the masked gods themselves, summoned by the head of the kachina cult. There are no other crimes. Theft rarely occurs and is a private matter. Adultery is no crime and the strain that arises from such an act is easily taken care of under their marriage arrangements. Homicide, in the one case that is remembered, was settled quickly by payments between the two families.

39] The priests of the high council, therefore, are not disturbed. They administer the main features of the ceremonial calendar. The successful prosecution of their plans could be blocked at every turn by an unco-operative minor priest. He would only have to sulk, refusing, for instance, to set up his altar or to furnish his kachina priest mask. The priestly council could only wait and defer the ceremonial. But everyone co-operates, and no show of authority is called for.

40] This same lack of personal exercise of authority is as characteristic of domestic situations as it is of religious. The matrilineal and matrilocal household of course makes necessary a different allocation of authority from that with which we are familiar. But matrilineal societies do not usually dispense with a male person of authority in the household even though the father does not qualify. The mother's brother as the male head of the matrilineal household is arbiter and responsible head. But Zuñi does not recognize any authority as vested in the mother's brother, and certainly not in the father. Neither of them disciplines the children of his household. Babies are much fondled by the men folk. They carry them when they are ailing and hold them in their laps evenings. But they do not discipline them. The virtue of co-operation holds domestic life true to form just as it holds religious life, and no situations arise that need to be drastically handled. What would they be? Marriage is in other cultures the almost universal occasion where some authority is exercised. But among the Pueblos it is arranged with little formality. Marriage elsewhere in the world involves property rights and economic exchange, and on all such occasions the elders have prerogatives. But in Zuñi marriage there are no stakes in which the elders are interested. The slight emphasis upon possessions among the Pueblos makes a casual affair not only of the elsewhere difficult situation of marriage but of a dozen others, all those which according to other cultural forms involve investment of group property for the young man. Zuñi simply eliminates the occasions.

41] Every arrangement militates against the possibility of the child's suffering from an Œdipus complex. Malinowski has pointed out for the Trobriands that the structure of society gives to the uncle authority that is associated in our culture with the father. In Zuñi, not even the uncles exercise authority. Occasions are not tolerated which would demand its exercise. The child grows up without either the resentments or the compensatory day-dreams of ambition that have their roots in this familiar situation. When the child himself becomes an adult, he has not the motivations that lead him to imagine situations in which authority will be relevant.

42] Therefore the initiation of boys is the strange event that it is in Zuñi, strange, that is, in comparison with the practices that are constantly met with in the world. For the initiation of boys is very often an uninhibited exercise of their prerogatives by those in authority; it is a hazing by those in power of those whom they must now admit to tribal status. These rites occur in much the same forms in Africa, in South America, and in Australia. In South Africa the boys are herded under men with long sticks who use them freely on all occasions. They must run the gantlet with blows raining upon them, they must expect constant blows from behind accompanied by jeers. They must sleep naked without blankets in the coldest months of the year, their heads, not their feet, turned toward the fire. They may not smear the ground to keep away the white worms that bite them at night. At the first signs of daybreak they must go to the pool and stay submerged in the cold water till the sun appears. They may not drink a drop of water for the three months of the initiation camp, they are fed with disgusting food. In compensation, unintelligible formulas are taught them with a great show of importance, and esoteric words.

43] In American Indian tribes so much time is not usually given to boys' initiation, but the ideas are often the same. The Apache, with whom the Zuñi have many relations, say that breaking a boy is like breaking a young colt. They force him to make holes in the ice and bathe, run with water in his mouth, humiliate him on his trial war parties, and generally bully him. The Indians of Southern California bury him in hills of stinging ants.

44] But in Zuñi the boy's initiation is never in any way an ordeal. It is thought to make the rite very valuable if the children cry even under the mild strokes they receive. The child is accompanied at every step by his ceremonial father and takes his strokes either clasped upon the old man's back or kneeling between his knees. He is given security by his accompanying sponsor, rather than pushed violently out of the nest, like the South African boy. And the final initiation ends when the boy himself takes the yucca whip and strikes the kachina as he has himself been struck. The initiation does not unload upon the children the adults' pitiful will to power. It is an exorcising and purifying rite. It makes the children valuable by giving them group status. The whipping is an act which they have seen their elders court all their lives as a blessing and a cure. It is their accolade in the supernatural world.

45] The lack of opportunities for the exercise of authority, both in religious and in domestic situations, is knit up with another fundamental trait: the insistence upon sinking the individual in the group. In Zuñi, responsibility and power are always distributed and the group is made the functioning unit. The accepted way to approach the supernatural is in group ritual. The accepted way to secure family subsistence is by household partnership. Neither in religion nor in economics is the individual autonomous. In religion a man who is anxious about his harvest does not offer prayer for the rain that will save it; he dances in the summer rain dances. A man does not pray for the recovery of his son who is ill; he brings the doctors' order of Big Fire Society to cure him. Those individual prayers that are allowed, at the personal planting of prayer-sticks, at the head-washings of ceremonial cleanliness, at the calling of the medicine men or a ceremonial father, have validity only because they are necessary parts of a larger whole, the group ritual to which they belong. They could no more be separated from it and still have power than one word could be taken from the long magic formulas and retain by itself the efficacy of the perfect prayer.

46] Sanction for all acts comes from the formal structure, not from the individual. A chief priest, as we saw, can plant prayer-sticks only as chief priest and at those times when he is known to be officially functioning. A medicine man doctors because he is a member of the cult of medicine men. Membership in that cult does not merely strengthen powers of his own, as is the case on the plains, but it is the sole source of his powers. Even the killing of Navajos is judged in the same way. A folktale tells a story of consummate treachery. A rich Navajo and his wife came to trade in a Zuñi household, and the men murdered him for his turquoise. "But they had not the power of the scalp"; that is, they did not join the war cult, which would have made it right for them to have perpetrated the deed. According to Zuñi thought there is institutional sanction even for this act, and they condemn merely the deed that does not avail itself of its institutional warrant.

47] The Zuñi people therefore devote themselves to the constituted forms of their society. They sink individuality in them. They do not think of office, and possession of priestly bundles, as steps in the upward path of ambition. A man when he can afford it gets himself a mask in order to increase the number of things "to live by" in his household, and the number of masks his kiva commands. He takes his due part in the calendric rituals and at great expense builds a new house to entertain the kachina priest impersonations at Shalako, but he does it with a degree of anonymity and lack of personal reference that is hard to duplicate in other cultures. Their whole orientation of personal activity is unfamiliar to us.

48] Just as in religion the acts and motivations of the individual are singularly without personal reference, so too in economic life. The economic unit is, as we have seen, a very unstable group of menfolk. The core of the household, the permanent group, is a relationship group of women, but the women are not the ones who function importantly in the great economic enterprises such as agriculture or herding, or even work in turquoise. And the men who are necessary in the fundamental occupations are a shifting group loosely held together. The husbands of the daughters of the household will return to their maternal households upon a domestic storm and will henceforth have no responsibility for feeding or housing their children whom they leave behind. There are, besides, in the household the miscellaneous male blood relatives of the female relationship group: the unmarried, the widowed, the divorced, and those who are awaiting the passing of temporary unpleasantness in their wives' households. Yet this miscellaneous group, whatever its momentary composition, pools its work in filling the common corn storeroom, and this corn remains the collective property of the women of the household. Even if some newly cultivated fields belong as private property to any of these men, all the men jointly farm them for the common storeroom just as they do ancestral fields.

49] The custom is the same in regard to houses. The men build them, and jointly, and they belong to the women. A man, leaving his wife in the fall, may be leaving behind him the house he has spent his year building and a full cornroom, the result of his season's farming. But there is no thought of his having any individual claim upon either; and he is not thought of as defrauded. He pooled his work in his household's, and the results are a group supply; if he is no longer a member of that group, that is his affair. Sheep are today a considerable source of income, and are owned by men individually. But they are co-operatively herded by groups of male kindred, and new economic motivations are very slow in making their appearance.

50] Just as according to the Zuñi ideal a man sinks his activities in those of the group and claims no personal authority, so also he is never violent. Their Apollonian commitment to the mean in the Greek sense is never clearer than in their cultural handling of the emotions. Whether it is anger or love or jealousy or grief, moderation is the first virtue. The fundamental tabu upon their holy men during their periods of office is against any suspicion of anger. Controversies, whether they are ceremonial or economic or domestic, are carried out with an unparalleled lack of vehemence.

51] Every day in Zuñi there are fresh instances of their mildness. One summer a family I knew well had given me a house to live in, and because of some complicated circumstances another family claimed the right to dispose of the dwelling. When feeling was at its height, Quatsia, the owner of the house, and her husband were with me in the living-room when a man I did not know began cutting down the flowering weeds that had not yet been hoed out of the yard. Keeping the yard free of growth is a chief prerogative of a house-owner, and therefore the man who claimed the right to dispose of the house was taking this occasion to put his claim publicly upon record. He did not enter the house or challenge Quatsia and Leo, who were inside, but he hacked slowly at the weeds. Inside, Leo sat immobile on his heels against the wall, peaceably chewing a leaf. Quatsia, however, allowed herself to flush. "It is an insult," she said to me. "The man out there knows that Leo is serving as priest this year and he can't be angry. He shames us before the whole village by taking care of our yard." The interloper finally raked up his wilted weeds, looked proudly at the neat yard, and went home. No words were even spoken between them. For Zuñi it was an insult of sorts, and by his morning's work on the yard the rival claimant sufficiently expressed his protest. He pressed the matter no further.

52] Marital jealousy is similarly soft-pedalled. They do not meet adultery with violence. A usual response on the plains to the wife's adultery was to cut off the fleshy part of her nose. This was done even in the Southwest by non-Pueblo tribes like the Apache. But in Zuñi the unfaithfulness of the wife is no excuse for violence. The husband does not regard it as a violation of his rights. If she is unfaithful, it is normally a first step in changing husbands, and their institutions make this sufficiently easy so that it is a really tolerable procedure. They do not contemplate violence.

53] Wives are often equally moderate when their husbands are known to be unfaithful. As long as the situation is not unpleasant enough for relations to be broken off, it is ignored. The season before one of Dr. Bunzel's visits in Zuñi one of the young husbands of the household in which she lived had been carrying on an extra-marital affair that became bruited about all over the pueblo. The family ignored the matter completely. At last the white trader, a guardian of morals, expostulated with the wife. The couple had been married a dozen years and had three children; the wife belonged to an important family. The trader set forth with great earnestness the need of making a show of authority and putting an end to her husband's outrageous conduct. "So," his wife said, "I didn't wash his clothes. Then he knew that I knew that everybody knew, and he stopped going with that girl." It was effective, but not a word was passed. There were no outbursts, no recriminations, not even an open recognition of the crisis.

54] Wives, however, are allowed another course of action which is not sanctioned in the case of deserted husbands. A wife may fall upon her rival and beat her up publicly. They call each other names and give each other a black eye. It never settles anything, and even in the rare cases when it occurs, it dies down as quickly as it has flared. It is the only recognized fist-fight in Zuñi. If on the other hand a woman remains peacefully with her husband while he conducts amour after amour, her family are angry and bring pressure to bear upon her to separate from him. "Everybody says she must love him," they say, and all her relatives are ashamed. She is disobeying the rules that are laid down for her.

55] For the traditional course is that of divorce. If a man finds his wife's female relatives uncongenial, he is free to return to his mother's household. It provides a means of avoiding domestic intimacy with individuals he dislikes, and he merely dissolves the relationships which he has found difficult to handle amicably.

56] If the Pueblos provide institutions that effectively minimize the appearance of a violent emotion like jealousy, they are even more concerned to provide Apollonian techniques at death. Nevertheless there is a difference. Jealousy, it is evident from the practices of many different cultures, is one of the emotions that can be most effectively fostered by cultural arrangements, or it can be outlawed. But bereavement is not so easily escaped. The death of a near relative is the closest thrust that existence deals. It threatens the solidarity of the group, calls for drastic readjustments, especially if the dead individual is an adult, and often means loneliness and sorrow for the survivors.

57] The Pueblos are essentially realistic, and they do not deny sorrow at death. They do not, like some of the cultures we shall discuss, convert mourning for a near relative into an ambitious display or a terror situation. They treat it as loss, and as important loss. But they provide detailed techniques for getting past it as quickly and with as little violence as possible. The emphasis is upon making the mourner forget. They cut a lock of hair from the deceased and make a smudge to purify those who grieve too much. They scatter black cornmeal with the left hand—associated with death—to "make their road black"; that is, to put darkness between themselves and their grief. In Isleta, on the evening of the fourth day, before the relatives separate after the death, the officiating priest makes a ground altar on which they put the prayer-sticks for the dead, the dead man's bow and arrow, the hairbrush used to prepare the body for burial, and articles of the dead man's clothing. There are, besides, the bowl of medicine water, and a basket of food to which everyone has contributed. On the floor, from the house door to the altar, the priests make a road of meal for the deceased to come in by. They gather to feed the dead man for the last time and send him away. One of the priests sprinkles everyone from the medicine bowl, and then opens the house door. The chief speaks to the dead men, bidding him to come and eat. They hear the footsteps outside and his fumbling at the door. He enters and eats. Then the chief sprinkles the road for him to leave by, and the priests "chase him out of the village." They take with them the prayer-sticks for the dead, the pieces of his clothing and his personal possessions, the hairbrush and the bowl of food. They take them outside the village and break the hairbrush and the bowl, burying everything out of sight. They return on a run, not looking behind them, and bolt the door against the dead by scratching a cross upon it with a flint knife to prevent his entrance. It is the formal breach with the dead. The chief speaks to the people telling them that they shall not remember any more. "It is now four years he is dead." In ceremonial and in folklore they use often the idea that the day has become the year or the year the day. Time has elapsed to free them of grief. The people are dismissed, and the mourning is over.

58] Whatever the psychological bent of a people, however, death is a stubbornly inescapable fact, and in Zuñi the Apollonian discomfort at not being able to outlaw the upheaval of death on the part of the nearest of kin is very clearly expressed in their institutions. They make as little of death as possible. Funeral rites are the simplest and least dramatic of all the rites they possess. None of the elaboration that goes into their calendric ceremonials is to be found on this occasion. The corpse is interred at once, and no priests officiate.

59] But a death that touches an individual closely is not so easily disposed of even in Zuñi. They conceptualize this persistence of grief or discomfort by the belief that the surviving spouse is in great danger. His dead wife may "pull him back"; that is, in her loneliness she may take him with her. It is exactly the same for a wife whose husband has died. If the survivor grieves he is the more liable to the danger. Therefore he is treated with all the precautions with which the person who has taken life is surrounded. He must isolate himself for four days from ordinary life, neither speak nor be spoken to, take an emetic for purification every morning, and go outside the village to offer black cornmeal with his left hand. He swings it four times around his head and casts it from him to "take off the bad happening," they say. On the fourth day he plants his prayer-sticks to the dead and prays her, in the one prayer in Zuñi that is addressed to an individual, either human or supernatural, to leave him at peace, not to drag him down with her, and to grant him

> All of your good fortune whatsoever,
> Preserving us along a safe road.

The danger that is upon him is not considered over for a year. During that time his dead wife will be jealous if he approaches a woman. When the year is up he has intercourse with a stranger and gives her a gift. With the gift goes the danger that has haunted him. He is free again, and he takes another wife. It is the same with a wife whose husband has died.

60] On the western plains mourning behaviour was at the furthest remove from such an anxiety display. It was a Dionysian indulgence in uninhibited grief. All their behaviour stressed rather than avoided the despair and upheaval that is involved in death. The women gashed their heads and their legs, and cut off their fingers. Long lines of women marched through the camp after the death of an important person, their legs bare and bleeding. The blood on their heads and the calves of their legs they let cake and did not remove. As soon as the corpse was taken out for burial, everything in the lodge was thrown on the ground for anyone to possess himself of. The possessions of the dead were not thought to be polluted, but all the property of the household was given away because in its grief the family could have no interest in things they owned and no use for them. Even the lodge was pulled down and given to another. Nothing was left to the widow but the blanket around her. The dead man's favourite horses were led to his grave and killed there while all the people wailed.

61] Excessive individual mourning also was expected and understood. After the interment a wife or a daughter might insist upon staying at the grave, wailing and refusing to eat, taking no notice of those who tried to urge her back to the camp. A woman, especially, but sometimes a man, might go out wailing alone in dangerous places and sometimes received visions that gave supernatural power. In some tribes women often went to the graves and wailed for years, and in later years still went on pleasant afternoons to sit beside them without wailing.

62] The abandon of grief for children is especially characteristic. The extremity of the parents' grief could be expressed among the Dakota by their coming naked into the camp, wailing. It was the only occasion on which such a thing could happen. An old writer says of his experience among other Plains tribes, "Should anyone offend the parent during this time [of mourning] his death would most certainly follow, as the man, being in profound sorrow, seeks something on which to wreak his revenge, and he soon after goes to war, to kill or to be killed, either being immaterial to him in that state." They courted death as the Pueblos pray to be delivered from the awful possibility of it.

63] These two attitudes at death are familiar types of contrasted behaviour, and most individuals recognize the congeniality of one or the other. The Pueblos have institutionalized the one, and the Plains the other. This does not mean, of course, that violent and uninhibited grief is called up in each member of a bereaved family on the western plains, or that in the pueblos after being told to forget he adjusts himself with only such discomfort as finds expression in breaking a hairbrush. What is true is that in one culture he finds the one emotion already channelled for him, and in the other the other. Most human beings take the channel that is ready made in their culture. If they can take this channel, they are provided with adequate means of expression. If they cannot, they have all the problems of the aberrant everywhere.

64] There is still another way in which the Apollonian ideal expresses itself in Pueblo institutions. They do not culturally elaborate themes of terror and danger. They have none of the Dionysian will to create situations of contamination and fear. Such indulgences are very common in mourning all over the world—burial is an orgy of terror, not of grief. In Australian tribes the nearest of kin fall upon the skull and pound it to bits that it may not trouble them. They break the bones of the legs that the ghost may not pursue them. In Isleta, however, they break the hairbrush, not the bones of the corpse. The Navajo, the people closest to the Pueblos, burn the lodge and everything in it at death. Nothing the dead man has owned can pass casually to another. It is contaminated. Among the Pueblos only his bow and arrow and his mili, the medicine man's fetish of a perfect corn ear, are buried with the dead, and the mili is denuded first of all its valuable macaw feathers. They throw away nothing at all. The Pueblos in all their death institutions are symbolizing the ending of this man's life, not the precautions against the contamination of his corpse, or against the envy and vindictiveness of his ghost.

65] Their cosmological ideas are another form in which they have given expression to their extraordinarily consistent spirit. The same lack of intensity, of conflict, and of danger which they have institutionalized in this world, they project also upon the other world. The supernaturals, as Dr. Bunzel says, "have no animus against man. Inasmuch as they may withhold their gifts, their assistance must be secured by offerings, prayers and magical practices." But it is no placation of evil forces. The idea is foreign to them. They reckon, rather, that the supernaturals like what men like, and if men like dancing so will the supernaturals. Therefore they bring the supernaturals back to dance in Zuñi by donning their masks, they take out the medicine bundles and "dance" them. It gives them pleasure. Even the corn in the storeroom must be danced. "During the winter solstice, when all ritual groups are holding their ceremonies, the heads of households take six perfect ears of corn and hold them in a basket while they sing to them. This is called 'dancing the corn' and is performed that the corn may not feel neglected during the ceremonial season." So too the great Dance of the Corn, now no longer performed, culminated in this enjoyment they had the means of sharing with the corn ears.

66] They do not picture the universe, as we do, as a conflict of good and evil. They are not dualistic. The European notion of witchcraft, in becoming domesticated in the pueblos, has had to undergo strange transformation. It derives among them from no Satanic majesty pitted against a good God. They have fitted it into their own scheme, and witch power is suspect not because it is given by the devil, but because it "rides" its possessors, and once assumed, cannot be laid aside. Any other supernatural power is assumed for the occasion calling it forth. One indicates by planting prayer-sticks and observing the tabus that one is handling sacred things. When the occasion is over, one goes to one's father's sisters to have one's head washed and is again upon a secular footing. Or a priest returns his power to another priest that it may rest until it is called for again. The idea and techniques of removing sacredness are as familiar to them as those of removing a curse were in mediæval times. In Pueblo witchcraft no such techniques of freeing oneself of supernatural power are provided. One cannot be quit of the uncanny thing, and for that reason witchcraft is bad and threatening.

67] It is difficult for us to lay aside our picture of the universe as a struggle between good and evil and see it as the Pueblos see it. They do not see the seasons, nor man's life, as a race run by life and death. Life is always present, death is always present. Death is no denial of life. The seasons unroll themselves before us, and man's life also. Their attitude involves "no resignation, no subordination of desire to a stronger force, but the sense of man's oneness with the universe." When they pray they say to their gods:

> We shall be one person.

They exchange intimate relationship terms with them:

> Holding your country,
> Holding your people,
> You will sit down quietly for us.
> As children to one another
> We shall always remain.
> My child,[1]
> My mother,[1]
> According to my words
> Even so may it be.

They speak of exchanging breath with their gods:

> Far off on all sides
> I have as my fathers life-giving priests [2]
> Asking for their life-giving breath,
> Their breath of old age,
> Their breath of waters,
> Their breath of seeds,
> Their breath of riches,
> Their breath of fecundity,
> Their breath of strong spirit,
> Their breath of power,
> Their breath of all good fortune
>   with which they are possessed,

[1] Gods are here addressed as the children of mortals no less than their parents.
[2] Supernatural beings; gods.

> Asking for their breath,
> Into our [3] warm bodies taking their breath,
> We shall add to your [4] breath.
> Do not despise the breath of your fathers,
> But draw it into your body. . . .
> That we may finish our roads together.
> May my father bless you with life;
> May your road be fulfilled.

The breath of the gods is their breath, and by their common sharing all things are accomplished.

68] Like their version of man's relation to other men, their version of man's relation to the cosmos gives no place to heroism and man's will to overcome obstacles. It has no sainthood for those who,

> Fighting, fighting, fighting,
> Die driven against the wall.

It has its own virtues, and they are singularly consistent. The ones that are out of place they have outlawed from their universe. They have made, in one small but long-established cultural island in North America, a civilization whose forms are dictated by the typical choices of the Apollonian, all of whose delight is in formality and whose way of life is the way of measure and of sobriety.

Questions

The clarity of arrangement in "The Pueblos of New Mexico" is the result of the clarity of the author's theme idea. Dr. Ruth Benedict, an eminent anthropologist, bases her essay on a thoroughgoing knowledge of Pueblo culture. Her account is far more, however, than an accumulation and survey of facts about the Zuñi. Rather it is an interpretation of an impressive mass of data; each individual item is placed in the position best calculated to support the general idea. Nothing is stuck in or tacked on.

In analyzing the essay the student should first get the concepts of "Dionysian" and "Apollonian" fixed firmly in his mind and then

---

[3] The medicine man's.   [4] The patient's.

attempt to see how these concepts are carried through each successive topic.

1. Who was Dionysus? Who was Apollo? Look up the words in an unabridged dictionary in order to understand the application of the terms "Dionysian" and "Apollonian" in this selection.

2. What is meant by "measure in the Hellenic sense" (paragraph 1)? Why does Dr. Benedict depend on Greek terms to define her ideas even though she is describing an American Indian civilization?

3. Dr. Benedict's article is not intended for an audience of specialists and her vocabulary is, on the whole, understandable to the layman; such technical terms as are used are usually explained in context. A few of the words, however, have a specialized meaning. Be sure you understand the way in which each of the following terms is used: *cultural mechanism* (paragraph 11); *affect* (paragraph 14); *comatose* (paragraph 16); *desacratizing* (paragraph 19); *ethos* (paragraph 20); *matrilineal* (paragraph 40); *matrilocal* (paragraph 40); *kachina* (paragraph 44).

4. Paragraphs 5 through 16 describe in considerable detail practices among Indian tribes other than the Pueblos. The general subject matter of these paragraphs is the vision-dream.

   a. What trait of character is illustrated by all the practices used to attain the vision-dream? Explain why this trait is properly called "Dionysian."

   b. What is the author's purpose in spending twelve paragraphs on non-Pueblo practices before she even begins to discuss the Pueblos?

   c. Within this section, how do paragraphs 10, 11, and 12 differ from the rest in subject matter?

   d. Paragraphs 13 through 16 are obviously a unit, for they all deal with the use of drugs and alcohol to achieve an ecstatic state. In what other way is the subject matter of these paragraphs distinguished from the practices described in paragraphs 5 through 9?

5. Assume that the following were substituted for the first three sentences of paragraph 17.

   The Pueblos, unlike other North American Indians, do not accept disruptive experiences and do not derive supernatural power from them.

This substituted sentence would be admissible as a transition. In what way is it less satisfactory than the author's fuller transitional method? Why is the author's method of particular importance in a long article?

6. Paragraph 17 begins a discussion of those practices in Pueblo civilization comparable to the practices already described among other North American Indians (paragraphs 5 through 16).

   a. Through what paragraph does this discussion extend?

   b. The order in which the use of specific stimulants is considered is not the same in the two sections. Can you see any reason for the change?

   c. Paragraph 22 is devoted to non-Pueblo practices. Do you think that this material could have been inserted in paragraph 5 where torture is first mentioned? Why or why not?

7. Read through the rest of the essay and mark all those paragraphs which are concerned with behavior in Indian tribes other than the Pueblo.

   a. What are the instances in which Dr. Benedict does not provide a contrast, or not a very full contrast, to the practice described among the Pueblos? Can you explain, in each instance, why such a contrast should be omitted or abridged?

   b. Would it have been possible for the author to collect all her material on contrasting Indian civilizations at the beginning of the essay? Explain your answer. Under what circumstances is it better for the writer to shift back and forth between the two main subjects compared, as in this selection?

8. Paragraphs 25 through 30 are concerned with the dance.

   a. In what way is the attitude toward dancing in tribes other than the Pueblo similar to their belief in the vision-dream?

   b. In what way is the use made of the dance among the Pueblos similar to their rejection of the vision-dream?

   c. There is a balanced contrast in paragraphs 25 through 27 and another in paragraphs 28 and 29. Explain the difference in method in the two sets of contrasts. Justify the order in which these paragraphs appear; i.e., why would it be difficult to place paragraphs 28 and 29 at the beginning of this section?

9. Consider paragraphs 32 through 39 as a unit. Several subjects are mentioned in this section—shamanism, the priesthood, self-

reliance, warfare, conformity. Explain carefully how these ideas are related and what the chief topic of the unit is.
10. In paragraphs 40 through 44, how is the specific matter of initiation related to the topic of this section? What is the topic and how is it related to the main Dionysian-Apollonian contrast?
11. Explain what the folktale about the Navajo in paragraph 46 is meant to illustrate.
12. Explain what is meant by sentence 2 of paragraph 50. What is "the mean in the Greek sense"? Why does Dr. Benedict speak of "cultural handling" rather than just of "handling"?
13. In the discussion of death (paragraphs 56 through 64), the author reverses her usual method in handling the contrast; i.e., she discusses the Pueblos first before describing practices surrounding death in other Indian cultures. Can you see any reason for this change in method?
14. In the concluding section (paragraphs 65 through 68) why are Pueblo ideas contrasted with the ideas of our civilization rather than with those of other Indian civilizations?
15. Assume that the concluding sentence read as follows:

They have made, in one small but long-established cultural island in North America, a formal, measured, and sober civilization.

Why is the revised sentence inferior to the original as a conclusion?

Suggested Assignments

Take any *one* topic in this article which interests you—the dance, death ceremonies, domestic relationships, and so on—and write an essay based on a comparison of Pueblo practices with those of our civilization.

After you have selected your topic, you will probably find that this is not an easy paper to write. We are so accustomed to taking our own cultural patterns for granted that it is hard for us to see a meaning in them. Try to analyze rather than merely to describe the practice you have selected.

When you have arrived at a satisfactory interpretation of our cultural pattern, a further question arises. Is your comparison governed by a real theme idea? Have you explained not only that the two civilizations are different, but *why* they are different?

3 Expression of Judgment and Opinion

H. L. MENCKEN

Education

NEXT to the clerk in holy orders, the fellow with the worst job in the world is the schoolmaster. Both are underpaid, both fall steadily in authority and dignity, and both wear out their hearts trying to perform the impossible. How much the world asks of them, and how little they can actually deliver! The clergyman's business is to save the human race from hell: if he saves one-eighth of one per cent., even within the limits of his narrow flock, he does magnificently. The schoolmaster's is to spread the enlightenment, to make the great masses of the plain people intelligent—and intelligence is precisely the thing   10 that the great masses of the plain people are congenitally and eternally incapable of.

2] Is it any wonder that the poor birchman, facing this labor that would have staggered Sisyphus Æolusohn, seeks refuge

"Education." Reprinted from *Prejudices: Third Series* by H. L. Mencken, by permission of Alfred A. Knopf, Inc. Copyright 1922 by Alfred A. Knopf, Inc.

from its essential impossibility in a Chinese maze of empty technic? The ghost of Pestalozzi, once bearing a torch and beckoning toward the heights, now leads down stairways into black and forbidding dungeons. Especially in America, where all that is bombastic and mystical is most esteemed, the art of pedagogics becomes a sort of puerile magic, a thing of preposterous secrets, a grotesque compound of false premises and illogical conclusions. Every year sees a craze for some new solution of the teaching enigma, at once simple and infallible—manual training, playground work, song and doggerel lessons, the Montessori method, the Gary system—an endless series of flamboyant arcanums. The worst extravagances of *privat dozent* experimental psychology are gravely seized upon; the uplift pours in its ineffable principles and discoveries; mathematical formulæ are worked out for every emergency; there is no sure-cure so idiotic that some superintendent of schools will not swallow it.

3] A couple of days spent examining the literature of the New Thought in pedagogy are enough to make the judicious weep. Its aim seems to be to reduce the whole teaching process to a sort of automatic reaction, to discover some master formula that will not only take the place of competence and resourcefulness in the teacher but that will also create an artificial receptivity in the child. The merciless application of this formula (which changes every four days) now seems to be the chief end and aim of pedagogy. Teaching becomes a thing in itself, separable from and superior to the thing taught. Its mastery is a special business, a transcendental art and mystery, to be acquired in the laboratory. A teacher well grounded in this mystery, and hence privy to every detail of the new technic (which changes, of course, with the formula), can teach anything to any child, just as a sound dentist can pull any tooth out of any jaw.

4] All this, I need not point out, is in sharp contrast to the old theory of teaching. By that theory mere technic was simplified and subordinated. All that it demanded of the teacher told off to teach, say, geography, was that he master the facts in the geography book and provide himself with a stout rattan. Thus equipped, he was ready for a test of his natural pedagogical genius. First he exposed the facts in the book, then he gilded them with whatever appearance of interest and importance he could conjure up, and then he tested the extent of their transference to the minds of his pupils. Those pupils who had ingested them got apples; those who had failed got fanned with the rattan. Followed the second round, and the same test again, with a second noting of results. And then the third, and fourth, and the fifth, and so on until the last and least pupil had been stuffed to his subnormal and perhaps moronic brim. 60

5] I was myself grounded in the underlying delusions of what is called knowledge by this austere process, and despite the eloquence of those who support newer ideas, I lean heavily in favor of it, and regret to hear that it is no more. It was crude, it was rough, and it was often not a little cruel, but it at least had two capital advantages over all the systems that have succeeded it. In the first place, its machinery was simple; even the stupidest child could understand it; it hooked up cause and effect with the utmost clarity. And in the second place, it tested the teacher as and how he ought to be tested—that is, for his actual 70 capacity to teach, not for his mere technical virtuosity. There was, in fact, no technic for him to master, and hence none for him to hide behind. He could not conceal a hopeless inability to impart knowledge beneath a correct professional method.

6] That ability to impart knowledge, it seems to me, has very little to do with technical method. It may operate at full function without any technical method at all, and contrariwise, the most elaborate of technical methods, whether out of Switzerland, Italy or Gary, Ind., cannot make it operate when it is not actually present. And what does it consist of? It consists, first, of a 80 natural talent for dealing with children, for getting into their minds, for putting things in a way that they can comprehend. And it consists, secondly, of a deep belief in the interest and importance of the thing taught, a concern about it amounting to a sort of passion. A man who knows a subject thoroughly, a man so soaked in it that he eats it, sleeps it and dreams it—this man can always teach it with success, no matter how little he knows of technical pedagogy. That is because there is enthusiasm in him, and because enthusiasm is almost as contagious as fear or the barber's itch. An enthusiast is willing to go to any trouble to impart the glad news bubbling within him. He thinks that it is important and valuable for to know; given the slightest glow of interest in a pupil to start with, he will fan that glow to a flame. No hollow formalism cripples him and slows him down. He drags his best pupils along as fast as they can go, and he is so full of the thing that he never tires of expounding its elements to the dullest.

7] This passion, so unordered and yet so potent, explains the capacity for teaching that one frequently observes in scientific men of high attainments in their specialties—for example, Huxley, Ostwald, Karl Ludwig, Virchow, Billroth, Jowett, William G. Sumner, Halsted and Osler—men who knew nothing whatever about the so-called science of pedagogy, and would have derided its alleged principles if they had heard them stated. It explains, too, the failure of the general run of high-school and college teachers—men who are undoubtedly competent, by the professional standards of pedagogy, but who nevertheless contrive only to make intolerable bores of the things they presume to teach. No intelligent student ever learns much from the average drover of undergraduates; what he actually carries away has come out of his textbooks, or is the fruit of his own reading and inquiry. But when he passes to the graduate school, and comes among men who really understand the subjects they teach, and, what is more, who really love them, his store of knowledge increases rapidly, and in a very short while, if he has any intelligence at all, he learns to think in terms of the thing he is studying.

8] So far, so good. But an objection still remains, the which may be couched in the following terms: that in the average college or high school, and especially in the elementary school, most of the subjects taught are so bald and uninspiring that it is difficult to imagine them arousing the passion I have been describing—in brief, that only an ass could be enthusiastic about them. In witness, think of the four elementals: reading, penmanship, arithmetic and spelling. This objection, at first blush, seems salient and dismaying, but only a brief inspection is needed to show that it is really of very small validity. It is made up of a false assumption and a false inference. The false inference is that there is any sound reason for prohibiting teaching by asses, if only the asses know how to do it, and do it well. The false assumption is that there are no asses in our schools and colleges today. The facts stand in almost complete antithesis to these notions. The truth is that the average schoolmaster, on all the lower levels, is and always must be essentially an ass, for how can one imagine an intelligent man engaging in so puerile an avocation? And, the truth is that it is precisely his inherent asininity, and not his technical equipment as a pedagogue, that is responsible for whatever modest success he now shows.

9] I here attempt no heavy jocosity, but mean exactly what I say. Consider, for example, penmanship. A decent handwriting, it must be obvious, is useful to all men, and particularly to the lower orders of men. It is one of the few things capable of acquirement in school that actually helps them to make a living. Well, how is it taught today? It is taught, in the main, by schoolmarms so enmeshed in a complex and unintelligible technic that, even supposing them able to write clearly themselves, they find it quite impossible to teach their pupils. Every few years sees a radical overhauling of the whole business. First the vertical hand is to make it easy; then certain curves are the favorite magic; then there is a return to slants and shadings. No department of pedagogy sees a more hideous cavorting of quacks. In none is the natural talent and enthusiasm of the teacher more depressingly crippled. And the result? The result is that our American school children write abominably—that a clerk or stenographer with a simple, legible hand becomes almost as scarce as one with Greek.

10] Go back, now, to the old days. Penmanship was then taught, not mechanically and ineffectively, by unsound and shifting formulæ, but by passionate penmen with curly patent-leather hair and far-away eyes—in brief, by the unforgettable professors of our youth, with their flourishes, their heavy down-strokes and their lovely birds-with-letters-in-their-bills.

You remember them, of course. Asses all! Preposterous popinjays and numskulls! Pathetic idiots! But they loved penmanship, they believed in the glory and beauty of penmanship, they were fanatics, devotees, almost martyrs of penmanship—and so they got some touch of that passion into their pupils. Not enough, perhaps, to make more flourishers and bird-blazoners, but enough to make sound penmen. Look at your old writing book; observe the excellent legibility, the clear strokes of your "Time is money." Then look at your child's.

11] Such idiots, despite the rise of "scientific" pedagogy, have not died out in the world. I believe that our schools are full of them, both in pantaloons and in skirts. There are fanatics who love and venerate spelling as a tom-cat loves and venerates catnip. There are grammatomaniacs; schoolmarms who would rather parse than eat; specialists in an objective case that doesn't exist in English; strange beings, otherwise sane and even intelligent and comely, who suffer under a split infinitive as you or I would suffer under gastro-enteritis. There are geography cranks, able to bound Mesopotamia and Beluchistan. There are zealots for long division, experts in the multiplication table, lunatic worshipers of the binomial theorem. But the system has them in its grip. It combats their natural enthusiasm diligently and mercilessly. It tries to convert them into mere technicians, clumsy machines. It orders them to teach, not by the process of emotional osmosis which worked in the days gone by, but by formulæ that are as baffling to the pupil as they are paralyzing to the teacher. Imagine what would happen to one of them who stepped to the blackboard, seized a piece of chalk, and engrossed a bird that held the class spell-bound—a bird with a thousand flowing feathers, wings bursting with parabolas and epicycloids, and long ribbons streaming from its bill! Imagine the fate of one who began "Honesty is the best policy" with an H as florid and—to a child—as beautiful as the initial of a mediæval manuscript! Such a teacher would be cashiered and handed over to the secular arm; the very enchantment of the assembled infantry would be held as damning proof against him. And yet it is just such teachers that we should try to discover and develop. Pedagogy needs their enthusiasm, their naïve belief in their own grotesque talents, their capacity for communicating their childish passion to the childish.

12] But this would mean exposing the children of the Republic to contact with monomaniacs, half-wits, defectives? Well, what of it? The vast majority of them are already exposed to contact with half-wits in their own homes; they are taught the word of God by half-wits on Sundays; they will grow up into Knights of Pythias, Odd Fellows, Red Men and other such half-wits in the days to come. Moreover, as I have hinted, they are already face to face with half-wits in the actual schools, at least in three cases out of four. The problem before us is not to dispose of this fact, but to utilize it. We cannot hope to fill the schools with persons of high intelligence, for persons of high intelligence simply refuse to spend their lives teaching such banal things as spelling and arithmetic. Among the teachers male we may safely assume that 95 per cent. are of low mentality, else they would depart for more appetizing pastures. And even among the teachers female the best are inevitably weeded out by marriage, and only the worst (with a few romantic exceptions) survive. The task before us, as I say, is not to make a vain denial of this cerebral inferiority of the pedagogue, nor to try to combat and disguise it by concocting a mass of technical hocus-pocus, but to search out and put to use the value lying concealed in it. For even stupidity, it must be plain, has its uses in the world, and some of them are uses that intelligence cannot meet. One would not tell off a Galileo or a Pasteur to drive an ash-cart or an Ignatius Loyola to be a stockbroker, or a Brahms to lead the orchestra in a Broadway cabaret. By the same token, one would not ask a Herbert Spencer or a Duns Scotus to instruct sucklings. Such men would not only be wasted at the job; they would also be incompetent. The business of dealing with children, in fact, demands a certain childishness of mind. The best teacher, until one comes to adult pupils, is not the one who knows most, but the one who is most capable of reducing knowledge to that simple compound of the obvious and the wonderful which slips easiest into the infantile comprehension. A man of high intelligence, perhaps, may accomplish the thing by a conscious intellectual feat. But it is vastly easier to the man (or woman) whose habits of mind are naturally on the plane of a child's. The best teacher of children, in brief, is one who is essentially childlike.

13] I go so far with this notion that I view the movement to introduce female bachelors of arts into the primary schools with the utmost alarm. A knowledge of Bergsonism, the Greek aorist, sex hygiene and the dramas of Percy MacKaye is not only no help to the teaching of spelling, it is a positive handicap to the teaching of spelling, for it corrupts and blows up that naïve belief in the glory and portentousness of spelling which is at the bottom of all successful teaching of it. If I had my way, indeed, I should expose all candidates for berths in the infant grades to the Binet-Simon test, and reject all those who revealed the mentality of more than fifteen years. Plenty would still pass. Moreover, they would be secure against contamination by the new technic of pedagogy. Its vast wave of pseudo-psychology would curl and break against the hard barrier of their innocent and passionate intellects—as it probably does, in fact, even now. They would know nothing of cognition, perception, attention, the sub-conscious and all the other half-fabulous fowl of the pedagogic aviary. But they would see in reading, writing and arithmetic the gaudy charms of profound and esoteric knowledge, and they would teach these ancient branches, now so abominably in decay, with passionate gusto, and irresistible effectiveness, and a gigantic success.

Questions

It would be pleasant to believe that the effectiveness of a piece of writing always depended on the soundness of the ideas and the clarity with which they were presented; but the fact is that thoughts which should be impressive and persuasive often fall flat because the writing is uninspired, while thoughts which are obvious or even unsound become splendid and convincing when they are presented by an author who knows how to employ the tricks of writing to advantage. So with H. L. Mencken's essay, "Education." Few people would agree with everything he says, but few would deny that his method of presentation is extraordinarily clever. The answers to the following questions should make evident some of the techniques involved in this cleverness.

1. Assume that the following paragraph were substituted for paragraph 1 of Mencken's essay:

One of the most difficult jobs in the world is that of the schoolmaster. He is underpaid, his profession is steadily falling in authority and dignity, and what he is trying to perform is almost impossible. The world asks a great deal of him. It demands that he make the whole population intelligent. Intelligence, unfortunately, is not as widespread as is generally supposed.

a. Point out specific differences between Mencken's first paragraph and the revised version printed above.

b. The clergyman is not mentioned again in the essay. Why does Mencken introduce him in paragraph 1? What relationship is Mencken implying between virtue and intelligence?

c. What approach to the subject of schoolteaching would the revised paragraph printed above lead you to expect? Why?

d. How does Mencken's introductory paragraph establish the tone of his essay?

2. Mencken uses an extended comparison in paragraph 1 and incidental comparison throughout the essay.

a. Identify *Sisyphus* (line 14). Do you know what Mencken means by *Sisyphus Æolusohn?* Explain the difference in effect between the phrase "facing this staggering labor" and the phrase that Mencken uses, *facing this labor that would have staggered Sisyphus Æolusohn.*

b. Suppose that lines 174-176 were rewritten as follows: "There are fanatics who love and venerate spelling as a patriot loves and venerates his flag." Why would the comparison be inappropriate? Explain what a comparison does in addition to emphasizing the central fact.

c. In line 56 could the word "learned" be substituted for the word *ingested?* What comparison is implied by the use of the word *ingested?* Where else in the paragraph is this comparison referred to?

d. Find other instances in which Mencken makes use of comparison and explain the function of each.

e. Of the comparisons referred to in *a, b,* and *c,* one is a simile, one a metaphor, and one an allusion. Look up the definitions of these terms and tell which is which.

3. Substitute a word or phrase for each of the following, retaining the sense of the original: *birchman* (line 13); *ghost of Pestalozzi* (line 16); *drover of undergraduates* (line 110); *emotional osmosis* (lines 186-187); *assembled infantry* (lines 197-198). In each instance, is the expression you have chosen as effective as Mencken's? Why or why not?

4. How does Mencken know that the clergyman can save only "one-eighth of one per cent." of his congregation (line 7)? What is his justification for using these precise statistics? Does he make use of this device elsewhere in the essay?

5. *a.* In paragraph 2 Mencken calls the art of teaching "a sort of puerile magic, a thing of preposterous secrets, a grotesque compound of false premises and illogical conclusions" (lines 20-22). Could any of the three phrases in this series be omitted without destroying the sense? Which phrase do you consider most essential? Why does Mencken use all three?

b. Assume that lines 164-166 were rewritten as follows:

But they loved penmanship, they were martyrs, fanatics, devotees of penmanship, they believed in the glory and beauty of penmanship.

Is the revised order as effective as Mencken's? Why or why not? Is Mencken following any principle in the order of his phrases?

c. Point out other examples in the essay, similar to those cited above, in which Mencken uses descriptive phrases in a series. Can you see any general principle governing his use of such phrases?

6. Ordinarily the frequent repetition of a word, particularly in student writing, implies a poor vocabulary or simply lack of effort.

a. How many times does Mencken use the word *half-wit* in paragraph 12? Could a synonym be substituted in any of these instances? Do you consider that his repetition of the word is justified?

b. Find other examples of Mencken's use of repetition.

7. Transition from paragraph to paragraph, a matter which often causes students trouble, is primarily dependent upon clarity of

thought. The exact method of transition, however, varies with the tone and purpose of the entire essay. Compare each of the following transitions with those Mencken uses and explain why Mencken's transitional phrase or sentence is better suited to his whole approach to his subject.

a. "Although these arguments may be granted, an objection still remains . . ." (*So far, so good. But an objection still remains . . .*) (line 118).

b. "In the old days, on the other hand, penmanship was taught . . ." (*Go back, now, to the old days. Penmanship was then taught . . .*) (lines 157-158).

c. "Persons possessed of such enthusiasm, despite the rise of 'scientific' pedagogy . . ." (*Such idiots, despite the rise of "scientific" pedagogy . . .*) (line 172).

d. "If the objection is raised that this would mean exposing our children to contact with monomaniacs, half-wits, and defectives, one may well answer that it makes little difference." (*But this would mean exposing the children of the Republic to contact with monomaniacs, half-wits, defectives? Well, what of it?*) (lines 203-205).

8. Review questions 1 through 7 and summarize the kinds of stylistic devices Mencken uses to emphasize his argument.

    a. Can you find any examples of other rhetorical methods which Mencken uses?

    b. In your opinion are any of these devices overemphatic? Is the argument weakened rather than strengthened at any point?

9. At one time figures of speech and other rhetorical devices were regarded as "ornamental"—that is, they were thought of not as something really essential to the thought, but as a sort of decoration added to make the writing more impressive or enjoyable. At the present time, it is usual to regard figures of speech as "functional" —that is, they are thought of as devices by which the author's thought—or more often his feeling—may be more adequately or more exactly expressed. Would you say that Mencken's figures of speech were ornamental or functional?

Suggested Assignments

1. Rewrite paragraph 2, divesting it in so far as possible of its rhetorical flourishes. In other words, present the essential idea of the paragraph in simple prose (see question 1). Be sure you understand all the words and allusions before you begin.
2. In an essay of your own, refute *one* of Mencken's arguments, using as persuasive a style as possible. You will probably produce a better composition if you confine yourself to one point and do not attempt to answer his whole argument.

ALEXANDER WOOLLCOTT

The Archer-Shee Case

FROM time to time, since the turn of the century, there has issued from the press of a publishing house in London and Edinburgh a series of volumes called the *Notable British Trials,* each volume dedicated to some case in the criminal annals of England or Scotland. Each would contain not only the testimony of witnesses, the photographs of exhibits, the arguments of counsel, the dicta from the bench, and the verdict of the jury, but also an introductory essay nicely calculated to enthrall those readers who collect such instances of human violence, much as other madmen collect coins or autographs or stamps.

2] The cases thus made available range all the way from the trials of the mutineers aboard the *Bounty* to the libel action

---

"The Archer-Shee Case." From *Long, Long Ago* by Alexander Woollcott. From *The Portable Woollcott.* Copyright 1939 by Alexander Woollcott, 1946 by The Viking Press, Inc. Reprinted by permission of The Viking Press, Inc., New York.

which, in the twilight of the Victorian era, grew out of a charge of cheating during a card game at a place called Tranby Croft, a gaudy lawsuit which agitated the entire Empire because it dragged into the witness box no less a personage, a bit ruffled and breathing heavily, than H.R.H. the Prince of Wales, who was later to rule and consolidate that empire as Edward VII. But for the most part, of course, the cases thus edited have had their origin in murder most foul, and they constitute not only an indispensable part of every law library but a tempting pastime to all of us whose telltale interest in poison and throat-cutting is revealed in no other aspect of our humdrum, blameless lives.

3] Now, as an avid subscriber to the series, I have long been both exasperated and puzzled by the fact that it contained no transcript of that trial which, more and more in recent years, has taken definite shape in my own mind as one of the most notable and certainly the most British of them all. Nowhere in England or America is there available in any library a record of the Archer-Shee case. The student eager to master its details must depend on such scattered odds and ends as he can dredge up from contemporary memoirs and from the woefully incomplete reports in newspaper files which already moulder to dust at the touch.

4] But within recent months, by a series of curious chances too fantastic to have been foreseen, a complete private record of the entire case has come into my possession, and it is my present plan, before another year has passed, to put it into print for the use of anyone who needs it as a light or craves it as a tonic. For the Archer-Shee case is a short, sharp, illuminating chapter in the long history of human liberty, and a study of it might, it seems to me, stiffen the purpose of all those who in our own day are freshly resolved that that liberty shall not perish from the earth.

5] In the fall of 1908, Mr. Martin Archer-Shee, a bank manager in Liverpool, received word, through the commandant of the Royal Naval College at Osborne, that the Lords Commissioners of the Admiralty had decided to dismiss his thirteen-year-old son George, who had been proudly entered as a cadet only a few months before. It seems that a five-shilling postal order had been stolen from the locker of one of the boys—stolen, forged, and cashed—and, after a sifting of all the available evidence, the authorities felt unable to escape the conclusion that young Archer-Shee was the culprit. Out of such damaged and unpromising material the Admiralty could scarcely be expected to fashion an officer for His Majesty's Navy. "My Lords deeply regret," the letter went on to say, "that they must therefore request you to withdraw your son from the College." This devastating and puzzling news brought the family hurrying to Osborne. Was it true? No, Father. Then why did the authorities accuse him? What had made them think him guilty? The bewildered boy had no idea. "Well," said the father in effect, "we'll have to see about this," little guessing then, as he was to learn through many a bitter and discouraging month, that that would be easier said than done.

6] What had made them think the boy a thief? The offish captain could only refer him to the Admiralty, and the Lords of the Admiralty—by not answering letters, evading direct questions, and all the familiar technique of bureaucratic delay—retired behind the tradition that the Navy must be the sole judge of material suitable for the making of a British officer. If once they allowed their dismissal of a cadet to be reviewed by an inevitably outraged family, they would be establishing a costly and regrettable precedent.

7] What the elder Archer-Shee found blocking the path was no personal devil, no vindictive enemy of his son, no malignant spirit. But he was faced with an opponent as maddening, as cruel, and as destructive. He was entering the lists against the massive, complacent inertia of a government department which is not used to being questioned and does not like to be bothered. He was girding his loins for the kind of combat that takes all the courage and patience and will power a man can summon to his aid. He was challenging a bureaucracy to battle.

8] At a dozen points in the ensuing struggle, in which he was backed up every day by his first-born, who was a Major and an M.P. and a D.S.O., a less resolute fighter might have been willing to give up, and one of smaller means would have had to. After all, the boy's former teachers and classmates at Stonyhurst, the Catholic college where he was prepared for Osborne, had welcomed him back with open arms, and, as allusions to the episode began to find their way into print, there were plenty of comfortable old men in clubs who opined loudly that this man Archer-Shee was making a bloody nuisance of himself. But you may also be sure that there were those among the neighbors who implied by their manner that the Navy must know what it was doing, that where there was so much smoke there must be some fire, that if the whole story could be told, and so forth and so forth. I think the father knew in his heart, as surely as anyone can know anything in this world, that his son was innocent. While there was a breath left in his body and a pound in his bank account, he could not let the youngster go out into the world with that stain on his name. He would not give up. Probably he was strengthened by his memory of how bitterly his little boy had wept on the day they took him away from Osborne. The father lived—by no more than a few months— to see the fight through.

9] The first great step was the retaining of Sir Edward Carson, then at the zenith of his incomparable reputation as an advocate. In his day, Carson was to hold high office—Attorney-General, Solicitor-General—to assume political leadership in the Ulster crisis—leader of the Irish Unionists in the House—to be rewarded with a peerage. It was part of the manifold irony of that crowded and stormy life, which ended in his death at eighty-one in 1935, that probably he will be longest remembered because of that hour of merciless cross-examination, in a libel suit at the Old Bailey, which brought down in ruins the towering and shaky edifice known as Oscar Wilde. But some there are who, when all else is forgotten, will rather hold Carson in highest honor for the good turn he once did to a small boy in trouble. He put all his tremendous power and implacable persistence and passionate hatred of tyranny at the service of Master Archer-Shee.

10] It was only after he had heard the boy's own story (and raked him with such a bracketing fire of questions as he was famous for directing against a witness) that he agreed to take the case at all. From that interview he rose, saying in effect, "This boy did not steal that postal order. Now, let's get at the facts."

11] This took a bit of doing. It was the nub of the difficulty that the small embryo officer had, by becoming a cadet, lost the rights of an ordinary citizen without yet reaching that status which would have entitled him to a court-martial. To be sure, the Admiralty by this time had resentfully bestirred itself to make several supplementary inquiries, but these were all *ex parte* proceedings, with the boy unrepresented by counsel, the witnesses unsubjected to the often clarifying fire of cross-examination. Even when the badgered authorities went so far as to submit their findings to the Judge Advocate General for review, they still kept the Archer-Shees cooling their heels in the anteroom.

I am commanded by the Lords Commissioners of the Admiralty to to acknowledge receipt of your letter relative to the case of George Archer-Shee, and my Lords desire me to say that the further enquiry is not one at which a representative of your side in the sense in which you use the word would be appropriate.

12] Well, even at the horrid risk of following a procedure which might be described as "inappropriate," Carson was determined to get the case into court, to make those witnesses tell their story not to a biased and perhaps comatose representative of the Admiralty but to a jury of ordinary men—above all, to tell it with the public listening. Resisting him in this was Sir Rufus Isaacs, later to become, as Lord Reading, Chief Justice of England, but then—in 1909 and 1910, this was—Solicitor-General and, unbecoming as was the posture into which it threw him, mysteriously compelled by professional tradition to defend the Admiralty's action at every step.

13] How to get the case into court? Carson finally had recourse to an antique and long-neglected device known as the Petition of Right. First he had to establish the notion that there had been a violation of contract—a failure of the Crown to keep its part of the bargain implied when, at some considerable expense to his folks and with a binding agreement on his own part to serve as an officer in the Navy once he had been trained for the job, the boy matriculated. But, contract or no contract, a subject may sue the King only under certain circumstances. If he approach the throne with a Petition of Right and the King consent to write across it "Let right be done," His Majesty can, in that instance and on that issue, be sued like any commoner.

14] Instead of welcoming such a course as the quickest way of settling the original controversy and even of finding out what really had happened to that fateful postal order, the Admiralty, perhaps from sheer force of habit, resorted to legal technicalities as a means of delay. Indeed, it was only the human impatience of the justices, to whom a demurrer was carried on appeal, that finally cut through the red tape. They would eventually have to decide whether or not a Petition of Right was the suitable remedy, but in the meantime, they asked, why not let them have the facts? Why not, indeed? It was all Carson was contending for. It was all the Archer-Shees had ever asked for. Later in the House of Commons, where he was to hear the intervention of the demurrer denounced as a tragic error, Sir Rufus took considerable credit to himself for having bowed to this call for the facts, but he was making a virtue of something that had been very like necessity.

15] Anyway, the trial was ordered. So at long last, on a hot day in July 1910—nearly two years after the postal order was stolen and too late for any hope of finding out who really had stolen it—the case came before a jury in the King's Bench Division, and the witnesses whose stories in the first place had convinced the Osborne authorities that young Archer-Shee was a thief must, with Sir Rufus vigilant to protect them, submit themselves to cross-examination by the most alarming advocate of the English bar.

16] By this time the case had ceased to be a local squabble, reported as a matter of professional interest in various service journals but showing up in the ordinary newspapers only in an occasional paragraph. Now it was being treated by the press, column after column, as a *cause célèbre,* and all the Empire was following it with bated breath. Carson was on his feet in open court speaking for the Suppliant:

His son was branded as a thief and as a forger, a boy thirteen years old was labeled and ticketed, and has been since labeled and ticketed for all his future life, as a thief and a forger, and in such investigation as led to that disastrous result, neither his father nor any friend was ever there to hear what was said against a boy of thirteen, who by that one letter, and by that one determination was absolutely deprived of the possibility of any future career either in His Majesty's Service, or indeed in any other Service. Gentlemen, I protest against the injustice to a little boy, a child thirteen years of age, without communication with his parents, without his case ever being put, or an opportunity of its ever being put forward by those on his behalf—I protest against that boy at that early stage, a boy of that character, being branded for the rest of his life by that one act, an irretrievable act that I venture to think could never be got over. That little boy from that day, and from the day that he was first charged, up to this moment, whether it was in the ordeal of being called in before his Commander and his Captain, or whether it was under the softer influences of the persuasion of his own loving parents, has never faltered in the statement that he is an innocent boy.

17] But these reverberant words had overtones which all Englishmen could hear. Now the case was being followed with painful attention by plain men and women slowly come to the realization that here was no minor rumpus over the discipline and punctilio of the service, indeed no mere matter of a five-shilling theft and a youngster's reputation, but a microcosm in which was summed up all the long history of British liberty. Here in the small visible compass of one boy's fate was the entire issue of the inviolable sovereignty of the individual.

18] The Archer-Shees had as their advantageous starting point the inherent improbability of the boy's guilt. There seemed no good reason why he *should* steal five shillings when he was in ample funds on which he could lay his hands at will by the simple process of writing a chit. But if, for good measure or out of sheer deviltry, he *had* stolen his classmate's postal order, it seemed odd that instead of cashing it furtively he would not only openly get permission to go to the post office, which was out of bounds, but first loiter about for some time in an effort to get a schoolmate to go along with him for company. But this inherent improbability, so visible from this distance, quite escaped the attention of the college authorities who, by the sheer momentum of prosecution, had hastily reached their own conclusion by another route.

19] When young Terence Back dolefully reported to the Cadet Gunner that the postal order which had arrived that very morning as a present from some doting relative was missing from his locker, the Chief Petty Officer at once telephoned the post office to find out if it had already been cashed. It had. Oh!

20] There followed a rush of officialdom to the post office and much questioning of the chief clerk, Miss Anna Clara Tucker, first there and later at the college by Commander Cotton, the officer in charge of the investigation. Now, Miss Tucker, had there been any cadets at the post office that day? Yes, two—one to buy a 15s. 6d. postal order, the other to buy two totaling 14s. 9d. And was it one of them who had cashed the stolen order? Yes, it was. Would the postmistress be able to pick him out? No. They all looked so alike, in their uniforms, that she wouldn't know one from the other. But this she could tell, this she *did* remember—the stolen order was cashed by the boy who had bought the postal order for fifteen and six. And which one was that? Well, her records could answer that question. It was Cadet Archer-Shee. (He had needed that order, by the way, to send for a model engine on which his heart was set, and to purchase the order he had that morning drawn sixteen shillings from his funds on deposit with the Chief Petty Officer, a sum which would not only buy the order but pay for the necessary postage and leave in his pocket some small change for emergencies.)

21] Thus to Commander Cotton—Richard Greville Arthur Wellington Stapleton Cotton, who, oddly enough, was later to command H.M.S. *Terrible*—thus to Commander Cotton, who reported accordingly to the Captain, and he, through Portsmouth, to the Admiralty, it seemed satisfactorily evident that the postmistress was ineluctably identifying Archer-Shee as the thief, or at least as the villain who had converted the stolen goods into cash.

22] On her testimony the authorities acted—innocently, if you like, and not without later taking the precaution to support it by the dubious opinion of a handwriting expert. But so muddle-headed was this investigation, and such is the momentum of prosecution the world around, that the very first *précis* of that testimony filed with the Admiralty was careful to omit, as perhaps weakening the evidence against the boy—so swiftly do departmental investigators change from men seeking the truth into men trying to prove a hasty conclusion—was careful to omit the crucial fact that at the college next morning, when six or seven of the cadets were herded past her for inspection, the postmistress had been unable, either by the look of his face or by the sound of his voice, to pick out Archer-Shee. This failure became patently crucial when, two years later on that sweltering July day, Carson, with artfully deceptive gentleness, took over Miss Tucker for cross-examination.

23] The cashing of the stolen order and the issuing of the order for fifteen and six had taken place at the same time? Well, one transaction after the other. Her records showed that? No, but she remembered. The two took place within what space of time? Well, there might have been interruptions. After all, she was in sole charge of the office at the time? Yes. There was the telephone to answer, telegrams to take down as they came over the wire? Yes, and the mail to sort. These matters often took her away from the window? Yes. Even into the back room? Sometimes. So sometimes, if one cadet should go away from the window and another step into his place during any one of the interruptions, she might not notice the exchange? That was true. And, since they all looked alike to her, one cadet in this very instance *could* have taken the place of another without her realizing, when she returned to the window, that she had not been dealing throughout with the same boy? Possibly. So that now she couldn't say it was Archer-Shee who had cashed the stolen order? She had never said that exactly. Nor could she even be sure, now that she came to think of it, that the stolen order had, in fact, been cashed by the same cadet who bought the order for fifteen and six? Not absolutely sure. That, in effect—here oversimplified in condensation, but in effect—was her testimony.

24] Well, there it was—a gap in her story wide enough to drive a coach through. As soon as he saw it—it would strike a mere onlooking layman that the Admiralty might well have asked these same questions two years before—Sir Rufus knew the jig was up. Wherefore, when court opened on the fourth day, he was soon on his feet announcing that he no longer wished to proceed with any question of fact. It takes no great feat of imagination to guess at the breathlessness in that courtroom as the Solicitor-General came to the point:

As a result of the evidence that has been given during the trial that has been going on now for some days, and the investigation that has taken place, I say now, on behalf of the Admiralty, that I accept the statement of George Archer-Shee that he did not write the name on the postal order, and did not cash it, and consequently that he is innocent of the charge. I say further, in order that there may be no misapprehension about it, that I make that statement without any reserve of any description, intending that it shall be a complete justification of the statement of the boy and the evidence he has given before the Court.

25] In return—perhaps a fair exchange haggled for behind the scenes—Carson went on record as holding the belief that the responsible persons at Osborne and at the Admiralty had acted in good faith and that not even the disastrous Miss Tucker had been wanting in honesty. He had merely sought to show that she was mistaken.

26] Then, while the jury swarmed out of the box to shake hands with Carson and with the boy's father, the exhausted advocate turned to congratulate the boy himself, only to find that he wasn't even in court. Indeed, the case was over and court had adjourned before he got the news. When, blushing and grinning from ear to ear and falling all over himself, he went to Carson's room in the Law Courts to thank him, the great advocate ventured to ask how in his hour of triumph the boy had happened to be missing. Well, sir, he got up late. It seems he went to the theater the night before and so had overslept. Overslept! For weeks Carson himself had hardly been able to get any sleep. Overslept! Good God! Hadn't he even been anxious? Oh, no, sir. He had known all along that once the case got into court the truth would come out. Carson mopped his brow. Then he laughed. Perhaps that *was* the best way to take such things.

27] Thereafter, of course, the boy's was not the only attention that wandered. All England may have been watching, but, after all, other current topics were not without their elements of public interest. For one thing, a new King was on the throne. The Edward who had written "Let right be done" across the Archer-Shee petition now lay in his tomb at Windsor, and his son George was only just beginning the reign which was to prove so unforeseeably eventful. Then, even as the case came to an end, another was ready to overshadow it. Indeed, on the very day when, on behalf of the Admiralty, Sir Rufus acknowledged the boy's innocence, Inspector Dew arrived in Quebec to wait for the incoming *Montrose* and arrest two of her passengers, a fugitive medico named Crippen and his dream-girl, Ethel Le Neve. Even so, thanks to the sounding board known as the House of Commons, neither the public nor the Admiralty was allowed to forget the Archer-Shee case. Indeed, news of its conclusion had hardly reached the House when several members were on their feet giving notice—due notice that England would expect some specific assurance that the lesson had been learned, that never again would a boy be thus cavalierly dismissed from Osborne without notice to his folks or a chance for adequate defense.

28] In this instance, of course, it was too late for anything but apology and indemnification. "This," one speaker said with apparently unconscious humor, "could be left to the generosity of the Admiralty." Another speaker—the honorable member for the Universities of Glasgow and Aberdeen—put it this way: "I am quite sure the Admiralty will do all in their power to redress the very terrible and almost irreparable wrong done to the boy, on such a wrong being brought to their knowledge." But this confidence proved to be naïve. Month followed month with no word of apology, no word even of regret, and, as for indemnification, no offer to pay more than a fraction of what the boy's father had already spent in his defense. Indeed, in the fitful discussion on this point, the Admiralty had even introduced the pretty suggestion that the nipping of young Archer-Shee's naval career in the bud had not been so very injurious, because he was not a promising student anyway. It looks, at this distance, like a bad case of bureaucratic sulks.

29] So in March and April of the following year the attack was renewed. By the quaint but familiar device of moving that the salary of the First Lord of the Admiralty (Mr. Reginald McKenna) be reduced by one hundred pounds, the honorable member for Kingston (Mr. Cave) started the ball rolling. Although the honorable member for Leicester, Mr. Ramsay MacDonald, was so far out of key as to call the motion an attempt to blackmail the Treasury (cries of "Shame! Shame!"), the resulting debate went to the heart of the matter and put in memorable and satisfying words just what many decent and inarticulate men had been wanting to have said about the case all along.

30] The relative passages in *Hansard* make good reading to this day, because all those who moved to the attack spoke as if nothing in the world could matter more than the question of justice to one small unimportant boy. The wretched legalism of the Admiralty's evasions received its just meed of contempt, with the wits of Sir Rufus Isaacs matched (and a bit more) by that same F. E. Smith who was later to become Lord Birkenhead and who, by the way, was at the time fresh from the defense of Ethel Le Neve at the Old Bailey. These members, together with Lord Charles Beresford and others, firmly jockeyed the unhappy First Lord into the position where he not only gave assurance that thereafter no boy at Osborne would ever be so dealt with—this he had come prepared to do—but went on record, at long reluctant last, as expressing in this case his unqualified regrets. He even consented to pay to the boy's father whatever sum a committee of three (including Carson himself) should deem proper. This ended in a payment of £7120, and with that payment the case may be said to have come to an end.

31] The case—but not the story. That has an epilogue. The characters? Most of them are gone. I don't know whatever became of poor Miss Tucker, but the elder Archer-Shee is gone, and Isaacs and Carson. Even Osborne is gone—Osborne where Victoria walked with Albert and one day plucked the primroses for Disraeli. At least its Naval College has gone out of existence, swallowed up in Dartmouth.

32] And the boy himself? Well, when it came to him, the author of the epilogue dipped his pen in irony. To say that much is tantamount to a synopsis. If you will remember that the boy was thirteen when they threw him out of Osborne and fifteen when his good name was re-established, you will realize that when the Great War began he was old enough to die for King and Country. And did he? Of course. As a soldier, mind you. The lost two years had rather discouraged his ambitions with regard to the Navy. August 1914 found him in America, working in the Wall Street firm of Fisk & Robinson. Somehow he managed to get back to England, join up with the Second Battalion of the South Staffordshire Regiment, win a commission as Second Lieutenant, and get over to France in time to be killed—at Ypres —in the first October of the War.

33] So that is the story of Archer-Shee, whose years in the land, all told, were nineteen. To me his has always been a deeply moving story, and more and more, as the years have gone by, a significant one. Indeed, I should like to go up and down our own land telling it to young people not yet born when Archer-Shee kept his rendezvous with death. You see, I know no easier way of saying something that is much on my mind. For this can be said about the Archer-Shee case: that it could not happen in any totalitarian state. It is so peculiarly English, this story of a whole people getting worked up about a little matter of principle; above all, the story of the foremost men of the land taking up the cudgels—taking up the cudgels against the state, mind you—because a youngster had been unfairly treated. It would have been difficult to imagine it in the Germany of Bismarck and the Wilhelms. It is impossible to imagine it in the Germany of Adolf Hitler.*

Questions

"The Archer-Shee Case" is a résumé of a lawsuit that has long since been settled. Master George Archer-Shee was acquitted of the charge of dishonesty, and Woollcott is certainly in hearty agreement with that acquittal. In what way, then, can his report of the case be regarded as "controversial"?

The essay is not, obviously, the same kind of controversy represented by Lincoln's speech (page 264) or Churchill's speech (page 286); that is, it does not present direct evidence on an undecided problem for the purpose of influencing opinion and thus helping to settle that particular problem. Rather, Woollcott reviews an old controversy, a controversy already settled, for the purpose of throwing light on a current issue, an issue by no means settled. What Woollcott chooses to select from the original mass of data on the case and the way in which he presents his evidence are determined by the fact that he is applying the material from an old controversy to a living question. Far from being a mere summarizer, he is a strongly opinionated writer directing the reader's attention to the contemporary problem of the rights of the individual versus the rights of the state.

1. The account of the case itself does not begin until paragraph 5.
    a. Do paragraphs 1 and 2 have any point other than to introduce the subject to the reader in a leisurely fashion? Suppose paragraphs 1 and 2 were omitted and the following appeared as the first sentence of the essay (replacing the first two sentences of paragraph 3).

    Although it is, I believe, the most notable of all British trials, nowhere in England or America is there available in any library a record of the Archer-Shee case.

    What would be the difference in effect?

* That there is dramatic interest as well as political significance inherent in this material is evidenced by Terence Ratigan's "The Winslow Boy," a play based on the Archer-Shee Case which was produced in New York in 1948.

b. What is the point of Woollcott's labeling the case "the most British of them all" (paragraph 3)?

c. Where does Woollcott explain his purpose in reviewing the case?

2. The story of George Archer-Shee, which runs from paragraph 5 through paragraph 32, can easily be divided into three sections chronologically. Point out the three sections and explain how the content of each differs.

3. Throughout his account of the case Woollcott's commentary is subtly mingled with the facts in such a way that the two can scarcely be disentangled. For example, in paragraph 5 the words "proudly" and "bewildered" are designed to arouse sympathy for George Archer-Shee before the reader has examined the evidence. In paragraph 6 the words "all the familiar technique of bureaucratic delay" are a judgment passed on the Navy's conduct. Can you point out other similar instances of incidental commentary?

4. Two paragraphs in the account of the case are wholly devoted to commentary. Point them out.

5. Woollcott prefers to review the case in his own words and quotes very sparingly from the actual documents. When he does insert a quotation, he has a particularly good reason for doing so.

a. What idea in the essay is particularly well illustrated by the quotation in paragraph 11?

b. Why is Carson's defense (paragraph 16) quoted verbatim instead of being summarized?

6. Explain what is meant by "microcosm" in paragraph 17.

7. What is the connection between the other current events mentioned in the beginning of paragraph 27 and the central point of the essay? Are they mentioned chiefly to give a picture of the era?

8. Explain what is meant by "the author of the epilogue dipped his pen in irony" (paragraph 32).

9. Consider each of the following as a statement of the central idea of the essay. If any of these statements appears to you incorrect or incomplete, be prepared to explain why.

a. In Great Britain the rights of any individual against the encroachment of the state are guaranteed.

    b. The German people are temperamentally incapable of considering the individual more important than the state.

    c. Even in a democracy only the rich are adequately defended against injustice on the part of the government.

    d. The complexities of the English legal system should be simplified.

10. Suppose the Archer-Shee case had been settled quickly and simply, with no bureaucratic delay and no legal difficulties. Would it then have served as an illustration of Woollcott's thesis?

Suggested Assignment

Do the exercise "The Borden Case" on page 350.

NICCOLO MACHIAVELLI

Corruption in a Commonwealth

I HAVE said before that a bad citizen cannot work grave mischief in a commonwealth which has not become corrupted. This opinion is not only supported by the arguments already advanced, but is further confirmed by the examples of Spurius Cassius and Manlius Capitolinus. For Spurius, being ambitious, and desiring to obtain extraordinary authority in Rome, and to win over the people by loading them with benefits (as, for instance, by selling them those lands which the Romans had taken from the Hernici), his designs were seen through by the senate, and laid him under such suspicion, that when in haranguing the people he offered them the money realized by the sale of the

"Corruption in a Commonwealth." From *Discourses on the First Decade of Titus Livius* by Niccolo Machiavelli; translated by Ninian Hill Thomson.

grain brought from Sicily at the public expense, they would have none of it, believing that he offered it as the price of their freedom. Now, had the people been corrupted, they would not have refused this bribe, but would have opened rather than closed the way to the tyranny.

2] The example of Manlius is still more striking. For in his case we see what excellent gifts both of mind and body, and what splended services to his country were afterwards cancelled by that shameful eagerness to reign which we find bred in him by his jealousy of the honours paid Camillus. For so darkened did his mind become, that without reflecting what were the institutions to which Rome was accustomed, or testing the material he had to work on, when he would have seen that it was still unfit to be moulded to evil ends, he set himself to stir up tumults against the senate and against the laws of his country.

3] And herein we recognize the excellence of this city of Rome, and of the materials whereof it was composed. For although the nobles were wont to stand up stoutly for one another, not one of them stirred to succour Manlius, and not one of his kinsfolk made any effort on his behalf; so that although it was customary, in the case of other accused persons, for their friends to put on black and sordid raiment, with all the other outward signs of grief, in order to excite pity for the accused, none was seen to do any of these things for Manlius. Even the tribunes of the people, though constantly ready to promote whatever courses seemed to favour the popular cause, and the more vehemently the more they seemed to make against the nobles, in this instance sided with the nobles to put down the common enemy. Nay the very people themselves, keenly alive to their own interests, and well disposed towards any attempt to damage the nobles, though they showed Manlius many proofs of their regard, nevertheless, when he was cited by the tribunes to appear before them and submit his cause for their decision, assumed the part of judges and not of defenders, and without scruple or hesitation sentenced him to die. Wherefore, I think, that there is no example in the whole Roman history which serves so well as this to demonstrate the virtues of all ranks in that republic. For not a man in the whole city bestirred himself to shield a citizen endowed with every great quality, and who, both publicly and privately, had done so much that deserved praise. But in all, the love of country outweighed every other thought, and all looked less to his past deserts than to the dangers which his present conduct threatened; from which to relieve themselves they put him to death. "Such," says Livius, "*was the fate of a man worthy our admiration had he not been born in a free State.*"

4] And here two points should be noted. The first, that glory is to be sought by different methods in a corrupt city, and in one which still preserves its freedom. The second, which hardly differs from the first, that in their actions, and especially in matters of moment, men must have regard to times and circumstances and adapt themselves thereto. For those persons who from an unwise choice, or from natural inclination, run counter to the times, will for the most part live unhappily, and find all they undertake issue in failure; whereas those who accommodate themselves to the times are fortunate and successful. And from the passage cited we may plainly infer, that had Manlius lived in the days of Marius and Sylla, when the body of the State had become corrupted, so that he could have impressed it with the stamp of his ambition, he might have had the same success as they had, and as those others had who after them aspired to absolute power; and, conversely, that if Sylla and Marius had lived in the days of Manlius, they must have broken down at the very beginning of their attempts.

5] For one man, by mischievous arts and measures, may easily prepare the ground for the universal corruption of a city; but no one man in his lifetime can carry that corruption so far, as himself to reap the harvest; or granting that one man's life might be long enough for this purpose, it would be impossible for him, having regard to the ordinary habits of men, who grow impatient and cannot long forego the gratification of their desires, to wait until the corruption was complete. Moreover, men deceive themselves in respect of their own affairs, and most of all in respect of those on which they are most bent; so that either from impatience or from self-deception, they rush upon undertakings for which the time is not ripe, and so come to an ill end. Wherefore to obtain absolute authority in a commonwealth and to destroy its liberties, you must find the body of the State already corrupted, and corrupted by a gradual wasting continued from generation to generation; which, indeed, takes place necessarily, unless, as has been already explained, the State be often reinforced by good examples, or brought back to its first beginnings by wise laws.

6] Manlius, therefore, would have been a rare and renowned man had he been born in a corrupt city; and from his example we see that citizens seeking to introduce changes in the form of their government, whether in favour of liberty or despotism, ought to consider what materials they have to deal with, and then judge of the difficulty of their task. For it is no less arduous and dangerous to attempt to free a people disposed to live in servitude, than to enslave a people who desire to live free.

Questions

Questions on the passage by Machiavelli will be found at the end of Croce's "Political Honesty."

BENEDETTO CROCE

Political Honesty

ANOTHER manifestation of the general failure to comprehend the true nature of politics is the persistent and ill-humoured demand that is made for "honesty" in public life.

2] An ideal sings in the souls of all the poor in spirit, and

"Political Honesty." From *The Conduct of Life* by Benedetto Croce, copyright, 1924, by Harcourt, Brace and Company, Inc.

finds expression in the unmusical prose of their diatribes, their oratory, and their utopias. They dream of a sort of areopagus, made up of honest men, to whom alone should be entrusted the affairs of State or nation. In this congress we should find chemists, and physicians, and poets, and mathematicians, and doctors, and just plain ordinary citizens, all, however, endowed with two qualities: nobility of intentions along with personal unselfishness; and training or ability in some branch of human activity not directly connected with politics proper. Politics, in the good sense of the term, should result rather from this cross-breeding of honesty with so-called "technical competence."

3] Just what kind of politics would be produced by this assortment of virtuous technicians there is, fortunately, no way of testing by experiment. History has never tried to realise this particular ideal, and seems to be in no great hurry to do so. It is true that every now and then—episodically, so to speak—groups more or less distantly resembling such elect company find themselves possessed of political power for short periods of time. Men loved and revered for their spotless probity and for their intellect and learning, are occasionally made heads of States. But they are at once put out of office again, with a doctorate in ineptitude added to their other titles. I need refer, in illustration, only to the Trinity, as it was dubbed, of "honest men" who made such botches in their respective countries, of the liberal revolutions of the first half of the nineteenth century: Lafayette in France, Espartero in Spain, and Guglielmo Pepe in the kingdom of Naples.

4] It is strange—though not so strange when we consider it in the light of the psychological explanations suggested above—that people should think in these terms in connection with politics only. When we are sick, when we must submit to a surgical operation, we never dream of hunting up an "honest man," or even an honest philosopher or mathematician. What we ask for and do our best to find is a doctor or a surgeon, and we will take him honest or dishonest as he happens to be, provided he is a competent physician with a discerning clinical eye and a surgical hand that does not falter. But in politics we demand not politicians, by which I mean experts in statesmanship, but honest men, trained, if they are trained, in something besides politics.

5] "But what is political honesty then?" it may be asked. Political honesty is nothing but political capacity; just as the honesty of the physician and the surgeon is their capacity as physician or surgeon, which prevents them from murdering their patients with a fatuity compounded of good intentions and impressive erudition in other fields.

6] "And is that all? Should not the public official be a man above reproach in every respect, wholly worthy of esteem? Can public affairs be left to persons not in themselves commendable?" The answer is that the shortcomings a statesman of competence or genius may have in spheres other than politics make him unavailable in those spheres but not in politics. In the rest of his life we are free to condemn him and treat him as an ignorant professor, an unfaithful husband, a bad father, a corrupt libertine, or anything else. In the same way we may censure a spendthrift, dissolute or immoral poet as a gambler, a rake, and an adulterer; but we must accept his poetry for what it is as poetry: the pure part of his soul, the aspect of his life with which he progressively redeems himself. After Charles James Fox, a roisterer and roué of the first order, had come into prominence as orator and leader in Parliament, he is said to have tried to set his private life in order, forsaking disreputable places of amusement in an effort to become a respectable gentleman. Straightway he felt his inspiration as a speaker fail him. He lost his zest for the political fray. And he recovered his normal efficiency only when he had gone back to his habitual manner of living. Well, what of it? The most we might do is to deplore an unfortunate physical and psychological constitution in a man that makes him feel the need of unusual excitements and indulgences in order to do his best work. But this would have no bearing on Fox's achievement as a statesman; and as he was a valuable public servant, England did well in giving him plenty of room in politics; though prudent parents could not be blamed if they kept their daughters out of his way.

7] "But that isn't the only thing," the objection further runs. "If we may ignore the private life of a statesman, how about actual dishonesty? This strikes at the roots of the very service he renders, and makes him a traitor to party or country. That is why we demand that he be privately, which means integrally, honest." However, we must not overlook the fact that a man blessed with genius or real capacity will take liberties with everything but not with what constitutes his passion, his love, his glory, the fundamental justification and purpose of his being. The poet will be careless of his manners or his morals; but if he is a real poet he will not compromise his art, he will not consent under any circumstances to write verse unworthy of him. And so it is with the politician and the statesman. Mirabeau used to get money from the Royal Court; but though he used the money for himself, he used the Court along with the National Assembly to further his idea of establishing in France a constitutional monarchy of the English type, neither absolutist nor demagogical.

8] "But supposing he is a political genius, who, despite his passion for his calling, yields to his lower instincts and ruins his work?" On this point there is nothing to be said. Here dishonesty coincides with bad politics, with political incompetence; and incompetence will be incompetence whatever its motives, good or bad, and regardless of the form it may take as innate and fundamental, or as momentary and incidental. So the great poet, for a price or to do a favour, might consent to write uninspired verses of adulation or "of occasion." In this case, however, he would no longer be a poet.

Questions

In reading the opinions of others, especially on controversial subjects, it is well to consider not only the obvious meaning of the passage, but all the implications and all the attitudes which lie behind it; sometimes the real significance of a statement is very different from what it seems to be at first glance. So too, in writing, we should scrutinize our statements carefully and make sure that we understand not only what we say, but the logical consequences of it. Consider, for instance, the essays by Machiavelli and Croce.

1. State the main idea of each essay in a single sentence.
2. From which point of view does Machiavelli regard public affairs, the ruler's or the citizen's? From whose point of view does Croce regard the matter? Who seems more concerned about the welfare of the community as a whole?
3. To whom does Machiavelli seem to be offering advice? What about Croce?
4. Are the opinions advanced by Machiavelli in this essay in harmony with the main ideas of his political philosophy, as they are summarized on page 359?
5. What is Machiavelli's attitude toward Spurius Cassius and Manlius Capitolinus? Does he consider their conduct vicious or merely imprudent?
6. What is Machiavelli's attitude toward the problem of corruption in a state? (Be sure you know what is meant by "corruption" in this context.)
7. What would Machiavelli have thought of the conduct of Charles James Fox? (This question can be answered better by reference to the summary on page 359 than by reference to the essay on corruption.)
8. What kind of misconduct is it which Croce considers allowable or at least pardonable in a statesman? Is it his intention to excuse the Tammany Hall type of thieving politician? Is the misconduct of Manlius and Spurius of the kind which he condones?
9. What conception of the politician is revealed in Croce's choosing to compare him to the doctor and the poet?
10. What supposed characteristic of human nature does Croce's whole argument rest upon?
11. Charles Stewart Parnell, a nineteenth-century Irish politician, attained to such a position of power and influence that he was called the "uncrowned king of Ireland"; but subsequently, because of a scandal in which he was involved with another man's wife, he lost many of his supporters and fell abruptly from his high position. What would Machiavelli and Croce probably have thought of this episode?
12. Neither Machiavelli's position nor Croce's is one with which a person brought up in the American democratic tradition would find himself in full agreement. But in the one case the disagree-

ment is a fundamental and almost irreconcilable one, while in the other case the disagreement is one over a specific issue, not over fundamentals; one is a quarrel over ends, the other over means. In which case is the difference fundamental, and why?

Suggested Assignments

1. Write an essay on some problem of local politics. Choose a specific problem, not a vague and general one, and make the essay an analysis, not an editorial. If possible, the discussion ought to be handled in such a way as to bring out some political principle which, like the principles discussed by Machiavelli and Croce, would be applicable in situations other than the one under discussion.
2. Do the exercise "Machiavelli in Our Time" on page 359.

ABRAHAM LINCOLN

Address at Cooper Institute

MR. PRESIDENT AND FELLOW-CITIZENS OF NEW YORK: The facts with which I shall deal this evening are mainly old and familiar; nor is there anything new in the general use I shall make of them. If there shall be any novelty, it will be in the mode of presenting the facts, and the inferences and observations following that presentation. In his speech last autumn at Columbus, Ohio, as reported in *The New-York Times,* Senator Douglas said:

2] Our fathers, when they framed the government under which we live, understood this question just as well, and even better, than we do now.

"Address at Cooper Institute." Delivered at Cooper Institute, New York, on February 27, 1860.

3] I fully indorse this, and I adopt it as a text for this discourse. I so adopt it because it furnishes a precise and an agreed starting-point for a discussion between Republicans and that wing of the Democracy headed by Senator Douglas. It simply leaves the inquiry: What was the understanding those fathers had of the question mentioned?

4] What is the frame of government under which we live? The answer must be, "The Constitution of the United States." That Constitution consists of the original, framed in 1787, and under which the present government first went into operation, and twelve subsequently framed amendments, the first ten of which were framed in 1789.

5] Who were our fathers that framed the Constitution? I suppose the "thirty-nine" who signed the original instrument may be fairly called our fathers who framed that part of the present government. It is almost exactly true to say they framed it, and it is altogether true to say they fairly represented the opinion and sentiment of the whole nation at that time. Their names, being familiar to nearly all, and accessible to quite all, need not now be repeated.

6] I take these "thirty-nine," for the present, as being "our fathers who framed the government under which we live." What is the question which, according to the text, those fathers understood "just as well, and even better, than we do now"?

7] It is this: Does the proper division of local from Federal authority, or anything in the Constitution, forbid our Federal Government to control as to slavery in our Federal Territories?

8] Upon this, Senator Douglas holds the affirmative, and Republicans the negative. This affirmation and denial form an issue; and this issue—this question—is precisely what the text declares our fathers understood "better than we." Let us now inquire whether the "thirty-nine," or any of them, ever acted upon this question; and if they did, how they acted upon it—how they expressed that better understanding. In 1784, three years before the Constitution, the United States then owning the Northwestern Territory, and no other, the Congress of the Confederation had before them the question of prohibiting slavery in that Territory; and four of the "thirty-nine" who afterward framed the Constitution were in that Congress, and voted on that question. Of these, Roger Sherman, Thomas Mifflin, and Hugh Williamson voted for the prohibition, thus showing that, in their understanding, no line dividing local from Federal authority, nor anything else, properly forbade the Federal Government to control as to slavery in Federal territory. The other of the four, James McHenry, voted against the prohibition, showing that for some cause he thought it improper to vote for it.

9] In 1787, still before the Constitution, but while the convention was in session framing it, and while the Northwestern Territory still was the only Territory owned by the United States, the same question of prohibiting slavery in the Territory again came before the Congress of the Confederation; and two more of the "thirty-nine" who afterward signed the Constitution were in that Congress, and voted on the question. They were William Blount and William Few; and they both voted for the prohibition—thus showing that in their understanding no line dividing local from Federal authority, nor anything else, properly forbade the Federal Government to control as to slavery in Federal territory. This time the prohibition became a law, being part of what is now well known as the ordinance of '87.

10] The question of Federal control of slavery in the Territories seems not to have been directly before the convention which framed the original Constitution; and hence it is not recorded that the "thirty-nine," or any of them, while engaged on that instrument, expressed any opinion on that precise question.

11] In 1789, by the first Congress which sat under the Constitution, an act was passed to enforce the ordinance of '87, including the prohibition of slavery in the Northwestern Territory. The bill for this act was reported by one of the "thirty-nine"—Thomas Fitzsimmons, then a member of the House of Representatives from Pennsylvania. It went through all its stages without a word of opposition, and finally passed both branches without ayes and nays, which is equivalent to a unanimous passage. In this Congress there were sixteen of the thirty-nine fathers who framed the original Constitution. They were John Langdon, Nicholas Gilman, Wm. S. Johnson, Roger Sherman, Robert Morris, Thos. Fitzsimmons, William Few, Abraham Baldwin, Rufus King, William Paterson, George Clymer, Richard Bassett, George Read, Pierce Butler, Daniel Carroll and James Madison.

12] This shows that, in their understanding, no line dividing local from Federal authority, nor anything in the Constitution, properly forbade Congress to prohibit slavery in the Federal territory; else both their fidelity to correct principle, and their oath to support the Constitution, would have constrained them to oppose the prohibition.

13] Again, George Washington, another of the "thirty-nine," was then President of the United States and as such approved and signed the bill, thus completing its validity as a law, and thus showing that, in his understanding, no line dividing local from Federal authority, nor anything in the Constitution, forbade the Federal Government to control as to slavery in Federal territory.

14] No great while after the adoption of the original Constitution, North Carolina ceded to the Federal Government the country now constituting the State of Tennessee; and a few years later Georgia ceded that which now constitutes the States of Mississippi and Alabama. In both deeds of cession it was made a condition by the ceding States that the Federal Government should not prohibit slavery in the ceded country. Besides this, slavery was then actually in the ceded country. Under these circumstances, Congress, on taking charge of these countries, did not absolutely prohibit slavery within them. But they did interfere with it—take control of it—even there, to a certain extent. In 1798 Congress organized the Territory of Mississippi. In the act of organization they prohibited the bringing of slaves into the Territory from any place without the United States, by fine, and giving freedom to slaves so brought. This act passed both branches of Congress without yeas and nays. In that Congress were three of the "thirty-nine" who framed the original Constitution. They were John Langdon, George Read, and Abraham Baldwin. They all probably voted for it. Certainly they would have placed their opposition to it upon record if, in their understanding, any line dividing local from Federal authority, or anything in the Constitution, properly forbade the Federal Government to control as to slavery in Federal territory.

15] In 1803 the Federal Government purchased the Louisiana country. Our former territorial acquisitions came from certain of our own States; but this Louisiana country was acquired from a foreign nation. In 1804 Congress gave a territorial organization to that part of it which now constitutes the State of Louisiana. New Orleans, lying within that part, was an old and comparatively large city. There were other considerable towns and settlements, and slavery was extensively and thoroughly intermingled with the people. Congress did not, in the Territorial Act, prohibit slavery; but they did interfere with it—take control of it—in a more marked and extensive way than they did in the case of Mississippi. The substance of the provision therein made in relation to slaves was:

1st. That no slave should be imported into the Territory from foreign parts.

2d. That no slave should be carried into it who had been imported into the United States since the first day of May, 1798.

3d. That no slave should be carried into it, except by the owner, and for his own use as a settler; the penalty in all the cases being a fine upon the violator of the law, and freedom to the slave.

16] This act also was passed without ayes or nays. In the Congress which passed it there were two of the "thirty-nine." They were Abraham Baldwin and Jonathan Dayton. As stated in the case of Mississippi, it is probable they both voted for it. They would not have allowed it to pass without recording their opposition to it if, in their understanding, it violated either the line properly dividing local from Federal authority, or any provision of the Constitution.

17] In 1819-20 came and passed the Missouri question. Many votes were taken, by yeas and nays, in both branches of Congress, upon the various phases of the general question. Two of the "thirty-nine"—Rufus King and Charles Pinckney—were members of that Congress. Mr. King steadily voted for slavery prohibition and against all compromises, while Mr. Pinckney as steadily voted against slavery prohibition and against all compromises. By this, Mr. King showed that, in his understanding, no line dividing local from Federal authority, nor anything in the Constitution, was violated by Congress prohibiting slavery in Federal territory; while Mr. Pinckney, by his votes, showed that, in his understanding, there was some sufficient reason for opposing such prohibition in that case.

18] The cases I have mentioned are the only acts of the "thirty-nine," or of any of them, upon the direct issue, which I have been able to discover.

19] To enumerate the persons who thus acted as being four in 1784, two in 1787, seventeen in 1789, three in 1798, two in 1804, and two in 1819-20, there would be thirty of them. But this would be counting John Langdon, Roger Sherman, William Few, Rufus King, and George Read each twice, and Abraham Baldwin three times. The true number of those of the "thirty-nine" whom I have shown to have acted upon the question which, by the text, they understood better than we, is twenty-three, leaving sixteen not shown to have acted upon it in any way.

20] Here, then, we have twenty-three out of our thirty-nine fathers "who framed the government under which we live," who have, upon their official responsibility and their corporal oaths, acted upon the very question which the text affirms they "understood just as well, and even better, than we do now"; and twenty-one of them—a clear majority of the whole "thirty-nine"—so acting upon it as to make them guilty of gross political impropriety and wilful perjury if, in their understanding, any proper division between local and Federal authority, or anything in the Constitution they had made themselves, and sworn to support, forbade the Federal Government to control as to slavery in the Federal Territories. Thus the twenty-one acted; and, as actions speak louder than words, so actions under such responsibility speak still louder.

21] Two of the twenty-three voted against congressional prohibition of slavery in the Federal Territories, in the instances in which they acted upon the question. But for what reasons they so voted is not known. They may have done so because they thought a proper division of local from Federal authority, or some provision or principle of the Constitution, stood in the way; or they may, without any such question, have voted against the prohibition on what appeared to them to be sufficient grounds of expediency. No one who has sworn to support the Constitution can conscientiously vote for what he understands to be an unconstitutional measure, however expedient he may think it; but one may and ought to vote against a measure which he deems constitutional if, at the same time, he deems it inexpedient. It, therefore, would be unsafe to set down even the two who voted against the prohibition as having done so because, in their understanding, any proper division of local from Federal authority, or anything in the Constitution, forbade the Federal Government to control as to slavery in Federal territory.

22] The remaining sixteen of the "thirty-nine," so far as I have discovered, have left no record of their understanding upon the direct question of Federal control of slavery in the Federal Territories. But there is much reason to believe that their understanding upon that question would not have appeared different from that of their twenty-three compeers, had it been manifested at all.

23] For the purpose of adhering rigidly to the text, I have purposely omitted whatever understanding may have been manifested by any person, however distinguished, other than the thirty-nine fathers who framed the original Constitution; and, for the same reason, I have also omitted whatever understanding may have been manifested by any of the "thirty-nine" even on any other phase of the general question of slavery. If we should look into their acts and declarations on those other phases, as the foreign slave trade, and the morality and policy of slavery generally, it would appear to us that on the direct question of Federal control of slavery in Federal Territories, the sixteen, if they had acted at all, would probably have acted just as the twenty-three did. Among that sixteen were several of the most noted antislavery men of those times—as Dr. Franklin, Alexander Hamilton, and Gouverneur Morris—while there was not one now known to have been otherwise, unless it may be John Rutledge, of South Carolina.

24] The sum of the whole is that of our thirty-nine fathers who framed the original Constitution, twenty-one—a clear majority of the whole—certainly understood that no proper division of local from Federal authority, nor any part of the Constitution, forbade the Federal Government to control slavery in the Federal Territories; while all the rest had probably the same understanding. Such, unquestionably, was the understanding of our fathers who framed the original Constitution; and the text affirms that they understood the question "better than we."

25] But, so far, I have been considering the understanding of the question manifested by the framers of the original Constitution. In and by the original instrument, a mode was provided for amending it; and, as I have already stated, the present frame of "the government under which we live" consists of that original, and twelve amendatory articles framed and adopted since. Those who now insist that Federal control of slavery in Federal Territories violates the Constitution, point us to the provisions which they suppose it thus violates; and, as I understand, they all fix upon provisions in these amendatory articles, and not in the original instrument. The Supreme Court, in the Dred Scott case, plant themselves upon the Fifth Amendment, which provides that no person shall be deprived of "life, liberty, or property without due process of law"; while Senator Douglas and his peculiar adherents plant themselves upon the Tenth Amendment, providing that "the powers not delegated to the United States by the Constitution" "are reserved to the States respectively, or to the people."

26] Now, it so happens that these amendments were framed by the first Congress which sat under the Constitution—the identical Congress which passed the act, already mentioned, enforcing the prohibition of slavery in the Northwestern Territory. Not only was it the same Congress, but they were the identical, same individual men who, at the same session, and at the same time within the session, had under consideration, and in progress toward maturity, these constitutional amendments, and this act prohibiting slavery in all the territory the nation then owned. The constitutional amendments were introduced before, and passed after, the act enforcing the ordinance of '87; so that, during the whole pendency of the act to enforce the ordinance, the constitutional amendments were also pending.

27] The seventy-six members of that Congress, including sixteen of the framers of the original Constitution, as before stated, were preëminently our fathers who framed that part of "the government under which we live" which is now claimed as forbidding the Federal Government to control slavery in the Federal Territories.

28] Is it not a little presumptuous in any one at this day to affirm that the two things which that Congress deliberately framed, and carried to maturity at the same time, are absolutely inconsistent with each other? And does not such affirmation become impudently absurd when coupled with the other affirmation, from the same mouth, that those who did the two things alleged to be inconsistent, understood whether they really were inconsistent better than we—better than he who affirms that they are inconsistent?

29] It is surely safe to assume that the thirty-nine framers of the original Constitution, and the seventy-six members of the Congress which framed the amendments thereto, taken together, do certainly include those who may be fairly called "our fathers who framed the government under which we live." And so assuming, I defy any man to show that any one of them ever, in his whole life, declared that, in his understanding, any proper division of local from Federal authority, or any part of the Constitution, forbade the Federal Government to control as to slavery in the Federal Territories. I go a step further. I defy any one to show that any living man in the whole world ever did, prior to the beginning of the present century (and I might almost say prior to the beginning of the last half of the present century), declare that, in his understanding, any proper division of local from Federal authority, or any part of the Constitution, forbade the Federal Government to control as to slavery in the Federal Territories. To those who now so declare I give not only "our fathers who framed the government under which we live," but with them all other living men within the century in which it was framed, among whom to search, and they shall not be able to find the evidence of a single man agreeing with them.

30] Now, and here, let me guard a little against being misunderstood. I do not mean to say we are bound to follow implicitly in whatever our fathers did. To do so would be to discard all the lights of current experience—to reject all progress, all improvement. What I do say is that if we would supplant the opinions and policy of our fathers in any case, we should do so upon evidence so conclusive, and argument so clear, that even their great authority, fairly considered and weighed, cannot stand; and most surely not in a case whereof we ourselves declare they understood the question better than we.

31] If any man at this day sincerely believes that a proper division of local from Federal authority, or any part of the Constitution, forbids the Federal Government to control as to slavery in the Federal Territories, he is right to say so, and to enforce his position by all truthful evidence and fair argument which he can. But he has no right to mislead others, who have less access to history, and less leisure to study it, into the false belief that "our fathers who framed the government under which we live" were of the same opinion—thus substituting falsehood and deception for truthful evidence and fair argument. If any man at this day sincerely believes "our fathers who framed the government under which we live" used and applied principles, in other cases, which ought to have led them to understand that a proper division of local from Federal authority, or some part of the Constitution, forbids the Federal Government to control as to slavery in the Federal Territories, he is right to say so. But he should, at the same time, brave the responsibility of declaring that, in his opinion, he understands their principles better than they did themselves, and especially should he not shirk that responsibility by asserting that they "understand the question just as well, and even better, than we do now."

32] But enough! Let all who believe that "our fathers who framed the government under which we live understood this question just as well, and even better, than we do now," speak as they spoke, and act as they acted upon it. This is all Republicans ask—all Republicans desire—in relation to slavery. As those fathers marked it, so let it be again marked, as an evil not to be extended, but to be tolerated and protected only because of and so far as its actual presence among us makes that toleration and protection a necessity. Let all the guaranties those fathers gave it be not grudgingly, but fully and fairly, maintained. For this Republicans contend, and with this, so far as I know or believe, they will be content.

33] And now, if they would listen—as I suppose they will not— I would address a few words to the Southern people.

34] I would say to them: You consider yourselves a reasonable and a just people; and I consider that in the general qualities of reason and justice you are not inferior to any other people. Still, when you speak of us Republicans, you do so only to denounce us as reptiles, or, at the best, as no better than outlaws. You will grant a hearing to pirates or murderers, but nothing like it to "Black Republicans." In all your contentions with one another, each of you deems an unconditional condemnation of "Black Republicanism" as the first thing to be attended to. Indeed, such condemnation of us seems to be an indispensable prerequisite— license, so to speak—among you to be admitted or permitted to speak at all. Now can you or not be prevailed upon to pause and to consider whether this is quite just to us, or even to yourselves? Bring forward your charges and specifications, and then be patient long enough to hear us deny or justify.

35] You say we are sectional. We deny it. That makes an issue; and the burden of proof is upon you. You produce your proof; and what is it? Why, that our party has no existence in your section—gets no votes in your section. The fact is substantially true; but does it prove the issue? If it does, then in case we should, without change of principle, begin to get votes in your section, we should thereby cease to be sectional. You cannot escape this conclusion; and yet, are you willing to abide by it? If you are, you will probably soon find that we have ceased to be sectional, for we shall get votes in your section this very year.

You will then begin to discover, as the truth plainly is, that your proof does not touch the issue. The fact that we get no votes in your section is a fact of your making, and not of ours. And if there be fault in that fact, that fault is primarily yours, and remains so until you show that we repel you by some wrong principle or practice. If we do repel you by any wrong principle or practice, the fault is ours; but this brings you to where you ought to have started—to a discussion of the right or wrong of our principle. If our principle, put in practice, would wrong your section for the benefit of ours, or for any other object, then our principle, and we with it, are sectional, and are justly opposed and denounced as such. Meet us, then, on the question of whether our principle, put in practice, would wrong your section; and so meet us as if it were possible that something may be said on our side. Do you accept the challenge? No! Then you really believe that the principle which "our fathers who framed the government under which we live" thought so clearly right as to adopt it, and indorse it again and again, upon their official oaths, is in fact so clearly wrong as to demand your condemnation without a moment's consideration.

36] Some of you delight to flaunt in our faces the warning against sectional parties given by Washington in his Farewell Address. Less than eight years before Washington gave that warning, he had, as President of the United States, approved and signed an act of Congress enforcing the prohibition of slavery in the Northwestern Territory, which act embodied the policy of the government upon that subject up to and at the very moment he penned that warning; and about one year after he penned it, he wrote Lafayette that he considered that prohibition a wise measure, expressing in the same connection his hope that we should at some time have a confederacy of free States.

37] Bearing this in mind, and seeing that sectionalism has since arisen upon this same subject, is that warning a weapon in your hands against us, or in our hands against you? Could Washington himself speak, would he cast the blame of that sectionalism upon us, who sustain his policy, or upon you, who repudiate it? We respect that warning of Washington, and we commend it to you, together with his example pointing to the right application of it.

38] But you say you are conservative—eminently conservative—while we are revolutionary, destructive, or something of the sort. What is conservatism? Is it not adherence to the old and tried, against the new and untried? We stick to, contend for, the identical old policy on the point in controversy which was adopted by "our fathers who framed the government under which we live"; while you with one accord reject, and scout, and spit upon that old policy, and insist upon substituting something new. True, you disagree among yourselves as to what that substitute shall be. You are divided on new propositions and plans, but you are unanimous in rejecting and denouncing the old policy of the fathers. Some of you are for reviving the foreign slave trade; some for a congressional slave code for the Territories; some for Congress forbidding the Territories to prohibit slavery within their limits; some for maintaining slavery in the Territories through the judiciary; some for the "gur-reat pur-rin-ciple" that "if one man would enslave another, no third man should object," fantastically called "popular sovereignty"; but never a man among you is in favor of Federal prohibition of slavery in Federal Territories, according to the practice of "our fathers who framed the government under which we live." Not one of all your various plans can show a precedent or an advocate in the century within which our government originated. Consider, then, whether your claim of conservatism for yourselves, and your charge of destructiveness against us, are based on the most clear and stable foundations.

39] Again, you say we have made the slavery question more prominent than it formerly was. We deny it. We admit that it is more prominent, but we deny that we made it so. It was not we, but you, who discarded the old policy of the fathers. We resisted, and still resist, your innovation; and thence comes the greater prominence of the question. Would you have that question reduced to its former proportions? Go back to that old policy. What has been will be again, under the same conditions. If you would have the peace of the old times, readopt the precepts and policy of the old times.

40] You charge that we stir up insurrections among your slaves. We deny it; and what is your proof? Harper's Ferry! John Brown!! John Brown was no Republican; and you have failed to implicate a single Republican in his Harper's Ferry enterprise. If any member of our party is guilty in that matter, you know it, or you do not know it. If you do know it, you are inexcusable for not designating the man and proving the fact. If you do not know it, you are inexcusable for asserting it, and especially for persisting in the assertion after you have tried and failed to make the proof. You need not be told that persisting in a charge which one does not know to be true, is simply malicious slander.

41] Some of you admit that no Republican designedly aided or encouraged the Harper's Ferry affair, but still insist that our doctrines and declarations necessarily lead to such results. We do not believe it. We know we hold no doctrine, and make no declaration, which were not held to and made by "our fathers who framed the government under which we live." You never dealt fairly by us in relation to this affair. When it occurred, some important State elections were near at hand, and you were in evident glee with the belief that, by charging the blame upon us, you could get an advantage of us in those elections. The elections came, and your expectations were not quite fulfilled. Every Republican man knew that, as to himself at least, your charge was a slander, and he was not much inclined by it to cast his vote in your favor. Republican doctrines and declarations are accompanied with a continual protest against any interference whatever with your slaves, or with you about your slaves. Surely, this does not encourage them to revolt. True, we do, in common with "our fathers who framed the government under which we live," declare our belief that slavery is wrong; but the slaves do not hear us declare even this. For anything we say or do, the slaves would scarcely know there is a Republican party. I believe they would not, in fact, generally know it but for your misrepresentations of us in their hearing. In your political contests among yourselves, each faction charges the other with sympathy with Black Republicanism; and then, to give point to the charge, defines Black Republicanism to simply be insurrection, blood, and thunder among the slaves.

42] Slave insurrections are no more common now than they were before the Republican party was organized. What induced the Southampton insurrection, twenty-eight years ago, in which at least three times as many lives were lost as at Harper's Ferry? You can scarcely stretch your very elastic fancy to the conclusion that Southampton was "got up by Black Republicanism." In the present state of things in the United States, I do not think a general, or even a very extensive, slave insurrection is possible. The indispensable concert of action cannot be attained. The slaves have no means of rapid communication; nor can incendiary freemen, black or white, supply it. The explosive materials are everywhere in parcels; but there neither are, nor can be supplied, the indispensable connecting trains.

43] Much is said by Southern people about the affection of slaves for their masters and mistresses; and a part of it, at least, is true. A plot for an uprising could scarcely be devised and communicated to twenty individuals before some one of them, to save the life of a favorite master or mistress, would divulge it. This is the rule; and the slave revolution in Hayti was not an exception to it, but a case occurring under peculiar circumstances. The gunpowder plot of British history, though not connected with slaves, was more in point. In that case, only about twenty were admitted to the secret; and yet one of them, in his anxiety to save a friend, betrayed the plot to that friend, and, by consequence, averted the calamity. Occasional poisonings from the kitchen, and open or stealthy assassinations in the field, and local revolts extending to a score or so, will continue to occur as the natural results of slavery; but no general insurrection of slaves, as I think, can happen in this country for a long time. Whoever much fears, or much hopes, for such an event, will be alike disappointed.

44] In the language of Mr. Jefferson, uttered many years ago, "It is still in our power to direct the process of emancipation and deportation peaceably, and in such slow degrees, as that the evil will wear off insensibly; and their places be, *pari passu*, filled up by free white laborers. If, on the contrary, it is left to force itself on, human nature must shudder at the prospect held up."

45] Mr. Jefferson did not mean to say, nor do I, that the power of emancipation is in the Federal Government. He spoke of Virginia; and, as to the power of emancipation, I speak of the slaveholding States only. The Federal Government, however, as we insist, has the power of restraining the extension of the institution —the power to insure that a slave insurrection shall never occur on any American soil which is now free from slavery.

46] John Brown's effort was peculiar. It was not a slave insurrection. It was an attempt by white men to get up a revolt among slaves, in which the slaves refused to participate. In fact, it was so absurd that the slaves, with all their ignorance, saw plainly enough it could not succeed. That affair, in its philosophy, corresponds with the many attempts, related in history, at the assassination of kings and emperors. An enthusiast broods over the oppression of a people till he fancies himself commissioned by Heaven to liberate them. He ventures the attempt, which ends in little else than his own execution. Orsini's attempt on Louis Napoleon, and John Brown's attempt at Harper's Ferry, were, in their philosophy, precisely the same. The eagerness to cast blame on old England in the one case, and on New England in the other, does not disprove the sameness of the two things.

47] And how much would it avail you, if you could, by the use of John Brown, Helper's book,* and the like, break up the Republican organization? Human action can be modified to some extent, but human nature cannot be changed. There is a judgment and a feeling against slavery in this nation, which cast at least a million and a half of votes. You cannot destroy that judgment and feeling—that sentiment—by breaking up the political organization which rallies around it. You can scarcely scatter and disperse an army which has been formed into order in the face of your heaviest fire; but if you could, how much would you gain by forcing the sentiment which created it out of the peaceful

---

* *The Impending Crisis in the South*, by H. R. Helper.

channel of the ballot-box into some other channel? What would that other channel probably be? Would the number of John Browns be lessened or enlarged by the operation?

48] But you will break up the Union rather than submit to a denial of your constitutional rights.

49] That has a somewhat reckless sound; but it would be palliated, if not fully justified, were we proposing, by the mere force of numbers, to deprive you of some right plainly written down in the Constitution. But we are proposing no such thing.

50] When you make these declarations you have a specific and well-understood allusion to an assumed constitutional right of yours to take slaves into the Federal Territories, and to hold them there as property. But no such right is specifically written in the Constitution. That instrument is literally silent about any such right. We, on the contrary, deny that such a right has any existence in the Constitution, even by implication.

51] Your purpose, then, plainly stated, is that you will destroy the government, unless you be allowed to construe and force the Constitution as you please, on all points in dispute between you and us. You will rule or ruin in all events.

52] This, plainly stated, is your language. Perhaps you will say the Supreme Court has decided the disputed constitutional question in your favor.* Not quite so. But waiving the lawyer's distinction between dictum and decision, the court has decided the question for you in a sort of way. The court has substantially said, it is your constitutional right to take slaves into the Federal Territories, and to hold them there as property. When I say the decision was made in a sort of way, I mean it was made in a divided court, by a bare majority of the judges, and they not quite agreeing with one another in the reasons for making it; that it is so made as that its avowed supporters disagree with one another about its meaning, and that it was mainly based upon a mistaken statement of fact—the statement in the opinion that "the right of property in a slave is distinctly and expressly affirmed in the Constitution."

* In the Dred Scott decision.

53] An inspection of the Constitution will show that the right of property in a slave is not "distinctly and expressly affirmed" in it. Bear in mind, the judges do not pledge their judicial opinion that such right is impliedly affirmed in the Constitution; but they pledge their veracity that it is "distinctly and expressly" affirmed there—"distinctly," that is, not mingled with anything else—"expressly," that is, in words meaning just that, without the aid of any inference, and susceptible of no other meaning.

54] If they had only pledged their judicial opinion that such right is affirmed in the instrument by implication, it would be open to others to show that neither the word "slave" nor "slavery" is to be found in the Constitution, nor the word "property" even, in any connection with language alluding to the things slave, or slavery; and that wherever in that instrument the slave is alluded to, he is called a "person"; and wherever his master's legal right in relation to him is alluded to, it is spoken of as "service or labor which may be due"—as a debt payable in service or labor. Also it would be open to show, by contemporaneous history, that this mode of alluding to slaves and slavery, instead of speaking of them, was employed on purpose to exclude from the Constitution the idea that there could be property in man.

55] To show all this is easy and certain.

56] When this obvious mistake of the judges shall be brought to their notice, is it not reasonable to expect that they will withdraw the mistaken statement, and reconsider the conclusion based upon it?

57] And then it is to be remembered that "our fathers who framed the government under which we live"—the men who made the Constitution—decided this same constitutional question in our favor long ago: decided it without division among themselves when making the decision; without division among themselves about the meaning of it after it was made, and, so far as any evidence is left, without basing it upon any mistaken statement of facts.

58] Under all these circumstances, do you really feel yourselves justified to break up this government unless such a court decision as yours is shall be at once submitted to as a conclusive and final rule of political action? But you will not abide the election of a Republican president! In that supposed event, you say, you will destroy the Union; and then, you say, the great crime of having destroyed it will be upon us! That is cool. A highwayman holds a pistol to my ear, and mutters through his teeth, "Stand and deliver, or I shall kill you, and then you will be a murderer!"

59] To be sure, what the robber demanded of me—my money—was my own; and I had a clear right to keep it; but it was no more my own than my vote is my own; and the threat of death to me, to extort my money, and the threat of destruction to the Union, to extort my vote, can scarcely be distinguished in principle.

60] A few words now to Republicans. It is exceedingly desirable that all parts of this great Confederacy shall be at peace, and in harmony one with another. Let us Republicans do our part to have it so. Even though much provoked, let us do nothing through passion and ill temper. Even though the Southern people will not so much as listen to us, let us calmly consider their demands, and yield to them if, in our deliberate view of our duty, we possibly can. Judging by all they say and do, and by the subject and nature of their controversy with us, let us determine, if we can, what will satisfy them.

61] Will they be satisfied if the Territories be unconditionally surrendered to them? We know they will not. In all their present complaints against us, the Territories are scarcely mentioned. Invasions and insurrections are the rage now. Will it satisfy them if, in the future, we have nothing to do with invasions and insurrections? We know it will not. We so know, because we know we never had anything to do with invasions and insurrections; and yet this total abstaining does not exempt us from the charge and the denunciation.

62] The question recurs, What will satisfy them? Simply this: we must not only let them alone, but we must somehow convince them that we do let them alone. This, we know by experience, is no easy task. We have been so trying to convince them from the very beginning of our organization, but with no success. In all our platforms and speeches we have constantly protested our purpose to let them alone; but this has had no tendency to convince them. Alike unavailing to convince them is the fact that they have never detected a man of us in any attempt to disturb them.

63] These natural and apparently adequate means all failing, what will convince them? This, and this only: cease to call slavery wrong, and join them in calling it right. And this must be done thoroughly—done in acts as well as in words. Silence will not be tolerated—we must place ourselves avowedly with them. Senator Douglas's new sedition law must be enacted and enforced, suppressing all declarations that slavery is wrong, whether made in politics, in presses, in pulpits, or in private. We must arrest and return their fugitive slaves with greedy pleasure. We must pull down our Free-State constitutions. The whole atmosphere must be disinfected from all taint of opposition to slavery, before they will cease to believe that all their troubles proceed from us.

64] I am quite aware they do not state their case precisely in this way. Most of them would probably say to us, "Let us alone; do nothing to us, and say what you please about slavery." But we do let them alone—have never disturbed them—so that, after all, it is what we say which dissatisfies them. They will continue to accuse us of doing, until we cease saying.

65] I am also aware they have not as yet in terms demanded the overthrow of our Free-State constitutions. Yet those constitutions declare the wrong of slavery with more solemn emphasis than do all other sayings against it; and when all these other sayings shall have been silenced, the overthrow of these constitutions will be demanded, and nothing be left to resist the demand. It is nothing to the contrary that they do not demand the whole of this just now. Demanding what they do, and for the reason they do, they can voluntarily stop nowhere short of this consummation. Holding, as they do, that slavery is morally right and socially elevating, they cannot cease to demand a full national recognition of it as a legal right and a social blessing.

66] Nor can we justifiably withhold this on any ground save

our conviction that slavery is wrong. If slavery is right, all words, acts, laws, and constitutions against it are themselves wrong, and should be silenced and swept away. If it is right, we cannot justly object to its nationality—its universality; if it is wrong, they cannot justly insist upon its extension—its enlargement. All they ask we could readily grant, if we thought slavery right; all we ask they could as readily grant, if they thought it wrong. Their thinking it right and our thinking it wrong is the precise fact upon which depends the whole controversy. Thinking it right, as they do, they are not to blame for desiring its full recognition as being right; but thinking it wrong, as we do, can we yield to them? Can we cast our votes with their view, and against our own? In view of our moral, social, and political responsibilities, can we do this?

67] Wrong as we think slavery is, we can yet afford to let it alone where it is, because that much is due to the necessity arising from its actual presence in the nation; but can we, while our votes will prevent it, allow it to spread into the national Territories, and to overrun us here in these free States? If our sense of duty forbids this, then let us stand by our duty fearlessly and effectively. Let us be diverted by none of those sophistical contrivances wherewith we are so industriously plied and belabored —contrivances such as groping for some middle ground between the right and the wrong: vain as the search for a man who should be neither a living man nor a dead man; such as a policy of "don't care" on a question about which all true men do care; such as Union appeals beseeching true Union men to yield to Disunionists, reversing the divine rule, and calling, not the sinners, but the righteous to repentance; such as invocations to Washington, imploring men to unsay what Washington said and undo what Washington did.

68] Neither let us be slandered from our duty by false accusations against us, nor frightened from it by menaces of destruction to the government, nor of dungeons to ourselves. Let us have faith that right makes might, and in that faith let us to the end dare to do our duty as we understand it.

Questions

1. What are the three sections into which the essay is divided? Why are they arranged in this order? Consider how the organization would be affected by the following considerations:

    a. The audience addressed was a Northern one.

    b. The first section, as the speech is now arranged, is of a somewhat dry and abstract character.

2. What is the proposition which Lincoln is trying to prove in the first section? What is the method of proof?
3. If, as Lincoln says in paragraph 30, we are not "bound to follow implicitly in whatever our fathers did," what is the point of the argument?
4. *a.* Why is paragraph 21 important to Lincoln's line of reasoning?

    b. Point out those sentences of paragraphs 8 and 17 in which this argument is foreshadowed.
5. Is twenty-one out of thirty-nine (paragraph 20) a sufficiently impressive majority for Lincoln's purposes? Is the silence of sixteen out of the thirty-nine a suspicious circumstance?
6. Would it be possible to place paragraphs 25 and 26 before paragraphs 8 through 24? Could the material in paragraphs 25 and 26 have been inserted after paragraph 13?
7. The second section is supposed to be an appeal to the South. Does Lincoln expect that the appeal will be successful? Why does he make it?
8. If Lincoln were really trying to win over the South in this passage, what changes in tone and language would be necessary?
9. Is any real argument advanced in paragraph 38?
10. What course of action is Lincoln urging upon the Republicans in the last section?

WINSTON S. CHURCHILL

The Munich Agreement

IF I do not begin this afternoon by paying the usual, and indeed almost invariable, tributes to the Prime Minister for his handling of this crisis, it is certainly not from any lack of personal regard. We have always, over a great many years, had very pleasant relations, and I have deeply understood from personal experiences of my own in a similar crisis the stress and strain he has had to bear; but I am sure it is much better to say exactly what we think about public affairs, and this is certainly not the time when it is worth anyone's while to court political popularity. We had a shining example of firmness of character from the late First Lord of the Admiralty two days ago. He showed that firmness of character which is utterly unmoved by currents of opinion, however swift and violent they may be. My hon. Friend the Member for South-West Hull [Mr. Law], to whose compulsive speech the House listened on Monday, was quite right in reminding us that the Prime Minister has himself throughout his conduct of these matters shown a robust indifference to cheers or boos and to the alternations of criticism or applause. If that be so, such qualities and elevation of mind should make it possible for the most severe expressions of honest opinion to be interchanged in this House without rupturing personal relations, and for all points of view to receive the fullest possible expression. Having thus fortified myself by the example of others, I will proceed to emulate them. I will, therefore, begin

"The Munich Agreement." From *Blood, Sweat, and Tears* by the Rt. Hon. Winston S. Churchill, courtesy of G. P. Putnam's Sons. The address was delivered in the House of Commons, October 5, 1938.

by saying the most unpopular and most unwelcome thing. I will begin by saying what everybody would like to ignore or forget but which must nevertheless be stated, namely, that we have sustained a total and unmitigated defeat, and that France has suffered even more than we have. The utmost my right hon. Friend the Prime Minister has been able to secure by all his immense exertions, by all the great efforts and mobilization which took place in this country, and by all the anguish and strain through which we have passed in this country—the utmost he has been able to gain for Czechoslovakia in the matters which were in dispute has been that the German dictator, instead of snatching the victuals from the table, has been content to have them served to him course by course.

2] The Chancellor of the Exchequer [Sir John Simon] said it was the first time Herr Hitler had been made to retract—I think that was the word—in any degree. We really must not waste time after all this long Debate upon the difference between the positions reached at Berchtesgaden, at Godesberg and at Munich. They can be very simply epitomized, if the House will permit me to vary the metaphor. One pound was demanded at the pistol's point. When it was given, £2 were demanded at the pistol's point. Finally, the dictator consented to take £1 17s. 6d. and the rest in promises of good will for the future.

3] Now I come to the point, which was mentioned to me just now from some quarters of the House, about the saving of peace. No one has been a more resolute and uncompromising struggler for peace than the Prime Minister. Everyone knows that. Never has there been such intense and undaunted determination to maintain and secure peace. That is quite true. Nevertheless, I am not quite clear why there was so much danger of Great Britain or France being involved in a war with Germany at this juncture if, in fact, they were ready all along to sacrifice Czechoslovakia. The terms which the Prime Minister brought back with him could easily have been agreed, I believe, through the ordinary diplomatic channels at any time during the summer. And I will say this: that I believe the Czechs, left to themselves and told they were going to get no help from the Western Powers, would have been able to make better terms than they have got after all this tremendous perturbation; they could hardly have had worse.

4] There never can be any absolute certainty that there will be a fight if one side is determined that it will give way completely. When one reads the Munich terms, when one sees what is happening in Czechoslovakia from hour to hour, when one is sure, I will not say of Parliamentary approval but of Parliamentary acquiescence, when the Chancellor of the Exchequer makes a speech which at any rate tries to put in a very powerful and persuasive manner the fact that, after all, it was inevitable and indeed righteous: when we saw all this—and everyone on this side of the House, including many members of the Conservative Party who are vigilant and careful guardians of the national interest, is quite clear that nothing vitally affecting us was at stake—it seems to me that one must ask, What was all the trouble and fuss about?

5] The resolve was taken by the British and the French Governments. Let me say that it is very important to realize that it is by no means a question which the British Government only have had to decide. I very much admire the manner in which, in the House, all references of a recriminatory nature have been repressed. But it must be realized that this resolve did not emanate particularly from one or other of the Governments but was a resolve for which both must share in common the responsibility. When this resolve was taken and the course was followed—you may say it was wise or unwise, prudent or short-sighted—once it had been decided not to make the defense of Czechoslovakia a matter of war, then there was really no reason, if the matter had been handled during the summer in the ordinary way, to call into being all this formidable apparatus of crisis. I think that point should be considered.

6] We are asked to vote for this Motion [1] which has been put upon the Paper, and it is certainly a Motion couched in very uncontroversial terms, as, indeed, is the Amendment moved from

---

[1] "That this House approves the policy of His Majesty's Government by which war was averted in the recent crisis and supports their efforts to secure a lasting peace."

the Opposition side. I cannot myself express my agreement with the steps which have been taken, and as the Chancellor of the Exchequer has put his side of the case with so much ability I will attempt, if I may be permitted, to put the case from a different angle. I have always held the view that the maintenance of peace depends upon the accumulation of deterrents against the aggressor, coupled with a sincere effort to redress grievances. Herr Hitler's victory, like so many of the famous struggles that have governed the fate of the world, was won upon the narrowest of margins. After the seizure of Austria in March we faced this problem in our Debates. I ventured to appeal to the Government to go a little further than the Prime Minister went, and to give a pledge that in conjunction with France and other Powers they would guarantee the security of Czechoslovakia while the Sudeten-Deutsch question was being examined either by a League of Nations Commission or some other impartial body, and I still believe that if that course had been followed events would not have fallen into this disastrous state. I agree very much with my right hon. Friend the Member for Sparkbrook [Mr. Amery] when he said on that occasion, "Do one thing or the other; either say you will disinterest yourself in the matter altogether or take the step of giving a guarantee which will have the greatest chance of securing protection for that country."

7] France and Great Britain together, especially if they had maintained a close contact with Russia, which certainly was not done, would have been able in those days in the summer, when they had the prestige, to influence many of the smaller states of Europe; and I believe they could have determined the attitude of Poland. Such a combination, prepared at a time when the German dictator was not deeply and irrevocably committed to his new adventure, would, I believe, have given strength to all those forces in Germany which resisted this departure, this new design. They were varying forces—those of a military character which declared that Germany was not ready to undertake a world war, and all that mass of moderate opinion and popular opinion which dreaded war, and some elements of which still have some influence upon the Government. Such action would have given strength to all that intense desire for peace which the helpless German masses share with their British and French fellow men, and which, as we have been reminded, found a passionate and rarely permitted vent in the joyous manifestations with which the Prime Minister was acclaimed in Munich.

8] All these forces, added to the other deterrents which combinations of Powers, great and small, ready to stand firm upon the front of law and for the ordered remedy of grievances, would have formed, might well have been effective. Between submission and immediate war there was this third alternative, which gave a hope not only of peace but of justice. It is quite true that such a policy in order to succeed demanded that Britain should declare straight out and a long time beforehand that she would, with others, join to defend Czechoslovakia against an unprovoked aggression. His Majesty's Government refused to give that guarantee when it would have saved the situation, yet in the end they gave it when it was too late, and now, for the future, they renew it when they have not the slightest power to make it good.

9] All is over. Silent, mournful, abandoned, broken, Czechoslovakia recedes into the darkness. She has suffered in every respect by her association with the Western democracies and with the League of Nations, of which she has always been an obedient servant. She has suffered in particular from her association with France, by whose guidance and policy she has been actuated for so long. The very measures taken by His Majesty's Government in the Anglo-French Agreement to give her the best chance possible, namely, the 50 per cent clean cut in certain districts instead of a plebiscite, have turned to her detriment, because there is to be a plebiscite too in wide areas, and those other Powers who had claims have also come down upon the helpless victim. Those municipal elections upon whose voting the basis is taken for the 50 per cent cut were held on issues which had nothing to do with joining Germany. When I saw Herr Henlein over here he assured me that was not the desire of his people. Positive statements were made that it was only a question of home rule, of having a position of their own in the Czechoslovakian State. No one has a right to say that the plebiscite which is to be taken in areas under

Saar conditions, and the clean cut of the 50 per cent areas—that those two operations together amount in the slightest degree to a verdict of self-determination. It is a fraud and a farce to invoke that name.

10] We in this country, as in other Liberal and democratic countries, have a perfect right to exalt the principle of self-determination, but it comes ill out of the mouths of those in totalitarian states who deny even the smallest element of toleration to every section and creed within their bounds. But, however you put it, this particular block of land, this mass of human beings to be handed over, has never expressed the desire to go into the Nazi rule. I do not believe that even now, if their opinion could be asked, they would exercise such an opinion.

11] What is the remaining position of Czechoslovakia? Not only are they politically mutilated, but economically and financially they are in complete confusion. Their banking, their railway arrangements, are severed and broken, their industries are curtailed, and the movement of their population is most cruel. The Sudeten miners, who are all Czechs and whose families have lived in that area for centuries, must now flee into an area where there are hardly any mines left for them to work. It is a tragedy which has occurred. There must always be the most profound regret and a sense of vexation in British hearts at the treatment and the misfortune which have overcome the Czechoslovakian Republic. They have not ended here. At any moment there may be a hitch in the program. At any moment there may be an order for Herr Goebbels to start again his propaganda of calumny and lies; at any moment an incident may be provoked, and now that the fortress line is turned, what is there to stop the will of the conqueror? Obviously, we are not in a position to give them the slightest help at the present time, except what everyone is glad to know has been done, the financial aid which the Government have promptly produced.

12] I venture to think that in future the Czechoslovak State cannot be maintained as an independent entity. I think you will find that in a period of time which may be measured by years, but may be measured only by months, Czechoslovakia will be engulfed in the Nazi regime. Perhaps they may join it in despair or in revenge. At any rate, that story is over and told. But we cannot consider the abandonment and ruin of Czechoslovakia in the light only of what happened only last month. It is the most grievous consequence of what we have done and of what we have left undone in the last five years—five years of futile good intentions, five years of eager search for the line of least resistance, five years of uninterrupted retreat of British power, five years of neglect of our air defenses. Those are the features which I stand here to expose and which marked an improvident stewardship for which Great Britain and France have dearly to pay. We have been reduced in those five years from a position of security so overwhelming and so unchallengeable that we never cared to think about it. We have been reduced from a position where the very word "war" was considered one which could be used only by persons qualifying for a lunatic asylum. We have been reduced from a position of safety and power—power to do good, power to be generous to a beaten foe, power to make terms with Germany, power to give her proper redress for her grievances, power to stop her arming if we chose, power to take any step in strength or mercy or justice which we thought right—reduced in five years from a position safe and unchallenged to where we stand now.

13] When I think of the fair hopes of a long peace which still lay before Europe at the beginning of 1933 when Herr Hitler first obtained power, and of all the opportunities of arresting the growth of the Nazi power which have been thrown away, when I think of the immense combinations and resources which have been neglected or squandered, I cannot believe that a parallel exists in the whole course of history. So far as this country is concerned, the responsibility must rest with those who have had the undisputed control of our political affairs. They neither prevented Germany from rearming, nor did they rearm ourselves in time. They quarreled with Italy without saving Ethiopia. They exploited and discredited the vast institution of the League of Nations and they neglected to make alliances and combinations which might have repaired previous errors, and thus they left us in the hour of trial without adequate national defense or effective international security.

14] In my holiday I thought it was a chance to study the reign of King Ethelred the Unready. The House will remember that that was a period of great misfortune, in which, from the strong position which we had gained under the descendants of King Alfred, we fell very swiftly into chaos. It was the period of Danegeld and of foreign pressure. I must say that the rugged words of the Anglo-Saxon Chronicle, written a thousand years ago, seem to me apposite, at least as apposite as those quotations from Shakespeare with which we have been regaled by the last speaker from the Opposition Bench. Here is what the Anglo-Saxon Chronicle said, and I think the words apply very much to our treatment of Germany and our relations with her. "All these calamities fell upon us because of evil counsel, because tribute was not offered to them at the right time nor yet were they resisted; but when they had done the most evil, then was peace made with them." That is the wisdom of the past, for all wisdom is not new wisdom.

15] I have ventured to express those views in justifying myself for not being able to support the Motion which is moved tonight, but I recognize that this great matter of Czechoslovakia, and of British and French duty there, has passed into history. New developments may come along, but we are not here to decide whether any of those steps should be taken or not. They have been taken. They have been taken by those who had a right to take them because they bore the highest executive responsibility under the Crown. Whatever we may think of it, we must regard those steps as belonging to the category of affairs which are settled beyond recall. The past is no more, and one can only draw comfort if one feels that one has done one's best to advise rightly and wisely and in good time. I, therefore, turn to the future, and to our situation as it is today. Here, again, I am sure I shall have to say something which will not be at all welcome.

16] We are in the presence of a disaster of the first magnitude which has befallen Great Britain and France. Do not let us blind ourselves to that. It must now be accepted that all the countries of Central and Eastern Europe will make the best terms they can with the triumphant Nazi power. The system of alliances in Central Europe upon which France has relied for her safety has been swept away, and I can see no means by which it can be reconstituted. The road down the Danube Valley to the Black Sea, the road which leads as far as Turkey, has been opened. In fact, if not in form, it seems to me that all those countries of Middle Europe, all those Danubian countries, will, one after another, be drawn into this vast system of power politics—not only power military politics but power economic politics—radiating from Berlin, and I believe this can be achieved quite smoothly and swiftly and will not necessarily entail the firing of a single shot. If you wish to survey the havoc of the foreign policy of Britain and France, look at what is happening and is recorded each day in the columns of *The Times*. Why, I read this morning about Yugoslavia—and I know something about the details of that country—

17] "The effects of the crisis for Yugoslavia can immediately be traced. Since the elections of 1935, which followed soon after the murder of King Alexander, the Serb and Croat Opposition to the Government of Dr. Stoyadinovitch have been conducting their entire campaign for the next elections under the slogan: 'Back to France, England, and the Little Entente; back to democracy.' The events of the past fortnight have so triumphantly vindicated Dr. Stoyadinovitch's policy . . ."—his is a policy of close association with Germany—"that the Opposition has collapsed practically overnight; the new elections, the date of which was in doubt, are now likely to be held very soon and can result only in an overwhelming victory for Dr. Stoyadinovitch's Government." Here was a country which, three months ago, would have stood in the line with other countries to arrest what has occurred.

18] Again, what happened in Warsaw? The British and French Ambassadors visited the Foreign Minister, Colonel Beck, or sought to visit him, in order to ask for some mitigation in the harsh measures being pursued against Czechoslovakia about Teschen. The door was shut in their faces. The French Ambassador was not even granted an audience, and the British Ambassador was given a most curt reply by a political director. The whole matter is described in the Polish Press as a political indiscretion committed by those two powers, and we are today reading of the success of Colonel Beck's blow. I am not forgetting, I must say, that it is less than twenty years since British and French bayonets rescued Poland from the bondage of a century and a half. I think it is indeed a sorry episode in the history of that country, for whose freedom and rights so many of us have had warm and long sympathy.

19] Those illustrations are typical. You will see, day after day, week after week, entire alienation of those regions. Many of those countries, in fear of the rise of the Nazi power, have already got politicians, Ministers, Governments, who were pro-German, but there was always an enormous popular movement in Poland, Rumania, Bulgaria and Yugoslavia which looked to the Western democracies and loathed the idea of having this arbitrary rule of the totalitarian system thrust upon them, and hoped that a stand would be made. All that has gone by the board. We are talking about countries which are a long way off. But what will be the position, I want to know, of France and England this year and the year afterwards? What will be the position of that Western front of which we are in full authority the guarantors? The German army at the present time is more numerous than that of France, though not nearly so matured or perfected. Next year it will grow much larger, and its maturity will be more complete. Relieved from all anxiety in the East, and having secured resources which will greatly diminish, if not entirely remove, the deterrent of a naval blockade, the rulers of Nazi Germany will have a free choice open to them as to what direction they will turn their eyes. If the Nazi dictator should choose to look westward, as he may, bitterly will France and England regret the loss of that fine army of ancient Bohemia which was estimated last week to require not fewer than 30 German divisions for its destruction.

20] Can we blind ourselves to the great change which has taken place in the military situation, and to the dangers we have to meet? We are in process, I believe, of adding in four years, four battalions to the British Army. No fewer than two have already been completed. Here are at least 30 divisions which must now be taken into consideration upon the French front, besides the 12 that were captured when Austria was engulfed. Many people, no doubt, honestly believe that they are only giving away the interests of Czechoslovakia, whereas I fear we shall find that we have deeply compromised, and perhaps fatally endangered, the safety and even the independence of Great Britain and France. This is not merely a question of giving up the German colonies, as I am sure we shall be asked to do. Nor is it a question only of losing influence in Europe. It goes far deeper than that. You have to consider the character of the Nazi movement and the rule which it implies. The Prime Minister desires to see cordial relations between this country and Germany. There is no difficulty at all in having cordial relations between the peoples. Our hearts go out to them. But they have no power. But never will you have friendship with the present German Government. You must have diplomatic and correct relations, but there can never be friendship between the British democracy and the Nazi power, that power which spurns Christian ethics, which cheers its onward course by barbarous paganism, which vaunts the spirit of aggression and conquest, which derives strength and perverted pleasure from persecution, and uses, as we have seen, with pitiless brutality the threat of murderous force. That power cannot ever be the trusted friend of the British democracy.

21] What I find unendurable is the sense of our country falling into the power, into the orbit and influence of Nazi Germany, and of our existence becoming dependent upon their good will or pleasure. It is to prevent that that I have tried my best to urge the maintenance of every bulwark of defense—first, the timely creation of an Air Force superior to anything within striking distance of our shores; secondly, the gathering together of the collective strength of many nations; and thirdly, the making of alliances and military conventions, all within the Covenant, in order to gather together forces at any rate to restrain the onward movement of this power. It has all been in vain. Every position has been successively undermined and abandoned on specious and plausible excuses.

22] We do not want to be led upon the high road to becoming a satellite of the German Nazi system of European domination. In a very few years, perhaps in a very few months, we shall be confronted with demands with which we shall no doubt be invited to comply. Those demands may affect the surrender of territory or the surrender of liberty. I foresee and foretell that the policy of submission will carry with it restrictions upon the freedom of speech and debate in Parliament, on public platforms, and discussions in the Press, for it will be said—indeed, I hear it said sometimes now—that we cannot allow the Nazi system of dictatorship to be criticized by ordinary, common English politicians. Then, with a Press under control, in part direct but more potently indirect, with every organ of public opinion doped and chloroformed into acquiescence, we shall be conducted along further stages of our journey.

23] It is a small matter to introduce into such a Debate as this, but during the week I heard something of the talk of Tadpole and Taper. They were very keen upon having a general election, a sort of, if I may say so, inverted khaki election. I wish the Prime Minister had heard the speech of my hon. and gallant Friend the Member for the Abbey Division of Westminster [Sir Sidney Herbert] last night. I know that no one is more patient and regular in his attendance than the Prime Minister, and it is marvelous how he is able to sit through so much of our Debates, but it happened that by bad luck he was not here at that moment. I am sure, however, that if he had heard my hon. and gallant Friend's speech he would have felt very much annoyed that such a rumor could even have been circulated. I cannot believe that the Prime Minister, or any Prime Minister, possessed of a large working majority, would be capable of such an act of historic, constitutional indecency. I think too highly of him. Of course, if I have misjudged him on the right side, and there is a dissolution on the Munich Agreement, on Anglo-Nazi friendship, of the state of our defenses and so forth, everyone will have to fight according to his convictions, and only a prophet could forecast the ultimate result; but, whatever the result, few things could be more fatal to our remaining chances of survival as a great

Power than that this country should be torn in twain upon this deadly issue of foreign policy at a moment when, whoever the Ministers may be, united effort can alone make us safe.

24] I have been casting about to see how measures can be taken to protect us from this advance of the Nazi power, and to secure those forms of life which are so dear to us. What is the sole method that is open? The sole method that is open is for us to regain our old island independence by acquiring that supremacy in the air which we were promised, that security in our air defenses which we were assured we had, and thus to make ourselves an island once again. That, in all this grim outlook, shines out as the overwhelming fact. An effort at rearmament the like of which has not been seen ought to be made forthwith, and all the resources of this country and all its united strength should be bent to that task. I was very glad to see that Lord Baldwin yesterday in the House of Lords said that he would mobilize industry tomorrow. But I think it would have been much better if Lord Baldwin had said that two and a half years ago, when everyone demanded a Ministry of Supply. I will venture to say to hon. Gentlemen sitting here behind the Government Bench, hon. Friends of mine, whom I thank for the patience with which they have listened to what I have to say, that they have some responsibility for all this too, because, if they had given one tithe of the cheers they have lavished upon this transaction of Czechoslovakia to the small band of Members, who were endeavoring to get timely rearmament set in motion, we should not now be in the position in which we are. Hon. Gentlemen opposite, and hon. Members on the Liberal benches, are not entitled to throw these stones. I remember for two years having to face, not only the Government's deprecation, but their stern disapproval. Lord Baldwin has now given the signal, tardy though it may be; let us at least obey it.

25] After all, there are no secrets now about what happened in the air and in the mobilization of our anti-aircraft defenses. These matters have been, as my hon. and gallant Friend the Member for the Abbey Division said, seen by thousands of people. They can form their own opinions of the character of the statements which have been persistently made to us by Ministers on this subject. Who pretends now that there is air parity with Germany? Who pretends now that our anti-aircraft defenses were adequately manned or armed? We know that the German General Staff are well informed upon these subjects, but the House of Commons has hitherto not taken seriously its duty of requiring to assure itself on these matters. The Home Secretary [2] said the other night that he would welcome investigation. Many things have been done which reflect the greatest credit upon the administration. But the vital matters are what we want to know about. I have asked again and again during these three years for a secret Session where these matters could be thrashed out, or for an investigation by a Select Committee of the House, or for some other method. I ask now that, when we meet again in the autumn, that should be a matter on which the Government should take the House into its confidence, because we have a right to know where we stand and what measures are being taken to secure our position.

26] I do not grudge our loyal, brave people, who were ready to do their duty no matter what the cost, who never flinched under the strain of last week—I do not grudge them the natural, spontaneous outburst of joy and relief when they learned that the hard ordeal would no longer be required of them at the moment; but they should know the truth. They should know that there has been gross neglect and deficiency in our defenses; they should know that we have sustained a defeat without a war, the consequences of which will travel far with us along our road; they should know that we have passed an awful milestone in our history, when the whole equilibrium of Europe has been deranged, and that the terrible words have for the time being been pronounced against the Western democracies: "Thou art weighed in the balance and found wanting." And do not suppose that this is the end. This is only the beginning of the reckoning. This is only the first sip, the first foretaste of a bitter cup which will be proffered to us year by year unless, by a supreme recovery of

[2] Sir Samuel Hoare.

moral health and martial vigor, we arise again and take our stand for freedom as in the olden time.

Questions

1. What was the immediate occasion of the speech? (It is not enough to say "the Munich Agreement.")
2. What is the principal theme of the address?
3. What is gained by combining in one address the unpleasant truths about Munich and the proposals for increasing the air force? How would the emotional impact of the speech be altered by the omission of the second topic?
4. Why are the consequences of the pact for Czechoslovakia and the Balkan countries discussed first and the consequences for England second?
5. Define clearly the foreign policy which Churchill is denouncing and the one which he proposes.
6. Define as exactly as you can the tone and feeling of the speech. Would a more passionate and rhetorical speech have been effective?
7. Describe as well as you can the personality revealed in the speech.
8. *a.* What is Churchill's attitude toward Prime Minister Chamberlain? Do the rather mild beginning and the courteous references throughout much soften the blow?

    b. At the time of Chamberlain's death (November 9, 1940), Churchill spoke of him as one who "acted with perfect sincerity according to his lights and strove to the utmost of his capacity and authority . . . to save the world from the awful, devastating struggle" of the Second World War. He concluded that Chamberlain was "one whom Disraeli would have called 'an English worthy'" (Speech in the House of Commons, November 12, 1940). How much contradiction is there between this praise and the severe blame of the Munich address?
9. In the speeches by Lincoln and Churchill we see two men faced with a common problem, a permanent problem of statesmanship and morality, and their attitudes toward the problem and their

solutions to it are not unlike. What is the problem and what is the solution?

Suggested Assignment

Write a short essay on some event in which the moral problem mentioned in question 9 is an issue. The subject need not be taken from politics or history; the problem manifests itself in ordinary life also.

PART TWO

Source Materials for Student Papers

A MYSTERIOUS DISAPPEARANCE *

From a Letter of Abraham Lincoln

[One way of testing one's ability as a writer, and especially one's ability to stick to a point and subordinate everything to a central purpose, is to take a story which someone has told in all its details and rewrite it as an illustration of an idea, keeping only such details as are necessary to bring out the main point. The story printed below is an excellent one for this purpose. It is taken from a letter written by Abraham Lincoln to his friend Joshua Speed and describes a case in which Lincoln had been concerned while he was practicing law in Springfield, Illinois. The story is told in an amusing fashion, but with such a mass of detail that it is sometimes hard to follow. Read the story and then, with the aid of the questions which follow, consider how it might be rewritten if it were to be used to illustrate an idea.]

Springfield, June 19, 1841

DEAR SPEED: We have had the highest state of excitement here for a week past that our community has ever witnessed; and although the public feeling is somewhat allayed, the curious affair which aroused it is very far from being even yet cleared of mystery. It would take a quire of paper to give you anything like a full account of it, and I therefore only propose a brief outline. The chief personages in the drama are Archibald Fisher, supposed to be murdered, and Archibald Trailor, Henry Trailor, and William Trailor, supposed to have murdered him. The three Trailors are brothers; the first, Arch., as you know, lives in town; the second, Henry, in Clary's Grove; and the third, William, in

---

* This exercise should be used in connection with the essay by Whipple on pages 3-6.

Warren County; and Fisher, the supposed murdered, being without a family, had made his home with William. On Saturday evening, being the 29th of May, Fisher and William came to Henry's in a one-horse dearborn, and there stayed over Sunday; and on Monday all three came to Springfield (Henry on horseback), and joined Archibald at Myers's, the Dutch carpenter. That evening at supper Fisher was missing, and so next morning some ineffectual search was made for him; and on Tuesday, at one o'clock P.M. William and Henry started home without him. In a day or two Henry and one or two of his Clary Grove neighbors came back for him again, and advertised his disappearance in the papers. The knowledge of the matter thus far had not been general, and here it dropped entirely, till about the 10th instant, when Keys received a letter from the postmaster in Warren County, that William had arrived at home, and was telling a very mysterious and improbable story about the disappearance of Fisher, which induced the community there to suppose he had been disposed of unfairly. Keys made this letter public, which immediately set the whole town and adjoining county agog. And so it has continued until yesterday. The mass of the people commenced a systematic search for the dead body, while Wickersham was despatched to arrest Henry Trailor at the Grove, and Jim Maxcy to Warren to arrest William. On Monday last, Henry was brought in, and showed an evident inclination to insinuate that he knew Fisher to be dead, and that Arch. and William had killed him. He said he guessed the body could be found in Spring Creek, between the Beardstown road and Hickox's mill. Away the people swept like a herd of buffalo, and cut down Hickox's milldam *nolens volens*, to draw the water out of the pond, and then went up and down and down and up the creek, fishing and raking, and raking and ducking, and diving for two days, and, after all, no dead body found.

2] In the mean time a sort of scuffling-ground had been found in the brush in the angle, or point, where the road leading into the woods past the brewery and the one leading in past the brickyard meet. From the scuffle-ground was the sign of something about the size of a man having been dragged to the edge of the thicket, where it joined the track of some small-wheeled carriage drawn by one horse, as shown by the road-tracks. The carriage-track led off toward Spring Creek. Near this drag-trail Dr. Merryman found two hairs, which, after a long scientific examination, he pronounced to be triangular human hair, which term, he says, includes within it the whiskers, the hair growing under the arms and on other parts of the body; and he judged that these two were of the whiskers, because the ends were cut, showing that they had flourished in the neighborhood of the razor's operations.

3] On Thursday last Jim Maxcy brought in William Trailor from Warren. On the same day Arch. was arrested and put in jail. Yesterday (Friday) William was put upon his examining trial before May and Lovely. Archibald and Henry were both present. Lamborn prosecuted, and Logan, Baker, and your humble servant defended. A great many witnesses were introduced and examined, but I shall only mention those whose testimony seemed most important. The first of these was Captain Ransdell. He swore that when William and Henry left Springfield for home on Tuesday before mentioned, they did not take the direct route—which, you know, leads by the butcher shop—but that they followed the street north until they got opposite, or nearly opposite, May's new house, after which he could not see them from where he stood; and it was afterward proved that in about an hour after they started, they came into the street by the butcher shop from toward the brick-yard. Dr. Merryman and others swore to what is stated about the scuffle-ground, drag-trail, whiskers, and carriage-tracks. Henry was then introduced by the prosecution. He swore that when they started for home, they went out north, as Ransdell stated, and turned down west by the brick-yard into the woods, and there met Archibald; that they proceeded a small distance farther, when he was placed as a sentinel to watch for and announce the approach of any one that might happen that way; that William and Arch. took the dearborn out of the road a small distance to the edge of the thicket, where they stopped, and he saw them lift the body of a man into it; that they then moved off with the carriage in the direction of Hickox's mill, and he loitered about for something like an hour, when William returned with the carriage, but without Arch., and said they had put him in a safe place; that they went somehow—he did not know exactly how—into the road close to the brewery, and proceeded on to Clary's Grove. He also stated that some time during the day William told him that he and Arch. had killed Fisher the evening before; that the way they did it was by him (William) knocking him down with a club, and Arch. then choking him to death.

4] An old man from Warren, called Dr. Gilmore, was then introduced on the part of the defense. He swore that he had known Fisher for several years; that Fisher had resided at his house a long time at each of two different spells—once while he built a barn for him, and once while he was doctored for some chronic disease; that two or three years ago Fisher had a serious hurt in his head by the bursting of a gun, since which he had been subject to continued bad health and occasional aberration of mind. He also stated that on last Tuesday, being the same day that Maxcy arrested William Trailor, he (the doctor) was from home in the early part of the day, and on his return, about eleven o'clock, found Fisher at his house in bed, and apparently very unwell; that he asked him how he came from Springfield; that Fisher said he had come by Peoria, and also told of several other places he had been at more in the direction of Peoria, which showed that he at the time of speaking did not know where he had been wandering about in a state of derangement. He further stated that in about two hours he received a note from one of Trailor's friends, advising him of his arrest, and requesting him to go on to Springfield as a witness, to testify as to the state of Fisher's health in former times; that he immediately set off, calling up two of his neighbors as company, and, riding all evening and all night, overtook Maxcy and William at Lewiston in Fulton County; that Maxcy refusing to discharge Trailor upon his statement, his two neighbors returned and he came on to Springfield. Some question being made as to whether the doctor's story was not a fabrication, several acquaintances of his (among whom was the same postmaster who wrote Keys, as before mentioned) were introduced as sort of compurgators, who swore that they knew the doctor to be of good character for truth and veracity, and generally of good character in every way. Here the testimony ended, and the Trailors were discharged, Arch. and William expressing both in word and manner their entire confidence that Fisher would be found alive at the doctor's by Galloway, Mallory, and Myers, who a day before had been despatched for that purpose; while Henry still protested that no power on earth could ever show Fisher alive. Thus stands this curious affair. When the doctor's story was first made public, it was amusing to scan and contemplate the countenances and hear the remarks of those who had been actively in search for the dead body: some looked quizzical, some melancholy, and some furiously angry. Porter, who had been very active, swore he always knew the man was not dead, and that he had not stirred an inch to hunt for him; Langford, who had taken the lead in cutting down Hickox's milldam, and wanted to hang Hickox for objecting, looked most awfully woebegone: he seemed the "victim of unrequited affection," as represented in the comic almanacs we used to laugh over; and Hart, the little drayman that hauled Molly home once, said it was too *damned* bad to have so much trouble, and no hanging after all.

5] I commenced this letter on yesterday, since which I received yours of the 13th. I stick to my promise to come to Louisville. Nothing new here except what I have written. I have not seen —— since my last trip, and I am going out there as soon as I mail this letter.

Questions

1. *a.* If Lincoln had been writing to another lawyer in the case to give him a clear account of all the facts bearing on the guilt or innocence of the Trailors, his report would have been somewhat different from the letter he wrote to Speed. He might very well have omitted some details as unimportant; the whole last part of the fourth paragraph (from "Thus stands this curious affair" to the end) might not have appeared. What other details might have been omitted in such a report? What details would be especially important?

b. A social psychologist interested in the behavior of crowds in a crisis or in community attitudes toward crime would find this affair interesting; but the points that would strike him and which he would wish to report would often be different from those which would catch the eye of the lawyer. The social psychologist would be especially interested in the actions of Porter, Langford, and Hart (paragraph 4). Why? What other details would receive his attention?

c. A reporter covering the case for a newspaper would probably feel obliged to prepare a much more condensed account than Lincoln's. What details might he feel justified in omitting?

2. Consider each of the following "theme ideas" in turn and tell which details you would include if you were retelling the incident to support the idea. (It is understood, of course, that certain facts must be included in any account to make the story comprehensible.)

   a. The rule that a man cannot be convicted of murder unless the body of the victim can be produced is a wise one.

   b. The behavior of a community in which a crime has been committed often betrays more pleasure in the excitement of catching and punishing a criminal than real zeal for justice.

3. Rewrite the narrative as an illustration of one of the ideas given above or of one which you yourself make up.

THE FUEGIANS *

❧ *From Darwin's "Voyage of the Beagle"*

[Although the selection from Darwin on pages 17-21 is complete in itself and gives a striking picture of life in Tierra del Fuego, it was not prepared originally as a complete essay, but is simply one entry in a journal which Darwin kept during the expedition of H.M.S.

* This exercise should be used with the essay by Darwin (pages 17-21).

Beagle around the world in 1831-1836. There are a number of other entries in which Darwin deals with the life of the Fuegians, and altogether there would have been ample material for a short treatise on the life of the country, if Darwin had had occasion to write one. In fact, an extended essay could still be written from the material Darwin has left us, and would offer interesting problems in organization. The more important entries dealing with the Fuegians are printed below. Read them with care and then, with the aid of the questions which follow, consider how the material might be turned into a formal essay on the subject.]

1] December 17, 1832. Having now finished with Patagonia and the Falkland Islands, I will describe our first arrival in Tierra del Fuego. A little after noon we doubled Cape St. Diego, and entered the famous strait of Le Maire. We kept close to the Fuegian shore, but the outline of the rugged, inhospitable Statenland was visible amidst the clouds. In the afternoon we anchored in the Bay of Good Success. While entering we were saluted in a manner becoming the inhabitants of this savage land. A group of Fuegians partly concealed by the entangled forest were perched on a wild point overhanging the sea; and as we passed by, they sprang up and waving their tattered cloaks sent forth a loud and sonorous shout. The savages followed the ship, and just before dark we saw their fire, and again heard their wild cry.

In the morning the Captain sent a party to communicate with the Fuegians. When we came within hail, one of the four natives who were present advanced to receive us, and began to shout most vehemently, wishing to direct us where to land. When we were on shore the party looked rather alarmed, but continued talking and making gestures with great rapidity. It was without exception the most curious and interesting spectacle I ever beheld: I could not have believed how wide was the difference between savage and civilized man: it is greater than between a wild and domesticated animal, inasmuch as in man there is a greater power of improvement. The chief spokesman was old, and appeared to be the head of the family; the three others were powerful young men, about six feet high. The women and children had been sent away. These Fuegians are a very different race from the stunted, miserable wretches farther westward; and they seem closely allied to the famous Patagonians of the Strait of Magellan. Their only garment consists of a mantle made of guanaco skin, with the wool outside; this they wear just thrown over their shoulders, leaving their persons as often exposed as covered. Their skin is of a dirty coppery red colour.

They are excellent mimics: as often as we coughed or yawned, or made any odd motion, they immediately imitated us. Some of our party began to squint and look awry; but one of the young Fuegians (whose whole face was painted black, excepting a white band across his eyes) succeeded in making far more hideous grimaces. They could repeat with perfect correctness each word in any sentence we addressed them, and they remembered such words for some time. Yet we Europeans all know how difficult it is to distinguish apart the sounds in a foreign language.

I have not as yet noticed the Fuegians whom we had on board. During the former voyage of the Adventure and Beagle in 1826 to 1830, Captain Fitz Roy seized on a party of natives, as hostages for the loss of a boat, which had been stolen, to the great jeopardy of a party employed on the survey; and some of these natives, as well as a child whom he bought for a pearl button, he took with him to England, determining to educate them and instruct them in religion at his own expense. To settle these natives in their own country was one chief inducement to Captain Fitz Roy to undertake our present voyage. The natives were accompanied by a missionary, R. Matthews; of whom and of the natives, Captain Fitz Roy has published a full and excellent account. Two men, one of whom died in England of the small-pox, a boy, and a little girl were originally taken; and we had now on board, York Minster, Jemmy Button (whose name expresses his purchase-money), and Fuegia Basket. York Minster was a full-grown, short, thick, powerful man: his disposition was reserved, taciturn, morose, and when excited violently passionate; his affections were very strong towards a few friends on board; his intellect good. Jemmy Button was a universal favourite, but likewise passionate; the expression of his face at once showed his nice disposition. He was merry and often laughed, and was remarkably sympathetic with anyone in pain: when the water was rough, I was often a little sea-sick, and he used to come to me and say in a plaintive voice, "Poor, poor fellow!" But the notion, after his aquatic life, of a man being sea-sick, was too ludicrous, and he was generally obliged to turn on one side to hide a smile or laugh, and then he would repeat his "Poor, poor fellow!" He was of a patriotic disposition; and he liked to praise his own tribe and country, in which he truly said there were "plenty of trees," and he abused all the other tribes: he stoutly declared that there was no Devil in his land. Jemmy was short, thick, and fat, but vain of his personal appearance; he used always to wear gloves, his hair was neatly cut, and he was distressed if his well-polished shoes were dirtied. It seems yet wonderful to me, when I think over all his many good qualities, that he should have been of the same race, and doubtless partaken of the same character, with the miserable, degraded savages whom we first met here. Lastly, Fuegia Basket was a nice, modest, reserved young girl, with a rather pleasing but sometimes sullen expression, and very quick in learning anything, especially languages. This she showed in picking up some Portuguese and Spanish, when left on shore for only a short time at Rio de Janeiro and Monte Video, and in her knowledge of English. York Minster was very jealous of any attention paid to her; for it was clear he determined to marry her as soon as they were settled on shore.

Although all three could both speak and understand a good deal of English, it was singularly difficult to obtain much information from them concerning the habits of their countrymen: this was partly owing to their apparent difficulty in understanding the simplest alternative. Everyone accustomed to very young children knows how seldom one can get an answer even to so simple a question as whether a thing is black *or* white; the idea of black or white seems alternately to fill their minds. So it was with these Fuegians, and hence it was generally impossible to find out, by cross-questioning, whether one had rightly understood anything which they had asserted.

2] December 25, 1832. Close by the cove, a pointed hill, called Kater's Peak, rises to the height of 1700 feet. The surrounding islands all consist of conical masses of greenstone, associated sometimes with less regular hills of baked and altered clay-slate. The cove takes its name of "Wigwam" from some of the Fuegian habitations; but every bay in the neighbourhood might be so called with equal propriety. The inhabitants, living chiefly upon shell-fish, are obliged constantly to change their place of residence; but they return at intervals to the same spots, as is evident from the piles of old shells, which must often amount to many tons in weight. These heaps can be distinguished at a long distance by the bright green colour of certain plants, which invariably grow on them. Among these may be enumerated the wild celery and scurvy grass, two very serviceable plants, the use of which has not been discovered by the natives.

The Fuegian wigwam resembles, in size and dimensions, a haycock. It merely consists of a few broken branches stuck in the ground, and very imperfectly thatched on one side with a few tufts of grass and rushes. The whole cannot be the work of an hour, and it is only used for a few days. At Goeree Roads I saw a place where one of these naked men had slept, which absolutely offered no more cover than the form of a hare. The man was evidently living by himself, and York Minster said he was "very bad man," and that probably he had stolen something. On the west coast, however, the wigwams are rather better, for they are covered with seal-skins.

3] January 19, 1833. At dinner-time we landed among a party of Fuegians. It was as easy to please as it was difficult to satisfy these savages. Young and old, men and children, never ceased repeating the word "yammerschooner," which means "give me." After pointing to almost every object, one after the other, even to the buttons on our coats, and saying their favourite word in as many intonations as possible, they would then use it in a neuter sense, and vacantly repeat "yammerschooner." After yammerschoonering for any article very eagerly, they would by a simple artifice point to their young women or little children, as much as to say, "If you will not give it me, surely you will to such as these."

At night we endeavoured in vain to find an uninhabited cove; and at last were obliged to bivouac not far from a party of natives. They were very inoffensive as long as they were few in numbers, but in the morning (21st) being joined by others they showed symptoms of hostility, and we thought that we should have come to a skirmish. An European labours under great disadvantages when treating with savages like these, who have not the least idea of the power of fire-arms. In the very act of levelling his musket he appears to the savage far inferior to a man armed with a bow and arrow, a spear, or even a sling. Nor is it easy to teach them our superiority except by striking a fatal blow. Like wild beasts, they do not appear to compare numbers; for each individual, if attacked, instead of retiring, will endeavour to dash your brains out with a stone, as certainly as a tiger under similar circumstances would tear you. Captain Fitz Roy on one occasion being very anxious, from good reasons, to frighten away a small party, first flourished a cutlass near them, at which they only laughed; he then twice fired his pistol close to a native. The man both times looked astounded, and carefully but quickly rubbed his head; he then stared awhile, and gabbled to his companions, but he never seemed to think of running away. We can hardly put ourselves in the position of these savages, and understand their actions. In the case of this Fuegian, the possibility of such a sound as the report of a gun close to his ear could never have entered his mind. He perhaps literally did not for a second know whether it was a sound or a blow, and therefore very naturally rubbed his head. Certainly I believe that many savages of the lowest grade, such as these of Tierra del Fuego, have seen objects struck, and even small animals killed by the musket, without being in the least aware how deadly an instrument it is.

4] January 22, 1833. At night we slept close to the junction of Ponsonby Sound with the Beagle Channel. A small family of Fuegians, who were living in the cove, were quiet and inoffensive, and soon joined our party round a blazing fire. We were well clothed, and though sitting close to the fire were far from too warm; yet these naked savages, though further off, were observed, to our great surprise, to be streaming with perspiration at undergoing such a roasting. They seemed, however, very well pleased, and all joined in the chorus of the seamen's songs: but the manner in which they were invariably a little behindhand was quite ludicrous. . . .

Jemmy was now in a district well known to him, and guided the boats to a quiet pretty cove named Woollya, surrounded by islets, every one of which and every point had its proper native name. We found here a family of Jemmy's tribe, but not his relations: we made friends with them; and in the evening they sent a canoe to inform Jemmy's mother and brothers. The cove was bordered by some acres of good sloping land, not covered (as elsewhere) either by peat or by forest trees. Captain Fitz Roy originally intended, as before stated, to have taken York Minster and Fuegia to their own tribe on the west coast; but as they expressed a wish to remain here, and as the spot was singularly favourable, Captain Fitz Roy determined to settle here the whole party, including Matthews, the missionary. Five days were spent in building for them three large wigwams, in landing their goods, in digging two gardens, and sowing seeds.

The next morning after our arrival (the 24th) the Fuegians began to pour in, and Jemmy's mother and brothers arrived. Jemmy recognised the stentorian voice of one of his brothers at a prodigious distance. The meeting was less interesting than that between a horse, turned out into a field, when he joins an old companion. There was no demonstration of affection; they simply stared for a short time at each other; and the mother immediately went to look after her canoe. We heard, however, through York that the mother had been inconsolable for the loss of Jemmy, and had searched everywhere for him, thinking that he might have been left after having been taken in the boat. The women took much notice of and were very kind to Fuegia.

5] February 6, 1833. Matthews gave so bad an account of the conduct of the Fuegians,* that Captain Fitz Roy determined

* I.e., when the Beagle returned to Woollya, where the missionary had settled.

to take him back to the Beagle; and ultimately he was left at New Zealand, where his brother was a missionary. From the time of our leaving, a regular system of plunder commenced; fresh parties of the natives kept arriving: York and Jemmy lost many things, and Matthews almost everything which had not been concealed underground. Every article seemed to have been torn up and divided by the natives. Matthews described the watch he was obliged always to keep as most harassing; night and day he was surrounded by the natives, who tried to tire him out by making an incessant noise close to his head. One day an old man, whom Matthews asked to leave his wigwam, immediately returned with a large stone in his hand; another day a whole party came armed with stones and stakes, and some of the younger men and Jemmy's brother were crying: Matthews met them with presents. Another party showed by signs that they wished to strip him naked and pluck all the hairs out of his face and body. I think we arrived just in time to save his life. Jemmy's relatives had been so vain and foolish, that they had showed to strangers their plunder, and their manner of obtaining it. It was quite melancholy leaving the three Fuegians with their savage countrymen; but it was a great comfort that they had no personal fears. York, being a powerful resolute man, was pretty sure to get on well, together with his wife Fuegia. Poor Jemmy looked rather disconsolate, and would then, I have little doubt, have been glad to have returned with us. His own brother had stolen many things from him; and as he remarked, "What fashion call that." He abused his countrymen, "All bad men, no sabe (know) nothing," and, though I never heard him swear before, "Damned fools." Our three Fuegians, though they had been only three years with civilized men, would, I am sure, have been glad to have retained their new habits; but this was obviously impossible. I fear it is more than doubtful whether their visit will have been of any use to them.

6] February 28, 1834. The Beagle anchored in a beautiful little cove at the eastern entrance of the Beagle Channel. Captain Fitz Roy determined on the bold, and as it proved successful, attempt to beat against the westerly winds by the same route which we had followed in the boats to the settlement at Woollya. We did not see many natives until we were near Ponsonby Sound, where we were followed by ten or twelve canoes. . . .

Some of the Fuegians plainly showed that they had a fair notion of barter. I gave one man a large nail (a most valuable present) without making any signs for a return; but he immediately picked out two fish, and handed them up on the point of his spear. If any present was designed for one canoe, and it fell near another, it was invariably given to the right owner. The Fuegian boy, whom Mr. Low had on board, showed, by going into the most violent passion, that he quite understood the reproach of being called a liar, which in truth he was. We were this time, as on all former occasions, much surprised at the little notice, or rather none whatever, which was taken of many things, the use of which must have been evident to the natives. Simple circumstances—such as the beauty of scarlet cloth or blue beads, the absence of women, our care in washing ourselves—excited their admiration far more than any grand or complicated object, such as our ship. Bougainville has well remarked concerning these people, that they treat the "chef-d'œuvres de l'industrie humaine, comme ils traitent les loix de la nature et ses phénomènes." *

7] March 5, 1834. We anchored in the cove at Woollya, but we saw not a soul there. We were alarmed at this, for the natives in Ponsonby Sound showed by gestures, that there had been fighting; and we afterwards heard that the dreaded Oens men had made a descent. Soon a canoe, with a little flag flying, was seen approaching, with one of the men in it washing the paint off his face. This man was poor Jemmy—now a thin haggard savage, with long disordered hair, and naked, except a bit of a blanket round his waist. We did not recognise him till he was close to us; for he was ashamed of himself, and turned his back to the ship. We had left him plump, fat, clean, and well dressed;

---

* "Masterpieces of human industry as they treat the laws of nature and its phenomena."

I never saw so complete and grievous a change. As soon however as he was clothed, and the first flurry was over, things wore a good appearance. He dined with Captain Fitz Roy, and ate his dinner as tidily as formerly. He told us he had "too much" (meaning enough) to eat, that he was not cold, that his relations were very good people, and that he did not wish to go back to England: in the evening we found out the cause of this great change in Jemmy's feelings, in the arrival of his young and nice-looking wife. With his usual good feeling, he brought two beautiful otter-skins for two of his best friends, and some spear-heads and arrows made with his own hands for the Captain. He said he had built a canoe for himself, and he boasted that he could talk a little of his own language! But it is a most singular fact, that he appears to have taught all his tribe some English: an old man spontaneously announced "Jemmy Button's wife." Jemmy had lost all his property. He told us that York Minster had built a large canoe, and with his wife Fuegia had several months since gone to his own country, and had taken farewell by an act of consummate villainy; he persuaded Jemmy and his mother to come with him, and then on the way deserted them by night, stealing every article of their property.

Jemmy went to sleep on shore, and in the morning returned, and remained on board till the ship got under weigh, which frightened his wife, who continued crying violently till he got into his canoe. He returned loaded with valuable property. Every soul on board was heartily sorry to shake hands with him for the last time. I do not now doubt that he will be as happy as, perhaps happier than, if he had never left his own country. Everyone must sincerely hope that Captain Fitz Roy's noble hope may be fulfilled, of being rewarded for the many generous sacrifices which he made for these Fuegians, by some shipwrecked sailor being protected by the descendants of Jemmy Button and his tribe! When Jemmy reached the shore, he lighted a signal fire, and the smoke curled up, bidding us a last and long farewell, as the ship stood on her course into the open sea.

Questions

1. *a.* Could any of the details in the entries you have just read have properly been introduced into the selection which appears on pages 17-21? In other words, are there any facts given here which bear upon the problem as to whether the Fuegians "enjoy a sufficient share of happiness" in their miserable environment "to render life worth having"?

   b. If any of these details were to be transferred to this selection, into which paragraph would each be inserted?

2. *a.* Suppose that Darwin had intended to write an essay to prove that a life of excessive physical hardship will make a race both intellectually and morally backward. Which details (in the entries given above and in the selection on pages 17-21) would he have been likely to include?

   b. What form of organization would be appropriate to such an essay? Would it be wise to discuss the physical hardships first and then the intellectual and moral shortcomings, or would the opposite arrangement be better?

3. Suppose now that Darwin, or someone using Darwin's material, had undertaken to write an essay which would give as complete an account as possible of all aspects of the life of the Fuegians. Here the problem of selection would be less urgent—nearly everything would go in; but the problem of organization would be a very hard one. It would be necessary, first of all, to classify the details under suitable headings and thus establish the chief divisions of the essay.

   a. Would the form of organization used in the selection on pages 17-21 serve for the longer essay? In what ways would it be inadequate?

   b. The headings used would doubtless include "food supply," "religion," "tools and weapons," and so on; extend the list until you you have enough headings to cover all the details which are important enough to be inserted.

4. It is not sufficient simply to invent enough headings to cover all the details; the headings must represent logical divisions of the material and should overlap as little as possible (they will overlap to some degree no matter how well they are chosen). Consider for

instance the following list: climate, food supply, environment, family life, famines, war, cannibalism, tools and weapons, religion, belief in future life, government, killing old women, intelligence. This list is illogical, because many of the headings are really not major divisions of the material at all, but should be treated as subdivisions under other headings. Thus "climate" is really one aspect of "environment," and "famines" should be a sub-heading under "food supply." Find other headings which might be changed into sub-headings.

5. The list of headings given in question 4 has another defect; the arrangement is poor and would produce a very confusing essay. "War" and "government," for instance, are related topics and ought to be brought together. Take the list which you prepared for question 3 and arrange the topics in their logical order, keeping related topics together. There should be some overall plan; the one used by Darwin in the selection on pages 17-21 is a good one, but others are possible.

6. Look up the rules for outlining in your composition handbook and prepare an outline for the essay described in question 3.

7. Write an essay based on Darwin's descriptions of Tierra del Fuego. A short essay unified around a theme idea (such as the one suggested in question 2) would probably prove more satisfactory than the long essay described in question 3.

MASTERS AND SERVANTS [*]

From the Diary of Samuel Pepys

["Each new sensation and impression was no longer a single, unrelated thing: it took its place in a pattern and sifted down to form certain observable cycles of experience." So Wolfe describes the intellectual development of his hero; but he might just as well have been

[*] It is suggested that this exercise be used with the essay by Thomas Wolfe (pages 26-32).

giving advice to a student just taking up composition. A very large part of the writing process consists in seeing patterns. If a writer can see a pattern in the material that he has before him, and still better, if he can express that pattern in the form of a "theme idea," then he is on the way to writing a successful paper. On the other hand, if he sees no pattern, if his material assumes no form in his mind but remains an amorphous mass, then the paper he produces cannot help but be vague and confused. Consider, for instance, the quotations given below. They are taken from the *Diary* of Samuel Pepys, an English public official of the second half of the seventeenth century, and describe his relations with his servants. There is material here for a rather amusing short theme; but before the theme can be written, some sort of order must be imposed on the material. Read the quotations, and with the aid of the questions which follow, try to make the pattern emerge.]

1] Jan. 16, 1660. Thence home, where I found my wife and maid a-washing. I staid up till the bell-man came by with his bell just under my window as I was writing of this very line, and cried, "Past one of the clock, and a cold, frosty, windy morning." I then went to bed, and left my wife and the maid a-washing still.

2] Aug. 14, 1660. At night home with my wife by water, where I made good sport with having the girl and the boy to comb my head, before I went to bed, in the kitchen.

3] Dec. 1, 1660. This morning, observing some things to be laid up not as they should be by the girl, I took a broom and basted her till she cried extremely, which made me vexed, but before I went out I left her appeased.

4] Aug. 26, 1661. This morning before I went out I made even with my maid Jane, who has this day been my maid three years, and is this day to go into the country to her mother. The poor girl cried, and I could hardly forbear weeping to think of her going, for though she be grown lazy and spoilt, yet I shall never have one to please us better in all things, and so harmless, while I live. So I paid her her wages and gave her 2*s*. 6*d*. over, and bade her adieu, with my mind full of trouble at her going.

5] Oct. 25, 1661. This day I did give my clerk Will a sound lesson about his forbearing to give us the respect due to a master and mistress.

6] Oct. 30, 1661. At my coming home I am sorry to find my wife displeased with her maid Doll, whose fault is that she cannot keep peace, but will always be talking in an angry manner, though it be without reason and to no purpose, which I am sorry for and do see the inconvenience that do attend the increase of a man's fortune by being forced to keep more servants, which brings trouble.

7] Feb. 24, 1662. So home and to supper, and then called Will up, and chid him before my wife for refusing to go to church with the maids yesterday, and telling his mistress that he would not be made a slave of, which vexes me.

8] April 18, 1662. This morning sending the boy down into the cellar for some beer, I followed him with a cane, and did there beat him for his faults, and his sister came to me down and begged for him. So I forebore, and afterwards, in my wife's chamber, did there talk to Jane [the sister] how much I did love the boy for her sake, and how much it do concern to correct the boy for his faults, or else he would be undone. So at last she was well pleased.

9] June 18, 1662. So home, and after some merry discourse with my wife and maids as I now-a-days often do, I being well pleased with both my maids, to bed.

10] Dec. 2, 1662. Before I went to the office my wife and I had another falling out about Sarah, against whom she has a deadly hate, I know not for what, nor can I see but she is a very good servant. Then to my office, and there sat all the morning, . . . and after dinner did give Jane a very serious lesson, against we take her to be our chambermaid, which I spoke so to her that the poor girl cried and did promise to be very dutifull and carefull.

11] Feb. 5, 1663. Then home to dinner, and did find it so well done, above what I did expect from my maid Susan, that I did call her in and gave her sixpence.

12] Oct. 29, 1663. This morning in dressing myself and wanting a band, I found all my bands that were newly made clean so ill smoothed that I crumpled them, and flung them all on the ground, and was angry with Jane, which made the poor girl mighty sad, so that I were troubled for it afterwards.

13] Sept. 9, 1664. My wife and Mercer and Tom and I sat till eleven at night, singing and fiddling, and a great joy it is to see me master of so much pleasure in my house, that it is and will be still, I hope, a constant pleasure to me to be at home. The girl plays pretty well upon the harpsicon, but only ordinary tunes, but hath a good hand; sings a little, but hath a good voyce and eare. My boy, a brave boy, sings finely, and is the most pleasant boy at present, while his ignorant boy's tricks last, that ever I saw. So to supper, and with great pleasure to bed.

14] Feb. 19, 1665. Lay in bed, it being Lord's day, all the morning talking with my wife, sometimes pleased, sometimes displeased, and then up and to dinner. All the afternoon also at home, and Sir W. Batten's, and in the evening comes Mr. Andrews, and we sung together, and then to supper, he not staying, and at supper hearing by accident of my mayds their letting in a rogueing Scotch woman that haunts the office, to helpe them to washe and scoure in our house, and that very lately, I fell mightily out, and made my wife, to the disturbance of the house and neighbours, to beat our little girle, and then we shut her down into the cellar, and there she lay all night. So we to bed.

15] July 30, 1666. Up, and did some business in my chamber, then by and by comes my boy's Lute-Master, and I did direct him hereafter to begin to teach him to play his part on the Theorbo [a musical instrument], which he will do, and that in a little time I believe. . . . Thence home; and to sing with my wife and Mercer in the garden; and coming in I find my wife plainly dissatisfied with me, that I can spend so much time with Mercer, teaching her to sing, and could never take the pains with her. Which I acknowledge; but it is because that the girl do take musique mighty readily, and she do not, and musique is the thing of the world that I love most, and all the pleasure almost that I can now take. So to bed in some little discontent, but no words from her.

16] Aug. 14, 1666. So home and dined, and after dinner, with my wife and Mercer to the Beare-garden, where I have not been, I think, of many years, and saw some good sport of the bull's tossing of the dogs: one into the very boxes. But it is a very rude and nasty pleasure. We had a great many hectors in the same box with us (and one very fine went into the pit, and played his dog for a wager, which was a strange sport for a gentleman), where they drank wine, and drank Mercer's health first, which I pledged with my hat off; and who should be in the house but Mr. Pierce the surgeon, who saw us and spoke to us. Thence home, well enough satisfied, however, with the variety of this afternoon's exercise; and so I to my chamber, till in the evening our company came to supper. We had invited to a venison pasty Mr. Batelier and his sister Mary, Mrs. Mercer, her daughter Anne, Mr. Le Brun, and W. Hewers; and so we supped, and very merry. And then about nine o'clock to Mrs. Mercer's gate, where the fire and boys expected us, and her son had provided abundance of serpents and rockets; and there mighty merry (my Lady Pen and Pegg going thither with us, and Nan Wright), till about twelve at night, flinging our fireworks, and burning one another and the people over the way. And at last our businesses being most spent, we into Mr. Mercer's, and there mighty merry, smutting one another with candle grease and soot, till most of us were like devils. And that being done, then we broke up, and to my house; and there I made them drink, and upstairs we went, and then fell into dancing (W. Batelier dancing well), and dressing, him and I and one Mr. Banister (who with his wife come over also with us) like women; and Mercer put on a suit of Tom's, like a boy, and mighty mirth we had, and Mercer danced a jigg; and Nan Wright and my wife and Pegg Pen put on perriwigs. Thus we spent till three or four in the morning, mighty merry; and then parted, and to bed.

17] May 18, 1667. Up, and all the morning at the office, and then to dinner, and after dinner to the office to dictate some letters, and then with my wife to Sir W. Turner's to visit The., but she being abroad we back again home, and then I to the office, finished my letters, and then to walk an hour in the garden talking with my wife, whose growth in musique do begin to please me mightily, and by and by home and there find our Luce drunk, and when her mistress told her of it would be gone, and so put up some of her things and did go away of her accord, nobody pressing her to it, and the truth is, though she be the dirtiest, homeliest servant that ever I kept, yet I was sorry to have her go, partly through my love to my servants, and partly because she was a very drudging, working wench, only she would be drunk. But that which did a little trouble me was that I did hear her tell her mistress that she would tell her master something before she was aware of her that she would be sorry to have him know; but did it in such a silly, drunken manner, that though it trouble me a little, yet not knowing what to suspect she should know, and not knowing well whether she said it to her mistress or Jane, I did not much think of it. So she gone, we to supper and to bed, my study being made finely clean.

18] Oct. 15, 1667. Before the play begun, my wife began to complain to me of Willet's confidence in sitting cheek by jowl with us at the theater; but I perceive she is already jealous of my kindness to Willet, so that I fear this girl is not likely to stay long with us.*

Questions

1. It is evident that the relationship between Pepys and his servants, and even between Pepys and his clerk, was very different from the relationship between employer and employee in America today. Along with all the disadvantages which we, from the point of view of the twentieth century, can see in the position of the seventeenth-century servant, there were certain compensations. What were the disadvantages and compensations?

* Jane, Will, Doll, Nell, Sarah, Susan, Mercer, Tom, Willet, and the "boys" and "girls" referred to throughout were all servants in the Pepys household. Will and Mercer should be regarded as somewhat superior to the ordinary servants, he being a clerk and she a kind of companion. Mrs. Mercer is Mercer's mother.

2. What, in general, was Pepys' attitude toward his servants? Is it a commendable one, or not so commendable?
3. What is there about the episodes of December 1, 1660, and October 29, 1663, which prevents us from regarding them as mere exhibitions of brutality?
4. What is meant by the term "paternalism" as applied to industrial life? Would it be appropriate to apply the word to Pepys' attitude toward his servants? (What is the etymology of the word?)
5. When you begin to see a pattern in the material, formulate the theme idea and write the paper.

AESOP'S FABLES *

[Popular literature is almost always an interesting subject for analysis, because it reveals a view of life that comes not from the insight of a great thinker or writer, but from the common experiences of what we call "the folk." Even fairy tales and fables, which nowadays are read by children if they are read at all, are of interest to the mature reader who can see behind their simple stories an expression of the fundamental passions and the primitive wisdom of mankind. So it is with the fables commonly attributed to Aesop, a Phrygian who is supposed to have lived about 600 B.C. A few of these fables are printed below. Read them carefully and then, with the aid of the questions which follow, plan an essay based on this material.]

1. THE WOLF AND THE CRANE

A Wolf had got a bone stuck in his throat, and in the greatest agony ran up and down, beseeching every animal he met to relieve him: at the same time hinting at a very handsome reward to the successful operator. A Crane, moved by his entreaties and promises, ventured her long neck down the Wolf's throat, and drew out the bone. She then modestly asked for the promised

---

* This exercise should be used with the essays "The *Golden Legend*" by Émile Mâle and "The Art of Donald McGill" by George Orwell.

reward. To which the Wolf, grinning and showing his teeth, replied with seeming indignation, "Ungrateful creature! to ask for any other reward than that you have put your head into a Wolf's jaws, and brought it safe out again!"

2. THE ANT AND THE GRASSHOPPER

On a cold frosty day an Ant was dragging out some of the corn which he had laid up in summer time, to dry it. A Grasshopper, half-perished with hunger, besought the Ant to give him a morsel of it to preserve his life. "What were you doing," said the Ant, "this last summer?" "Oh," said the Grasshopper, "I was not idle. I kept singing all the summer long." Said the Ant, laughing and shutting up his granary, "Since you could sing all summer, you may dance all winter."

3. THE COUNTRYMAN AND THE SNAKE

A Countryman returning home one winter's day, found a Snake by the hedge-side, half dead with cold. Taking compassion on the creature, he laid it in his bosom and brought it home to his fireside to revive it. No sooner had the warmth restored it, than it began to attack the children of the cottage. Upon this the Countryman, whose compassion had saved its life, took up a mattock and laid the Snake dead at his feet.

4. THE FIGHTING-COCKS AND THE EAGLE

Two young Cocks were fighting as fiercely as if they had been men. At last the one that was beaten crept into a corner of the hen-house, covered with wounds. But the conqueror, straightway flying up to the top of the house, began clapping his wings and crowing, to announce his victory. At this moment an Eagle, sailing by, seized him in his talons and bore him away; while the defeated rival came out from his hiding place, and took possession of the dunghill for which they had contended.

5. THE DOG AND THE SHADOW

A Dog had stolen a piece of meat out of a butcher's shop, and was crossing a river on his way home, when he saw his own shadow reflected in the stream below. Thinking that it was another dog with another piece of meat, he resolved to make himself master of that also; but in snapping at the supposed treasure, he dropped the bit he was carrying, and so lost all.

6. THE WOLF AND THE LAMB

As a Wolf was lapping at the head of a running brook, he spied a stray Lamb paddling at some distance, down the stream. Having made up his mind to seize her, he bethought himself how he might justify his violence. "Villain!" said he, running up to her, "how dare you muddy the water that I am drinking?" "Indeed," said the Lamb humbly, "I do not see how I can disturb the water, since it runs from you to me, not from me to you." "Be that as it may," replied the Wolf, "it was but a year ago that you called me many ill names." "Oh, Sir!" said the Lamb, trembling, "a year ago I was not born." "Well," replied the Wolf, "if it was not you, it was your father, and that is all the same; but it is no use trying to argue me out of my supper." And without another word he fell upon the poor helpless Lamb and tore her to pieces.

7. THE LION AND THE MOUSE

A Lion was sleeping in his lair, when a Mouse, not knowing where he was going, ran over the mighty beast's nose and awakened him. The Lion clapped his paw upon the frightened little creature, and was about to make an end of him in a moment, when the Mouse, in pitiable tone, besought him to spare one who had so unconsciously offended, and not stain his honorable paws with so insignificant a prey. The Lion, smiling at his little prisoner's fright, generously let him go. Now it happened no long time after that the Lion, while ranging the woods for his prey, fell into the toils of the hunters; and finding himself entangled without hope of escape, set up a roar that filled the whole forest with its echo. The Mouse, recognizing the voice of his former preserver, ran to the spot, and without more ado set to work to nibble the knot in the cord that bound the Lion, and in a short time set the noble beast at liberty.

8. THE TORTOISE AND THE EAGLE

A Tortoise, dissatisfied with his lowly life, when he beheld so many of the birds, his neighbors, disporting themselves in the clouds, and thinking that, if he could but once get up into the air, he could soar with the best of them, called one day upon an Eagle and offered him all the treasures of Ocean if he could only teach him to fly. The Eagle would have declined the task, assuring him that the thing was not only absurd but impossible, but being further pressed by the entreaties and promises of the Tortoise, he at length consented to do for him the best he could. So taking him up to a great height in the air and loosing his hold upon him, "Now, then!" cried the Eagle; but the Tortoise, before he could answer him a word, fell plump upon a rock, and was dashed to pieces.

9. THE SICK STAG

A Stag that had fallen sick lay down on the rich herbage of a lawn, close to a wood-side, that she might obtain an easy pasturage. But so many of the beasts came to see her—for she was a good sort of neighbor—that one taking a little, and another a little, they ate up all the grass in the place. So, though recovering from the disease, she pined for want, and in the end lost both her substance and her life.

10. THE CRAB AND HER MOTHER

Said an old Crab to a young one, "Why do you walk so crooked, child? Walk straight!" "Mother," said the young Crab, "show me the way, will you? and when I see you taking a straight course, I will try and follow."

11. THE LION AND THE FOX

A Fox agreed to wait upon a Lion in the capacity of a servant. Each for a time performed the part belonging to his station; the Fox used to point out the prey, and the Lion fell upon it and seized it. But the Fox, beginning to think himself as good a beast as the master, begged to be allowed to hunt the game instead of finding it. His request was granted, but as he was in the act of making a descent upon a herd, the huntsmen came out upon him, and he was himself made the prize.

12. THE LION, THE ASS, AND THE FOX HUNTING

The Lion, the Ass, and the Fox formed a party to go out hunting. They took a large booty, and when the sport was ended bethought themselves of having a hearty meal. The Lion bade the Ass allot the spoil. So dividing it into three equal parts, the Ass begged his friends to make their choice; at which the Lion, in great indignation, fell upon the Ass, and tore him to pieces. He then bade the Fox make a division; who, gathering the whole into one great heap, reserved but the smallest mite for himself. "Ah! friend," said the Lion, "who taught you to make so equitable a division?" "I wanted no other lesson," replied the Fox, "than the Ass's fate."

13. THE WOLVES AND THE SHEEP

Once on a time the Wolves sent an embassy to the Sheep, desiring that there might be peace between them for the time to come. "Why," said they, "should we be forever waging this deadly strife? Those wicked Dogs are the cause of all; they are incessantly barking at us, and provoking us. Send them away, and there will be no longer any obstacle to our eternal friendship and peace." The silly Sheep listened, the Dogs were dismissed, and the flock, thus deprived of their best protectors, became an easy prey to their treacherous enemy.

14. THE BELLY AND THE MEMBERS

In former days, when all a man's limbs did not work together as amicably as they do now, but each had a will and way of its own, the Members generally began to find fault with the Belly for spending an idle luxurious life, while they were wholly occupied in laboring for its support, and ministering to its wants and pleasures; so they entered into a conspiracy to cut off its supplies for the future. The Hands were no longer to carry food to the Mouth, nor the Mouth to receive the food, nor the Teeth to chew it. They had not long persisted in this course of starving the Belly into subjection, ere they all began, one by one, to fail and flag, and the whole body to pine away. Then the Members were convinced that the Belly also, cumbersome and useless as it seemed, had an important function of its own; that they could no more do without it than it could do without them; and that if they would have the constitution of the body in a healthy state, they must work together, each in his proper sphere, for the common good of all.

15. THE MONKEY AND THE CAMEL

At a great meeting of the Beasts, the Monkey stood up to dance. Having greatly distinguished himself, and being applauded by all present, it moved the spleen of the Camel, who came forward and began to dance also; but he made himself so utterly absurd, that all the Beasts in indignation set upon him with clubs and drove him out of the ring.

16. THE MOLE AND HER MOTHER

Said a young Mole to her mother, "Mother, I can see." So, in order to try her, her Mother put a lump of frankincense before her, and asked her what it was. "A stone," said the young one. "O, my child!" said the Mother, "not only do you not see, but you cannot even smell."

17. THE HORSE AND THE STAG

A Horse had the whole range of a meadow to himself; but a Stag coming and damaging the pasture, the Horse, anxious to have his revenge, asked a Man if he could not assist him in punishing the Stag. "Yes," said the Man, "only let me put a bit in your mouth, and get upon your back, and I will find the weapons." The Horse agreed, and the Man mounted accordingly; but instead of getting his revenge, the Horse has been from that time forward the slave of Man.

18. THE TRAVELERS AND THE PLANE-TREE

Some Travelers, on a hot day in summer, oppressed with the noontide sun, perceiving a Plane-tree near at hand, made straight for it, and throwing themselves on the ground rested under its shade. Looking up, as they lay, towards the tree, they said one to another, "What a useless tree to man is this barren Plane!" But the Plane-tree answered them, "Ungrateful creatures! at the very moment that you are enjoying benefit from me, you rail at me as being good for nothing."

19. THE MICE IN COUNCIL

Once upon a time the Mice being sadly distressed by the persecution of the Cat, resolved to call a meeting, to decide upon the best means of getting rid of this continual annoyance. Many plans were discussed and rejected; at last a young Mouse got up and proposed that a Bell should be hung round the Cat's neck, that they might for the future always have notice of her coming, and so be able to escape. This proposition was hailed with the greatest applause, and was agreed to at once unanimously. Upon which an old Mouse, who had sat silent all the while, got up and said that he considered the contrivance most ingenious, and that it would, no doubt, be quite successful; but he had only one short question to put, namely, which of them it was who would bell the Cat?

20. THE GOOSE WITH THE GOLDEN EGGS

A certain Man had the good fortune to possess a Goose that laid him a Golden Egg every day. But dissatisfied with so slow an income, and thinking to seize the whole treasure at once, he killed the Goose; and cutting her open, found her—just what any other goose would be!

21. THE THIEF AND THE DOG

A Thief coming to rob a house would have stopped the barking of a Dog by throwing sops to him. "Away with you!" said the Dog; "I had my suspicions of you before, but this excess of civility assures me that you are a rogue."

22. THE EAGLE AND THE JACKDAW

An Eagle made a swoop from a high rock and carried off a Lamb. A Jackdaw, who saw the exploit, thinking that he could do the like, bore down with all the force he could muster upon a ram, intending to bear him off as a prize. But his becoming entangled in the wool, he made such a fluttering in his efforts to escape, that the shepherd, seeing through the whole matter, came up and caught him, and having clipped his wings, carried him home to his children at nightfall. "What bird is this, father, that you have brought us?" exclaimed the children. "Why," said he, "if you ask himself, he will tell you that he is an Eagle; but if you will take my word for it, I know him to be but a Jackdaw."

23. THE BOY AND THE FILBERTS

A certain Boy put his hand into a pitcher where great plenty of Figs and Filberts were deposited; he grasped as many as his fist could possibly hold, but when he endeavored to pull it out, the narrowness of the neck prevented him. Unwilling to lose any of them, but unable to draw out his hand, he burst into tears, and bitterly bemoaned his hard fortune. An honest fellow who stood by gave him this wise and reasonable advice: "Grasp only half the quantity, my boy, and you will easily succeed."

24. THE LION AND HIS THREE COUNCILLORS

The Lion called the Sheep to ask her if his breath smelled: she said Ay; he bit off her head for a fool. He called the Wolf and asked him: he said No; he tore him in pieces for a flatterer. At last he called the Fox and asked him. Truly he had got a cold and could not smell.

25. THE FOX AND THE CROW

A Crow had snatched a good piece of cheese out of a window and flew with it into a high tree, intent to enjoy her prize. A Fox spied the dainty morsel, and thus he planned his approaches. "O Crow," said he, "how beautiful are thy wings, how bright thine eye! how graceful thy neck! thy breast is the breast of an eagle! thy claws—I beg pardon—thy talons, are a match for all the beasts of the field. O! that such a bird should be dumb, and want only a voice!" The Crow, pleased with the flattery, and chuckling to think how she would surprise the Fox with her caw, opened her mouth. Down dropped the cheese! The Fox, snapping it up, observed as he walked away, that whatever he had remarked of her beauty, he had said nothing yet of her brains.

26. THE LION AND THE BULLS

Three Bulls fed in a field together in the greatest peace and amity. A Lion had long watched them in the hope of making a prize of them, but found that there was little chance for him so long as they kept all together. He therefore began secretly to spread evil and slanderous reports of one against the other, till he had fomented a jealousy and distrust amongst them. No sooner did the Lion see that they avoided one another and fed each by himself apart, then he fell upon them singly, and so made an easy prey of them all.

27. THE OLD WOMAN AND HER MAIDS

A thrifty old Widow kept two Servant-maids, whom she used to call up to their work at cock-crow. The Maids disliked exceedingly this early rising, and determined between themselves to wring off the Cock's neck, as he was the cause of all their trouble by waking their mistress so early. They had no sooner done this, than the old lady, missing her usual alarm, and afraid of oversleeping herself, continually mistook the time of day, and roused them up at midnight.

28. THE BOASTING TRAVELER

A Man who had been traveling in foreign parts, on his return home was always bragging and boasting of the great feats he had accomplished in different places. In Rhodes, for instance, he said he had taken such an extraordinary leap, that no man could come near him, and he had witnesses there to prove it. "Possibly," said one of his hearers; "but if this be true, just suppose this to be Rhodes, and then try the leap again."

29. THE WOLF AND THE HORSE

As a Wolf was roaming over a farm, he came to a field of oats, but not being able to eat them, he left them and went his way. Presently meeting with a Horse, he bade him come with him into the field; "For," said he, "I have found some capital oats; and I have not tasted one, but have kept them all for you, for the very sound of your teeth is music to my ear." But the Horse replied: "A pretty fellow! if Wolves were able to eat oats, I suspect you would not have preferred your ears to your appetite."

30. THE WOLF AND THE SHEPHERDS

A Wolf looking into a hut and seeing some shepherds comfortably regaling themselves on a joint of mutton observed, "A pretty row would these men have made if they had caught me at such a supper!"

31. THE ASTRONOMER

An Astronomer used to walk out every night to gaze upon the stars. It happened one night that, as he was wandering in the outskirts of the city with his whole thoughts rapt up in the skies, he fell into a well. On his holloaing and calling out, one who heard his cries ran up to him, and when he had listened to his story, said, "My good man, while you are trying to pry into the mysteries of heaven, you overlook the common objects that are under your feet."

Questions

1. The first stage in the preparation of an essay of this kind is a thorough study of the material. One way to begin is to classify the stories according to their themes and the lessons which they teach.

    a. What human failing is dealt with in fables 1, 3, 17, and 18? What lesson is enforced in fables 8, 11, 14, 15, 16, and 22? Classify the other fables into suitable categories. (A few may not be classifiable and may have to stand alone.) State briefly what lesson each fable or group of fables is meant to teach.

    b. Would there be any point in making a classification of the fables according to the animals who figure in them? Are the fables really about animals, or do the animals stand for something else?

2. It is not enough to perceive the individual lessons which these fables teach; one must try to arrive at some conclusions about the spirit and character of the whole group.

    a. What is the general attitude of the fables toward friendship and gratitude? Is fable 7 typical of the group?

b. What attitude toward government and authority is suggested by the fables about lions and wolves?

c. What view of human nature is implied by your answers to *a* and *b*? Is this view assumed in any other fables besides those dealing with friendship and power?

d. Could fables 8, 11, 15, and 22 have been produced in a thoroughly democratic society?

e. Characterize the spirit of the fables in a compact statement. What sort of life would a man lead who modeled his conduct on these stories?

3. The main problem which a person writing an essay on this kind of material would face is the problem of working in summaries of a certain number of the fables. There are several possible methods:

    a. Summarize all the fables very briefly.

    b. Summarize only a few, but treat those few thoroughly. One or two might be quoted in entirety.

    c. Summarize a few thoroughly and refer briefly to a number of others.

    Which method seems best? Which is the poorest? Which method does Mâle (page 135) use?

4. Select one of the following as the subject of your own theme; whether you choose *a, b,* or *c,* you will find the essays by Orwell (page 124) and Mâle (page 135) useful as models.

    a. An analysis of the ideas and attitudes which lie behind Aesop's Fables.

    b. An analysis of the ideas and attitudes which lie behind Grimm's Fairy Tales.

    c. An analysis of the appeal made by one of the following types of pulp fiction: (1) Westerns; (2) detective stories; (3) horror stories; (4) science fiction (i.e., stories involving trips to imaginary planets, inventions of the twenty-first century, and so on); (5) stories of "true" romance. You should confine yourself to stories in *one* of these classifications, and you will probably find it necessary to read about a dozen such stories before you can see the pattern emerging or arrive at any general conclusions.

WOMEN OF THE NEAR EAST*

From the Letters of Lady Mary Wortley Montagu

[The Greek view of women, which is so well described in Dickinson's essay, has sometimes been referred to as "Oriental" in spirit; and certainly there are points of resemblance between the attitudes and practices of the Greeks and those which prevailed for centuries—and indeed still prevail—in Mohammedan countries. One writer who has given a spirited picture of the life of women in an Eastern country is Lady Mary Wortley Montagu, who visited Turkey in 1717 as wife to the English ambassador. Her husband's high position caused her to be respected and gave her opportunities for observation which Christians were seldom accorded in those days, and her own intellect and literary skill made her an excellent observer and reporter. Some selections from her letters are printed below; there is material in them for an interesting short essay on the condition of women in Turkey. Read the selections and then, with the aid of the questions which follow, plan an essay which could be written from this material.]

1] Belgrade, Feb. 12, 1717; to Mr. Pope. We are lodged in one of the best houses, belonging to a very considerable man among them. My only diversion is the conversation of our host, Achmet Beg. I have frequent disputes with him concerning the difference of our customs, particularly the confinement of women. He assures me, there is nothing at all in it.

2] Adrianople, April 1, 1717; to the Countess of Bristol. The Grand Signior's eldest daughter was married some few days before I came; and, upon that occasion, the Turkish ladies display

---

* This exercise should be used in conjunction with "The Greek View of Woman" by Dickinson (pages 151-159).

all their magnificence. The bride was conducted to her husband's house in a very great splendour. She is widow of the late Vizier, who was killed at Peterwaradin, though that ought rather to be called a contract than a marriage, not having ever lived with him; however, the greatest part of his wealth is hers. He had the permission of visiting her in the seraglio; and, being one of the handsomest men in the empire, had very much engaged her affections.—When she saw this second husband, who is at least fifty, she could not forbear bursting into tears. He is a man of merit, and the declared favourite of the Sultan (which they call *mosáyp*), but that is not enough to make him pleasing in the eyes of a girl of thirteen.

3] Adrianople, April 1, 1717; to the Countess of Mar. I cannot forbear admiring either the exemplary discretion or extreme stupidity of all the writers that have given accounts of the Turkish ladies. 'Tis very easy to see that they have more liberty than we have. No woman, of what rank soever, being permitted to go into the streets without two muslins; one that covers her face all but the eyes, and another that hides the whole dress of her head. You may guess how effectually this disguises them, so that 'tis impossible for the most jealous husband to know his wife when he meets her.

4] Adrianople, April 1, 1717; to the Countess of Mar. Upon the whole, I look upon the Turkish women as the only free people in the empire: the very Divan pays a respect to them; and the Grand Signior himself, when a pasha is executed, never violates the privileges of the *harém* (or women's apartment), which remains unsearched and entire to the widow. They are queens of their slaves, whom the husband has no permission so much as to look upon, except it be an old woman or two that his lady chooses. 'Tis true their law permits them four wives; but there is no instance of a man of quality that makes use of this liberty, or of a woman of rank that would suffer it.

5] Adrianople, April 1, 1717; to Mr. Pope. I am very glad I have it in my power to satisfy your curiosity, by sending you a faithful copy of the verses that Ibrahim Pasha, the reigning favourite, has made for the young princess, his contracted wife, whom he is not yet permitted to visit without witnesses, though she is gone home to his house. He is a man of wit and learning; and whether or no he is capable of writing good verse himself, you may be sure, that, on such an occasion, he would not want the assistance of the best poets in the empire. Thus the verses may be looked upon as a sample of their finest poetry; and I don't doubt you'll be of my mind, that it is most wonderfully resembling *The Song of Solomon,* which was also addressed to a royal bride.

TURKISH VERSES ADDRESSED TO THE SULTANA, ELDEST DAUGHTER OF SULTAN ACHMET III

The nightingale now wanders in the vines:
Her passion is to seek roses.
I went down to admire the beauty of the vines:
The sweetness of your charms has ravish'd my soul.
Your eyes are black and lovely,
But wild and disdainful as those of a stag.

II

The wish'd possession is delay'd from day to day;
The cruel Sultan Achmet will not permit me
To see those cheeks more vermilion than roses.
I dare not snatch one of your kisses;
The sweetness of your charms has ravish'd my soul.
Your eyes are black and lovely,
But wild and disdainful as those of a stag.

III

The wretched Pasha Ibrahim sighs in these verses:
One dart from your eyes has pierc'd thro' my heart.
Ah! when will the hour of possession arrive?
Must I yet wait a long time?
The sweetness of your charms has ravish'd my soul.
Ah! Sultana! stag-ey'd—an angel amongst angels!
I desire,—and, my desire, remains unsatisfied.—
Can you take delight to prey upon my heart?

IV

My cries pierce the heavens!
My eyes are without sleep!
Turn to me, Sultana—let me gaze on thy beauty.
Adieu! I go down to the grave.
If you call me I return.
My heart is hot as sulphur; sigh, and it will flame.
Crown of my life! fair light of my eyes!
My Sultana! my princess!
I rub my face against the earth;—I am drown'd in scalding tears—
I rave!
Have you no compassion? Will you not turn to look upon me?

6] Adrianople, April 18, 1717; to the Countess of Mar. I was invited to dine with the Grand Vizier's lady, and it was with a great deal of pleasure I prepared myself for an entertainment which was never given before to any Christian. I thought I should very little satisfy her curiosity (which I did not doubt was a considerable motive to the invitation) by going in a dress she was used to see, and therefore dressed myself in the court habit of Vienna, which is much more magnificent than ours. However, I chose to go *incognita,* to avoid any disputes about ceremony, and went in a Turkish coach, only attended by my woman that held up my train, and the Greek lady who was my interpretess. I was met at the court door by her black eunuch, who helped me out of the coach with great respect, and conducted me through several rooms, where her she-slaves, finely dressed, were ranged on each side. In the innermost I found the lady sitting on her sofa, in a sable vest. She advanced to meet me, and presented me half a dozen of her friends with great civility. She seemed a very good woman, near fifty years old. I was surprised to observe so little magnificence in her house, the furniture being all very moderate; and, except the habits and number of her slaves, nothing about her that appeared expensive. She guessed at my thoughts, and told me that she was no longer of an age to spend either her time or money in superfluities; that her whole expense was in charity, and her whole employment praying to God. There was no affectation in this speech;

both she and her husband are entirely given up to devotion. He never looks upon any other woman; and, what is much more extraordinary, touches no bribes, notwithstanding the example of all his predecessors. He is so scrupulous in this point, that he would not accept Mr. Wortley's present, till he had been assured over and over again that it was a settled perquisite of his place at the entrance of every ambassador.

.   .   .   .

I returned her thanks, and soon after took my leave. I was conducted back in the same manner I entered; and would have gone straight to my own house; but the Greek lady with me earnestly solicited me to visit the *kiyàya's* lady, saying, he was the second officer in the empire, and ought indeed to be looked upon as the first, the Grand Vizier having only the name, while he exercised the authority. I had found so little diversion in this *harém*, that I had no mind to go into another. But her importunity prevailed with me, and I am extreme glad that I was so complaisant.

All things here were with quite another air than at the Grand Vizier's; and the very house confessed the difference between an old devote and a young beauty. It was nicely clean and magnificent. I was met at the door by two black eunuchs, who led me through a long gallery between two ranks of beautiful young girls, with their hair finely plaited, almost hanging to their feet, all dressed in fine light damasks, brocaded with silver. I was sorry that decency did not permit me to stop to consider them nearer. But that thought was lost upon my entrance into a large room, or rather pavilion, built round with gilded sashes, which were most of them thrown up, and the trees planted near them gave an agreeable shade, which hindered the sun from being troublesome. The jessamines and honeysuckles that twisted round their trunks, shed a soft perfume, increased by a white marble fountain playing sweet water in the lower part of the room, which fell into three or four basins with a pleasing sound. The roof was painted with all sorts of flowers, falling out of gilded baskets, that seemed tumbling down. On a sofa, raised three steps, and covered with fine Persian carpets, sat the *kiyàya's* lady, leaning on cushions of white satin, embroidered; and at her feet sat two young girls, the eldest about twelve years old, lovely as angels, dressed perfectly rich, and almost covered with jewels.

. . . .

She [the *kiyàya's* lady] was dressed in a *caftán* of gold brocade, flowered with silver, very well fitted to her shape, and showing to advantage the beauty of her bosom, only shaded by the thin gauze of her shift. Her drawers were pale pink, green and silver, her slippers white, finely embroidered: her lovely arms adorned with bracelets of diamonds, and her broad girdle set round with diamonds; upon her head a rich Turkish handkerchief of pink and silver, her own fine black hair hanging a great length in various tresses, and on one side of her head some bodkins of jewels. I am afraid you will accuse me of extravagance in this description. I think I have read somewhere the women always speak in rapture when they speak of beauty, but I cannot imagine why they should not be allowed to do so. I rather think it a virtue to be able to admire without any mixture of desire or envy. The gravest writers have spoken with great warmth of some celebrated pictures and statues. The workmanship of Heaven certainly excels all our weak imitations, and, I think, has a much better claim to our praise. For me, I am not ashamed to own I took more pleasure in looking on the beauteous Fatima, than the finest piece of sculpture could have given me.

She told me the two girls at her feet were her daughters, though she appeared too young to be their mother. Her fair maids were ranged below the sofa, to the number of twenty, and put me in mind of the pictures of the ancient nymphs. I did not think all nature could have furnished such a scene of beauty. She made them a sign to play and dance. Four of them immediately began to play some soft airs on instruments, between a lute and a guitar, which they accompanied with their voices, while the others danced by turns. This dance was very different from what I had seen before. Nothing could be more artful, or more proper to raise certain ideas. The tunes so soft!—the motions so languishing!—accompanied with pauses and dying eyes! half-falling back, and then recovering themselves in so artful a manner, that I am very positive the coldest and most rigid prude upon earth could not have looked upon them without thinking of something not to be spoken of.

· · · · · · ·

When the dance was over, four fair slaves came into the room with silver censers in their hands, and perfumed the air with amber, aloes-wood, and other scents. After this they served me coffee upon their knees in the finest japan china, with *soucoupes* of silver, gilt. The lovely Fatima entertained me all this time in the most polite agreeable manner, calling me often *Guzél sultanum,* or the beautiful sultana, and desiring my friendship with the best grace in the world, lamenting that she could not entertain me in my own language.

When I took my leave, two maids brought in a fine silver basket of embroidered handkerchiefs; she begged I would wear the richest for her sake, and gave the others to my woman and interpretess. I retired through the same ceremonies as before, and could not help fancying I had been some time in Mahomet's paradise, so much I was charmed with what I had seen.

7] Constantinople, May 29, 1717; to the Abbé Conti. Any woman that dies unmarried is looked upon to die in a state of reprobation. To confirm this belief, they reason, that the end of the creation of woman is to increase and multiply; and she is only properly employed in the works of her calling when she is bringing forth children, or taking care of them, which are all the virtues that God expects from her. And, indeed, their way of life, which shuts them out of all public commerce, does not permit them any other. Our vulgar notion, that they do not own women to have any souls, is a mistake. 'Tis true, they say they are not of so elevated a kind, and therefore must not hope to be admitted into the paradise appointed for the men, who are to be entertained by celestial beauties. But there is a place of happiness destined for souls of the inferior order, where all good women are to be in eternal bliss. Many of them are very superstitious, and will not remain widows ten days, for fear of dying in the reprobate state of a useless creature. But those that like their liberty, and are not slaves to their religion, content themselves with marrying when they are afraid of dying.

8] Belgrade Village, June 17, 1717; to the Lady ——. You desire me to buy you a Greek slave, who is to be mistress of a thousand good qualities. The Greeks are subjects, and not slaves. Those who are to be bought in that manner, are either such as are taken in war, or stolen by the Tartars from Russia, Circassia, or Georgia, and are such miserable, awkward, poor wretches, you would not think any of them worthy to be your housemaids. 'Tis true that many thousands were taken in the Morea; but they have been, most of them, redeemed by the charitable contributions of the Christians, or ransomed by their own relations at Venice. The fine slaves that wait upon the great ladies, or serve the pleasures of the great men, are all bought at the age of eight or nine years old, and educated with great care, to accomplish them in singing, dancing, embroidery, etc. They are commonly Circassians, and their patron never sells them, except it is as a punishment for some very great fault. If ever they grow weary of them, they either present them to a friend, or give them their freedom. Those that are exposed to sale at the markets are always either guilty of some crime, or so entirely worthless that they are of no use at all. I am afraid you will doubt the truth of this account, which I own is very different from our common notions in England; but it is no less truth for all that.

9] Belgrade Village, June 17, 1717; to the Lady ——. If one was to believe the women in this country, there is a surer way of making one's self beloved than by becoming handsome; though you know that's our method. But they pretend to the knowledge of secrets that, by way of enchantment, give them the entire empire over whom they please. For me, who am not very apt to believe in wonders, I cannot find faith for this. I disputed the point last night with a lady, who really talks very sensibly on any other subject; but she was downright angry with me, that she did not perceive she had persuaded me of the truth of forty stories she told me of this kind; and at last mentioned several ridiculous marriages, that there could be no other reasons assigned for. I assured her, that in England, where we were entirely ignorant of all magic, where the climate is not half so warm, nor the women half so handsome, we were not without our ridiculous marriages; and that we did not look upon it as anything supernatural when a man played the fool for the sake of a woman. But my arguments could not convince her against (as she said) her certain knowledge, though, she added, that she scrupled making use of charms herself; but that she could do it whenever she pleased; and, staring in my face, said (with a very learned air), that no enchantments would have their effect upon me; and that there were some people exempt from their power, but very few. You may imagine how I laughed at this discourse; but all the women here are of the same opinion. They don't pretend to any commerce with the devil; but that there are certain compositions to inspire love.

10] Constantinople, Sept. 1, 1717; to Mr. Pope. The women are not so closely confined as many have related; they enjoy a high degree of liberty in the bosom of servitude, and they have methods of evasion and disguise that are very favorable to gallantry; but after all, they are still under uneasy apprehensions of being discovered; and a discovery exposes them to the most merciless rage of jealousy, which is here a monster that cannot be satiated but with blood. The magnificence and riches that reign in the apartments of the ladies of fashion here, seem to be one of their chief pleasures, joined with their retinue of female slaves, whose music, dancing, and dress amuse them highly;—but there is such an air of form and stiffness amidst this grandeur, as hinders it from pleasing me at long run, however I was dazzled with it at first sight.

11] Pera of Constantinople, Jan. 4, 1718; to Mrs. Thistlethwayte. Without any exaggeration, all the women of my acquaintance that have been married ten years, have twelve or thirteen children; and the old ones boast of having had five-and-twenty or thirty a-piece, and are respected according to the number they have produced. When I have asked them sometimes, How they expected to provide for such a flock, they answered,

That the plague will certainly kill half of them; which indeed generally happens, without much concern to the parents.

12] Pera of Constantinople, March 10, 1718; to the Countess of Mar. I went to see the Sultana Hafitén, favourite of the late Emperor Mustapha, who, you know (or perhaps you don't know) was deposed by his brother, the reigning Sultan Achmet, and died a few weeks after, being poisoned, as it was generally believed. This lady was, immediately after his death, saluted with an absolute order to leave the seraglio, and choose herself a husband from the great men at the Porte. I suppose you may imagine her overjoyed at this proposal. Quite contrary: these women, who are called, and esteem themselves, queens, look upon this liberty as the greatest disgrace and affront that can happen to them. She threw herself at the Sultan's feet, and begged him to poignard her, rather than use his brother's widow with that contempt.

13] Constantinople, ——, 1718; to the Countess of ——. 'Tis very pleasant to observe how tenderly all voyage-writers lament the miserable confinement of the Turkish ladies, who are perhaps freer than any ladies in the universe, and are the only women in the world that lead a life of uninterrupted pleasure exempt from cares; their whole time being spent in visiting, bathing, or the agreeable amusement of spending money, and inventing new fashions. A husband would be thought mad that exacted any degree of economy from his wife, whose expenses are no way limited but by her own fancy. 'Tis his business to get money, and hers to spend it; and this noble prerogative extends itself to the very meanest of the sex. Here is a fellow that carries embroidered handkerchiefs upon his back to sell, as miserable a figure as you may suppose such a mean dealer, yet I'll assure you his wife scorns to wear anything less than cloth of gold; has her ermine furs, and a very handsome set of jewels for her head. They go abroad when and where they please. 'Tis true they have no public places but the bagnios, and there can only be seen by their own sex; however, that is a diversion they take great pleasure in.

14] Constantinople, ——, 1718; to the Countess of ——. I do not think the Turks deserve the barbarous character we give them. I am well acquainted with a Christian woman of quality who made it her choice to live with a Turkish husband, and is a very agreeable, sensible lady. She is a Spaniard, and was at Naples with her family when that kingdom was part of the Spanish dominion. Coming from thence in a felucca, accompanied by her brother, they were attacked by the Turkish admiral, and taken. He married her, and never took any other wife, and (as she says herself) she never had any reason to repent the choice she made. He left her some years after one of the richest widows in Constantinople. But there is no remaining honourably a single woman, and that consideration has obliged her to marry the present admiral, his successor.

Questions

1. Before using material such as this, it is well to consider the character and reliability of the reporter.

    a. As far as one can judge from the material itself, what sort of person is the writer? Does she appear to have any prejudices or preconceptions which might color her reporting of the facts? (A review of the questions on the selection from Lady Montagu in Part One [pages 70-71] may help to answer this question.)

    b. Is the wife of an ambassador likely to be shown much of the less attractive side of the life of the country? What limitations would her position place on her opportunities as an observer?

2. Another problem which arises in connection with an essay of this kind is the scope and character of the material itself.

    a. Do the letters deal with all classes of Turkish society, or only one class?

    b. Is the material chiefly concerned with the feelings and attitudes of the women, or with the external aspects of their life?

    c. Is there sufficient material here for an essay on "The Turkish View of Women"? (Be sure you understand the exact significance of the title; cf. question 2 on page 159.) What kind of source material, largely used in Dickinson's essay, is almost completely absent here? Did Dickinson have any material comparable to Lady Montagu's letters?

3. Once the material has been surveyed, it is time for the writer to form his own judgment of the problem and formulate his theme idea. Consider the following as possible theme ideas.

a. The life of the women of Turkey seemed strange to an English woman.

b. Women's life in Turkey had a good side and a bad side.

c. Women's life in Turkey was one round of luxury and pleasure.

d. Women's life in Turkey tended to develop a passionate and luxurious disposition without developing intellectual and spiritual qualities.

e. The degree of relative contentment which characterized the lot of the Turkish woman of the eighteenth century should prevent us from assuming that because a way of life is different from ours it is therefore less fortunate.

f. Those who regard women as essentially empty and frivolous should note that these qualities seem to be most marked in those societies which, like the Turkish, most repress and confine women.

g. Although in most societies men have maintained a kind of domination over women, human nature prevents this domination from ever becoming complete, even in such societies as the Turkish, where women are closely confined.

Any one of these theme ideas represents a defensible point of view toward the material. They differ greatly, however, in the interest they arouse and the depth of thought they display; some would lead to well unified essays, whereas others would be likely to lead to nothing but a string of facts. Comment on each of the ideas.

4. After the writer sees clearly in his own mind the point which he intends to prove, he must select the material to support the point. Take one of the theme ideas in question 3 and select from the letters those details which would illustrate the idea.

5. The arrangement of the material should always be carried out with reference to the main point of the essay. Thus the second theme idea (*b*) listed in question 3 calls for a very simple kind of organization with the essay divided into two main sections, one concerned with the bad side of Turkish life, and one with the good.

The fourth theme idea (*d*) also suggests an essay divided into two sections; what would they be?

6. *a.* One obvious way of organizing such material as that given in the letters would be to arrange the details under such topics as "dress," "entertainment," "housing," "courtship," and so on. Is there any theme idea listed in question 3 for which this form of organization would be suitable?

b. Another possible form would be that of a narrative—for instance, the imaginative reconstruction of a day in the life of a Turkish lady. Would this arrangement fit any of the theme ideas given in question 3?

7. Formulate a theme idea which expresses your own judgment on the way of life described in the letters. Select the material which is needed to illustrate the idea and decide on a form of organization. If your instructor so directs, write the essay.

THE BORDEN CASE *

A Summary Statement by the Editors

[On the following pages there appears an array of facts, arranged chiefly in chronological order, concerning the Borden murder case. In planning a theme based on this case, the student is in the position of any writer using controversial material to support his own interpretation. He is confronted by the fundamental problems of the selection and arrangement of facts.]

SUMMARY OF THE CASE. The Borden case is one of the most famous murder trials in the history of American crime. On Au-

---

* The facts given here are adapted principally from a summary of the Borden case by John H. Wigmore in *The American Law Review* (Vol. XXVII [1893], pp. 819-845). A popular account of the crime can be found in Edmund Pearson's *Studies in Murder* (New York, 1924).

gust 4, 1892, Andrew Jackson Borden, aged 70, and his wife, aged 64, were murdered in their home in Fall River, Massachusetts. The body of Mr. Borden was found on the sofa in the downstairs sitting room; that of Mrs. Borden, in the upstairs guest room, between the bed and dressing table. Both the Bordens had been murdered in the same way: the murderer had undoubtedly used an axe or similar instrument and had struck repeated blows.

Miss Lizzie Andrew Borden, aged 32, Andrew Borden's daughter by a former marriage, was accused of the double killing. On June 20, 1893, after a trial which aroused the passionate interest of the entire nation, she was declared "not guilty." No one ever confessed himself the murderer.

FACTS IN THE CASE. (1) The Bordens lived in a house on Second Street, an unpretentious frame structure without a bathroom. The plan of the house is given on p. 352. (A photograph of the house appears in *Life* magazine [Aug. 2, 1948, p. 61]). The absence of hallways in this house is important. On the ground floor a person entering by the kitchen door would have had to pass through the kitchen and thence either through the sitting room or through the dining room and sitting room, or through the dining room, sitting room, and parlor to reach the front entry. On the second floor, passage from the rear to the front was not possible; the door between Mr. and Mrs. Borden's room and Lizzie's room was locked on both sides. (2) Andrew Jackson Borden, retired merchant, was a prominent person in Fall River. He was President of the Union Savings Bank, director in several mills, and owner of a good deal of real estate. His fortune was estimated at $300,000. (3) Mr. Borden's domestic arrangements were as follows: After the death of the first Mrs. Borden, the mother of Lizzie and her sister Emma, Mr. Borden, in 1865, married Miss Abby Durfee Gray. Abby Gray Borden, at the time she was murdered, was a short, heavy set woman, 64 years old. Emma Borden, aged 41, unmarried, and Lizzie Borden, aged 32, unmarried, lived with their father and stepmother. At the time of the murder a servant, Bridget Sullivan (called "Maggie" by the Bordens) had been in the Borden household for about three years. (4) On the day of the murder Miss Emma Borden

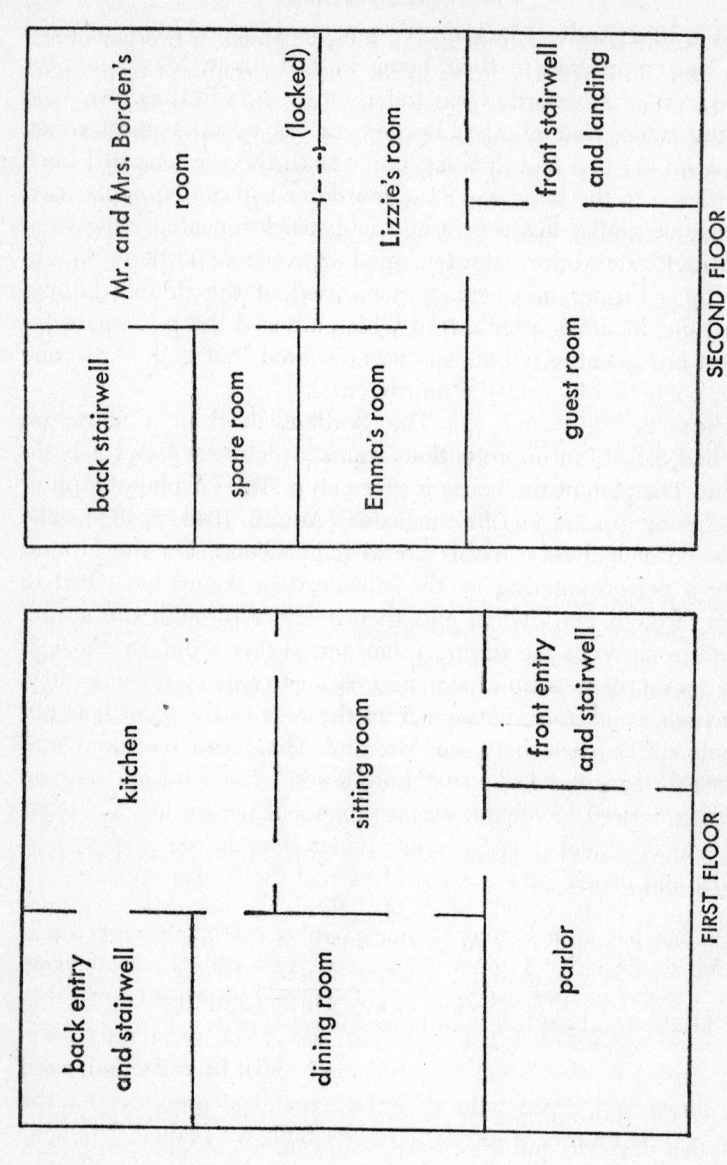

was visiting friends in Fairhaven. John V. Morse, a brother of the first Mrs. Borden and a guest in the house, was absent from quarter to eight until after the murder had been reported to the police, just before noon. He had been calling on a nephew and niece in another part of town. His alibi was found valid.

(5) On Tuesday night, August 2, Mr. and Mrs. Borden were suddenly seized with violent attacks of vomiting. (6) On Wednesday morning, August 3, a woman, identified by the druggist and by-standers as Lizzie Borden, tried to buy prussic acid at a local drugstore. She said she wanted it to keep moths from a sealskin cape. The druggist told her:

Well, my good lady, it is something we don't sell unless by a prescription from the doctor, as it is a very dangerous thing to handle.

(The court excluded this evidence.) (7) On Wednesday evening, August 3, Lizzie Borden paid a call on Miss Alice Russell, a close friend. Part of the conversation follows:

Miss Borden said: "I have made up my mind, Alice, to take your advice and go to Marion, and I have written there to them that I shall go, but I cannot help feeling depressed; I cannot help feeling that something is going to happen to me; I cannot shake it off. Last night we were all sick; Mr. and Mrs. Borden were quite sick and vomited; I did not vomit, and we were afraid that we have been poisoned; the girl did not eat the baker's bread and we did, and we think it may have been the baker's bread."

Miss Borden also suggested that the milk might have been poisoned and continued,

"Father has been having so much trouble with those with whom he has dealings that I am afraid some of them will do something to him; I expect nothing but that the building will be burned down over our heads. The barn has been broken into twice."

[Miss Russell's testimony]

(8) On the morning of August 4, which proved to be a brutally hot day, Mr. and Mrs. Borden and John V. Morse ate breakfast together. Mr. Morse left the house at 7:45. Shortly after this

Lizzie came down and started to eat breakfast. Mr. Borden went upstairs to his room, Mrs. Borden began tidying the house, and Bridget went out into the yard to vomit. When the servant returned she found Lizzie absent and Mrs. Borden dusting; Mr. Borden had apparently left the house to go downtown. At about 9:30, after having given Bridget instructions to wash the downstairs windows, Mrs. Borden went upstairs to put pillow cases on the bed in the guest room. This was the last time she was seen alive. Bridget fetched window washing equipment from the barn and cellar; when she returned, the downstairs rooms were empty. She closed all the downstairs windows and then began washing them, inside and out. (9) When Mr. Borden returned home, at about 10:30, he found the screen door at the kitchen entry hooked from the inside. Bridget let him in by the front door, which was triply bolted. At the same time she heard Miss Lizzie Borden, upstairs on the front landing, laughing or exclaiming. (Two rooms opened on the second-floor front landing: Lizzie's room and the guest room.)

(10) Mr. Borden took the key to his own room, went up by the back stairs, came down shortly, and entered the sitting room. Bridget began to wash the dining room windows and Lizzie set up an ironing board in the dining room. The following conversation occurred:

She [Lizzie] said, "Maggie, are you going out this afternoon?" I said, "I don't know; I might and I might not; I don't feel very well." She says, "If you go out, be sure and lock the door, for Mrs. Borden has gone on a sick call and I might go out too." Says I, "Miss Lizzie, who is sick?" "I don't know; she had a note this morning; it must be in town."

[Bridget Sullivan's testimony]

No evidence of the existence of this note or of the person who had sent it was ever found.

(11) Shortly before 11 Bridget went up the back stairs to her room to lie down. She admitted that she may have dozed a little. Ten or fifteen minutes later she heard a cry from downstairs.

Miss Lizzie hollered: "Maggie, come down." I said, "What is the matter?" She says, "Come down quick, father's dead. Somebody's come in and killed him."

When Bridget asked Lizzie where she had been when the murder occurred, the latter replied,

"I was out in the yard, and heard a groan, and came in and the screen door was wide open."

[Bridget Sullivan's testimony]

(12) Without seeing the corpse, Bridget was sent for the family physician, Dr. Bowen, and for Miss Russell, the close friend on whom Lizzie had called the previous evening. Mrs. Churchill, a neighbor, and Dr. Bowen soon arrived on the scene. By 11:15 the police were informed of the tragedy. (13) Bridget suggested that she should be sent to look for Mrs. Borden and tell her what had happened. Lizzie replied:

"Maggie, I am almost positive I heard her coming in. Won't you go upstairs to see."

[Bridget Sullivan's testimony]

Accompanied by Mrs. Churchill, Bridget mounted the front stairs. On the far side of the guest room, between the bed and dressing table, the body of Mrs. Borden was discovered.

(14) Both victims had been murdered in the same way. Mr. Borden's body was found on the sofa in the sitting room; ten wounds from a cutting instrument wielded with a swing had been inflicted on his head. Blood was spattered on the wall next to the sofa, on a picture on the wall, on the kitchen door near his feet, and on the parlor door. Medical testimony later established the fact that Mrs. Borden had been killed between one and two hours earlier than her husband. She had received nineteen head and neck wounds, thirteen of which had penetrated the skull. There were blood spots on two walls and more than seventy-five spots on the dressing table. (15) When search was made later, two hatchets and two axes were found on the premises. The handles of three of these tools were marked with ragged portions which would have made cleansing impossible.

The handle of the fourth tool was in part broken off, in part covered with ashes.

(16) The Fall River police officers were not accustomed to handle murder cases. On the day of the crime half of them were out of town on their annual picnic. Officer Allen, the first policeman to arrive at the Borden house, hurriedly returned to the police station to report the crime, leaving no guard on the house. When Allen's report brought other policemen to the premises, the persons in the house were not searched. No thorough search of the house was made until Saturday, August 6. (17) Friends and policemen repeatedly asked Lizzie where she had been at the time of her father's murder. She told one officer that she had been in the loft of the barn looking for sinkers for a fishing line and had heard no noises from the house. Another policeman, Officer Medley, testified that the dust on the loft floor showed no traces of footprints at the time of his investigation. Since other witnesses maintained that they had climbed up into the loft before him, and since he could not prove the time of his visit, his evidence was discredited. It was noted that the barn was intolerably hot on a summer day.

(18) On August 6, the same day on which funeral services were held for the murdered couple, the city Marshal informed Lizzie that she was suspected of the crime. Most of the information that she had given to police officers before her apprehension and at the coroner's inquest was excluded by the court at her trial on the grounds that such statements were not made voluntarily. (19) One of the chief points in Lizzie's favor was the absence of bloodstains on any of her clothing. Experts testified that whoever had wielded the cutting instrument would necessarily have been spattered with blood. Miss Borden turned over to the police a plain dark blue silk dress which she said she had been wearing Thursday morning. Some witnesses believed that she had been wearing a figured blue cotton dress, but could not be positive. Miss Russell testified that when she visited Lizzie on the Sunday morning following the murder (police officers were out in the yard at the time) Lizzie burned an old skirt. Lizzie's explanation was, "I am going to burn this old thing up; it is

covered with paint." The prosecution failed to prove that this skirt was the dress (or part of the dress) that Lizzie was wearing on the morning of August 4.

(20) Several vagrants were reported to have been observed near the scene of the crime. A boy thought he had seen a man jump over the back fence of the Borden premises. On August 16 a witness reported that he came upon a strange looking man on a farm four miles from town. The vagrant was said to be carrying an axe and muttering, "Poor Mrs. Borden." He was never found. (21) On the day following the murder, Emma and Lizzie Borden publicly offered a reward of $5000 to anyone who could secure the arrest and conviction of the person who had entered their house and killed their parents.

(22) One of the chief points in the case of the prosecution was motive. Emphasis was placed not only on the fact that Lizzie would inherit a fortune but also on the dissensions existing in the Borden household. The daughters sometimes took their meals alone and there had been quarrels over money matters. To a police officer who asked Lizzie on Thursday, "When did you last see your mother?" Lizzie replied, "She is not my mother. My mother is dead." (23) One of the chief points in the case of the defense was the good character of the accused, the impossibility that any woman of her background could have committed such brutal murders. She was a church member in good standing and active in various charitable organizations. The Reverend Mr. Buck and the Reverend Mr. Jubb, her pastors, became her firm supporters. (24) Miss Lizzie Borden, in accordance with the prerogative of American law, did not take the stand in her own defense. (25) When the jury, after deliberating a little over an hour, declared Miss Borden "not guilty," the decision was applauded by newspapers all over the country. Typical of the tone of editorial opinion is the following comment.

Such was the frightful ingenuity of the amateurish detectives and the ambitious prosecutors of Fall River, that they have fixed upon her [Lizzie Borden] a stigma which can never be wholly removed. . . . The protection of the good name of the innocent is more important by far than the condign punishment of the guilty. It would be a good thing if the friends of Lizzie Borden should undertake to give emphasis to this sound principle by persuading her to bring damage suits against the most perniciously active of her detractors.

(Review of Reviews, Aug. 1893)

(26) Soon after the acquittal, Emma Borden went to Fairhaven to live. Lizzie moved to a spacious, ten-room house about a mile and a half from her former home. There she led a quiet, solitary life until her death on June 1, 1927. (27) In her will, besides substantial bequests to her caretaker, to servants, and to friends she left $30,000 to the Animal Rescue League of Fall River and $2000 to the same league in Washington, D. C.; she established a trust fund for the perpetual care of her father's grave. (28) The Borden case continues to be a source of literary interest. At the time of the trial an anonymous ditty gained currency all over the country.

> Lizzie Borden took an axe
> And gave her Mother forty whacks;
> When she saw what she had done,—
> She gave her Father forty-one!

In 1933 a play, *Nine Pine Street,* was inspired by the murder. In 1948 the Ballet Theater in New York produced Agnes de Mille's ballet, *Fall River Legend,* based on the tragedy.

Suggestions for the Student

1. SELECTION AND ARRANGEMENT OF FACTS. Which facts shall the writer choose? In what order shall they be arranged? Which facts should receive emphasis? The student can answer none of these fundamental questions until he has decided upon his theme idea, the idea that will govern his whole presentation of the material.

2. THEME IDEA. To sift the evidence and decide to his own satisfaction that "Miss Borden was guilty" or "Miss Borden was not guilty" or "Miss Borden's guilt was not proven" is part of the writer's job, but it does not provide him with a theme idea. A satisfactory theme idea should have a significance extending beyond the immediate material; in other words, it should suggest the application of the facts given to other instances.

The writer may use one of the following suggestions or evolve a theme idea of his own.

a. The twentieth-century attitude toward a woman suspected of murder is far less sentimental than that of the nineteenth century.
b. Circumstantial evidence, however impressive, is not conclusive.
c. Social and religious prejudices often sway the feelings of jurymen.
d. No mass tragedy or natural disaster exercises on the public mind a fascination equal to that of an unusual murder case.
e. The attraction which a brutal murder case can exercise over the mind of a nation is proof that the veneer of civilization is thin.

3. POINT OF VIEW. Through whose eyes shall the facts be presented? The point of view of an omniscient, impartial twentieth-century investigator is the most obvious possibility. The selection and arrangement of facts will be very different, however, if the writer chooses to view the evidence through the eyes of a newspaper reader in 1892; or of a juryman; or of Officer Allen; or of Emma Borden; or of Lizzie herself.

4. WRITING. The facts are expressed here as baldly as possible, without emphasis or coloring. The student should not copy the words of this summary. He should rewrite the facts that he selects in accordance with his own purpose.

MACHIAVELLI IN OUR TIME *

A Summary Statement by the Editors

[Niccolo Machiavelli (1469-1527), author of the selection on pages 256-259, is also the author of *The Prince*, a book which is sometimes considered the first treatise on power politics. In it he describes, with hardly any moral disapproval, the methods which he thinks most ef-

* This exercise should be used in conjunction with the selections by Machiavelli and Croce (pages 256-264).

fective in securing and retaining political power. The successful ruler, according to Machiavelli, must stop at nothing. Along with a strong, well-trained intellect and unusual courage and resolution, he must possess a cold and ruthless temper which will enter readily into any act of cruelty or violence. He must be shrewd and cunning, capable of any deceit and prepared to break his most sacred word whenever it is to his advantage. At the same time, the Machiavellian must take the utmost care to mask his real intentions behind an appearance of strict virtue. He must justify his cruelties and deceits by specious pretexts; he must practice a strict economy in his wrongdoing, and never indulge in any vice or commit any injustice which is likely to offend men without bringing any solid good in return. In fact, the mere need for self-preservation may lead such a politician to provide good government; for although the ruler must realize that popular favor is an unstable base on which to found his power, he must also remember that a prince who protects the lives and property of his subjects is much more likely to remain in power than one whose tyrannical acts constantly excite men to treason and rebellion. The Machiavellian, indeed, is not necessarily a bad ruler; he is simply one who is determined to have power and who is completely unscrupulous about the means he uses in getting it.

[This work has enjoyed a constant popularity and an equally constant notoriety ever since it was written; it has been widely read and widely denounced. Just how much its principles have actually been practiced is hard to say, especially since the most successful Machiavellian is the one who is least Machiavellian in appearance. There are, however, a discouragingly large number of statesmen even in our own time who bear a suspicious resemblance to the Machiavellian type, and it is interesting to consider how far their characters and actions are those of the ruler described by Machiavelli. Take some statesman or politician whose conduct seems to you to conform to the Machiavellian pattern, collect material on his career,* and write an essay on that statesman as a Machiavellian ruler. If necessary, you may use the summary of Machiavelli's thought given above, but it would be better to read *The Prince* itself; it is short, readily available, and thoroughly interesting.]

* Your composition handbook will give directions for finding material in the library.

Analytical Table of Contents

PART ONE: Models

The first Section of *A Writer's Reader* contains finished pieces of writing that the student is to study in order to understand the process by which they came into being. Since in most composition courses the student is first asked to write on material drawn from his own experience, the first Section begins with

1 ESSAYS BASED ON DIRECT OBSERVATION

The first problem in writing an essay is the choice of suitable details; accordingly, the first four pieces in this section are provided with questions which emphasize the importance of this problem and assist the student in finding a solution to it.

> Edwin P. Whipple *Webster and the Neighbors*
> —a passage of the simplest kind, a general statement with an illustrative narrative; but as the questions show, the writing of even such a simple piece involves the careful selection of details if unity is to be attained.
>
> George Crabbe, Jr. *Life at Parham*
>
> Nathaniel Hawthorne *Two Weddings*
>
> Benjamin Franklin *Principle and Practice*
> —more complex passages, emphasizing again the problem of selecting suitable details.

From the problem of selection of material, the student proceeds to the problem of organization, the arrangement of material. The next four selections are provided with questions which stress this problem.

Charles Darwin *Tierra del Fuego*
—the problem of organization presented in an elementary form: details are grouped under a few broad headings which correspond to the paragraph divisions.

Marjorie Kinnan Rawlings *Environment*

Thomas Wolfe *Race and Occupation*
—more complex passages, involving such problems as transition, emphasis, and digression.

Theodore Roosevelt *In the Cattle Country*
—a difficult problem in organization, in which the difficulty arises not from any subtlety of thought or feeling, but simply from the quantity and variety of the details.

Although the selection and arrangement of material to fit the main purpose constitute a large part of the writing process, the author's personality, his thoughts, ideas, and emotions, are also of importance, and the author must be conscious of them if he is to avoid inconsistencies of tone and content. This point is illustrated by the group of passages which follow.

Mark Twain
Lady Mary Wortley Montagu
Alexander William Kinglake   } Five Travelers in the Near East
Sir Richard Burton
R. B. Cunninghame Graham

—here we see the difference in coloring and emphasis that may appear in the description of the same or similar objects when presented by writers of different interests or personalities.

Each essay treated so far has been used to illustrate some broad problem of composition. But an essay is not written merely to illustrate rhetorical problems; it is a unique thing with its own problems and purposes. Therefore, each of the last three essays in this section is analyzed as a special case.

George Gissing *Retrospect*
>—an example of the degree of complexity and conscious art which may lie behind the briefest and simplest piece of prose.

Robert Louis Stevenson *Despised Races*
>—some unusual problems of unity, arrangement, and tone.

Carlo Levi *Matera*
>—implying thought through description.

By this time, through the study of relatively simple selections in which the main ideas are supported by material drawn from observation, the student should have a fair understanding of the writing process and should be ready to apply his understanding to the more complex essays in

2 ESSAYS BASED ON READING OR INVESTIGATION

Most composition courses include some work on the "research essay" or "library paper"—work in which the student studies before he writes. The present Section has the double purpose of providing models for this kind of writing and of serving as a review of the principles of composition set forth in Section 1. With one exception, the essays are of a type that a student might write, even though they are above student level in quality.

The selections are arranged according to subject matter; the first three deal with historical subjects.

George Macaulay Trevelyan *The Value of History*

Francis Parkman *Braddock's Defeat*

James Anthony Froude *Sir Humfrey Gilbert*
>—three selections which form a convenient unit: Trevelyan holds up an ideal of historical writing, and Parkman and Froude provide examples to test against the ideal. A comparison between Parkman and Froude will

serve to show to what degree historical narrative reflects the interests and prejudices of the writer.

The next four selections deal with art and literature.

Lewis Mumford *Thomas Jefferson, Architect*
—a simple essay of architectural criticism that shows the application of a general critical rule to a specific instance.

George Orwell *The Art of Donald McGill*
—the questions accompanying this essay on "popular" art are designed to show how a critical work of real seriousness and significance can be drawn out of the most unpromising material.

Émile Mâle *The "Golden Legend"*
—a simple kind of literary criticism, made up of generalization and summary.

Sir Walter Raleigh *Robert Louis Stevenson as Romancer*
—too impressionistic to be a safe model; it is included to show the special difficulties involved in literary criticism.

The last three selections in the section, which deal with human customs and habits, belong to the field of social studies:

G. Lowes Dickinson *The Greek View of Woman*
—especially useful for the discussion of sources and quotations.

Sir Walter Scott *Ghosts*
—interesting in its classification of specific illustrations. There is room for argument concerning the efficacy of Scott's pattern of organization.

Ruth Benedict *The Pueblos of New Mexico*
—an exceptionally long essay in which a great variety of material has all been successfully unified around a theme idea.

3 EXPRESSION OF JUDGMENT AND OPINION

Although the editors feel that beginning writers had better stick to exposition and avoid such complex forms of writing as argumentation, they also feel that the beginner needs to be aware of the problems involved in controversial writing, whether considered from the writer's or the reader's point of view. The selections in Section 3 raise many of these problems.

H. L. Mencken *Education*
—a notable example of the manipulation of language for the purpose of imposing opinions and emotions on the reader.

Alexander Woollcott *The Archer-Shee Case*
—an example to prove that an essay which appears to be straight reporting or summary may have strongly controversial implications.

Niccolo Machiavelli *Corruption in a Commonwealth*

Benedetto Croce *Political Honesty*
—selections to show that a writer's opinion on a given point may sometimes be less important than the assumptions that lie behind that opinion.

Abraham Lincoln *Address at Cooper Institute*
—among the problems raised here are the handling of a closely reasoned argument and the arrangement of the parts for emotional effect.

Winston S. Churchill *The Munich Agreement*
—worthy of attention here is the speaker's control over emotion, both his own and that of his audience.

PART TWO: *Source Materials for Student Papers*

The exercises in this section consist of the raw materials, the unassimilated facts out of which essays are made (see the Preface for further comment). As Walter Map says, "The individual reader must shape the rough material which is set out here; through his efforts it may assume a pleasant pattern. I carry in the food from the hunt; it is up to you to prepare the tasteful dishes" (*De Nugis Curialium*).

The first three exercises go with Section 1 of Part One.

> A MYSTERIOUS DISAPPEARANCE *From a Letter of Abraham Lincoln*
>> —designed for use with the selection by Whipple, this exercise requires the student to convert a rambling, non-expository narrative into an expository one. The emphasis is on the selection of detail.
>
> THE FUEGIANS *From Darwin's "Voyage of the Beagle"*
>> —designed for use with the selection by Darwin, this exercise serves to introduce the problem of the arrangement of detail.
>
> MASTERS AND SERVANTS *From the Diary of Samuel Pepys*
>> —for use with the selection by Wolfe. In the first two exercises immediately above it was assumed that the writer had an idea to present and was searching for illustrative material; this exercise shows how an idea can be drawn from the material.

The next two exercises go with Section 2 of Part One.

> AESOP'S FABLES
>> —here is material for a simple type of literary criticism, with suggestions for handling this kind of material, including the problem of using summary and quotation.

Analytical Table of Contents 367

WOMEN OF THE NEAR EAST *From the Letters* of *Lady Mary Wortley Montagu*
—this exercise emphasizes the problems of evaluating material and securing interest and significance in the theme idea.

The last two exercises go with Section 3 of Part One.

THE BORDEN CASE *A Summary Statement by the Editors*
—here the problem of reasoning from evidence comes in.

MACHIAVELLI IN OUR TIME *A Summary Statement by the Editors*
—the last exercise is actually a jumping-off place for a "library" paper.

Most of the material given in the exercises is "primary" source material, of which several kinds are represented: facts reported by an outside observer (*The Fuegians, Women of the Near East*); facts reported by a participant (*A Mysterious Disappearance, Masters and Servants*); literary matter (*Aesop*).

4 essays p. 3 - 15 -

Rollow - p 22
Roosevelt - p 34
Ruth Benedict
Darwin - p 17 - p 310
Wolfe - p 26

grammatical -

blue book